I0742679

THE TERAS TACTICS

LUCIEN BURR

THE TERAS TACTICS
Lucien Burr

All rights reserved.
No part of this book may be used or reproduced in any manner without written permission of the publisher, except for the purpose of reviews.

Cover Art by Clown Saint
Internal Art by M.E. Morgan
Edited by Drew McBlain

This book is a work of fiction and as such all characters and situations are fictitious. Any resemblance to actual people, places or events is coincidental.

print ISBN: 978-0-6455494-8-5

Category (Adult Fiction)
Genre (SFF/ Dystopian / Romance / LGBT)

ALL RIGHTS RESERVED © LUCIEN BURR 2022 – 2024

LESSON RECAP

Cassius Jones has spent the last five years of his life living behind the safety of London's wards, the last protected bastion for humanity in England. But this placement must be earned. His brother Thaddeus was a graduate Hunter, destined to patrol and cull the growing population of the *teras*, mythic monsters most prominently drawn from Greco-Roman mythology. Cassius and Thaddeus stumble upon a hybrid, a creature not clearly drawn from any one myth, and Cass's world changes forever.

The University, which trains Londoners in the ways of survival, opens its doors to *xenos*—those who live beyond the wards—for the first time in a long while. London is getting overcrowded, and anyone living there must prove their worth. Cassius, who has dreamed of being a Scholar safe behind the wards, is pressured to choose the dangerous Hunter mantle instead.

But first, he must get through the trials.

A patrol attended by Thaddeus goes wrong. Cassius leaves the safety of London in pursuit of his brother, only to find him dying, mauled by a *manticore*. Three *xenos* come to his aid: Fred and Silas Lin, and Leo Shaw.

Cassius is instantly drawn to Mr Shaw, who at first believes Cassius knows more about the trials than he lets on.

After giving their blood to the University, they learn that if they flee, they will be tracked down by Blood Hunters, a subset of the Hunter mantle who have pledged to keep the University's secrets safe by eliminating runaways.

Cassius joins up with Londoners Victoria Bennet and Bellamy Taylor, convincing them to add Silas, Fred, and Leo to their merry band.

Cassius makes a deal with Dean Drearton to secure the tower rooms that Thaddeus instructed him to acquire with his dying wish. Here, he finds some supplies left by his brother, including hints about the trials.

Cassius witnesses a suicide and puts the young man out of his misery. He tries to find solace in the campus chapel and then heads for the library, as mentioned in his brother's note. He spies a flicker of someone in the hallway that can't be there.

A relationship with Leo starts to blossom.

From here, he finds the *automaton* Meléti, a *teras* of knowledge, one of Daedalus' creations, that tends to the University's library. When Meléti asks for memory as payment, we learn of Cassius' time in Hull before the wards with his abusive father.

We learn about the first trial.

In Summary:

The band suffer through the trials, trying to learn more about the University. Cassius and Leo begin a relationship. In the third trial, Cassius sacrifices Bellamy to save Victoria. He loses his left arm killing the *Nemean Lion*. His arm is replaced with a prosthetic. The band goes up against the final trial—the *manticore*. Cassius' betrayal is revealed to the group, but no one else owns up for any wrongdoing they've committed.

Silas dies.
Fred loses her leg.
Leo loses part of his cheek.
Victoria is thrown backwards into a tree.

Just when the end is surely near, something creaks from the forest. A new creature emerges.

It kills the *manticore*. Cassius instantly feels a connection to it. He speaks to it. He asks it what it wants.

It tells him.

Vengeance.

❈ I ❈

LESSON ONE

"*Vindicare.*"

Fingers crack and drag around the edge of my vision. Three hands, then four, then nothing but the fingers themselves. They sprout in fractal infinities, curling in on each other, scuttling over my eyelids. I cannot fight them off. My breath is short and sharp as they dash across my skin. I jerk back as they begin to caress my face, my neck, my chest; I throw myself backwards as the touch becomes intimate. I can't allow this. I don't want—this.

With a jolt, I land in the freezing snow. It is the dead of night in winter, and I am naked. My skin is sallow and thin; bright blue veins snake serpentine over my limbs. The longer I look at my arms, the less convinced I am of my own solidity. I am turning to glass. I will break at any moment.

"*Vindicare.*"

Nightmare, heavy, black—this part of my mind plunged months ago into near-complete darkness and has been swamped in the gloom ever since. But at night, in these dreams, the shadows yawn and stretch to encroach further, to make me *worse*. To make me suffer.

The nightmare's oily black tendrils creep across my mind. They take root in me. Bury deep. I fear this recurrent dream is corrupting me so innately I might not even realise when I'm too far gone—either broken and empty or so ruthless I cannot recognise myself.

I often see the bodies of my fallen comrades. Their blood is on my hands, and it flows ceaselessly, sinking into the grooves on my palms and clogging beneath my fingernails. The nightmare shows me Bellamy, a half-stretch from the door, begging me to help him, admonishing me for leaving him, damning me to hell. Or I see Peter Drike despondent, broken, dying alone as a *stygian* rips his eyes from his sockets.

But often, these dreams are only flavouring, an overture for the true nightmare, which is this: thick snow, an endless expanse of bone-white exploding in all directions, moonlight reflecting off the ground and the claustrophobia of the endless needle-thin trees. And in the centre of it all, that thing.

That damned creature creaking in amongst the frozen birches, brooding over humanity and warning me very plainly about what it wants. The hybrid.

It has hounded me for two months, visiting me almost every night, slipping seamlessly into the liminality of the dream world to stalk me there. I no longer know if it's real or not. Don't judge me for that. I'm not an idiot.

But I am haunted.

I stand before it now, shivering, nude, at its mercy. And tonight, it looms impossibly large over me, like God looking down. It snorts, and thousands of flayed, disembodied fingers scuttle down the birch trees until every branch has transformed into another set of crawling digits, until the bark peels and plops down into the snow. Endless fingers reach for me. It doesn't take long for them to crawl up my leg. Bloody flesh, wet, warm. I start to suffocate in it.

Vengeance marks me with blood; I become tainted with the stuff.

Through the gaps of the swarm of fingers, I meet its eye.

Once more, it tells me: *"Vindicare."*

The weight of the word strikes me again. The layering of it, the heaviness of the sentiment—it is not just revenge it wants.

To punish, to liberate, to lay claim to—what? What does it want?

Why do I feel it is coming for all of us?

Why do I feel there is nothing to be done to stop it?

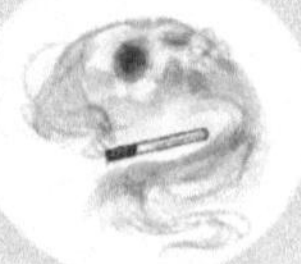

LESSON TWO

Sharp air burns in my lungs. Frigid, like I'm alone in Sherwood and shivering. I jolt awake, and I'm shaking so violently that I think I've wandered outside, that I'm convulsing to death in the snow.

But I haven't. I'm in bed. I'm alive. Tears are in my eyes and my body aches as if I've been running. Taking stock, I can see I've kicked my way out of the covers, and now I am lying in my own feverish sweat.

Delightful.

I have to laugh because, in the dark, the shadows are not my friends. Not behind the wards—not after what this place has done to me. Scanning for creatures lurking in the room— no matter the improbability—I start to slow my breathing. A twiggy, naked branch scratches at the window. By the bright blue pressing against the dark sky, it must be close to dawn, but this low light still sends the jerking shadows of that tree dancing across the room. I squeeze my eyes shut and open them.

A bulky silhouette stands at the end of the bed, unmoving.

I stare back. My primitive brain freezes with fear, and my muscles tense, my body readying itself to launch out of the bed. Sweat pools in my lower back and on my forehead, but the air is rapidly cooling it already.

The figure reaches out—

God, I can hear my heart—

And gently touches my foot.

I exhale.

The wind picks up outside and howls mournfully. I shuffle and sit back against the headboard, and he moves to sit beside me. The cramped single bed groans with the added weight.

"I woke you," I murmur.

He leans forward so the waking dawn light catches his face, and when he grins, it is dazzling, sharp canines gleaming with a smile that could blind.

Leo Shaw whispers back to me, "There are worse things to wake to."

"And better things," I say.

He grins again, but when he kisses me, exhaling against my lips, there's a force to it.

He wants me. Wants to have me. It's been weeks—nearly three now. His hand slides beneath my shirt, warm, his callouses peeling, and he squeezes against the jutting bone of my pelvis, moving his lips to my neck.

And bites.

"Leo," I hiss sharply, and he laughs breathlessly against my jaw.

"Would you two shut up?"

I exhale sharply. In the shadows of the room, another form moves, roughly rolling over on their bed.

We have the absolute joy of sharing the room with seven others. Gone are the false pretences awarded to us during the trials: we are here to learn, not for luxuries. I slip out of the sweat-covered sheets, don my uniform, step into rainboots, and wrap myself tightly in my Mackintosh. I nod Leo towards the door.

It's too close to dawn to sleep anyway.

Blistering cold blows straight through my jacket and shirt beneath it. We hunker down and pick a direction to walk in.

The dawn light is weak and filters softly outward in a blue-orange stretch.

Now that our blood has been marked as students, we are free to cross the Janus threshold—and it is in this inner sanctum we have been sequestered. From the outside, the University is a disjointed mess of sandstone, connecting vaguely together in a circle around a courtyard. In reality, the majority of those buildings are behind a magical ward. We first encountered it two months ago when we petitioned a graduate Artificer to help us in the trials. Whether she knows it or not, she saved our lives.

Mine and Leo's, at least.

"Where are we going?" Leo asks.

I reach into my pocket for one of my thin and hastily rolled cigarettes. Tobacco is sparse these days. Much of Newstead, several days north from here, used to cultivate it. A few farms in Suffolk and Norfolk did, too. No official reason has been given for the lack, but I feel the strain. Either the crops have failed, been destroyed —or abandoned.

I like none of those options.

Still, I am addicted to the damn stuff, and I can't stop smoking without the heavy dissatisfaction of life crawling into my throat. I nudge Leo, and he puts his hands out, cupping my match from the rain and wind. He's not looking at me as he does it. It's second nature now. We walk like this most mornings, pressing out into the cold and rain, finding corridors to talk in, to sit silently, or to fuck—though we haven't done much of that lately, and I want to rip off my skin. The more days pass, the more certain I am that he finds me hideous. Like Dorian Gray, every misdeed brands itself on my body until he can only see me as *murderer*. I would prefer he sees me as a body. Something to be fucked. If I cannot have all of him, I at least want that. Desirability feels so much more significant than love in this world. Love kills you. Love has you risking your life for a comatose father and a mother who barely cares for you.

Sex might at least get you closer to heaven.

I instinctively turn us to the *automaton's* library, which means stepping through one of the Janus Gates and into the outer rim of the campus. We move through a covered walkway. A blind arcade is superimposed on the right wall for decoration, but the left is an open series of connecting arches that look out to another set of sandstone buildings and green grass. It's picturesque in this morning haze, and the rain splits the light beautifully, misting everything with glow. At the end is one of the wards that separates the inner campus from the outer.

As we walk towards it, Leo nudges me.

"Will you tell me what you dreamed of this time?"

The hybrid's eyes flash in my brain, void-like and everexpanding. I hear the stillness of the forest in which it waits, the grinding of its joints as it slouches towards London's walls.

And then I inhale my cigarette deeply and burn away that image with crisp, bitter tobacco. I sniff at Leo and say, as nonchalantly as I can manage, "Do you care?"

He shrugs and grimaces. In the light, I see the stretch of the skin that was hastily knitted together on his left cheek. The *manticore's* wound is everpresent: those scars peek out behind the leather patch Leo wears to cover the rest of it. An unknittable hole that bares his teeth.

"I care if it's haunting you."

I look at him. "Does it haunt you?" I ask, and I want to convey the weight of it. Of the deaths. We bear the scars, but it's not equal. Of the few around campus whose limbs needed replacing, only a handful sport anything near in craftsmanship to mine. We are cowled with debt, but there are rumours that some are paying the same price for a limb made of steel as one made of marble and Artificer's magics.

So, in asking if Leo is haunted, I mean it threefold. First by the trials themselves, second by our actions in them, and thirdly by the outcome. A hierarchy we don't understand is unfolding before us. An inner society neither of us have any grip on. If I was Leo's compass in the trials, I'm nothing to him now. I have no insight to offer. The University is its own world.

"Of course it does," he says, and he grips my shoulder with fondness. But I cannot be sure he knows what I mean.

Technically, we are all equal now. Londoners, and workers, and *xenos*. In Drearton's London, which has always been about class, only fools would believe it.

The corridor ends abruptly in the Janus Gate, which is foggy, an abyssal swirl that looks like a passage to another plane of being. The world on the other side of it coalesces with a blue haze in the courtyard beyond. This gate is the true rite of passage—any unconfirmed blood that passes these wards has the pleasure of spontaneously combusting. We are allowed to pass back and forth until the new cohort of trial-takers begins. Usually, they are spread a year apart, but now it's only a handful of months before the new lot are set to begin. I suspect this will move up again.

Too many of us are dying out of London's wards, and no one is telling us why.

I breathe deep and walk through the gate. My body is still hit with shivers as it passes through. Doorways and arches already have power—the liminality of the threshold, the change of states that passing over allows. Except when I move through the wards, there is a very distinct moment of being nowhere. It feels unlike liminality. This is an absence, an abyss, and my stomach flips in horror every time I pass over it; I can feel every nerve blooming, every blood vessel expanding, every pore on my skin as if all my particles have gained sentience and realised simultaneously, with waking horror, their own mortality.

And then it's done.

The first time, most of us threw up. The nausea passes quicker now. Leo stumbles in after me with a heavy sigh.

"Hate that in the morning," he says, looping an arm over my shoulders. I tense because it's unusual for him to be intimate outside of bedrooms. I spin and stop him from walking. Surprised, he looks down at me, then over his right shoulder, where the chapel sits.

"Are you taking me to church, Mr Jones?"

I haven't set foot in God's realm for months. It is simple: I don't go to church anymore. I don't pray. God has forsaken me, so I forsake him, and now I worship nothing except this: carnality. Pleasure. Men. Every fucking breath I take—all of it is a luxury I laud with every inhale.

But Leo knows all this and is just being smart. He often likes to bring up what we did in that chapel, but at least he understands that kind of worship.

"Of a sort," I say, slipping a finger into his and tugging him along to the left.

When he sees we're headed to the library, he blinds me with one of those bewildering smiles, eyes heavy and canine glinting.

"I can't tell if you're saying that as a scholar or a whore," because, of course, I would liken a library to a church—as equally as I would a man—and of course, Leo knows I love it when he speaks to me so candidly. I love that embracing ferocity has made me unashamed: I love feeling joy for what I am for the first time. I love revelling in it.

"Want to find out?" I ask and speed ahead of him to Meléti's realm.

No one is visiting the library this early. Knowing what we know now, both times we visited the library during the trials, there were very likely people studying—we just lacked the means to see them. Personal wardstones act like the Janus gate does and, whilst on campus and in our possession, will allow only the initiated to see us. In any case, all the lights of the library blinker on in a cascading rush. It's empty, as expected, save for the *automaton*. Meléti whirrs over to us from some hidden area.

The *automaton* feeds on information the way others feed on flesh, refusing to help without an offering. It asks, "How can I help you today, Mr Jones?"

So I tell it, "We require no help, Meléti. You may go."

This is a trick we've been taught, so long as we are content to wander. And since neither Leo nor I are here to study, I'm grateful when the *automaton* spins unhappily on its heels and retreats without another word. When it rounds a corner, I take Leo's hand and drag him up the stairs.

There's almost three hours before we have to be anywhere. Two and a bit if we want to eat. But I'm barely thinking of anything but my cock in Leo's throat—vulgar, yes, maybe, *sorry*, but my thoughts are fraught with this. Even after two months, Leo and I aren't anything more than this. We use one another. We give, we take, and it is a reciprocal, mutual exchange. I keep it physical. I am very careful to keep my heart away from him. It probably isn't working, but I am trying very hard. Because I am ruthless now.

And everything I do is for myself.

We stumble into a row, already scrambling with our clothes. Leo shoves me against one of the shelves, and the books fall against one another with dull thuds. A three-day-old ache shivers up my spine, and I hiss out, "Gentle, darling, I'm sore."

Leo laughs against my teeth. "When have you ever wanted it gently?"

I wrap my arms around him, pulling him close, but it's not enough; I want him to crawl inside my ribcage. I want him to tear me apart.

We are both so hungry our kisses are practically violent, tongues and teeth and nails tearing to get to flesh. Like this, he pushes me to the ground, old floorboards creaking in angry protest with my dropped weight. I sprawl, thighs apart, so obvious and eager. Leo drops to his knees between my open legs with heavy-lidded eyes.

"Look at you," he murmurs, breathing hard, and I can almost hear the word *slut* sitting ready on his tongue. I sit up, pull him close, and eat the word out of his mouth, swallowing it before he can say it, taking its essence into me; I will be his slut. For him, for myself, in my pursuit of *ekstasis—to be outside of one's body, to transcend*—then I will rip pleasure from this moment.

He crawls between my legs, and I kick off my shoes behind his back. He goes to work on my trousers, and I reach out for purchase along the floor, bracing myself because I am straining already, pent-up. But instead of a grip, my fingers meet paper. Our little dance has books falling from the shelves, and I pick up the little bound treatise. Leo asks me to arch; he tugs my trousers down and off. My cock twitches against the fabric of my smalls.

Leo slips his fingers into the waistband and is about to pull it free when I ask, "Shall I read to you as you work?"

Leo jolts. He looks up, and his eyes dart from the manuscript to my steady gaze. Something flickers in his eyes

—resolve buckling, perhaps—and a disbelieving, airy laugh sounds. "What?"

I know how I look. I'm spread out, coat abandoned. I'm in a vest, a shirt, and an undone tie. Socks still on. I'm stretched out beneath him, legs wide and inviting and desperate, with my cock torturously hard, precum wetting my smalls as the head strains against its confines. Gripping the little treatise—I'm a tease.

"You're mad," he says, but there's no reproach in his words. He's looking at me and panting like he's run the field. Leo's just as pent-up as me. *Slut*. We're the same.

"We have to keep our studies up," I murmur. Leo exhales noisily; he's craving it so badly that *that* ridiculous comment makes his own cock throb. The motion catches my eye; I stare at the form of him pressing through his trousers.

I raise the manuscript. "Well?"

"Hips," he says in answer. I press up, and he drags my smalls down and off. Cold air pricks my cock, and I jolt, but then Leo's breath is warming me. I crane to look down, and we lock eyes; it's so bright in here that there's no hiding. His eyes are hungry as he stares up at me from under his brow, and he starts gently tonguing the slit, cleaning up all my leaking precum with slow diligence.

"Oh."

I arch out of instinct and necessity, my right hand snaking down to press Leo down onto me. But he resists, insistent on this slowness. He knows me and my body, knows I'll be bucking into his throat the instant he lets me. He must want to drag it out. It's killing me. My grip softens so ridiculously that the treatise nearly falls out of my hands. How long will I last like this? It's been weeks—I know I don't have long. But I love teasing Leo, so I pretend I'm a good student. A very good boy. I open the manuscript and read it to him.

I sigh as his tongue runs the length of my cock, gulping as I say, "Um, *On encountering a pit of mutated cerastes-class teras.*"

Leo pulls away, saliva-covered lips curling up as he says, "Oh, how incredibly hot."

I laugh and close the book—Leo splays a hand on my belly, nails digging in enough for me to yelp.

"What?" I hiss, but my body betrays me when more precum beads at the head of my cock.

"You promised you'd read to me, so read," Leo says, collecting the beads on his tongue with another languorous lick. I exhale and buck, and he jerks his lips back out of the way, staring at me until I make eye contact. Leo's gaze darkens suddenly. "Be a good boy and do what you're told."

"*Fuck*," I manage. Shakily, I bring the treatise closer to my face. Leo still hasn't taken all of me in his mouth. He works down, laving at my balls and sucking there instead.

A weak, high noise escapes my throat. Wobbly, I say, "Uh, *I, Sir William S. J. Peterman, had the twinned misfortune and joy—* oh, fuck—*of stumbling upon a pit of mutated cerastes. Some were pulled straight from their myths untouched, but others had broken from their legends twisted.* Shit, Leo, I really can't—"

Flush against my cock, he whispers, "Did I tell you to stop?"

I swallow, involuntarily grinding my hips forward. "No."

"No, *what?*"

I bite my lips, rocking my hips into the air and the empty space where his mouth was a moment ago. He won't give me what I want until I say it. Even if this title isn't quite true— we are only first-years, after all—something about it makes Leo more focused, more intensely aroused than usual. I look down at him and whisper, "No, Hunter Shaw."

Leo surges forward and takes the length of me down his throat, arching hungrily towards the hilt. I moan loud—*fuck*, that caught me off guard—and my cock jumps against his tongue. Some high-pitched sound escapes my throat, and I grind up so fast I make him gag. Saliva leaks from his mouth. I feel it dripping warmly onto my balls. I clamp my right hand on his head to keep him from pulling away, and with my left, I raise this stupid fucking treatise and start to read. My voice comes out an erratic wobble. Leo is making me read about mutations, an extra horn jutting out of a back. What looked to be a malformed leg twitching in disuse. A single leathery wing, barely more than skin. What we might class as hybrids now, fifty years before that giant talking beast chatted to me in Sherwood Forest.

No, no—I can't think about this. I am fucking Leo's throat, and his lips are soft and warm and vicelike, and there are hybrids in my head.

If I develop a goddamn fetish over this—

But then Leo does *something,* half-swallowing my cock. I can feel his throat bob, and he gags again, loudly moaning. I crane forward to see his own cock is out, slick with precum and desperately fucking up into the palm of his hand.

Fuck.

I drop the stupid treatise and shove both hands down into his wavy, thick hair, rocking up with my hips. We both moan, Leo another beautifully strangled sound and me a low growl from the bottom of my lungs. We find a wet, loud rhythm, and I am grinding down hard, using his throat, feeling the beauty in desecration and depravity, bodily savagism in the sweat of my flesh, something holy and primordial in using my body like this. In taking him, in being unabashed about what I want.

"*God,*" I pant above him, "Leo—*Leo*—"

My hips snap forward in a final thrust as I come, moan clipped and gasping, legs near strangling as I squeeze the back of his neck. I feel him tense, and warmth covers my cock, my ass, as he spills over me.

When I release him, Leo moans; I have wrecked that pretty face. His cheeks are wet with tears and saliva and cum, flushed bright pink, and his tongue is gently spilling from his lips.

"Come here," I say, sitting up to drag him closer. I taste myself on him as he kisses me indolently, pulling away only to put his cum-covered fingers in my mouth. I taste the both of us, and God shivers, which is how I know it's good.

"You're so beautiful," Leo says, finger under my chin, "Hunter Jones."

But I am looking at beauty; fucked, spent, and breathing hard. I am looking at the most beautiful thing in this God-forsaken world, and every beautiful thing the *teras* have stolen from us was born again in this Adonis.

I'm about to say something back when Meléti whirrs towards us. Its beady eyes assess us, and if an *automaton* could be reproachable, that would be the look this creature wears.

"You have made a mess in the library," it says.

And Leo looks up defiantly, grinning, and licks his lips. "Actually, Meléti, I think you'll find I swallowed it all."

LESSON THREE

A fist collides with my cheek.

I scream as pain reverberates through my jaw and down my neck. The punch whips my body around, and I stumble, half collapsing. My hands rush out to brace my fall, seeping into the cold sludge as my knees collide with the stone. When I cough, bloody spittle sprays out.

Fucking horrid pivot from my otherwise blissful morning.

"Yield yet?"

I glance over my shoulder. I'm wheezing, lungs on fire, and I know my wan skin will be blooming beautifully with a mottled bruise, but I refuse to show how much pain I'm in. My assailant is a second-year student Hunter by the name of Don Wamsley—a stupid name for a stupid man. He is Peter Drike after a year of torture, a rotten thing made worse by a rotten institution.

"Eat my ass, Don," I say, and stand up straight.

He only grins wider, happy to keep wailing on me.

This is every second morning of my life. With consistent food and consistent training, we will be made Hunters. I came here scrawny, underfed, and heavily dependent on tobacco and alcohol. Now, I have an ounce of muscle on me —but fuck you, you can pry stiff drinks and cigarettes from my cold, dead hands.

The Hunter cohort is continuously changing in size, with a stream of new students coming each year and a dozen or so Hunters dying each month. This is why we are trained together: there is no waiting anymore. The secrets learned in third-year classes are dying with their Hunters, and so first-years have been thrown into it all. Swim or sink; fight or be torn apart—rather literally.

Three claps ring out—Don calling for my attention. "Come on, Jones, we don't have all day."

I ready myself, new leather boots sliding back in the sleet. My marble prosthetic clanks, and when I shake the cold off the arm, it briefly locks out, twisting my shoulder socket to an unpleasant angle. I used to love this kind of weather; I would find peace in the gloom and rain. But now, the cold locks up my manmade joints, so this weather only serves to remind me how angry I still am.

Good thing violence is encouraged in this class.

Don has barely broken a sweat. He assesses me, and I can see Thaddeus in his stare. In looking at me, he can calculate where I'll move, which hand I favour, where my swing will land before I've even thrown the punch. This type of hand-to-hand combat isn't useful against *teras*, but that's not what this training is for. This is about learning strategy, honing your awareness of movement and fighting so you might side-step a strike that would otherwise eviscerate you from chest to groin.

I don't move first. I block out everything else, everyone else sparring around us. Only we exist in this little corner of the sleet-covered terrace. But all the concentration in the world isn't enough for me to sidestep Don's movement.

He rushes at me. I flinch, losing a good second of reaction

time. Then he's shoving me against the wall, grip tight around my throat, lifting me up—I'm too weak to do anything but kick uselessly. My vision goes hazy, and my brain panics. Everything in me wants to live and is flailing. I start scratching at his hands, hard marble hand beating down on his fingers, but he just stares at me, eyes gleaming and so open with their hate.

"That's what I thought," he sneers. "Maybe I should do us all a favour and get rid of you now. *Faggot.*"

Fine. If he wants to call me that, he'll get the full experience. So, I do what I do best and grab his fucking dick.

Don makes a sound like he's dying.

He's so surprised that he drops me, but I don't let go. I can feel his flaccid cock in my hands, and right now, the damn bastard is so shocked I'm even touching him at all that he isn't fighting back.

"Haven't been touched in a while, Don?"

Don lets go, intending to strike me with both fists. He wrenches an arm back, and I know he'll hit me hard and fast, so I drop to the ground in a low squat. I butt into his knees, and I have to topple myself forward just to unbalance him; he has the grounding of a building, rooted like a damn tree. I throw myself into him with everything I have, and we go down together. Air screams out of him in a breathy wheeze as his back meets the ground, and he latches his legs around me, holding me close as he punches down on my back.

I am ashamed to say my body knows this. There is a familiarity in a beating because I grew up like this, with a man three times my size taking out his hatred of this world on me—I know pain. I know how to withstand it. I compartmentalise the thudding, the brutal aches along my spine, and wait for Don to fatigue. When he slows, I twist my head and bite through the vest, teeth boring into the soft flesh of his hip. He screams, and his legs dislodge from around me. I scrabble back, punching as hard as I can with my prosthetic arm; a spray of blood hits me in the eye, and I stand up, panting.

Don lies there for a minute before sitting up, a dangerous look in his eye. I've just slightly split his top lip apart. His lips curl off his teeth; blood oozes into his gums as he gives me a sharp smile.

"Good," he says, spitting over his shoulder. Some of my blood has mingled with the wool of his trousers. I have blood all over my shirt. I brace myself for another one of his attacks, but when he stands, Don just brushes his hands on his trousers and claps me on the back. "Need to work your upper body more, though. It's where you're weakest."

And that's the difference between Peter and Don; Don is so fucking sure of himself that he's happy to give me little wins. I may be *faggot* to him, but I made it this far, and that makes me useful. Peter would have gotten up and beaten me to a pulp, but Don knows there's a shortage of people willing to head out of the wards. He has the strength to destroy something vital in my body and certainly has the hatred of me and my preferences to follow through, but a Hunter losing a week or more to injury doesn't just mean losing a week of training. These days, it means one less decent Hunter on the field, and that could mean the difference between Don living or dying. And if we were ever to work together on a kill, you want to make sure your fellow Hunters are as good, if not better, than you are.

So, all of us walk this fine line between training to our utmost limits and making sure we can still function the next day.

Our training happens in a small sleet-covered terrace built high in the building dedicated to Hunter studies. Getting up here means crossing over a thin trench with a high parapet. The same parapet walls of the terrace where we fight.

Professor Bedelia Dexter, the only one who can bestow the Mantle of Hunter on any of us, observes from a balcony raised above the courtyard where she can watch, order, and grade us—the former of which being something that happens constantly. Exams still happen, both written and physical, but the University isn't interested in people who can excel in controlled settings. The numerous potential outcomes of locking untrained would-be students in rooms with *teras* are tantamount to that.

The courtyard is fitted out specifically for Hunters' physical training: weapon racks, training dummies, open space for sparring, steep slopes, and balance beams. No *teras*, at least not on the regular. The real things are reserved for third-years and graduates.

With my sparring done, I turn to watch others work. Namely Leo, of course, because I'm a whore for him; for seeing him like this. He's stripped down to his white shirt with his sleeves rolled up, but he's sweating through it anyway, despite the cold. Slick with it, translucent; it slides against his chest, every swing of his arms tugging up the shirt and exposing his belly. I exhale greedily at the sight of him. Blood trickles down from his knuckles. A mottled bruise shines high on his right cheekbone.

He's sparring with a fresh graduate who comes up to his chin, taller than me and far, far stronger. Her name is Sutton D'Avore, and she claims an unbroken heritage to Angelica D'Avore, the first Hunter, now a lauded saint, an angel, an agent of God. Angelica's direct descendant has tawny skin, is broad with a thick torso, and has the exact kind of attitude you would expect from someone whose great-grandmother is London's exalted one.

She's strong and fast, scars lining her forearm. She's been out of the wards too many times to count. Even though she just graduated, she's been in command of her own Hunting party, the groups of graduates and a few student Hunters who seek out large threats and remove them, or head out on patrols.

I watch Leo and her spar. They both have pure strength in their favour, and neither of them is knocked back much by their opponent's hits. Leo clips her shoulder, and she hisses with fury, spinning around to kick him. He stumbles, recovers slowly, and Sutton takes advantage. Her next strike hits the leather patch covering his cheek wound, and Leo howls with pain, tearing it free. Even from this distance, I can see him gnash his teeth together, his pink tongue pressing out of the hole. Blood spots the skin around the puckered flesh. This is a tactic in itself because everyone who isn't a degenerative little trollop like yours truly flinches at the sight of Leo's face. It sparks fear in most people.

(I am not most people.)

Desire is a type of violence, you know, a carnal coveting, possession. It has a corruptive power to it, the ability to twist goodness and morality, to sunder one from God. From goodness itself. So when I look at Leo, knowing I have forsaken God already, watching bruises and blood and rage leak from his very being, it lights a fire in my groin.

He's just about to retaliate when Professor Bedelia's voice cuts over the lot of us.

"*Enough!*" she calls. I crane my neck to look at her. She's lithe and sinewy, her stark white hair long enough now to tie into a low, tiny ponytail. Like me, she's down a limb; her left leg is missing. She was next to the dean when I bargained for our rooms in the trials, and I suspect greatly she planted the idea of the *manticore* in that fucker's head. But so be it; I am one of these people now. So long as I don't think too hard about this place, I can survive it.

All of us go quiet and turn to her. There are less than a

hundred of us present, with most graduates and third-years on rotating patrols.

"Change of plans today," she clicks her tongue, leaning forward on the stripped wooden banister. "Next class will be with Hardinge."

I frown. Professor Hardinge teaches the Scholar's mantle. All of us have limited classes with the disciplines outside our chosen mantle, just enough to maintain basic knowledge on the field if need be. But these lessons are few and far between and always scheduled well in advance.

Something else is going on.

Leo and I share a look, but no one, not a single person, asks for clarification. That's not how it works here. You do as you're told.

"What are you waiting for?" Professor Dexter spits.

And with that resounding close to our order, we go.

LESSON FOUR

There is beauty in the academic wing, in the architecture and the books. The very scent of it hurts me in a base, intrinsic way. This should have been my life.

I like to think myself stronger for choosing Hunter, but in the end, all I did was follow my brother's dying order. The child in me, the innocent, craved this life of study. But necessity dictates otherwise. I will learn to kill the *teras* threat. I will live to be older than thirty.

I won't die.

All these thoughts swim in my head as we walk into the grand academic wing. It is a massive, sprawling hall with bright arched windows sitting high on both long sandstone walls. In perfect symmetry, four incredibly long wooden tables span the hall's length. Probably six hundred students could sit, seven hundred if you weren't worried about comfort.

The roof looks like the inside of an upside-down ship, curved with decorated partitions divided at strict intervals. A dozen portraits of lauded graduates sit dusty, high up on the walls, and twin-headed lamps dot the tables.

Our Hunter cohort files in later than the others, but I see Healers and Artificers, too, dotted in between the Scholars, identified by the colour of their uniform and the year patch sewn into their vests.

Hunters are given blacks, Healers blue vests, Scholars a tawny sandstone, and Artificers a rather upsetting maroon. (No, it doesn't really matter because we're here learning to fight actual hellish creatures, but these uniforms do not fit anyone well, except perhaps for Leo.) Instinctively, I duck my head; part of me longs to see Victoria or Fred, but neither of them has much to do with me anymore.

"Come on," Leo grabs my back and manoeuvres us through the tight crowd of bodies. The chatter is loud, and no one tells us to quiet down, so it only gets worse, pitching until all words slur together in a soupy cacophony. Leo drives us forward so we're near the opposite end of the hall, where the professor's podium sits empty. Leo seats us together at the top of the last vacant table, now being claimed by the Hunter cohort. Each mantle is divided and spread out on separate tables—though with less than a hundred of us Hunters present; we are overbearingly obvious. A few straggling Healers spill from the ends of their tightly packed table to take up the free end of ours; they are by far the largest cohort, behind Scholars and then Artificers. But there is no doubt there exists a large lack of balance in our disciplines.

Leo makes a clicking noise for my attention, and without saying a word, I know which way to look. We can do this now, our own language that we've learned between gasps and touches. I know what most of his sounds mean.

But for this, I wish I didn't. Two tables across from us is Victoria.

I freeze. I haven't seen her in two months, nearly three. Her hair is done up in an intricate braid on the crown of her head, her cheeks full and rosy brown. She looks healthy.

Good, even. But there is a distinct wan look to her under eyes that betrays her. She wears the Healer blues and is scribbling something furiously in a notebook, ignoring the chaos of the hall.

And my heart betrays the coldness I have adopted by thudding hard when I see her.

At once, everything is dredged up, everything, all the blackness of the trials—Bellamy reaching out, Victoria screaming, *oh God. God. I loved him. I swear it.*

Leo stupidly says, "You should—"

I exhale like he's punched me, and he shuts up.

"Absolutely fucking not," I grumble. This schism is not something to be reconciled. That is a decision I made and will bear alone.

I am the blackguard of their trials; everyone left alive is alive because of me. I will happily sit in that righteousness, and it is far easier to bear it knowing there is a hint of something good there. I saved her damn life—but that friendship is dead.

"I only meant. . ." Leo begins and trails off, and I wonder if he could one day love me. Is that what love is? He sees me and fucks me and knows deep down misery lives in my gut, so he pushes me back towards friends? I don't know, and I don't know why I'm so scared of Leo thinking of me as anything more than a body to take pleasure in.

"I know," I say, and do not elaborate—I need more than his mouth to cure these thoughts. I need to make time for him to rail all this nonsense out of my skull.

I am saved from further bullshit when Professor Hardinge mounts the podium.

He is a shadow given human form, lanky and tall, but he makes himself smaller in an almost self-reproachful way, curling his shoulders down so he looks like a standing lamp. He is forty-something, though last year I thought he looked much older by the way he stood; exhaustion and stress have burrowed into his skin and made themselves known in severe lines entrenched in his forehead and dark circles so deep that when the shadows sit in them, it looks like he's smudged soot beneath each eye.

When he opens his mouth, his voice bellows, easily travelling the length of the hall.

"Morning," he says with a nod. "We have with us here every enrolled student from years one to three who is not on rotating patrol, which numbers us nearly six hundred. We so rarely get to see the lot of you together, so this is a blessing." He says this flatly, as if obligated to make mention of us, but there's a tinge in his tone. I sit up straighter. "You all know. . .what's been happening."

A murmur starts up immediately. There is hot debate about what is known and what isn't. The first-year dormitories are chaotic when it comes to gossip, and the third-years feed us a consistent stream of nonsense. I've heard talk of farms burning and *teras* luring Londoners out beyond the wards. I want none of these to be true, though, and so I've tried not to think about it.

I've only been here two months. Surely, if it was significant, the University would tell us.

Without waiting for the chatter to die down, nor apparently willing to explain anything further, Professor Hardinge raises his fingers and clicks once.

In answer, the doors at the end of the hall open again, and a swarm of Scholars, made known by their bycoket hats glinting with embroidery, flood the hall. Where graduate Hunters embroider their hunting coats with their kills, graduate Scholars do the same on their hats for tomes: volumes whose knowledge they have subsumed, or on occasion, the depiction of a *teras* which said Scholar is an expert of the genus. In this way, I know there are a dozen or so graduate

Scholars rushing through us, with a few third-years doing the same. Each one is carrying a silver tray with them.

The smell instantly makes me ill.

Most of the hall recoils, bodies naturally shivering with disgust as the intense pickle scent wallops us. Formaldehyde.

I understand slowly.

There are so many trays that it takes me a moment to comprehend the sheer enormity of what has happened. Each tray has a small, somewhat malformed body on it. They are *teras*. Small *teras*—but nothing tugged purely from myth. At first I guess they are all F tier, by their size (not that that says much about viciousness). But then there's a whole range of them that they're impossible to classify. The worst part is they're not only from the Greco-Roman mythos. Something resembling a *selkie* and an insect lands on the table with the Healers. Someone shouts when a *cyclops-brùnaidh* skirts by us.

The Scholars move to place trays in front of four of us, but that means a hundred, a hundred-and-fifty *teras* have been killed for whatever this is. Voices go up high and curdle in not-quite screams. First-years, after what we've witnessed in the *trials,* jolt at the sight. We haven't been exposed to *teras* since our final trial. But the third-years make noises of surprise, too, even the Scholars who weren't assigned the task of carrying out the trays. I am briefly lulled by the knowledge no one knows what's going on.

Except for when I hear Don just across from me turn to a friend and say, "*Hybrid.*"

Hybrid.

A flash of fleshy fingers curling out from antlers reaches towards my mind. I flinch in the chair.

When the tray lands before us, I grip Leo's arm. It's instinctive and embarrassing and made all the worse because I've gripped him with the prosthetic, so I skirt closer and grab him again with my right. I need the anchorage of his body touching my own. Leo, who is always calm. Leo, who makes the difficult decisions and is never burdened by the horror—because my heart lurches upwards with complex heaviness: it is a lump of grief, guilt, and fear, the very remains of my blackened hope ready to spew forth from my mouth. I'm breathing heavily. Leo gently pushes his arm back over so he can rest his hand on the top of my right thigh. He squeezes the muscle without looking at me, eyes fixed on the dead thing before us, and he winces only once after I release my grip.

Briefly, I see what's on the tray. A single *Stygian bird* made bulbous as if stung by dozens of bees, with a horn jutting out from its sternum. But its feathers are plucked away around the horn, its belly holding an unsettling translucence, looking more like a thin membranous sack than anything solid.

Leo squeezes my thigh again.

I don't know enough about Leo to feel this close to him. I know his body more than I know his mind, but at least I can be certain of his steadiness. A rock for me to cling to.

But I can't rely on that or on him. Ruthlessness is expected; ruthlessness is the only way. So I let go and curl my right hand in a fist until my own nails are lancing the soft middle of my palm.

"Calm down, Jones," Don says with a grin. He grabs the fat, mucus-filled body of the hybrid and leans across the table to wave it at me. Wet plaps sound as the flesh slides together. "They're already dead."

Snickers go up at the same time Leo stands. He's grabbed the scalpel from the tray.

I stand up half a second later. I can't have Leo protecting me like this. I reach across the table, narrowly avoiding the wet, bulbous body of the hybrid against my skin, and tug Don closer until his neck is precariously close to the scalpel.

"Barbarians," a graduate Scholar mutters near me as she puts a tray down for the next group of Hunters.

"Faggots, actually," I say loudly, which makes her jump. I don't dare break eye contact with Don, but I see her hesitating in my periphery, just as I can see Professor Hardinge look our way. This would have killed me once, but I am not here to go prostrate before a saint of knowledge. I am here to make my vessel deadly, and if that means embracing barbarous desires, then so be it. If I had my gun, I'd point it at Don's damn head. "That's your problem, isn't it? Not that I find this eldritch mutation disgusting, but that I have sex with men."

Don flinches like I'm the devil, like my words have a corruptive power to them. He half turns his head as if to survey the surrounding crowd.

He doesn't want anyone to hear.

To prove my point, Don dumps the wet mass of flesh on the tray and splays his hands on the table, staining the beautiful wood with formaldehyde and whatever is naturally excreting from that creature's unnatural pores.

Don pitches his voice low. "My issue, Jones, is that you're making us look weak. All the more so if you have your boyfriend protecting you."

Weak? I glance over Don's shoulder—we have a lot of attention now. Eyes are on us. And three tables away, Victoria is looking too.

Fuck. Don't think about her—you don't know her anymore. But if anyone knows I'm not weak, it's the woman whose boyfriend I sacrificed.

I shove Don back. "I'll let you lecture me on weakness after you take a cock up your arse," I spit, which leaves Don blinking. He gives a breathy laugh, but there is anger in his eyes, an affronted rage burning through him.

"Thank you, student Hunters, for your riveting display of

foolishness and savagery. Always a welcome reminder to the rest of the mantles exactly what our distinction is."

Professor Hardinge says all this with his eyes locked on me. In the depths of my stomach, I feel a seed of shame split apart and attempt to take root. But I raise my chin, and I don't look away from him.

"Fucking bastard," Leo mutters, and I don't know whether he means Don or the professor. He still has the scalpel clutched in his bone-white grip.

"Everyone should have a tray in sight," the professor says, continuing like nothing's happened. "I'm sure you're all bright enough to recognise none of these creatures fit perfectly in any genus of known *teras*." He pauses as if to let this information settle before he adds, "This means the *teras* are mutating."

Most of us are silent, but there are some spurred to speak through their fear. Because what does it mean? What does it mean if we've assumed for years the *teras* have slipped into our world? They have forever defied Earth's rules—but now they are changing. And it's so much worse than the professor thinks because it's not just mutation, is it?

It's evolution.

I sit there, having looked Vengeance in its eyes, and I already know how things are going to go. The University had an open call last year. It knew things were getting bad. Now it's found a hundred-odd hybrids like it's nothing.

These are only F tier. What happens if a *manticore* mutates? What happens if a *scylla* does?

What happens if the *teras* get *stronger?*

I see Leo in the corner of my eye as he starts to breathe heavier. He is looking around the room, eyes darting from horror to horror, eyes unfixed and unfocused. For a moment, it's like looking at a stranger. Leo isn't like this; he wrenched

me back from the ledge just a handful of minutes ago. Is this.
. . panic?

"Hey," I whisper. I touch his arm with my flesh one, squeezing around his bicep. I watch in real-time as he settles, unlocking himself from the foggy vice grip of the attack. He looks down at his hand. His grip must have shifted because the scalpel has sliced open his right palm. He drops the bloody thing onto the table with a clatter and unceremoniously undoes his tie, using it to wrap his hand.

"Do you need a Healer?"

"No," he whispers, unnecessarily focused on wrapping up his palm. He's not looking at me. I want him to; I want to see his eyes, but whatever I just witnessed is a vulnerability he already regrets me viewing. Eyes are the windows to the soul and all that. Leo will let me know his body but not his mind.

Don is looking at us over his shoulder when I look up. I have a blinding moment of desire, a vision where I stand up and pierce his neck with the scalpel.

But that would mean one fewer Hunter.

"You'll be taking turns to dissect them," the professor is saying. I undo my hair, which is long enough that the braid sits below my collarbone. I ground myself by tying it back up tightly, eyes fixed on Professor Hardinge as he goes through the details.

We are to look for abnormalities in the body structure and identify what they are changing into as best we can. It's a thought experiment, at best, because how the fuck can we know?

The professor steps down from his podium and immediately comes to our table. I go tense, expecting another lecture, expecting to look someone I respect in the eye and pretend I am never uncertain of my convictions.

But then I realise someone is behind me. I jolt and turn. Dean Drearton stands waiting at my back.

I didn't hear him approach at all.

"I haven't explained more," Professor Hardinge says across from me.

"Quite alright," the dean says, smiling softly. He talks to the ten of us at this part of the table, saying, "Every mantle is looking for something different. Healers will need to know how to fix you lot up should hybrids appear on the field. Scholars need to study these news aberrations. Artificers—well, it's just good for them to know how to work if a limb is severed at a particular angle or by particular teeth. But it's you Hunters who must learn these creatures. We know the best defence against a *Stygian bird*—get them away from the pack, stay close together, wear thick leathers to limit the impact of their beaks. But if they become something else, our methods will have to change."

The dean moves to clap me on the back. "So, start to learn what might change, and then imagine that a whole lot bigger."

He does it again with that awful, cheery tone of his. Then, he moves on and starts the speech again for the next group of Hunters. We sit in silence until his voice is little more than a distant rumble.

"Cut it first, Cass," Don says.

I pick up the bloody scalpel without wiping Leo's blood away. It might as well be my blood; it has a place on my skin. Somewhere in it is him. His origin, his life source. When I pick up that scalpel and hold it hovering over the fleshy aberration, I make myself think of Leo's sticky blood as a crutch. Something human and strong.

I press the blade against the translucent sack, and it ruptures bladder-like, skin popping and unfolding and fluid splashing over the table. Rancid water and bloody pus pour out over the tray. All of us reel away with sudden nausea.

Someone vomits. The stench pervades and spreads near us until the whole table is shouting about it.

"Jesus fucking Christ," I mutter, pressing my nose into my sleeve.

Leo looks at me and laughs, though he looks about as sick as the rest of us. I flip the scalpel so its handle faces him, and he takes it from me. My hands are covered in his blood. His eyes linger on me. I see in them something Leo doesn't want to surface, something I see every time I mention the hybrid that stalked us in Sherwood Forest. In passing the instrument back to him, in our extended eye contact, a sort of covenant is made. A trade of sorts. I give Leo what he needs to cut his fear away.

He turns to the open carcass and makes a neat cut from groin to neck. Then, with an expert move, he cracks the sternum of the bird, so when he peels back the flesh, putting his hands inside it, the ribcage flares open like wings.

And I look at him and see something erotic about this. Do not judge me—love is a violent act. Every touch, every fuck, is about power—about taking it or giving it up. There is nothing quite so compelling and emasculating and beautiful as being torn apart. I want Leo's hands to make a cavity in my chest. I want him to tear my heart out and take a bite. I watch him rip open the hybrid's ribcage and expose all its organs. But I covet this haruspicy for myself. I want him to be my haruspex; I want to be his. Perhaps it would be the only way to ever learn anything deep about Leo Shaw. I should cut him open, read his liver, and make assumptions about that man's desires and past and future, all from the organs living inside him.

"Its heart is rotten," Leo says glumly. He picks it out with his bare hands. The tiny thing is putrid, unnaturally black and green, shrivelled as if from the inside.

"Check its liver," I whisper. Leo turns to me, as does Don.

Don snickers. He knows what I mean to do. "You can't be serious."

I flash him a look. "These creatures are pulled from myth. Even these hybrids. You can laugh at haruspicy, but in this world, I think that would be foolish. What say you, Hunter Shaw?"

I flush immediately—I've called him the title he has only earned in my bed—but Leo, thankfully, doesn't react. Don's lip curls up at an angle, full of disdain, but I think seeing Leo like this, with his forearms covered in blood and a scalpel in his hand and an eviscerated *teras* spread out in front of him— there is power in that image. Whether or not they understand it, whether or not it is erotic for them as it is for me, Leo owns this moment.

"I say you're right, Mr Jones," he says, with a malicious little grin flashed Don's way.

Don's friend says nothing but stands up somewhat eagerly to peer into the open corpse, and Don sighs in acquiescence. He leans across the table, further than necessary, to look inside the hybrid's exposed stomach. I think he's reaching for the scalpel, but his fingers glide over Leo's hand to rest on the bloody bandage he's made of his tie. They stare at each other, and Leo's fingers go slack as he offers up the scalpel. A shiver runs through me, a sharp jolt of jealousy and fire. What the fuck?

It feels like a covenant has been tainted. Necrosis festering in flesh. I see Don's eyes shift down Leo's chest; he smiles to himself like he's in private before he brings the scalpel down and makes a cut.

Oh, so that's how it is. Perhaps Don is a faggot too.

And a nasty, vindictive bastard to boot.

Don cuts and puts his hands inside. But he's an expert, and I watch somewhat furiously as he reaches in and, fingers dipped in viscera, pulls back the liver.

"Need a bronze liver," I murmur, "a diagram. I don't know —I only read about this."

"Not a haruspex yourself, Jones?" Don says. His sleeves are rolled back, and he's clutching the organ in his hands. His short, cropped hair is slick against his forehead in thin spikes. He looks like a predator in this moment.

Out of nowhere, a diagram appears over my shoulder— the exact copy of the *Piacenza Bronzeleber,* the Liver of Piacenza. When I turn, Dean Drearton is looking at the four of us with a shine in his eye; I haven't seen such a glimmer for months. I have barely seen the man himself.

"Very good, Mr Wamsley," Dean Drearton says.

Leo flashes me a look and gestures to me with the bloody scalpel he's picked up again. "All Mr Jones, sir."

Don's eyes slide to Leo and darken, but I turn to meet the dean's assessing gaze. He's so close to me it's like I have him pressed against the wall, *manticore* stinger to his neck. I wonder if he thinks of this when he leans back ever so slightly.

I could have fucking killed you. Never forget it.

But his gaze becomes a smile. The dean looks at me and nods. "Of course it was. Well done, Jones."

I lean over the diagram without reply and try not to let that comment in. But I love to be praised; I crave it carnally, and I feel some cold, improperly sealed tile dislodge in my heart; I do not want Drearton's affections, but I can't help desiring them. I can't help the swell of my heart when pride inflates it.

"Flip the liver," I tell Don. He hesitates. "The flat side. The visceral side."

He stares at me, and it might be hatred, or it might be something else I see flaring in his eyes. I tap the bronze diagram, which shows the visceral side of the liver divided into forty regions, with each bearing the names of one or more of the Etruscan gods. This diagram is an ancient heaven, a bridge, an amalgamation of flesh and divinity. I look at the mess of viscera Don is covered in and wonder if I am meant to see God.

"That's what they *did*," I spit. "So do it."

Don swallows and flips it. "You are quite the scholar," he says, but he does not mean this kindly.

I meet his stare and wink, which is brave; he might take that out on me next time we spar. But instead of waiting for whatever expression clouds his face, I balk and drag my gaze down to the liver in his hands. I only know one thing about Etruscan divination. I don't know how to read any other part of this diagram, only the top right of the liver—the head, the *caput iocineris*, marked by a triangular geometric structure— which, of course, doesn't actually exist so prominently on the liver. I end up having to lean forward to squint better at the flesh. Drearton looms behind me. I feel Leo's eyes watching, too. Asking for help is simultaneously an option and not.

I want to be able to do this myself.

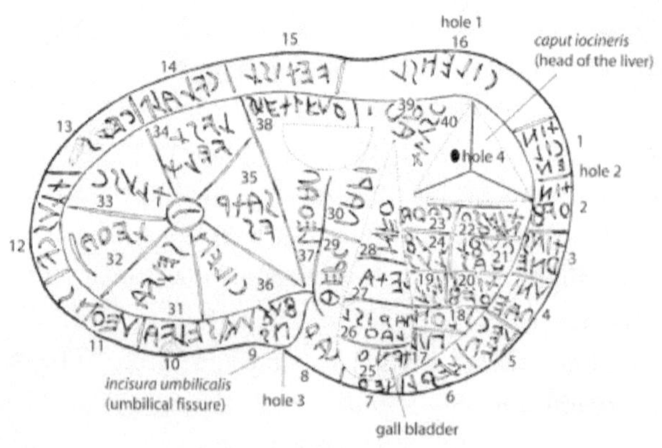

"Can you tilt it? To your right?"

Don does this. It doesn't help me at all. I think I'm sweating a bit, an exhibition under everyone's stares.

I swallow heavily. "Do you think you could just lean forward more?"

He does this as well. But something isn't right about this liver. Something is missing.

"How about—"

"Jones, I swear to God," Don mutters. "I can feel this thing fucking melting."

I lean back suddenly and turn to the dean. He's watching me carefully, his gaze that usual unsettling calm. But something sits poised behind his pupil, waiting for me to speak. It has a predator's quality: haunches tense, waiting. It lurks there, ready to pounce.

I am staring straight at him when I say, "It doesn't have the *caput*."

The dean nods ever so slightly just as Leo starts asking questions. Wet flesh plops onto the platter as Don drops the organ with poorly disguised disgust. I turn back just as he's looking around for somewhere to wipe his hands.

The dean clicks a finger above his head. "Towel for Mr Wamsley," he says, and a Scholar appears with one in hand. Don gets to wiping. I sit bodily down in my seat.

"What does it mean?" Don crows, rubbing uselessly at his blood-stained fingers.

The dean doesn't answer but looks pointedly at me; everything is still a test here. I am being trialled even now.

"It's an omen," I say. "A bad one. The Etruscans always looked for it first. And if it's missing, then. . ."

I flick my eyes up to the dean, who nods once, smallest smile tweaking his lips upwards.

"Then even worse things are to come," Leo murmurs.

And the dean says nothing to this except to nod again.

◈

"OF COURSE BAD things are to come. We didn't need a fucking bird liver to tell us that."

"But why'd we have to *cut everything open* if it didn't mean something?"

The Hunter's common room is alive with clamour. Almost everyone who was present in the hall is here now, crammed in and chatting, debating about what it all means. This room is on the second floor of the Hunter building and takes up most of it in a long stretch of open space. Grand gothic windows span every wall except for one that has been covered by heavy red curtains to keep the warmth in. One small arched window above the fireplace is curtainless, but nothing can be seen in the pitch-black night. Occasionally, the lamplight illuminates a droplet, but beyond that, there's nothing.

Oak study tables and uncomfortable wooden chairs line the outer walls, and big lounges fill the centre. Multiple hand-woven carpets of various colours cover the hardwood floor.

The fire crackles low, and I am squeezed against the arm of one of the several mismatched lounges. Leo squeezes close against me and some other person is packed against him. Part of me has stopped listening because Leo's thigh is flush against mine, and what happened in that hall has seeded me with worry. When I have that panic in me, the type that erases sense, I want to forget about it. Physically.

Leo's pinkie finger half grazes against mine. I want to eat him; I want to fuck right here in front of everyone.

But I slow my breathing and close my eyes because I'm not insane. I'm just desperate.

Over the debate, Leo clears his throat.

"You're missing the point," he says, and for some reason, everyone grows quiet. I understand, from a perverted standpoint; I'm so used to doing what he tells me in bed that power always imbues his words. But everyone else here seems to feel it, too. Leo shifts, sighs, and looks at me. "It's not that bad things are coming. We knew that last year. We knew that with the Open Call. It's that it's in their organs. It's that badness is twisting the *teras* away from myth. Away from what we know."

Sutton, who is the closest thing to a Hunter of legend among us, says, "Shaw's right. Jones could read the liver, and it still *meant* something. It still followed the legends we know. But that won't happen much longer. We won't be able to predict anything. There is a great and upsetting chance that everything we've studied for years will come to mean nothing."

All that finesse. All that training. For what?

Perhaps the only thing that will protect any of us is brute strength. Ruthlessness.

And everyone who died in the trials—the fight for that distinction, that focus on separating us into people good enough to fight—will mean nothing, too. Drearton would have been better off letting everyone who wanted to in.

Is it a farce to think we can stop the *teras* with our numbers dwindling as they are?

I tilt my head towards Leo and wonder how right he was, whether there is any real way to game this institution or this world. In a few short weeks, we'll be assigned to a patrol squad on a rotating basis, first-years shadowing graduate teams patrolling the immediate area beyond the wards and ensuring a safe distance between London and the *teras*. It terrifies me, but only dully. It's not like I haven't done it before. Thaddeus used to take me out with him—illegally, I might add. Less than a year ago, before he was gutted, he took me to Watford.

Where I encountered and killed my first hybrid.

I bow forward over my knees, suddenly exhausted. This

world has been changing under our noses for God knows how long, and we still lack the knowledge to defend ourselves.

The door to the common room opens, and Sutton shoots up. All of us turn as one to spy the newcomer. Then, several more of us stand.

A patrol has returned.

Unconsciously, I get to counting. Six Hunters stroll in. They've either bathed or encountered nothing on their patrol; all of them are pristine.

Don's face appears between us; he drapes his arms over mine and Leo's shoulders and grins when we both turn his way. Under his touch, I tense up, but Leo is relaxed and uncaring, or perhaps relaxed and enjoying it. I lean forward a little further and watch Don's thumb lazily stroking over Leo's defined shoulder. Little shit.

"Hunter Agrawal's party. He's one of the oldest Hunters we have. Came here from India," Don tells us. Age might as well be an indicator of prowess. The older you are, the more *teras* you've survived. "Looks like all of them are back, too. Except for one."

"Thank you, Wamsley," Leo says with a small smile. He catches my eye and quirks a brow; I must look furious.

Sutton stands up to meet Hunter Agrawal. He's in his mid-twenties. Indian—no wonder I've never heard of him. The University likes to make its prized graduates palatable. Even if the colonisation of India was greatly hindered by *teras* and became a failed occupation a decade before my birth, England still wishes to be an empire.

"Drearton's ordered more patrols," Hunter Agrawal says. His voice carries with hardened confidence as he shucks his Hunter coat and tricorn. It shines with embroidered silver thread: *griffin, kelpie, hydra, siren*. A smattering of smaller *teras* like *stygians*. And a *manticore*.

I freeze at that. You may embroider any *teras* you survive an encounter with. You don't have to kill it.

I wonder if Agrawal was there when Thaddeus died. I wonder if he gave the order to abandon my brother, gutted and exposed.

"Means longer shifts for third-years," he continues. He points to a few people whose names I haven't memorised. "You'll be shadowing graduate Hunters. We'll be buffing these patrols out with second-years. First-years, too. Thrown straight into the deep end," he adds, with what I think is a hint of reproach. "Questions?"

A dozen voices start up, all of them second- or third-years who have at least some standing in Agrawal. I haven't seen him or any of his party before, which suggests they've been stationed at an outpost. But these other Hunters respect him greatly.

"Are the reports true?" Sutton asks outright and loudly. "About the farms. The tobacco we can withstand,"—speak for your damn self— "but the crops. . ."

"What did you see out there? Where were you posted?"

The questions rise up like this, and Leo shifts forward with interest. I look at him, trying to take comfort in the sharp line of his jaw. I don't want to listen to any of this, or I don't want any of it to be real. I want to study Latin, learn myths, and fight small, easy *teras* for a pinch of glory. I don't want war.

But Leo is intrigued. His eyes shine with light, with want, like the kind of lust I get for his body. I still don't know what happened to him out there in Southend. I've learned nothing more, learned no further than his throwaway, *"Oh, it's very simple, actually. There's no one left that I love."*

Someone bursts through the door, panting. Sticky silence clings to the air around us. Agrawal turns. His face falls at the sight of her. At once, he and the other Hunters turn to crowd her, shielding this newcomer from the rest of the Hunter cohort.

She must be the last of their group.

"What do you suppose that's about?" Leo murmurs.

Don pulls back, fingers grazing over our shoulders as he stands. I crane to look at him, but his face is cold and serious, devoid of anything flirtatious or bullying. He stares at the group of Hunters.

"Nothing good," he whispers.

Leo and I exchange a glance and turn to give our full attention to Agrawal. Without pomp or ceremony, he spins back to us, hand over his mouth.

"Liverpool Outpost has fallen," he says.

And the whole common room descends into screams.

❧

"IT'S DAYS AWAY," Don murmurs an hour later. The common room is empty save for the dregs of us. Agrawal led most of the graduates, as well as the third- and second-years, to the dean. Some emergency meeting; whoever's left has decided to drink or smoke or fuck, because what's the point?

There are many outposts dotted throughout England. They are small, roughly built holds meant for Hunters to camp out in, clear, and move on. Some of the more prominent ones, like Liverpool, Birmingham, and Norwich, have permanent watchers. They are very rarely abandoned. The fact that Liverpool has fallen suggests an attack. A wave of *teras* descending on seasoned Hunters.

Liverpool to London is over a week's walk away. But we're not talking about humans here. And none of us really know what to do if whatever took out Liverpool is headed our way.

"You're the biggest idiot in this entire room, Wamsley."

Sutton claps Don on the back of the head as she walks by. "Sitting here in your own piss isn't going to do a thing."

Don is quick to anger. He's so quick that he's out of his seat and spitting over his shoulder before Sutton's had time to turn around and square him up. Both of them have muscle, but Sutton has a unique kind of brawn that makes her torso look like armour.

"You going to prove her right, Wamsley?" Leo coos beside me, lilt and all. I jump; he only uses that fucking tone when he's flirting.

Wamsley doesn't flinch, but he steps back and raises his chin, giving Sutton enough room to turn without fear he'd deck her in the back of the head. She leaves us all with a withering stare.

"Get some rest. All of you. We don't know when they're going to hit."

"You really think—" I start to say and cut myself off in a choke. We haven't said the word yet. None of us have, not even Agrawal.

Sutton stares at me like she's seeing me for the first time. "You should cut your hair," she says. Then she turns and walks out the door. "Nothing worse than being dragged along the ground by your hair."

"Fuck this," Don says a beat later. He shoves a finger at me. "Fuck you," and then to Leo, "And fuck you."

Leo laughs. "Oh, what did we do, Wamsley?" But Don is stalking out of the common room, too. Leo opens his arms. "Wamsley!"

The common room door slams closed.

"Jesus Christ," Leo swears beneath his breath. He stands to retrieve an abandoned bottle of crappy, homebrewed rum from the mantlepiece, popping the stopper open with a thumb. I watch him take a swig turned away from me, and I feel my stomach growling not with hunger but with anxiety; this terrible, twisting, jealous rot that wants to corrupt me.

"Why are you flirting with him?" I say, with a tacked-on laugh, to keep it light-humoured and joking and not so devastatingly pathetic.

Leo flashes me a smile. "I like to watch him squirm."

No denial. No backtracking. Whatever. I lean forward with my hand outstretched, and Leo places the bottle in it. I drink deeply.

"By morning, we'll have assignments," Leo says with a deep sigh. "Patrols, and hunting, and classes on top of that." He slaps a hand down on my thigh. "Doesn't leave much time for fun."

I smile despite myself because I'm a whore, but the lust dies quietly when I think about what's happening. Should I crawl into his lap and let him have me here? Should I pretend like I'm not jealous or scared? Or is the world changing in such a way that nothing may ever be alright again?

"What is it?" he asks.

I know the answer, but I still ask: "You think they'll send us right out?"

Leo shrugs. He gestures back for the bottle. I want to pour it straight into his mouth. "Maybe not far," he murmurs after a swig. "Maybe not to outposts. But you're smart, Cass. You know they'll throw us into the mix early."

He is right; certainty takes root in my belly. And then the fear becomes a swirling mix of anxiety and despair. It pushes dully against my ribcage, pressing out from the inside. Nausea and fear and sadness—I feel them all distantly, not because they aren't there, but because they are burrowing deep, maggot-like, chewing on my good sense and security to make me unstable and hollow.

I take a sharp, deep breath; I'd been holding stale air in

my lungs for too long. Leo raises a questioning brow. He looks. . . sad, in a way. Disappointed.

Perhaps I would be disappointed, too, if the body I wanted to fuck had too many emotions.

"I just wish I had a cigarette," I say finally. "I wish I didn't have to ration it." I wish I had ten; I wish I could smoke them all at once and drown in their smoke.

"You do," Leo says with a frown, reaching for another swig.

"No," I say, with a little chuckle. Tobacco is rare, and I already keenly feel the lack of it. "It's too precious now with the farms gone. And I have a feeling I'm going to become a really awful person when it's gone for good."

Headaches, snapping, withdrawals. Full body shakes. I'm irrational already—but haven't I always been?

Perhaps I'll return to alcoholism.

"Just have one, Cass."

I shake my head, and Leo sighs loudly. Though, when I look up, a tiny smile curls his lips.

"I was going to leave it," Leo murmurs. He shifts, putting the bottle down so he can reach down into his pocket. "Until we got back from first patrols, at least. Or until you really needed it. But if you need it now..."

He pulls something out of his pocket and hands it to me.

A rectangle of silver sits in his palm. I frown, not understanding, and it takes a few blinks for the shape to clarify.

It's a cigarette case.

Then Leo flips it open, and it's near overflowing with pre-rolled cigarettes.

I exhale in a rush, "Holy fuck, you are godly," and Leo laughs, pulling one out and pressing it between my lips. I don't smoke it right away. I put it between my fingers and pick the case up from Leo's palm, turning it over so it catches the light.

It's heavily embossed, and with the way things are right now, it must have cost a fortune. But trades are the currency here—and I'm scared of whatever this cost him.

I swear Leo can read my mind because he says, "You've taught me how to bargain for deals around here."

I flinch—I bargained our lives for a set of rooms, for the chance to read my brother's letter—but there's no malice in his eyes.

"What did you trade, your body?" I joke, and Leo does something with his brows and a low laugh that makes my groin hot.

"I don't think you'd like that very much if my teasing of Don Wamsley is anything to go by."

Is that all it is? I want to ask but don't in case I don't like the answer.

"What did you trade, Hunter Shaw?"

Leo says, without so much of a change of tone, "A vial of *manticore* poison," like it was dirt, or feathers, or as common as stones. As if it wasn't something I gave him to protect himself.

"*What?*"

I stare at him.

Leo hacked the stinger off the *manticore*'s corpse, and after I threatened the dean with it, we got it processed. We extracted the paralysing poison into four vials, and because I was a little bit infatuated, I split them evenly.

Now I have two, and Leo is down to one—for cigarettes. For me.

I can't look at him. "Why?"

Nonchalantly, like it's nothing, "Because you saved my life. Oh, and I don't like owing favours."

I glance up and catch his smile. "A cigarette case for your life?"

His eyes darken, heavy-lidded and desire-filled. "Not good enough?"

"Not even close," I say. I lean over to kiss him and drag his lip away with my teeth. "You'll have to make it up some other way."

"Woe is me," he says in an exhale. I could lean forward again. I could put my hand on his stomach. And he would wrench me over into his lap.

But instead, I blink and look down at the case properly. Flowers and snakes fill it. I raise a brow. "Snakes?"

"I was trying to find something phallic shaped, but alas…" he trails off, then breaks into a laugh at whatever look is on my face. "I'm joking, Cass. I wasn't exactly spoiled for choice. It was Sutton's; she's trying to give them up."

"It doesn't matter." I shake my head and look down at it again. "It's beautiful."

I stare at the little beady eye of the snake embossed in the silver, and I'm scared to look up. I'm scared that when I look at Leo next, nothing will have changed. He will kiss me, and he will fuck me, but he won't let me know him. He won't let it become anything, and neither will I.

But if I have to keep telling myself that, how true can it be?

The lounge creaks as his weight shifts. His warm hand comes to rest on my wrist. "What is it?" he asks softly, with worry in his voice.

And I've never been more scared than in that moment.

Not when Bellamy died, or Silas, or when Vengeance stared into my soul. I am scared now because I'm afraid to be loved and equally afraid to be unworthy of it.

Ruthless. You have to be ruthless. Leo has already told me what kind of man he is. What kind of man he wants to be. But what if I could change that? What if he's decided loving me is just as ruthless as never showing me his heart?

"Cassius?"

"It's beautiful." The words spill out in haste. I put the case down. "More beautiful than I probably deserve."

"Don't say that."

"Leo," I say sharply. I force myself to look at him. "Don't get me pretty gifts. Don't—muddle things."

His eyes move from wide and questioning to dark and sure. He leans back and briefly becomes someone else—that unknowable boy he used to be in Southend before I met him on the road in front of my brother's corpse. "Why not? Why shouldn't I? I wanted you to have it."

"And what does it mean?"

A flicker of disappointment flashes in his eyes. I hate it when he looks at me like that. "It's a gift, Cassius."

It means nothing. It means everything. *Shut up. Shut the fuck up before he says outright what you're afraid to learn.*

I want to ask: *But does it mean you love me? Does it mean I'm worth something to you?*

And does it matter, really, when the world is falling apart? If he wants me, he should be able to have me. I want him; I should be able to have him. Who cares about love? Who cares?

The cigarette case is a gift. I put the cigarette he plucked out for me back in my mouth.

"Then let me give you one back," I murmur around it.

He stays very still as I lean over. My fingers slip beneath the leather patch covering the eternal wound in his cheek.

"What are you doing," he whispers, not a question. Forefinger and thumb on his chin, I turn his head until the red gum glistens and the teeth shine, a beautiful cutaway of his perfect face.

I light the cigarette with a match sparked over the hardwood table in a tiny defiance of the sanctity of this institution. An empire of water marks and heat stains has already marched over this sad wood, but I am determined to leave a mark of my own. And once lit, it is instantaneous bliss.

The tobacco is different, slightly sweeter, but once it reaches my throat and becomes an intangible burn, a bright hotness in my throat, I hold my breath and drag Leo forward into a kiss.

This is self-destructive. This is exactly what I need and exactly what will be my end, but I open my mouth anyway and exhale into Leo's throat. I try to get all of it out: smoke, anxiety, inconsistency, emotion; I wish to be a cavern. To be that, I must excavate all this useless weight out of me. Ruthless and hollow. It's the only way I'll live.

But why shouldn't I have fun too?

Wisps of smoke creep out from the gap in Leo's face, tendrils crawling from between his teeth before he exhales heavily in surprise.

"You're disgusting," he tells me. For half a moment, he sounds like my father—which should unnerve me. It doesn't. I make friends with the twinkle in Leo's eye and perch my tongue against my canines. Lust blooms through his pupil. Leo cracks a smile. "Do it again."

So I do. I breathe smoke into his mouth over and again until the cigarette is down to a nub, and Leo takes it from my hand, squashes it underfoot, and roughly pulls me into his lap. His new-earned strength is apparent; he half lifts me, half drags until I'm safely sat between his legs, and without care for where we are—the visibility afforded by the bright lights, the open space, the fact anyone might walk in—he grinds up against me with a low moan. And I grind back in answer. It feels juvenile in a sense, awkward and desperate and ruttish, the way it used to be for me in cold alleys, fumbling in the dark. But this is temerarious. Bold. I almost want him here, fucked over the lounges or the carpet, and loud enough to draw an audience.

Reckless in another way.

My breaths are short and desperate, and I'm straining hard from the thought alone. Leo grazes his palm across my cock and leans close.

"I want to fuck you," he murmurs against my neck, hot mouth murmuring. "Right here."

With a kind of obligation, I say, "But—"

And without softness, hands on my ass, he grinds up so I can feel the hungry press of his cock between the cleft. Eagerness drowns out everything else. I hastily unbuckle my trousers. We are a sudden mess of limbs as I awkwardly fumble to wrench mine off, and the twinkle in Leo's eyes speaks to me with a particular sinful vernacular; I see in my mind's eye what he wants to do to me. How precisely he wants to ruin me. With one leg raised to rip off a trouser leg, I tilt my body weight to the other side to shimmy off the other. Leo watches all this, seemingly relaxed and unhurried, but as soon as the pants are off, he reaches up to the tie around my neck and yanks me forward. I collapse against him, half exposed and flushed, but he looks at me like I'm godly and pure, with the kind of reverence I used to reserve for God, and I want nothing more than to let him have me right now.

His hands slip under my shirt. Rough callous catches on my skin, and the bandage around his right hand scratches me. He presses unknowingly against a days-old bruise somewhere on my upper back. At the same time, his left hand has snaked around my thigh. He grips it possessively.

"Is saliva enough?" he whispers, and no, probably not, but I almost want it to hurt.

"Yes," I murmur, hips moving, "Yes."

He slips his hand out from under my shirt and puts his fingers to my lips. I open readily. Leo pushes two inside and tips my head back until I can barely see him, until he has the arched view of my throat, bobbing as I suck. All the while, he stares with his brows up and mouth open like he's in awe of me. We hold each other's gaze. Time slows itself for us, letting me look at the freckles blooming under his tanned skin, at how fluffy his hair is getting. But the lust in his eyes has its own gravity, and I'm drawn inevitably to them. I want to feed his hunger. I want to make sure he never starves again.

Leo exhales, like something heavy has just been lifted from his chest. He slips his fingers out and makes another noise as a string of saliva slips free of my lips. His cock throbs against my belly, and in answer, a bead of my precum wells against his skin. Leo moves his hand instantly to brush against the head.

I hiss at the sudden sensation, rocking involuntarily forward, fingers gripping the nape of Leo's neck. His breath is hot against my skin, and he waits no longer to push his fingers close to me. I shuffle and spread my legs and lower myself greedily against his fingers as he pushes in, and I refuse to look away from him.

"Fuck yourself on my fingers," he whispers rather sweetly —there's no need for an order or a threat because I want to. I drag myself up and down, grunting against the sharp spark of pleasure, the catch of his fingernail near the prostate; I don't stop.

"That's a good boy," he murmurs, tongue perched against the corner of his mischievous smile. "Look at you."

I flush and close my eyes. Sometimes, the eye contact is too much; I'm afraid he'll know me too well. He'll learn the intricacies of my degenerate soul, and I won't be able to be anything except his dog.

His bitch in heat—because I'm certainly nothing like that already.

Without warning, Leo pulls his fingers free. He stands

upright and takes me with him. My heart flies to my throat, thinking we've been caught, but before I can even turn to check that we're alone, he puts himself behind me.

"*Ah...*"

My head is wrenched back when he laces his fingers in my hair. His other hand wraps around my belly. And just as the pressure releases at my scalp, he pushes down on my neck and shoves me roughly onto the lounge.

I fall, spread-legged, the top half of my uniform a crumpled mess. I grip the seat and look over my shoulder at him; he's standing back and touching himself in long, slow strokes, watching me with that heavy-lidded stare of his. And the hunger in him scares me suddenly: that he can look at me messy and sprawled and so fucking desperate and find he's hungry enough to want me.

Leo crowds forward and moves me into another angle with ease as if I were a doll. He puts his knees on either side of me, and pushes inside.

I can't help the convulsive roll of my eyes as I take him. Leo makes a low hum of approval and fucks fully into me in a hard thrust.

"*Shit,*" I gasp. The pain is a bright ache. Sense briefly comes back to me—we are going to get caught, I cannot for the life of me stay quiet, I am going to moan until we have an audience, and then I am going to kill myself—but then Leo slides out and fucks forward again, and the thought withers and dies under a starburst of pained pleasure. He grazes against my prostate, and my body is forced into pleasured relaxation. My eyes are still lost somewhere in the heavens, and when he wrenches my head back so he can slip a hand around my throat, I arch so violently that I hear my spine pop in protest. My arm aborts in an attempt to reach back for him; he catches it, slips his fingers in mine, and drives us both into the couch.

I ignore the revenant of my faith as it rears up in horror at how reckless we're being. But faith is an easy thing to bury when desire has corroded the blockade. Neither guilt nor God is strong enough to cleanse me now. Neither Satan nor the hounds of hell will catch me; for I am briefly immortal in the only way that matters; in the way of the flesh, which in this life is *every fucking thing.*

"You feel so good," Leo murmurs, grunting, lost in his own rhythm. "You feel so fucking good."

There's an answering twitch between my legs; I start fucking myself on his cock, thrusting back with pathetic desperation. I can't help it. I want it too much to stop. So I shove my body weight onto one hand, pressing desperately against the cushions, and thrust my hips back, grabbing my aching cock with my other hand.

Leo takes over.

"Not yet," he says and pulls out. He forcibly moves my hand away. I whimper—God, *pathetic*—and let him puppet me into an even more exposing position. With one leg on the ground and the other crammed into the corner of the couch, Leo urges my hips up. I have to bite my tongue so I don't die, so that the part of me that wants to cower from this indecency doesn't take over, but Leo takes his time looking at me, teasing me, thumb stroking in and out of my ass before the way I tense around his finger makes him hiss. Quickly, I feel Leo's cock press down again, and he pushes inside me.

This new angle is so deep I finally moan loudly, my voice smothered by the lounge and the rain and the crackling fire. Something near my pelvis aches, but it's dulled by the heat in my body, and the loud want for ecstasy stifling everything else. When Leo slams forward again, I spasm with a strangled, high noise. My hands fumble against the lounge, desperate to find a grip that might keep me tethered to this reality. Leo moves the hair away from the back of my neck and kisses me as he moves incessantly and then unkindly, the force of his thrusts becoming so violent I'm worried I'll call God's name instead of his. I'll find my faith again in the moments before I come; I'll beg for help and for orgasm in the same breath.

But then I'm moving too, hips grinding desperately against the lounge. The tiniest bit of friction against my cock drives me insane. Distantly, I'm astounded by the kind of sounds escaping me: suddenly, I don't care who hears me. I don't care who knows I'm getting fucked within an inch of my life—for I am desired, and I am being had, and at the end of the world, what greater value can a body have than that?

Leo hears how close I am, or he feels it; pleasure modulates my voice, my body, and it's obvious he has me on the edge. He rips my head back by my hair—*Christ,* I scream out—and my next whimper makes him come in a blinding bull rush. My gaze goes hazy; I barely have to touch myself before I'm coming, too, catching the wet heat in the palm of my hand.

My knees are shaking at the end of it. Leo slides out and collapses onto the floor, positioning himself so his head can rest on the cushions. He reaches out blindly and pats my leg, and I crawl off to sit by him.

He is looking at me, so I look back. I feel the carpet beneath me and see the light of the fire warping light and shadows behind Leo's head. I smell the age of this room and hear the rain outside. In the afterglow, every sense works to shape an illusion I can rest in. Gone is the truth of our fate tomorrow. I pretend as I did the night before our final trial, that perhaps Leo and I might talk to one another as partners and that we might find solace in one another over the years of our study here.

That we might live.

"What is it?" Leo asks. His finger skims my chin, and he

smiles at me, still out of breath. I watch the rise and fall of his beautiful, sweat-drenched chest. He makes a face. "Cass?"

I force a smile and shake my head, undoing the rest of the buttons on my sweat-drenched shirt and loosening the tie. No tomorrow is promised; I should know that by now.

"I think you nearly killed me," I say instead of everything else I want to.

"And endure the fun and whimsy of this world all on my lonesome?" Leo grins. He leans forward and kisses me. "Never."

But that is Leo Shaw's prerogative, and I would do well to remember it.

Recklessness before all.

Recklessness before love.

And most definitely recklessness before me.

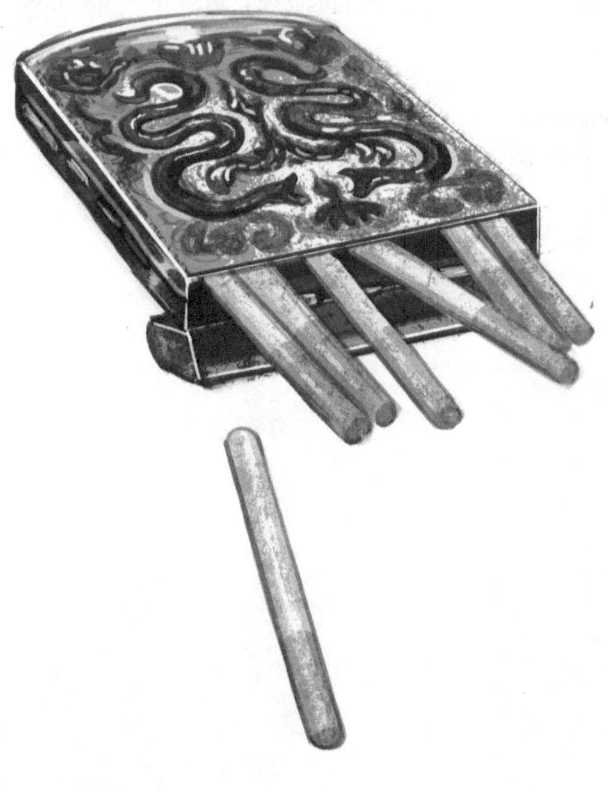

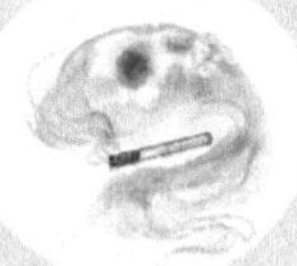

LESSON FIVE

"Come on, Jones, don't let me down."

The library is filled with first-years deep in their books and several second-years supervising us. Meléti skirts between the narrowly placed study tables like blood in a vein, responding instantly to requests and orders. For scheduled study, the *automaton* gets nothing from us. But if we wish to study outside of the set subject, it will likely try to wriggle information out of us.

Don speaks to me, and he is far too close to my ear. I smell honey on his breath, a luxury food he must have squirrelled away. Like my cigarettes, more and more of us are dipping into stashes. I glance up at him and meet his eye.

"You don't like the way I study?" I ask. I think I'm probably amongst the most well-read here, besides the Londoners I've started calling 'career graduates'. They could hide a bit during the trials, but they reek of their upbringing now: Horace and Virgil and Cicero and Herodotus and Thucydides at the forefront of their minds. I feel most comfortable with a book in hand, a dictionary I can thumb through when vocabulary slips away from me. But they have precious years I never had, and the privilege of education drilled into them. No *teras* threat to contend with. No hunger, no constant anxiety. Now, they possess the kind of intelligent mind I will strive towards forever. Latin and Greek roll of their tongues like first languages. Their minds are as consistent as a beating heart, metronome steady, and I feel like a floating rib, in constant limbo, not even attached to the sternum.

I wish Don would pick on them, but there's nothing there to critique.

"Not at all," Don whispers. "Though from what I've heard, you're rather loud when you study with a partner."

I've been sore all morning for obvious reasons. It hurts to sit; it hurts to walk. My hips ache, and my ass stings, and I—don't care. Or rather, I quite enjoy it, if just for the fucked-up truth that this pain is proof Leo wanted me to fuck me hard.

I turn bodily to face Don. "For a man so upset by my nature, you do spend an awful lot of time invested in my faggotry."

Don's nostrils flare. He glances over his shoulder, like anyone will care what he's up to when it's likely an army of *teras* are marching towards London.

"Just study hard," he snaps and fucks off.

How Don became our supervisor, I'm not sure—but I suspect it's because he's the most emotionally volatile out of all the second-years. A few second-year Hunters are dotted around, and every other first-year is spread throughout the library. More than once I think I've spotted the shaggy cut of Fred Lin, and I've quickly turned away. Better not to perceive her at all than to make eye contact.

I am meant to be focusing, but Leo chose to actually apply himself to the books and has thus isolated himself in some corner on the upper level. I have taken this personally. Fred and Victoria are certainly around, and I'm terrified to see them. I think how awful it will be in a few months when I am studying for an arbitrarily silly test and see panicked applicants stumbling into this place. With personal ward-stone in hand, they won't see me. I will have to bear witness alone as someone else falls to the *automaton*'s bullshit. That is the cycle of this place. I endure it, and instead of helping anyone else, I will let the next lot endure it, too.

But at least, if I am around in a few months' time to witness this, it means London is still standing. And at this point, who knows if that's a pipedream.

We are, obviously, researching *teras*. Copies of the final report made before Liverpool Outpost fell have been circulated, and now we're investigating every fine detail of it.

It reads:

Came after first strike of midnight. Black dogs, monstrous teeth, howling. Men on horseback, no skin, screams like ocean waves. We flee —Liverpool has fallen.

Godspeed.

The woman who returned late in Agrawal's crew had a copy of it. As we were told, at least one of Liverpool's Hunters made it to an outpost between Liverpool and Manchester; the report was passed to Manchester Outpost, and a copy was sent to the major outposts at Sheffield, Birmingham, Nottingham, and London via pigeon post. Several riders were sent out to the smaller outposts lacking the birds. There has been no word from the north.

It didn't take any of us long to realise something was wrong with the report. The descriptions alone are too far removed from the norm of our threat. A horde of monstrous black dogs emerging from the mist. A fleshy, skinless beast galloping forward, with a scream like waves crashing on rock.

I pause once more at that line. Skinless, fleshy—I think instantly of Vengeance, and the finger-like prongs reaching for me—*stop thinking about that.*

Focus.

After midnight. An inescapable throng of *teras*. There's no doubt about it.

It was an organised attack.

The Scholars' work now is to develop defensive techniques, but it's all hands on deck. We Hunters are to read the descriptions, draw our own conclusions regarding what myths they originate from, and determine if there are any weaknesses written down for us. This is the evolution of the University now: all of us must be brilliant. All of us should be all-rounders. All of us should expect to be deployed; all of us should expect war.

My palms are clammy with the thought. I have to shake out my hands and wipe them on my trousers before I return to the books I have spread out before me.

I don't bother with the black dogs, not at first—my interest is in the fleshy beast slouching towards London. It isn't Greek. It isn't Roman. It isn't even English.

It's Scottish. Orkney.

Nuckelavee.

I don't know much about it. Most of the native *teras* were driven away by the sheer number of Greco-Roman *teras*. Part of me knows I should draw conclusions, that I should recognise either an unsettling treaty forming between various myths, or an evolutionary shift, or *something* that might explain this new dynamic. The resurgence of old beasts.

But holding space for these thoughts means they can fester, and I'll be inevitably useless when my mind is overrun by an army of skinless *nuckelavee* led by that tall, pronged, new beast, seeking *vindicare*.

I spend a few minutes reading about the *nuckelavee*. Myths say its breath can wilt crops—just what London needs—and that from afar, it might look like a rider on a horse.

Walter Traill Dennison wrote an account a few years ago

— "Orkney Folklore, Sea Myths"—after speaking to a man named Tammas, who encountered and survived the creature.

The account reads:

"The lower part of this terrible monster, as seen by Tammie, was like a great horse, with flappers like fins about his legs and a mouth as wide as a whale's from which came breath like steam from a brewing kettle. He had but one eye as red as fire.

On him sat, or rather seemed to grow from his back, a huge man with no legs and arms that nearly reached to the ground. His head was as big as a clue of simmons, and this huge head kept rolling from one shoulder to the other as if it meant to tumble off.

But what to Tammie appeared most horrible of all was that the monster was skinless...the whole surface of it showing only red, raw flesh, in which Tammie saw blood, black as tar, running through yellow veins, and great white sinews, thick as horse tethers, twisting, stretching, and contracting, as the monster moved.

....

The mouth of the monster yawned like a bottomless pit..."

Tammas escaped by jumping into the freshwater loch. The *nuckelavee* should be contained by freshwater—it shouldn't be able to cross. Likewise, I read accounts that say another mythical spirit, Sea Mither, contains the *nuckelavee* in summer months. Who knows if any of this is still relevant? Evolution might mean an end to every weakness, and I feel that fear in me corrode something vital: the willpower keeping me together. I roughly close the book and focus on breathing and not falling apart so completely before my colleagues, before Don.

Who is looking at me, I realise. Looking not with the disgust I've come to expect from his breed of bully but with a quiet acknowledgement. He nods at me, just once, and it feels like a momentary armistice. I nod back.

We both know there are bigger battles to face than the animosity between us.

"Agrawal's done," a Hunter declares from the door. We all spin to the sound. The second-years nod and move to collect little slips of folded paper—our first assignments.

The Hunter hands them out and slips further into the library. As the second-years move insect-quick, handing out assignments, the Hunter clears his throat.

"I am Len Hayes of Agrawal's party. Graduated in '97." That makes this his third year as a fully-fledged Hunter. "Dean Drearton has confirmed that patrols will still go ahead: third-, second-, and first-years will be joining us. And so will members of other disciplines."

Whispers start up instantly. The *automaton* makes a sharp, droning noise that scares everyone back into quiet. Hayes waits with his hands behind his back. I see his black coat shimmer with his embroidered *teras*. He must be twenty-five or so, but his face is sullen and lined. When he gestures next, I see he's wearing gloves, and I wonder if he is like me. Whether his bones belong to him, or whether they're made of porcelain or marble or wood. Whether he feels indebted to the University, or whether he hates it.

I don't know why I think of this, nor why it makes my left arm ache at the point of the bitten-off ulna. Absentmindedly, I massage the joint and wait for Don to hand me my fate.

"Each patrol will have a smattering of student Scholars, Artificers, Healers—I don't want to *fucking* hear it," Hayes says roughly, raising a hand towards a sound of outrage somewhere to my right. "Drearton's kept us alive this long, and Drearton is correct in thinking that we must utilise every discipline in this war. Before you ask, no, we will not be overflowing with every individual discipline. Names are on your sheets; doesn't matter if you know no one, you will trust them. Every name on that list is an ally. Anyone who receives a slip of paper is heading out tonight. Everyone else, expect your assignments tomorrow."

Just as he finishes, Don hands me my paper. So, tonight, then. I take it in my hand and stare down at it, and it feels akin to holding the pages of the Bible between my forefinger and thumb. Something holy sits in these words, something bigger than me. A shiver runs down my spine, and I look up to the upper levels of the library. I spot him. Leo stares down, his forehead pressed against the banister. He has no paper in his hand.

Leo gives me a nod of his own. *Ruthless*, he mouths to me. I nod back and pretend 'ruthless' is Leo's way of showing love.

My hands are shaking. I put down the note and waste another cigarette calming my nerves. I slip the beautiful case from my pocket, light one, breathe, breathe, breathe.

Then, I open the paper and say, "Shit."

❧ 6 ❧

LESSON SIX

Fog whips up in white whorls as the horses trot towards Cripplegate.

We ride out in silence, which is good because I'm still sore from that brutal fuck and end up thinking about it every painful trot.

Get your thoughts in order, Cass. You're probably about to die.

The night air is sharp with a cold bite, and all of London is huddled indoors. Most of the ward is quiet. The news of impending *teras* has spread, I guess, but so too have the coping mechanisms of the University. Last night's sounds are echoed beyond the campus: revelry and fucking and laughter weave through the night air to us, even when many other buildings are quiet. Most of London sits empty now. The remaining useful few still need to cope, and everyone copes with doom differently.

Though I should stop thinking like this. Nothing has been confirmed. Nothing is certain. Liverpool might have been a singular, terrible thing.

"First-years, I want you in the middle," Sutton calls from ahead. There are five of us Hunters in total: two graduates—

Sutton, a fresh meat graduate, and Fraser, who is another of Agrawal's crew. He is wiry and unsettlingly tall, in his early twenties, but pockmarked by scars. His Hunter robes shine iridescent beneath the moonlight with silver wisps detailing his conquests. The embroidery only covers the mantle. Which is still exceptional—I am not judging. I just wish there was a Hunter well into his forties whom I might imprint onto, a well-seasoned survivor, proof that I might live beyond thirty. And I could form a little psycho-sexual bond with him that would be enough armour for whatever we might face out here.

But alas.

Besides the graduates, there is a second-year woman with shorn hair. She hasn't given me her name. The other first-year Hunter with me is called Eddie Green. It took me a moment to place him, and when I did, a great sickness twisted up my belly.

Because I shot his roommate in the head.

Green watched a suicide; Dean Drearton handed him a bottle to numb the sight and encouraged me to pull the trigger of my brother's gun. Every time Green looks at me, his eyes bulge. I suspect I'm burned into that memory; I am irrevocably intertwined.

We are to be met at Cripplegate by the patrollers from other disciplines. I see them rise out of the mist, waiting for us in a quiet, uneasy group split into thirds, standing apart from one another. Two fortified towers frame the portcullis of Cripplegate, closed to the bitter, dangerous night beyond. Torches pulse softly from sconces lining the wall, offering foggy gaslight against the dark gloom. It is in this dampened light that I see my new comrades: a singular first-year Artificer, two Scholars, a first-year and a third-year, each marked by the year patch peeking beneath their discipline's coloured cloaks, and then the Healers. Two of them. A third-year woman with a stern face and prominent nose, dark hair cut short and severe around her pale face.

And Victoria.

When I see her, I think about diving headfirst off my horse in the hope my neck will crack at just the right angle, and I never have to be confronted about the whole I-let-Bellamy-be-torn-to-shreds-and-used-his-corpse-as-a-distraction thing. But she is poised in such a way, with her shoulders back and her hair plaited, lovely blue cloak draped over the horse's flank, that it looks like Victoria Bennet could never even entertain a violent thought.

Her eyes say otherwise. They glance in my direction, just for a moment, and are aflame with concentrated furore; like the Erinyes, "divinities implacable, doom-laden"—blood is on my hands, and she will hound me for eternity over it. I am the man chased to the ends of the earth by the Furies for my sins. Or at least I should be. What happened in the trials has had no ramifications, and not even Victoria seems to have the energy to act on the anger in her heart.

"Right," Fraser says as he pulls on his horse's reins, bringing the gelding to a stop. No time for pleasantries or introductions, apparently. "This is how this works. Any non-Hunter—no matter your year grade, no matter if you've patrolled with us before—will ride in the middle. Sutton pulls up the rear; I lead. Two volunteers for the dark lanterns," — hands are raised before Fraser finishes— "and keep chatter to the minimum. This morning's patrol had no *teras* sightings, so let's hope it's an easy one. Questions?"

No one says anything. Fraser waits a moment longer, then clicks his horse into a trot.

Cripplegate's portcullis shudders up for us, and we burst forth in a colourful motley, our cloaks billowing out with the wind. Briefly, I see Drearton's vision in the unification of our disciplines: a beautiful militia, a new Crusade as God's agents defeat Satan's beasts. I understand in that singular moment how war might work in the University's favour, if not in London's. If we win, there is no force strong enough to knock Drearton from his perch. He will be London's saviour, and every person who ever spoke against him, every protest that questioned his actions, will be discredited.

But I have no time to dwell on this. Nausea sinks into my skin; it's as if the world changes instantly once we're beyond the wardstones' protection. How real that feeling is, I'm not sure, except I find myself believing in London's safety the way I used to worship God. If every prayer of mine could bolster our defences, I would be on my knees, prostrating before Drearton in every waking moment.

Desperation is not the best quality for a Hunter to foster —but it is my ever-present companion, whatever form it takes.

We ride in silence for an hour. Darkness swallows us, but the horses know the path and canter confidently onward, unafraid. The dark lanterns provide just enough illumination for us to travel by but not enough to draw unwanted attention. They come with a shield that can be raised if we need to conceal the light quickly. But I still feel as if something is watching us the entire time we are moving.

When Fraser raises a hand for us to slow, it all becomes much worse. I don't know where we are, beyond the general knowledge we've been riding northwest, in the direction of Harrow and Watford, but—and I am thankful for this—not to the towns themselves.

I don't want to see what became of Watford. If anyone was brave enough to haul the meat of those bodies into a mass grave to start again. If life continued in that town after I know what happened there.

That was the last time Thaddeus was proud of me. I can never go back.

Stop it. None of this matters anymore. This sadness does nothing for you; it won't even keep you alive.

I swallow my emotion because that part of me is right. We've slowed down, well away from the target, the place we must reach before we're clear to turn around and head back to safety. Fraser can sense something in the dark.

The lanterns throw a terrible yellow haze that shrouds us like a lace veil, but the deep night sits above us, its own unconquerable dominion, and it seems I can't quite extricate myself from God because His Word comes unbidden into the echo chamber of my mind:

Your enemy, the devil, prowls around like a roaring lion looking for someone to devour.

And I feel as I did every other time I've left London's wards; that something is not right.

Because Vengeance is close.

I can feel it, in the way I once felt the Holy Spirit settle in my bones, in the way lust is imbricated in my soul; with the quiet, crippling despair I felt upon seeing my brother split open and steaming in the bloody snow. I shudder, and I see Victoria shudder, too. It is the first time she looks at me in months with something other than hatred.

But is fear any better?

And then I look down. Her cloak is open like the rest of ours, but she's not in uniform. Not in the usual uniform, anyway. She wears a long, thin, muslin skirt in deep blue. It sits high-waisted over her stomach and rounds out. For just a moment, I forget the *teras* pressing against the dark veil of the night, and I remember her nearly three months earlier crying beneath that great oak outside the library, weeping, speaking in a rush, saying, "I suddenly can't stand him. I can't stand any of this. I can't stand myself," and I had thought it was all about the trials and the awful knowledge of what the institution wanted us to become.

But it was more than that.

None of us had noticed.

"You're pregnant," I say.

Victoria opens her mouth. Her horse stamps beneath her.

A scream splits the air.

Several clicks sound as the well-trained among us instinctively draw their guns. I pull two weapons in a flurry: Thaddeus' flintlock and a dagger I've coated with *manticore* poison. I wrench my head towards the sound and realise it's gone dark. Someone's dropped a lantern. The whole rear flank has been eaten by shadow, and all we have in order to understand the state of things is a flurry of sound: whinnying, stamping, confused and agitated humans stumbling about.

"Get together," Fraser hisses. He makes a few noises with his mouth; no one who knows what the signal means responds. I hear him curse when I get close, and I'm thankful the remaining lantern bearer—the first-year Artificer—is terrified and shaking. It means I won't have to see the fear grow in my superior's eyes.

The horses are spooked. I look around for the other Hunters. For a moment, I only see Fraser, and I imagine what it would mean if everyone else were dead.

We stay still. All of us breathe shallowly. With the little torchlight, I squint into the dark, gun raised and arm shaking. Adrenaline tries to bludgeon away everything I've ever learned—but I have survived a *manticore*. I will not die here today.

The air is filled with blood, acrid and sickly sweet, and another scent that, when I breathe deep, makes my stomach flip.

A reek of ocean brine

By God, do not be a *nuckelavee.*

It's too far from the ocean. The *nuckelavee* doesn't cross freshwater. I know by now the way anxiety poisons rationality; I slow my breathing, let the animal part of me yawn and stretch and sink into its senses. It is something else; those dogs, maybe. Black Shuck, or one of the many ghastly black hounds recorded in British folklore. I don't know anything about it or how to kill it. I spent my whole life assuming the Greco-Roman plague had driven back everything native. Now I am a fucking child. A terrified, fucking child.

Something shifts out of the grey fog. Unthinking, I pull back the hammer on the flintlock, arm swivelling towards the sound. But then Sutton gallops out of the shadow with a bleeding Green slung over her horse. Fraser snatches the torch from the Artificer's hands and waves it closer to them. The stolen light lets us see the damage. Sutton is pale and tight-lipped. Green bobs unresponsive over the horse's back behind her. I get a glimpse of what I assume is the remains of Green's horse—torn open, tongue lolling out. Tendons pulled away. It had only been a second. Hadn't it? One second, and the horse was dead.

"Report," Fraser hisses, eyes darting wild around us. Sutton is spooked. "*Report,* Hunter."

"We saw nothing," she whispers. "But I felt it rush past. Ground-based and large. Fast, too. That's it. Green flung himself at me. But Lydia..." Sutton turns around to stare into the dark.

I glance down. Blood has splattered her horse's flank; some of it flows from Green's destroyed calf. Bone puckers through.

"Down a Healer," Victoria whispers beside me. "You?"

I murmur back tersely, "A Hunter. Second-year."

Lydia. That was the name she didn't share.

Victoria brings her horse towards Sutton's. "If I don't do this now, he'll bleed to death."

Fraser nods. "Then do your job. Artificer!" Fraser hisses as he hands the torch back to the poor boy. "Determine whether Green will need a new leg. Hunters, dismount."

Fraser helps Sutton move Green to the ground.

I am shaking as I slide off. The cold air wicks the sweat off me and makes my palms freeze. The prosthetic aches at the joint, too; I wonder if it can freeze over and what I'll do if it locks up when the dark beast slouches out of the dark for my throat.

The instant Green is on the ground, Fraser ducks to the tree line. The poor Artificer leans ever so slightly forward, eyes moving between Green's convulsing body and the dark rise of the trees. Fire glow illuminates the tumbled underbrush, trees snapped in a shuddering display of force, both horizontally and vertically, as if something very large has barrelled through the forest. Fraser cracks off two twiggy branches from a fallen tree and darts back out of the black, dense ridge.

"Can't see anything. But I can feel it watching. Agreed?" He clicks his fingers in my direction. I nod, even if I can't tell the difference between paranoia and Hunter senses. His voice is barely above a whisper when he orders us next: "Horses should have emergency lanterns. Check the packs."

"Light," Victoria calls.

Fraser nods at the Artificer, who runs over to help Victoria mend our broken Hunter. I turn to my horse—well-trained but stamping, unsettled and upset—to throw open the satchel and fish around inside. I find a tiny lantern and matches. When lit, the lantern offers only the softest gaslight glow, dreamlike and hazy, for us to survive by.

A high-pitched chitter erupts from the treeline.

We turn in unison, shoddy lanterns raised against opaque blackness. My gut reacts first. I don't know how to explain it except that the limbic cortex of my mind crawls forward, dragging its lizard body out of the shadowy constitution of my brain. Cassius as I know him, as he presents himself, retreats; what's left is my body. And it has only fear, paranoia, desperate primate senses.

Intrinsically, my body takes a step back.

"It's there," I whisper. Fraser makes a noise and clicks his tongue, a near-silent order to retreat. All of us move back. We are a fleshy, panicked wave pressed close to Victoria and the Artificer who work to save Green's young life.

"We should retreat," the Artificer says softly. He's not even looking at us. Fraser cuts him off with a hiss. His eyes are focused on the ridge. I notice Sutton drawn towards it, too; she slumps forward as if her body is a ragdoll or as if something from the dark is tugging at her. I watch her take a step forward. She wheezes. The sound rumbles out of her, sounding as if a string is tied around her lungs and being knotted tighter and tighter.

Fraser shifts his focus to her, too.

"Sutton," he hisses sharply. She shoots upright with a sharp gasp.

"*Barghest*," she wheezes, voice gravely like she's scrabbling for air. "It's a *barghest*."

Black dog, North England. That's all I know of it.

"*Barghest?*" Fraser clarifies. He sighs like he's tired, like he would rather be anywhere else. And then Victoria echoes his question and sighs in the same way.

She stands up from Green's body. He's still bleeding out. She hasn't been able to staunch it. She and Fraser look at each other; the wind keens, and a sharp howl answers it. Victoria and Fraser don't flinch. The horses stamp and whinny, eager to leave.

"What is it?" The Artificer shifts his weight and stares back, past all of us to the darkened ridge.

"*Barghest* wounds never heal," whispers Victoria. She tears her eyes away from Fraser now, back to Green. He convulses on the ground. Victoria looks up like she's expecting someone —the other Healer who's been dragged off.

"That's one myth," Fraser says back, his voice just as low. "But it's the one that came through."

"Well, he has no chance." Victoria bends down and shucks Green out of his embroidery-free Hunter coat, even as he's choking on blood. I creep forward. The full extent of his wounds is on show; frothy blood bubbles out of the cuts on his chest. He could have been saved if these cuts had been caused by a normal *teras*. Couldn't he? There's a slither of one at his neck. A gouge on his chest. Blood has soaked through his shirt. It's not coagulating. He'll succumb to the blood loss, and our Healer knows it; Victoria knows it. She covers his face before he's even dead so none of us have to watch as he chokes his way into oblivion.

How horrible is that? The helplessness. The knowledge that nothing can be done. How limited we are by our humanity, how easily culled.

We all turn around as if Green is already dead. Victoria's face is impassive. Where's the girl from three months ago? The one collapsing from her fear, the one desperate and scared, begging that girl to leave the dead boy behind before the *harpy* skinned her?

As dead as Bellamy, some angry, twisted part of me spits. *As dead as the father of her unborn fucking child.*

"Are we Hunting?" Sutton mutters.

The Artificer shudders. "Maybe we should retreat."

But I look to Fraser, who is God at this point—God to all of us; I should go to my knees and beg for him to spare my life—but I already know.

We are staying to fight.

"D'Avore, and, uh," he clicks his fingers at me.

Weaky, I supply, "Cassius Jones."

He blinks, fingers frozen. He gives me a nod, an acknowledgement. "Thaddeus' brother," he murmurs. "You killed the *manticore* that killed him."

That's not true, not in any way that matters. I survived the encounter the same way Fraser did. At the end of my first year, I could have it embroidered on my Hunter coat if I wanted. But I would have to carry the weight of the lie, the truth of what killed the beast. And I can't hold any more space for Vengeance in this head than I do already.

When I don't reply, Fraser nods with something of approval. "Good. D'Avore, Jones. I'll take point. You'll flank. Artificer, Healer," he hasn't bothered to learn their names, "Stay with the horses."

The Artificer shivers with relief. Victoria is staring down, enraptured by Green's death throes.

"Weapons out," Fraser tells them. "We'll be too far away to save you."

That shakes the two of them. I watch Victoria blink rapidly and come back to herself. She reaches into her blue coat and pulls out a knife. Her brown skin turns nearly white with the strength of her grip around the handle.

The lantern light is paltry, and carrying them only makes us a target. Fraser has us leave them with the horses, and orders us towards the hill.

Sutton and Fraser have the advantage. They can see something or sense it. All I have is my paranoia. I squint into caliginous Erebus and imagine the beast lurking in the immense abyssal night. Crouched low, we creep into the tree line.

This is too much like the trials and nothing like them. The forest stretches out like an impossibly large arena. I'm used to greenhouses and great halls, confined spaces to fight and die in. But when we move from the clearing into the trees, something in me unlocks. It feels—familiar. Like the birch trees creaking, claustrophobically close together, and some unknowable creature rattling and groaning out of them.

At once, I have two feelings in me. The first is to be expected: pure fear. But the other is strangely close to relief. My body knows this type of terror, and it unfolds around the memory of it. I make an anchor out of the familiarity. I think about how fast this creature is and take out the *manticore* poison dagger in my left hand, holding it close to my face so I might, at the very least, scratch the thing before it rips into me.

Fraser stops moving. He breathes so deeply I can hear his lungs expand with the crisp night air. I still myself as Sutton does the same, and then I follow suit and breathe deep. It's so dark I can hardly see my own hand. So I close my eyes and listen. The cold makes the trees groan. I hear something like chains rattling against one another. But there are no birds or creatures, no trills, no ambient life. Everything has fled. In this eerie, impossible quiet, I find myself not praying to the Christian God but to Nyx herself, *mêter melaina,* and her home wrapped in dark clouds.

And then there is the cracking like a great slab of ice has split apart in front of us, and I open my eyes. Fraser shoots. His flintlock sparks. In the split second it takes for the bullet to hurtle out of the barrel, I see a distended, bloody jaw opening over Fraser's arm. Instinct has me fire. Two shots go off as Sutton reacts too, her shot quicker than mine. The light from our pistols illuminates a bulbous, bloodshot eye hidden in the shaggy mass of black fur. The *barghest* screams. Blood, gore, flesh; a rain of it splatters on me, and it smells like Watford again, with half-rotten, stinking pulp clinging to my hair and face. The *barghest* lashes out. I have only the sense of its hulking body swiping towards Sutton. She throws herself back to avoid a yellowed hook claw and fires again. Fraser gets close, and the *barghest's* voice twists high in a strangled yelp. I dive forward beside Fraser and stab with the *manticore* poison dagger. Its body shudders, frozen suddenly by the paralysing poison. I feel Fraser more so than I see him. He's looking at me rather than the *teras* at our feet. It's Sutton who steps forward and shoots the *barghest* in the head.

The noise rips Fraser out of whatever thought had captivated him. He shoots it, too, and nudges the body with his foot. It doesn't react.

"Good," he says. "Let's go."

Sutton and I are panting. Sweat pools at the back of my neck and my brow; it runs into my eye. And my heart is racing the way it does when I am fucked: this holy euphoria. I feel alive.

But Fraser's lack of ceremony spooks me. There are no congratulations, no acknowledgement of the swift kill. We stalk back out to the others. Victoria has her gun pointed firmly and unshakingly at the tree line. When we emerge, she jolts, pulling back at the last second.

I hear Fraser make an approving noise under his breath. I wonder how it is that, out of all of us, Victoria Bennet is the one most accepting of her new life? I watch her start to pack up the horses. She considers leaving Green untouched, then pulls the Hunter robe free and stuffs it into her horse's pack. Not out of kindness but for the resources.

If this is war, she'll need to make bandages out of anything she can.

I think again of the girl I used to know. Do I have a hand in her death, too?

"Well done, Mr Jones," she murmurs when I get close. I open my mouth to respond—and fail because I have too much to say—but her eyes shift away from me to Fraser. "Shit."

I swing around. Shit.

A red cut has opened on his cheek, and another down his left arm. They don't look particularly deep, but Fraser is grimacing as he kneels before a lantern and opens the door.

He glances up at Victoria as if he's asking her opinion or her permission. And all she does is shrug.

He doesn't get angry at this. He doesn't look upset. With a profound resignation, Fraser pulls a cautery iron free of the horse's pack. He begins to heat the metal.

"Would you?" he whispers without looking her way. But Victoria goes to him, kneeling beside him, and takes the rod from his fingers. Neither one flinches as she cauterises the wounds.

"Will that work?" the Artificer murmurs, and no one answers him because no one knows. Blood could still be pooling beneath the skin. But so long as Fraser can make it back to London, behind the Janus Gate, he will survive, for there is a fast-acting magic there. Magic, or some other kind of power. Something that will knit him back together.

I look back at Green's almost-corpse. He still shudders. Blood has wept from his open mouth, and his skin is already sickly pale.

A few more minutes and he'll be dead.

After that, we ride back. And we are halfway way to London when the storm starts. By the time we arrive, the ground outside London's wall is muddy. It means there's nothing, no footprints or tracks, to tell us who exactly it was that cut the man in half.

LESSON SEVEN

The body is open and steaming in the frigid, rainy night, but you wouldn't notice that from afar. It is slumped like a drunkard might be, hand braced against the stone of the gate for support, almost comical in its position. But the truth of it, knowing he was so close to the gates, to London's relative safety, makes it feel—personal.

And then comes the nature of the corpse.

When we return from patrol, we find London in shambles. The great fear overcomes me immediately: the wardstones have been breached. We are at war. But as we get closer and see instead several Hunters and Healers milling outside of Cripplegate, the fear shifts to something less immediate. The feeling is insidious. So rarely is any care given to anything outside of London's gates that this feels momentous.

They surround the corpse. From the looks of it, no one has tried to move it. I don't understand why until we're even closer.

Lanterns spin in our direction, four hammers drawn in percussive synchronicity as guns are raised in our direction.

There's a beat where there is no sound except heavy breathing and the rain. The moment stretches tensely as no one moves. It is only when Fraser whistles that the waiting cohort opens up to us. They relax at first, until someone with a keen eye squints through the dark and marks our small numbers.

"What the fuck happened to you?"

"*Barghest*," Fraser calls over the rain. His cheek is burning and scorched from the cauterisation. No blood has seeped through, but we still can't be sure this will heal anything. He barely reins in his horse before he dismounts; some Worker peels out of the shadows to take the horses away as the rest of us climb down into the mud. "And what's happened to him?"

Here, the cluster cracks open, and people peel off to either side to expose the upright body. I don't recognise this milling group of people. Most have their faces covered against the storm anyway. But I do recognise, of course, the dean.

Drearton is smothered in an oily black coat so heavy in its layers that the wind barely moves it. He's dressed in a tall-necked Mackintosh and a wide-brimmed hat, and when he turns, his face is submerged in shadow, save for his right eye, which glints when it falls on me. He spins rather enthusiastically and calls out, "Mr Jones. Survived your first patrol?"

"Evidently," I mutter, with more vitriol than strictly necessary. I feel the weight of the *manticore* poison dagger at my hip. And I have to wonder if I made the right decision when I took it away from his neck.

But better the devil you know, right? Still, when Drearton slips an arm around me, sweetly as if I haven't mouthed off, my whole body tenses like I've met Medusa's eye, like every tendon and working muscle in my body has been petrified. I can't tell if fear or disgust drives the feeling.

"What happened to the rest?" Drearton asks, still chipper. Fraser takes off his tricorn hat with a sweeping bow.

"I regret to report heavy losses, Dean Drearton," he says with genuine solemnity. "Those who you see before you are the only ones to survive our patrol."

And Drearton, for the sheer brilliance of his understanding smile and look of pity, makes the mistake of gripping my left shoulder rather tightly. We have lost Hunters. Healers. This affects him. This hurts.

Drearton is afraid.

"No matter—or rather, there will be time to mourn later. We have a pressing issue propped up against this wall. Come."

He gives me no choice because he hasn't lessened his grip. He simply walks forward again, and I move with him.

I crane around for Victoria, who lingers behind Fraser. I see her with her blood-covered hand on her stomach and imagine the bump of a growing life moving beneath her hand. She doesn't meet my gaze. She doesn't turn to look at the corpse. Instead, she looks out the way we've come.

Don't you dare. Don't you dare try to run.

"Well?" Drearton murmurs. I spin back to face the body.

For a good moment, there is nothing out of the ordinary. Call it cognitive dissonance, or a wilful sort of desperation— my eyes don't see the seams, and thus fear cannot take root in me. But the way I felt before Vengeance stalked out of the birch trees shivers through me again. A primordial knowing. An innate cognisance—something is profoundly wrong.

"See it?" Drearton asks. His cadence is gentle. With slow precision, he raises his fingers to the corpse. "Touch him, Mr Jones."

I know better than to flinch, and I know better than to question him. No one else utters a word, so they must have learned the same lesson. Drearton's word is as close to gospel as we have: I walk forward. The dead Englishman is pallid, skin a sickly off-white with a texture reminiscent of crumbling pressed flowers. One eye is halfway rolled to the back of his head, and his mouth hangs open. I step around him, more unconsciously than following any train of thought. His long coat is open at the front. I glance down his arm—and pause.

His hand is brown.

Not unnaturally so: it's a beautiful colour, like pressed earth after rain. And I realise slowly that this hand cannot belong to the Englishman at all.

All at once, he comes undone. The body unravels. The head slides backwards, an arm drops and the torso tumbles off with a softened thud against the sleet-covered ground. The legs buckle together, twitching as if still alive, and drop to their knees, exposing an oozing cross-section of thighs. Both femurs are beautifully even. There's no puckering, torn flesh. It's a clean cut.

Someone behind me loudly throws up.

I look up to meet Drearton's eye. He's watching me carefully. Even when the noise from the others grows exponentially, I can't help but feel how I react here if it was a test.

I hold myself still and go someplace else—somewhere nice, somewhere bodiless, until the churning in my stomach grounds me, and I have to think about pleasure. I think about sex. I think about food. I know the current sight is not conducive to that kind of mood; I know that. But it helps. It helps to think that my body has a use. If I can't let it react the way it wants, then I will turn this surplus of emotion towards something else.

Fraser whispers, "What could have done this?"

"Not what," Drearton says, pulling that scrutinising gaze away from me. "Who."

Fraser glances at Sutton with a look that screams, "What the actual fuck is he talking about?" and I feel the most camaraderie with them I have this whole night. Not even a *barghest* fight can compete with disdain for the dean.

"Cultists. The Cult of the Rift. They take *teras* and stitch them together. Now, they're doing the same to humans. Londoners."

Which is—bullshit. Can't he see the seamless cuts? The perfection with which this corpse has been pushed together?

When no one moves, the dean eyes each of us.

"What are you waiting for?" he snaps his fingers. The person who a moment ago was loudly vomiting springs upward shakily. The dean looks at her, "Round them up, then."

❧

THE WITCH HUNT makes me ill. I hear drunken revelry become something else: a dark chorus of screams and shouts. And this is only the beginning. This is only what I hear on the shadowy, wet walk back to the campus. Victoria disappeared immediately, so this walk I take alone.

You might ask: you went back to the University? Yes. I think nothing short of divine intervention would have made me try to stop what Drearton was doing. Because how could I stop a witch hunt? If the dean's word is gospel, then an order holds even more weight. Godliness weaves through his authority. And if God has abandoned us, at least Drearton never will.

The cultists will be rounded up. Come morning, a decision will be made.

I know as sure as breathing that someone will be killed.

But tonight, I can't care about it. I can't bring myself to expend the emotion. My body feels heavy, first with regular fatigue, and then with this great weight—I can hardly describe it. Apathy. But also everything, every possible feeling. I'm just not allowed to know the names of them all. Their gravity drags me close to sleep.

But I force myself to stay awake. I want a drink. A cigarette. A fuck. I want Leo to say nothing to me, ask no questions of me, and fuck me senseless. I want to feel only my body. I want to become only my body. So I trudge through the campus ground, thinking only of him and letting desire guide me like a beacon.

By the time I reach the common room, it's empty. I think perhaps Leo has gone to bed early, which frustrates me, because that room is full of other people. I almost consider crawling into bed with him anyway when a noise grabs my attention. I hear a laugh—his laugh—in one of the smaller rooms off the hall, which is used for private study. And so I go.

I hear voices and I perch outside the door, craning to hear them through the wood.

"Because you can't always have wanted this."

"Why not?"

"For one thing, it wasn't possible. If the world hadn't gone to piss and shit, there would have been no Calling. No Calling, no Leo Shaw before me right now."

"No Leo Shaw before you right now and no glorious company; how very sad such a thought must feel to you, Don."

There's a scoff—and if a scoff could sound layered, with want and tension, it would be that sound. I imagine Don poised with his glass to his lips, eyes falling over Leo unabashedly. Leo staring back—I stop the thought.

I know what night-time does to Leo. I know how he lets the shadows through his pores and how much more alive he is in the dark.

I'm afraid of what might happen when Don realises this, too.

I push the door open.

They are on opposite sides of the room, but my heart races as if I've found them a tangle of limbs. I realise I am shaking. How fucking embarrassing. Green bled to death from an immortal wound, I hunted a *barghest*, I watched a patchwork corpse fall apart, Victoria is fucking pregnant—but it's the thought that Leo might want someone else that makes this world all too much.

I don't look at him—I can't—and I make a beeline for the bottle in his hand.

"Please," I say. My voice sounds stupidly small and brittle. Leo's grip relaxes, and I drink and drink and drink until his hands gently pull the bottle down and away from me. I gasp like I've been running. I can't stop struggling to breathe.

Why is everything, all at once, too much for me?

"What's happened? Don, get the door."

"Fuck, I can go." I am vaguely aware as Don moves towards the door; I think I start to calm down.

But Leo says, "No. Stay. He's just come back from patrol."

I've slumped down to the floor at this point, and I look at Leo, lowering himself to hover over me, neck and jaw stretched out as he tells Don to stay. God, he is a vision. I reach out and touch the rounded corner of his jaw as it meets his ear. He catches my fingers rather roughly, but he kisses the back of them.

Don makes an affronted noise.

Leo is mine. Or at least, my body is his.

"I want him out," I say.

Don scoffs. The bottle he's holding sloshes as he tilts it back. "Well, now I don't want to go."

Leo says nothing but gives Don a little nod towards the door. I watch Don's face fall. He expected Leo to be on his side. Ambrosia floods my system; bliss is not meant for this mortal body. Leo is choosing me.

"Fuck you, Shaw. And you, especially, Jones. Tell me what the fuck happened."

Neither one of us say anything. Don rolls his eyes. "Oh, you fucking faggots."

That gets me up. Don't ask me why—I've called myself the same slur in front of Don's face. But it's the goddamned irony of it, isn't it? Don alone, making eyes at my lover. Don draping himself over my shoulder and whispering in my ear. Like Peter Drike, but worse—Don knows exactly what he is, and he hates himself for it.

Well, I know him the way I know every one of my kind. I know what that look in his eye means. I know it is desire. So I stand up, leap awkwardly over Leo, and slam Don back against the wall.

"Shut the fuck up!"

Whack. His head snaps back against the wall. He curses at me, pushing back against one side of my chest. Don is far stronger than me, but he's already off balance, and I am laying into him with my shoulder. I slide my forearm up and press it securely against his neck.

"You could just leave us alone. Couldn't you? But you won't. And I know why, Wamsley. I fucking know why. If you won't admit it to yourself, let me say it outright."

I do him the courtesy of leaning close, of breathing against his neck. I wonder if he wants to fuck me. I wonder if he wants Leo to fuck him. I wonder, after tonight, after watching bits of bodies tumble apart, after the impossibility of this war we are stumbling into, if I shouldn't just reach down and touch him.

"How badly you must want him to fuck you."

Pain hits me first before I can register what has happened. Don has spun me. The back of my skull aches and throbs from the force with which he pushed me. And his fingers are wrapped around my throat.

Don squeezes without mercy.

I gasp, and I laugh. I taste blood. I can't breathe and I'm laughing, and Leo is shouting something—and I know I'm right. Leo pulls him off.

"Jesus, man, would you stop?"

Don has his hands up. He looks stressed. I lick the blood from my lips.

"I'll go," he says roughly.

"*Barghest* attack," I say, to get him to stay. Don hovers and looks back at me. Leo murmurs another 'Jesus' under his breath. "The patrol fell apart. We killed it, but not before it killed two Hunters and a Healer. Fraser was wounded, too, but I think the magic of this pocket place will heal him."

Don sucks his teeth. "Fuck."

"Drearton's clearing out the Cult of the Rift after a body comprised of various people was found propped up against the wall. *Outside* the wards. I watched it fall to bits. It's all feeling inevitable. It's all too much. And I have to conserve my cigarettes, and God knows how much alcohol is left—you two should conserve those bottles—so why don't you just —stay?"

Don stares at me. Leo stares at me, too. I think only Leo gets my meaning, because when I glance his way, there's that signature quirk in his brow.

"No," Don says with a sigh. "We patrol tomorrow. And Drearton, fuck—there'll be an execution. Bright and fuckin' early. So I'll sleep, or—"

I don't even like Wamsley. The most attractive thing about him is his size. But he doesn't know what he's doing, not the way Leo does; his aggression is unmoored. He doesn't know how to use it to get what he really wants because he is afraid of what he really wants, the way I used to be.

But I want Leo. And Leo is entertaining Don, so now I want Don, too. I want to control the energy between them; I want to corrupt it and turn it towards me. I want to be wanted so desperately that I do this:

I step forward as Don is still talking, wrap my hand around the back of his head, and bring him down into a kiss.

Don slaps me across the face. He staggers back, wan, shaking. He looks between Leo and me, breathing heavily like he's seen something grotesque. He is still holding his hand squarely where my cheek used to be. I think I've broken him. God, that feels good.

Who would have thought, after years of back-alley fucks and desperate fondling, that I might have power like this now. That kiss must have been decidedly injurious to Don's armour, for his self-understanding is infantile. A baby before the reality of his desires. I have years and years and years of self-loathing. I haven't turned my back on God; I urge him to look down on me. I want an audience for my blasphemy, for ruthlessness.

This world is fucking ending. I have to take what I want.

Don turns to leave. He makes it to the door when I say: "Wait."

He waits. Compelled either by a lust suddenly unfettered or by my voice, which even I hear has a new tone to it. Commanding.

By now, I've turned to Leo. My fingers gently pry his shirt open. In this moment, Leo only has eyes for me.

What are you doing? His gaze asks me. *Why are you doing this?*

It's impulsive, crass, whorish—everything I've ever learned is screaming at me to stop; God is screaming at me, and the devil, too. But this? This I can control. When everything else is crumbling away from me, I can choose to whore myself out if I want to.

And I do want to.

Leo's eyes aren't judging me. They are equally, if not more, carnally challenging. I slip his shirt open and start at his neck. I graze the skin with my tongue. I plant kisses along his jaw and run my hands over his chest. Don makes a low noise that might be a moan, and both Leo and I respond to it. I push closer to the skin of Leo's neck and move down, first to the collarbone, which presses out from under his skin in a beautiful valley, and then to the pink rise of his nipples.

In my periphery, Don takes his hand off the doorknob and moves it down to the keyhole.

He locks the door.

"Bad night, darling?" Leo asks as I tongue his nipple. I graze my teeth too firmly, and the gentle grip on my hair changes. He wrenches my head up. I hiss and pant; I should be embarrassed. I should be begging Leo to stop.

But I started this, and Don is still watching me, and Leo grabs my face roughly and slaps my cheek so hard I briefly see stars. Harder than Don did. Fuck—why does that make me *so*—

"Are you joining us this evening, Wamsley, or will you be our voyeur?" Leo asks casually. He still has my head wrenched back. I'm making small, animalistic noises; I'm on the tips of my toes, and I have to hold onto Leo for support. There is nothing graceful about the way I'm standing or the noises I am making. He makes me an animal, a dog to be thrown around, punished, trained. Leo's gaze flickers down to me, and he smiles—smiles like he's proud, which sends a complicated ball of heat to my groin. While he waits for Don's reply, Leo lets me go and steps back to roll his shirt sleeves up. His shirt is open, and now his strong forearms are exposed, long fingers gliding the shirt sleeves up into neat bands that make his forearms bulge. A vein pulses along his right arm, and that's where my attention is when Leo kicks the inside of my ankles and drives my legs apart. My breath comes out rough and ragged as Leo moves to strip me. His strong hands manoeuvre me free of my belt, the damp Hunter's cloak, the white shirt beneath it slick with my sweat and red with blood that isn't mine. Thank God for Leo Shaw. He roughly tugs my trousers off, and then I'm standing only in my pants and my socks. Leo grabs my hips and pulls my backside against him so he can rut against me.

Here, the flush starts up. I'm in two minds—one scared and embarrassed, and the other on the verge of begging for it. I close my eyes because it's easier that way, but Leo catches me. He grabs me by the cheek and turns my face towards Don.

"Eyes open, darling," he whispers hoarsely. "Or you'll miss out on all the fun."

Don and I lock eyes. A flush the colour of a bruise pommels both his cheeks.

One of Leo's hands wraps around the back of my skull; he makes sure I'm looking at Don, at the tenting of his trousers. And then, one-handedly, Leo takes my pants off.

My cheeks burn with learned shame, and then with the lust that gets off on this. I make a disgraceful noise and trip over my own feet. Leo shushes me, presses his lips to the side of my face.

"Never seen you like this, Mr Jones," he murmurs, tongue gliding over my ear. "How pretty you look all exposed."

He pulls my hair hard, and I moan, eyes fluttering closed, and then he shoves himself roughly against my backside, grinding once, twice, groaning out a soft laugh. Something about it—about the way Leo holds himself and me beneath him, about the control he has, gives the whole situation a certain gentility. A gentility that falls apart the instant you think about it, but—there is a grace to him. To this. I no longer feel in control. I feel wild, unhinged, a slave to my lust. But Leo controls it. Leo controls *me*.

"I need an answer, Wamsley," Leo murmurs, teeth grazing

down my neck. I shudder. I arch back; Leo's hand presses into the divot at my hips, controlling my desperate thrust.

Don starts to say something and has to clear his throat. Leo pauses in expectation.

"Watch," Don says, voice quiet, dripping with lust and guilt. There's a distant flash of lightning outside, the deep rumble of thunder breaking in the distance, and Don jerks back like God himself has just cast him out of Eden.

But he does not leave.

Leo laughs, honey-rich with genuine glee. "Then we'll have to put on a show."

I have to bite back the intense urge to go to my knees and take off Leo's trousers. That's not what—I'm meant to do. It's not really what I want to do. I want Leo to guide me, to control me, and he does. In an almost ritualistic fashion, Leo's hand glides up to my neck, where Don's hands were moments before.

"Breathe deep," Leo whispers to me. My heart flutters— we haven't done this before. Leo's other thumb wipes a bit of blood from my lip. He pops it in his mouth, sucks it clean, and says, "Wamsley. Since you wanted to do this so badly. Tell me when to stop."

I'm halfway through my deep, preparatory breath when those words register. No—my life is in Don's hands. My life is in the hands of a man who likely hates me.

"What," Wamsley manages. His eyes look glazed as if he's in a dream. He's made no attempt to touch himself. Both his hands are useless leaden weights by his side, but his cock is straining—and he's looking at me with this confusing amalgam of pity and desire and—jealousy.

Leo's hands clamp down hard.

I jerk back in surprise. He's pressing first against the vessels on either side of my neck, which makes my vision blurry, but he also presses down on the trachea. Hard. I can't breathe. I feel my eyes roll back, fluttering against the front of my skull. And my body—my wretched whore of a body—reacts with pleasure. My grunt becomes a moan. My cock jerks. Just as it's getting good, Don says, "S-stop."

Leo lets go. All the air hits me in a rush. I half choke on it, keeling forward. Leo scoops me back by the waist and kisses my cheek.

"Alright, Mr Jones?"

I rasp out, "Fucking splendid, Mr Shaw."

With no conscious intention, I feel myself *grinning*. Leo walks around me, a smile on his own face.

"You liked that," he says with wonder, taking my chin in his hands. "No, you *loved* that."

My mouth is open and panting. Leo drags his eyes over to Don.

"What about you, Wamsley? Enjoying the show?"

Don says nothing, but he's breathing heavily—his cock is probably aching.

Without looking at me, Leo puts a hand on my shoulder and pushes me onto my knees. I go down dazed and delirious and still smiling. Onehandedly, Leo undoes his own trousers and slips the belt out in a fluid, snappish motion. *Crack*. The leather comes together right beside my head, and I shiver with fear—but Leo's already dropped the belt, slipped his hand inside, and taken his cock out. He taps the side of my face with it, smearing his precum over my cheek. I open my mouth, chase the head of his cock as he pulls it over my cheek. Leo's other hand clings to my hair, tugging me closer and away from the tip in a puppeteering game. I must look stupid. Desperate. A ruttish whore; God, please, make me one.

"Please," I murmur.

"You want it?" Leo's voice turns coy and sweet. I nod, over

and over. Leo's thumb ghosts over the bump in my throat. I swallow.

"Beautiful," Leo murmurs.

My cock gives a heavy twitch in response.

"Ahh," Leo says, and I make the noise. His thumb presses my jaw open wide, and he guides his own cock into the wet heat of my mouth. I arch, neck straining to take all of him.

"Mhm!" I choke. Leo's eyes roll back with the rest of his head, and he pushes down into me with staggering force. I choke with every thrust—my stomach flips, I make a noise like something dying—but I'm delirious. My eyes roll over to Don.

Who is touching himself in earnest.

I moan so loud and long that Leo hisses, hips pumping hard as my moan vibrates up his length. Don is touching himself, eyes on me, eyes on Leo's cock thrusting in and out of my mouth, watching me take it, take all of it, *fuck*—

Hot tears edge out of the corners of my eyes. I convulse, on the edge of vomiting as Leo stuffs me with his cock. I start fucking up into my own hand, desperate—that little friction is enough to get me close. Leo hammers down in a final sprint, and I am crying, jaw working sloppily, aching and choking.

"Ah, God," Leo pants. His head lolls forward. "Oh, fuck, Cass, here it comes."

Then, clipped and gasping, Leo buries himself to the hilt and comes. I moan, eyes rolling back as I come a moment later.

Leo is panting, breathless. I'm in a daze as he pulls out of me. Saliva and a string of cum I didn't swallow joins my lips to the tip of Leo's cock. We look at each other and laugh.

"Good boy, Mr Jones."

"I do try my best, Mr Shaw."

And we laugh again. Leo bends down and kisses me, slow

and languorous, like he truly cares about me. When he pulls back, I'm still looking at him, hoping for another moment of this intimacy.

But Leo is looking back at our voyeur.

Don stands there, the front of his trousers wet. He is flushed red, sweat beading on his forehead.

"Thank you for joining us, Wamsley. Thoughts on the show?"

But now that he's come, Don is full of rage and regret. I know it well. I know how insidious shame is.

Don says nothing. He turns on his heel, unlocks the door, and steps out like nothing has happened at all.

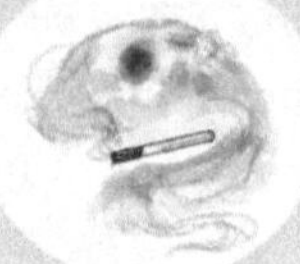

LESSON EIGHT

The Latin word for execution is *exsecutiō,* an agent noun denoting the performer of the action of the verb. From *exsequor. Ex* - out. *Sequor* - follow. To follow. To carry out. To fulfil.

To fulfil a promise.

You can see ritual running through that word, can't you? I can. And this type of execution—this ceremonial and very public execution—has all the trappings of something ancient.

Even in this world inured to cruelty, what the dean plans to do is horrific. Overnight, whilst I was wilfully distracting myself with Leo and Don, a few Cult of the Rifters have been found. A few of them were Workers, some of them family members of graduate Hunters, who either through money or skill had avoided Drearton's initial cull of London. I can't imagine any of them are glad of that now. Four are standing on hastily built scaffolds, but none of us can tell who they are. They've been dressed in the remains of *teras*—a taxidermied *griffon* head, a mask made of patchwork fur, one cowled and given a *hydra* headdress, and the final in a strange amalgam of *stygian* wings so that only their eyes show through the mask. An angel ripped from the Bible itself, haunting with its terror.

I doubt they dressed themselves, though it is the narrative Drearton shouts out for us all to hear. These traitors are shameless. These traitors bow to the *teras* and to Satan, not to God.

It's barely dawn. We are, all of London, gathered outside St Paul's Cathedral. Drearton claims none of us are packed inside because of the surety of blood, but there are rumours that they're already setting the cathedral up as an infirmary. If this execution is meant to strengthen humanity's resolve, the sight of a war hospital wouldn't help shore us up.

The scaffold is built directly in front of the cathedral, so the dome looms above all of us. The sun looks like a half-scrambled yolk spilling over the sky, and it's a bitter morning. Every student and graduate of the University is draped in their mantles—hats and cloaks, a sea of us packed close around the scaffold. My stump of an arm aches in this cold, especially where the prosthetic joins flesh. Frost creeps along the porcelain and chills the skin. Whatever nerves are there spark and ache, and I reach over to clutch the arm, fingers pressing against the joint.

Behind us stands the rest of London—Workers, family. They're packed tight, but they are barely a shadow of how the city used to be. Still, a substantial space has been left between us and them. Blood Hunters flank us at interspersed points. I've never seen them in our Hunter cohort. Their black mantles are shot through with red thread. They are marked differently, and they keep themselves separate; I wonder what their training consists of. I wonder how one becomes a Blood Hunter and whether they hunt *teras* as well as people. If I get closer to them and squint at their mantles, will I notice that their victories consist of human forms over *teras?* Will I see the broken bodies of the trial victims and students and graduates they have wrangled in the place of the beasts that the rest of us have to conquer?

How uniquely twisted do they have to be to act as Drearton's personal army over defenders of humanity?

The Blood Hunters face what's left of London's populace. There's barely anyone who can't be of some use. I haven't turned around to look at them. My mother might be there. My father, in his chair, dead-eyes, glazed—I'm surprised they haven't killed him yet.

He's of no use to the city anymore. Neither is she. Neither are so many of us. But for now, Drearton keeps the promises he used to lure us into the trials last year. In any case, I fear humanity is going to die here, fish in a barrel, our light snuffed out, clawing at each other and at *teras* and praying to a God who has so thoroughly abandoned us—

Leo grabs my shoulder.

I gasp, glancing up at him, catching the rapid rise and fall of my chest. He urges my hand down from my opposite shoulder and clutches it, all without looking my way; his eyes are fixed securely on the scaffold ahead of us, but his hand in mine is a comfort. I squeeze it. I can see his breath frosting with each rise and fall of his chest, and I try to make a meditation of watching him. *Don't think about your parents. Don't think about anything else. Don't think about death.*

But how can I not?

"A sad day," Drearton's voice booms. It carries in London's waking silence, rebounding off the cathedral and the buildings around us until all sharp edges of his words are bludgeoned; rounded noise booms out around us. "But a necessary one! London: here are the provocateurs, the criminals who seed dissent amongst us. They worship *teras*, beasts of Satan. Satanists in disguise come to defile this house of God! Come to let the *teras* destroy us all!"

There's only one way this can go. Nuance is dead: it

doesn't *matter* if they aren't because, at this point, prayer is all we have. Desperate wishing up to a God who has long abandoned us. I feel the swell, the mounting hysteria. The crowd behind us shouts and crows. I hear the Blood Hunters call out to one another in Latin, warning each other to be wary, but the crowd isn't angry. This is—joy.

The realisation slows me until I remember Drearton is their saviour. Like Moses, he has delivered his people, and he is about to do it again. The first of the cultists is brought down from the platform. Four horses wait. Their riders are the executioners and Blood Hunters, who always seem to deal with people and never *teras*.

Why have any of them agreed to this?

"Fred," Leo murmurs.

My mouth dries instantly. "What?"

Leo bobs his head. "Over there."

I freeze. *Don't*—part of my mind says, the logical part, and then the rest of me overrides it. I spin my head around to follow Leo's gaze.

She isn't looking at me, but it still hurts to look at her. Fred Lin has shaved her hair even shorter, buzzed to the scalp. I can't see her new leg; I can't see anything else about her. But she has her hood down and bunched around her shoulders, and so many around her wear their mantle cowls up as if to hide from God's judgement. Not Fred. Of course, not Fred. She will face what is to come head-on.

I haven't seen her since graduation. Which feels like eons ago now. An impossible expanse of time stretching out before us; I haven't seen her since she woke up, drenched in her own sweat, smelling of sick and disease with her leg missing and her brother dead.

I wish we'd never met you.

I know. I want to say it again: *I know. I wish you'd never met me, either. I'm sorry. Don't watch this execution—you don't need to be reminded of Bellamy. Of Silas.*

But why should Fred ever listen to me again?

The cultist, the one in the *griffon* head, has their limbs tied to four separate ropes. They struggle weakly. Ever so faintly, I can hear the sounds of their cries muffled behind the mask and again by what must be a gag.

Still London crows. A few of us begin to sway with it; do they not know what's coming? Has the rumour not spread to each and every one of us? It's all I've heard all morning.

Spectacular justice, it's called.

Drearton is going to rip them apart. Limb from limb. What happens on the scaffold will not be contained to the scaffold. The ritual will not end here; it does not begin here. I see it all in this brilliant moment. I am out of my body, and I know I am Drearton's soldier and that he likes to think of himself as God's. That in the face of time and chaos and primordial darkness, this is nothing but a blip. What happens here is more inevitable proof of humanity's violence. This institution, the *teras*, this world: it can't happen any other way.

No one will stop Drearton because Drearton isn't the problem. I could have slit his neck, and it wouldn't have mattered. The University is ungovernable. We are all too scared of death. We will all cling to the hope the University can provide. So, when the wave of hysteria builds and builds, and I can feel God at the edges of my periphery reaching for me, I let it happen.

I let Him in.

Because somehow, I am meant to find God here, in the pulled-apart bodies and the blood and the entrails, like a *haruspex*.

Leo faintly squeezes my hand, and I hold tight. The bodies around us tense and crane to watch as each mounted

Blood Hunter is handed one of the four ropes. The cultist is pulled taut into a spread eagle, and their cry becomes breathy and panicked, an incessant in-and-out wheeze as they brace themself for an agonising death.

It is so much crueller than a bullet or a hanging. Drowning, asphyxiation—there is a corporeality to this ritual that disgusts me. Like the body deserves a tenfold punishment. Like the soul must wade through its own blood and guts, be doused in its own fleshy evisceration, and push up through the clouds dripping viscera before it can plop into heaven.

The horses snort and stamp. Drearton says, "Ride!"

Four whipcracks resound, echoing back to us off marble and stone. Four horses ride in opposite directions.

The scream is instant and somehow still bellowing behind the mask and gag; the fear triumphs through the muffling gag, ripping through. The cultist's voice rattles like death is taking root before the first limb tears. Flesh ripping has a resonance to it, a wet crunching—I jolt as remembered pain bolts down my left arm, half of which is rotting in the putrefied body of a *Nemean Lion*. It sounds like that. It sounds like a *manticore* crunching through vertebrae. A decapitation. A body falling limp. I haven't looked away from the cultist, and somehow, in the blink of an eye, I see Bellamy. I see Silas. I see them both oscillating in and out of the world, struggling, screaming, voices pitched impossibly high. A crack echoes out as a hip bone shatters.

I glance at Fred.

And in the screams, I know we both hear Silas; that final, strained pitch of the vocal cords, that desperate cry before his head was severed from his neck. I remember the body falling limp, arms dropping, legs going slack. Did I even see that? I couldn't have; it was night, so much was happening. But I remember it, the way Fred is remembering it now. She looks at me, and I know she is cursing me. I feel the weight of it, a hex writhing through my limbs. She looks so tired. I wonder how many hours a night she spends hoping I die.

I wish we'd never met you.

"Cass," Leo murmurs. "Alright?"

"No."

He doesn't press. He just follows my line of sight.

"Ignore her," he murmurs.

I start to think, *why should I?* But then Leo says, uncharacteristically, "Ignore all of it. Trust me, it's easier that way."

I turn to look at him. I see there's a fine sheen of sweat on his brow. His breathing is measured and steady, but in that forced way: he's holding himself tense deliberately, like anything less than absolute stillness will see him break. I do something a little selfish, then—I reach out and grab at his hand with my other. He's curled it into a fist, and I slip my fingers between that defensive lock, thumb pressing firmly against the soft flesh of his wrist where I can feel his pulse.

The skin twitches. The heart rate is rapid and panicked, and I realise I recognise this kind of reaction because I have seen it so often, both in myself and anyone who's survived this long. Most especially in the *xenos*.

Leo is panicking.

"Leo," I say.

The mention of his name makes him inhale in answer. He pulls his eyes away from the squelching, gruesome scene and looks at me with a small frown. Before he's even spoken, I know he's misunderstood me.

"Because you've apologised," he says, answering a question I didn't ask. "And it's not really your fault. It could have been any of us."

My interest in Leo—in what happened to him outside London's walls and how he's reacting now—has overridden my upset at the sight of Fred. It's even trumped the blood-curdling sound of flesh, entrail, and blood plopping unceremoniously onto the ground as four limbs are torn from the torso.

I forgot how easily Leo forgives, how easily necessity overrides guilt for him. It takes everything in me not to put my head on his chest. I could leech comfort from him. I could become him, steal that attitude and his sensibilities, and move on. Silas is dead. Fred hates me for it.

The world is fucking ending. Who cares anymore? How many of us will still be alive when it's all over?

I'm supposed to be ruthless. Remember?

But if I have to keep reminding myself, how ruthless can I fucking be?

Some commotion begins on the scaffolding, where the other three condemned begin to panic. It is perhaps the most natural reaction out of anyone here. The audience, myself included, accepts the violent outcome. But there is still life in their bodies! There is still hope, and want, and desire! One of them—the one sporting the *hydra* headdress—leaps down from the scaffolding and attempts to bolt. Both his feet and hands are bound, so it's a miracle that he doesn't go prone on impact. I don't see the landing, but I see his head briefly disappear as he stumbles, ankle twisting, and then the Blood Hunters are on him.

A cry sounds as sharp and true as the pitched whistle of an arrow shooting too close to the ear. The signal spurs the horsed Blood Hunters into action. One leans back in the saddle, draws a sword from a sheath, and cuts through the rope he's been dragging, suspending a bloodied left arm pulled from the *griffon* cultist's limp torso. It swings back into the dirt, stone, and viscera. Now freed, the Blood Hunter nudges their gelding's flank and trots it in place. Ahead only twenty paces hobbles the condemned cultist, and the Blood Hunter drives their horse forward, unholsters a flintlock pistol from their left side, and fires a shot. I see the arterial spray as the bullet punctures through the cultist's shoulder. The scream muffles and gurgles in his throat as he drops. For good measure, the Blood Hunter rides forward and drives their blade through the other shoulder, skewering the man— and then he keeps riding.

No clean deaths allowed.

The scene unfolds like this: in some sick synchronicity, the remaining horsed Blood Hunters release the viscera they are dragging and return to their initial points. The fourth, half carrying and half dragging the *hydra* cultist, gallops forward. The skewered man screams. His legs kick impotently in the air. Blood gushes out of both shoulders, dripping onto the stone, and his arms weakly press against the hilt. The force of the gallop has driven him back against the base of the sword, and in a fit of desperate insanity, he moves his hands up to the blade and willingly cuts his hands raw in an attempt to pull himself free.

The effort does nothing for him. The Blood Hunters move to tie his limbs to each horse.

But now, the remaining two cultists give in fully to their panic. They both leap from the scaffolding and hobble off in separate directions. This causes the Blood Hunters separating the London crowd from the University to split off; two from each end rush to intercept them. The Londoners howl, cackle, roar. I instinctively step back—the air feels different. Leo must feel it, too, because he pulls me in front of him and puts his other hand on my waist.

"Might have to run, Mr Jones, if it gets too messy," he murmurs in my ear. His voice is calm, but his heartrate betrays him, rapid and fearful against my back.

I want to quip back; I want him to think I'm just as calm, too. But I'm not, and I can't pretend as easily as he can. I can't even hold my faith at bay. In an old habit, I reach for that old comfort: *God, do not forsake me.*

"Leo," I say because this is the greatest and most tangible comfort I have here. I have him, or part of him. I have, at times, his body. I clutch at the arm around my waist.

And then the wardstones flicker.

Just for a moment. Just a brief giving up of their power. They pulse, and I watch as the blue sheen across the city evaporates, like dozens of gas lamps being snuffed out; the quality of the sky shifts, and I *know* as the others around me know.

Something is happening to the magic.

I don't look at Leo. I don't look at anyone but Dean Drearton. His face is pale, eyes bulging and wide, neck craned upwards. I feel my heart reach an impossible, anguished speed—this can't be happening. This can't be happening. Without the wardstones, what are we but sitting ducks?

"Cassius," Leo says. I turn to look at him.

Something else is staring back at me.

I flinch in its arms, but it holds me steady. Whatever I'm looking at isn't registering cleanly, and I don't understand for a long time that what I'm seeing—who I'm seeing—is familiar.

Vengeance stares at me.

All of London disappears. It is only the two of us. Vengeance with its curved, upsetting body. The antlers creak like the birch trees of Sherwood Forest as the gargantuan body bends towards me, and the strange forestry of its fingers cracks and moves in anticipation. When it's close enough, it caresses my face with a strange kindness.

"*Vindicare,*" it whispers to me. "*Intellexistine?*"

Vengeance. Did you understand it?

"*Probe,*" I tell it. Very well. I claim I understood it very well, because even if I don't know the specifics, I know its revenge will be ritualistic. Then, severely and bravely, I say, "Te hinc amove."

Remove yourself from here.

It's the closest I can get to demanding it leave us alone. It snorts at me, nostrils flaring so wide I think part of my head could fit inside. It does not move, and nothing else exists; I can't look away from its dark grandeur.

I ask it: "*Quamobrem hic es?*"

What brings you here.

Vengeance's jaw cracks open wide, its head splitting into two, the top half snapping back wildly. It screams and groans, and the sound is so human I flinch.

"*Nos aegre facis,*" this new voice says. Previously, Vengeance has sounded like an impossible choral haunting, and now it's as if one of those voices has battled its way to the front.

Vengeance says, *You provoke us. You make us angry.*

I feel very suddenly insane. We provoke you? This was our world, our home, our lives—you, you fetid, rotten creatures! You are pests! You are mildew in the crops; you are gangrene on the body of Christ; you are meant to be cut out. Burned out. Destroyed.

I say none of it, but anger surges in me, and then I remember distantly the screech of the *harpy*—the only other *teras* I've had the misfortune of speaking to.

I had asked it, as it screamed and haunted around the greenhouse, "*Cur non discedis?*"

Why don't you leave?

It had told me, "Iuppiter me non audit. Sorores meae me non audiunt"

Jupiter does not hear me. My sisters do not hear me.

And I'd thought it was trapped in the greenhouse, that it had been telling me it couldn't escape the greenhouse.

But what if it was more than that?

What if it couldn't leave London? This world?

What if none of them can?

I open my mouth to ask Vengeance when the vision fades.

Roughly, I am thrown back into the world. Nausea, rotten adrenaline, and panic; all of it collides in my body, and I buckle, sliding down against Leo's side.

"Jesus," he mutters, catching me. "Mr Jones, it's over, now. It's over."

Belatedly, I realise he's talking about the torture. About the executions. The chatter of the crowd is immense, vigorous, alive, and wild with an electric wonder at what they've witnessed. The University cohort moves around us, swelling as they depart. The dean is gone. I don't know how long I've been standing there, transfixed by something no one else can see, but over the heads of those departing, I see the bloody, pulpy mess of body and limbs spread out over the marble. The twisted torsos of the dead crumple at awkward angles, their heads still covered by the cult masks.

I don't know why, but I walk forward.

"Mr Jones," Leo says, grip slipping as I walk forward. "Cassius. God."

I hear him following me. He tries to wrench me back, but I go down into a squat before one of the bodies, the one in the *hydra* mask. Squatting in amongst viscera reminds me of Watford. It reminds me of my brothers.

Would he be happy with all of this, I wonder? Would Thaddeus be the University's staunch defender? Would he be violent and angry and burning with a rage he could place nowhere else but in my hands?

I'm sorry. I don't know what I'm doing, and I don't think I can do anything differently. Something isn't right, and I don't know how to stop it.

My thoughts are interrupted by a viscous aching in my arm—the prosthetic, at the point of its joining, begins to throb and pulse suddenly. I hiss and look over at it.

Leo says, "Cassius, get up."

I ignore him. I ignore the way his voice hardens. I ignore

the pain, I ignore Vengeance, I ignore everything but the *hydra*—the woman, really. She's waifish. She's drowning in the scrappy, oversized clothes they've put her in. Her neck is pale and exposed, the only bit of skin I can see, and it's red with welts and speckled with her own blood. Angry, infected stitches protrude from her neck. Flies are already making a meal of her.

"They sewed it on," I say suddenly. "They sewed her into the mask."

Leo sighs behind me. It's a horrible way to die. A horrible way to be buried, if they bury them at all.

I can't help it. I say a prayer for her. I pray for all of them. God forsook them, and I am sorry for it.

I should have killed Dean Drearton when I had the chance.

"Cassius—"

"Why can't you have even an ounce of empathy?" I snap. I look back over my shoulder.

Leo deflates. His eyes show he's—hurt, I think. Wounded. But he snuffs out that bit of vulnerability with a blink.

"You were panicking. You were feeling it, too," I say. "You hate this as much as I do, and you pretend to be above it. You won't tell me what happened to you out there beyond the wards, but I can *feel it*, Leo. You've been inside me. I know you. Why can't you just—"

I don't even know what I'm asking. I'm breathing hard; everything feels hot. My head throbs.

Leo finds something to say. He gasps and laughs, and I hear his voice crack—which scares me, scares me so thoroughly that I'm completely transfixed before him. His eyes are wide and weepy, and he gestures out to the bloody mess of bodies. "Because perhaps the idea that the *teras* are the work of Satan or witches is not something Drearton dreamed up by himself. Maybe I've seen this all before. Maybe I see what's happening in London and recognise the hysteria, and maybe I know there's nothing I can do to stop it. Maybe I know there's no point in even trying because the *teras* are going to starve us out or breach the wards, and either way, we're dead. Maybe I just want to—survive as long as I can. Maybe I just want to fuck and drink and revel in adrenaline because there's no point in fighting or trying anymore."

I look at him. I look at him, I *look at him*, and I want him to feel it; the same tear in my heart, the same anger. The upset. How dare he! How dare he. Leo has claimed neutrality and apathy for so long. He has been untouchable by all of this. And it's a lie!

My stomach twists violently, and heat burns through my whole body. All my limbs begin to shake. Fury is untameable.

I say, "How disappointing," because what else is there to say. Leo has always been a mystery, but he's also been distant. Aloof. Despondent and detached and surviving the way a shade or a ghost might: haunting the peripheral, never engaging fully. He feels it just as keenly as I do. He feels it, and he won't share it with me. I realise, maybe for the first time, he's just as scared as me.

It is the first time in months that I miss God.

And then I pass out.

※ 9 ※

LESSON NINE

"And how the hell was I supposed to know?"

I wake suddenly in the dim orange glow of an unfamiliar room. Hissed whispers scratch around in my head, with the grating pressure of a sword being drawn from a scabbard. It's like I've had bottles upon bottles of wine; a heaviness in my head, the back of my neck, and a delayed aching separation between my eyes and my comprehension: every time I blink and twist, it takes too long to comprehend the shift in direction. My mind is slow to catch up.

A woman, voice sharp and spasming with barely controlled anger: "Because you've been undressing him, that's why!"

I blink rapidly and turn my head.

I am in heaven. I know this because it's all gold and white and soft light. I'm warm and cosy and staring up at beauty, at a great arching ceiling and endless circles patterned with gold tesserae suns. Stained glass, membranous and delicate, and roundness in the architecture, in domed tops and bowing corners, so it's like I'm in a holy womb, with all the parental comfort I always craved but was never given.

St Paul's Cathedral.

It had been greatly threatened by a conflagration that had spread in London in 1666, and because London is still medieval in its layout—an overcrowded warren of vein-thin streets laid in rat king knots and winding alleys—the fire could have destroyed humanity's final bastion with ease. But thankfully, it had been contained quickly. I shudder to think what would have happened—where all of us would be now or how humanity might have survived if London had burnt.

In the case of this place, I am grateful it survived for selfish reasons. It's like a homecoming. I close my eyes, and I feel God at the edges of my mind, at the edges of this cathedral—and I didn't have to crawl back to him because he found *me*. He brought me here. He remembered His child.

I almost cry. I know I shouldn't—I know it doesn't matter the way it used to and that I can't ever really love Him the way I used to. I know I must stay angry, and I know I have a right to be: if He has any sway over this world, then I am righteous in my fury. Part of me resents feeling anything good or joyous at being in His house; another part wants to go to sleep the way a babe might in the arms of his mother. Familiarity and comfort: that's what God remains to me.

"Well, Victoria, I'm not exactly focused when I'm *taking off his clothes*."

I blink again, hearing Leo clearly. I twist down to look at him—and he is unfamiliar in this house of God. He's only ever been blasphemous on holy ground before, and I see him shifting uncomfortably, an air of agitation swelling in his joints and making him step and shake out his hands.

I'm in a hospital ward—the great basilica of St Paul's is, as I suspected, now a makeshift infirmary. The pews have been pushed to the side, piled so haphazardly it's like a giant tidal wave has moved through: Moses parting the seas. I like that they're still in here, like this holy place could ever return to

God after this. Blood and rot and dying children; what's godlier than that?

Victoria and Leo stand nearby, locked in defensive and rapid conversation about me. I blink again, wondering if Vengeance did something—if that encounter with it in my mind has affected my body in some tangible way. But as I twist my head, I see the join between my prosthetic and my flesh is inflamed.

Infection.

Shit.

I hadn't noticed. How had I not noticed? It's been stiff and upsetting since the moment I earned it, but it hasn't ached the way an infection often does. None of the sting. None of the fire.

"Cassius," Victoria whispers. I flinch, and they're both looking at me. Victoria is still in her healer cloak; the rise of her belly is concealed beneath. Has Leo has spotted it yet. She looks—lovely. Her brown skin glows under the refracted gold light. "How are you feeling?"

She comes towards me. The cot is low to the ground, and she lowers herself carefully.

"Don't," I say—or attempt to say. My voice comes out hoarse and throaty, and Victoria shushes me even if I'm sounding rude, and she is so kind I could cry.

"I've put a salve on you," she says. "You were feverish." She reaches out to check it, the back of her hand against my forehead, and tuts and sighs. "Still are. It hasn't broken yet."

"I didn't. . ."

I don't know what I'm trying to say or what I'm trying to defend. I'm on the verge of tears suddenly. Leo lurks behind her, watching me with a pinched expression. He seems hesitant, and I wonder if he knows I've seen him there. I wonder if he's thinking about coming forward himself and holding my hand—which is dramatic and overly intimate for us. It's not the kind of care we have for one another's bodies.

We could be happy, in a way, I think about saying. *You and me. We could trust each other and be soft together, and it wouldn't matter —the vulnerability would be temporary because you're right, Leo Shaw. We're all going to die.*

We're all going to die.

I gasp—I'm crying.

"Shit," I say. "Fuck."

"Does it hurt?" Victoria asks. She gnaws at her lips, and her eyes show that she means it. She cares. After everything, after Bellamy—I don't deserve it.

"I'm sorry," I say, and I mean it for everything. For being alive. I want to—hurt myself suddenly. Hit my head. Beat my thighs. I squeeze my eyes shut and breathe, breathe, breathe.

What I did was necessary. Whether I believe that or not, it's done. I can't change it.

It's done.

What I need to focus on is Vengeance. The *teras*. The inevitable brewing war.

"How long do I have to be here?" I ask. My walls have gone up, and Victoria must feel it, too, because she flinches and pulls away. She sighs and stands up, face twisting with the effort. "Until I say so. Your body might be rejecting the prosthetic—which is unusual, given all the magic. If it's no different in the morning, I'll be sending you to the Artificers."

Fred. Fred became an Artificer. I grimace. The only thing I can hope for is that Fred Lin is not around when I present my fucked little arm for help.

"We should go," Victoria says. I realise she's talking to Leo, and I try to sit up.

"What," I cough out. "What's going on?"

"Patrol," Victoria says. She wipes her hands on the front of her cloak.

I shake my head at her. "What are you doing? You've already gone."

"Well, I'm going again."

She's not looking at me as she speaks.

Leo's brow furrows as he looks between the two of us. "What is it?"

Victoria spins towards me, and there's a warning in her eyes. I could say plenty of things now, but I mostly want to say: *Jesus Christ, Victoria, you're pregnant.*

Wait.

That's not—that's not *why* she's going again, is it?

Mouth running dry, I say instead, "It's just. She's already been. Not two nights ago, with me."

Victoria gnaws on her lip again. She looks away. A door somewhere slams closed, and there is laughter and chatter; some other Healers, I think. Victoria turns towards the sound as she says, "Well, I volunteered."

"Why?" Leo snorts. "Are you trying to get killed?"

He says it with levity, but Victoria doesn't answer. She doesn't turn back to us at all, and I wonder if she *is* trying to die.

I don't know what she thinks about her pregnancy. Is it Bellamy's legacy, or is it a burden for her to bear? Is it a parasite? Is it something she even wants?

I'm not in any place to ask.

"Anyway," Victoria says when she glances back. She looks at me first and orders: "Stay in bed. Someone will come by to check on you tonight, and I'll poke my head in after patrol."

If you return, I don't say.

She puts a hand on her hip and leans back, face twisted as she rubs at a knot in her shoulder. Leo sees it too, and something about the arch of her back, the light, and the way the cloak drapes over the swell registers in his face. His eyes go wide, and his lips pinch together thinly.

Leo Shaw doesn't say a word.

Victoria glances between us and mistakes the silence for something altogether far nicer. "Right," she says, and she offers me a sad sort of smile that gets chased off her face by something dreary and despondent. Her eyes darken, and she plays with her hands. "Right, I'll leave you two alone. Leo, I'll be outside."

Victoria Bennet walks away without another word. What must she be thinking, I wonder, when she sees Leo and me?

It must upset her. It must. . .irritate her. That whatever we have—something fairly fresh, ill-formed, and in many ways as noxious as *Fed Felen*—might survive when her and Bellamy didn't.

Which is all extremely fair and reasonable. If I was her, I'd be mad by now. I barely have much of a hold on my sanity as it is.

Leo is lurking over me in an uncomfortable way. Looking at him from this low angle, I realise how much his body has changed in the last three months. He has grown fast. Muscle clings to his body. But with the speed of his growth, an awkwardness has been bred in him, like something cancerous eating at his natural grace. Leo knew his old body well, and it showed in every movement, in the way he carried himself. Now, the added muscle seems like a cloak of its own. Leo hasn't quite learnt how to stand with it. How to sit in it. How to *own* it.

I see him turn his head to follow Victoria—wait, says my heart. Wait.

My skin goes hot. My head is aching—I can't stand this.

"Cigarette," I prompt him. "Please."

He snaps his attention back to me, and I go giddy; it's blissful under his gaze. He seems grateful for the suggestion and lurches forward to rummage through my clothes. My mind registers my nakedness quickly—I'm only in my pants, and the bedsheet is probably twenty years old, yellowed and scratchy thin cotton thrown over me more so for my modesty than to protect against the chill. A woollen blanket has been folded at the end of the cot, but I'm too sweaty to think about bundling up. I struggle to sit up, pushing one-handedly upright. I hold the prosthetic at a strange angle so it touches neither my body nor the bed itself. The sheet falls lax in my lap. I should be freezing in this cavernous cathedral; the holy cavity is as empty as Jesus' tomb when the great rock rolled away. Sitting upright has gravity working against me, and I suddenly feel far more feverish—far less certain of anything. I blink away some dizzying spots and think: *the heat of my skin is like God's touch. I am warm because He wants me warm.*

"Here." Leo has lit a cigarette. He urges it close to my lips, leveraging them apart as gently as a kiss. I turn towards him like the eager lover I am.

Ad omnem libidinem projectus homo—a man addicted to every lust.

I take a drag, and my eyes flutter closed. "Thank you," I croak out.

And then Leo does something unexpected. He hovers and then jolts towards me. Leo Shaw leans over and kisses me on the forehead.

I stare at him. He stares back. The cigarette burns down between us.

A conflicted rise of emotion swells up in me. Right before a patrol—he does this right before a patrol. He's seen people torn apart today, seen me faint, offered me a sliver of who he was before—something is wrong.

"You don't," I say and stop. *Calm down. He's fucked you in a confessional booth; a kiss on the forehead is nothing.* After another languid drag of the cigarette, a manufactured moment of laxity, I continue, "You don't normally do that. I hope you're not planning on dying."

He snorts and reaches out for the cigarette. Our fingers brush together, and I wish I had a magic touch where I could siphon all his thoughts through his skin. Leo smokes in silence, no longer coughing. "I plan on very little these days," he murmurs.

I know what he means. I know there's an unspoken, insidious truth to it, too—that we have very little hope of winning this war. But part of me, a yawning and eager chasm, wants Leo to say something else. Something about me.

You didn't plan on liking me, Leo Shaw, but perhaps you like me more than you first realised. Say it. *Say* it.

But he wouldn't be Leo Shaw if he did.

He hands the cigarette back to me with a smile and stands, dusting ash off his legs as he goes. He waves and turns to leave.

"Wait," I yell. My voice is reedy and embarrassing, pitched high as the cathedral takes the echo. I hear it get thinner and thinner as it reverberates around the empty arches, like a soul trying to scramble up to God.

Leo looks back over his shoulder.

"I'm sick of this, actually," I say. "If you die, I'll be quite pissed off, I think."

Leo frowns, but the corners of his lips twitch up in a devious smile. "Oh?"

"Yes. Rather. So," I tap the cigarette on the metal edge of the cot and watch the ash fall onto the holy ground—blasphemy, blasphemy, blasphemy, "I reckon we should make a deal."

Leo turns fully around now. He's always liked games, even if they never play to his strengths.

"What are you suggesting, Mr Jones?"

"I want to know you."

I say it so plainly that it shocks both of us. In the ensuing pause, I cough and undermine myself by making light of it. "I—I want you to tell me about your past. About what happened out there."

The smile vanishes from his face. "No."

"Leo—"

"There's nothing you could offer," he says, "that would make me say yes." His eyes turn dark. "No knowledge I can't learn about on my own. No trial I can't beat without you. No hole you haven't already offered up for me to fuck. What do you think would be an equivalent exchange? You've offered everything to me freely already, and that was your choice. It's not my fault you have nothing left to give." His hands are flexing and unflexing at his side; nausea and a stinging, vibrant pain shoot knifelike through my gut. "So no, Jones. No. It's better—it's just better like this."

He turns and leaves. I shake in the afterglow of his wrath; I shake because he's reminded me of my father and Thaddeus. That insidious anger and a very particular cut of violence.

How fucking wrong could I be. Leo Shaw doesn't—doesn't care about me at all.

The fever makes it all so much worse. My mind is a swampland. I cannot wade through. I can't do anything. Maybe I should vomit. Maybe I should get up and kill myself. Kill myself right here—I don't know, I'm panicking, I'm embarrassed, I'm ashamed, I thought he—

I press the burning end of the cigarette into my stomach and burn the skin. I'm able to breathe my first full lungful of air in minutes. I gather myself and slow my breathing.

I burst into tears.

"DEAD?"

I wake with a start and somehow manage to keep my eyes shut. I had fallen asleep. I cried all broken and pathetic for what seemed like hours, and sleep must have crept up on me, pried my fingers from my hollow face and tugged the waking will from me. The grief of the betrayal—of Leo's words, but also my own stupidity—seems at least blunter after I wake.

A hand presses to my forehead, and then two fingers touch my lips. I breathe slowly, trying to mimic the rise and fall of someone in a deep sleep.

Someone shifts, and I feel a body move away from me. "No," a shrill voice announces. I don't recognise it. "Fever's broken."

"Good. Good. Off you go, then, girl."

This second voice, though, chills me because it's Drearton. Why is he here? Why has he come to check on me? I am just another of his pawns.

Only you're not. You threatened him. You would have killed him.

I wish I had. Or, at least, I wish I had the *manticore* poison dagger on me now. It must be wrapped up in my clothes. Does Drearton know about it? Does he know Leo Shaw and I extracted the *teras'* paralysing poison for ourselves?

Would he use it on me if he knew?

My body revolts. It takes everything not to jolt. *Breathe. Breathe.* I've done this before. I've pretended to sleep to save my life before: I've let Thaddeus take the wrath of my father and pretended to sleep through his cries. I've forced myself to relax as *teras* poke and prod at our shabby hovel. So this? This I can do.

I relax my jaw, relax every tight muscle, and I imagine that I'm in some eternal sleep.

Endymionis somnum dormire: to sleep the sleep of Endymion, the shepherd preserved by Selene. Death and sleep are siblings.

"That one's not nearly as godly as he'd have you believe."

A new voice, somewhere further into the cathedral. The statement is answered by a derisive snort and footsteps leading away from me. I risk opening my eyes.

St Paul's is dark, save for the paltry light of candles, their weak glow offering little by way of visibility. Instead, the dark, voluminous shapes of the cathedral bear down on me from above. I blink rapidly, trying to ground myself.

My cot is positioned in the centre of the cathedral, making it absolutely impossible for me to slip off and sneak around. But at least I have some vantage to every corner—so long as Drearton and this new voice don't walk too far from me.

Luckily, they don't.

The cathedral is awash in blue light, snuffed out at times by an impenetrable shadow. The moonlight gleams through the coloured stained glass, and this reveals the silhouettes of Drearton and this newcomer, a figure propped up against one of the columns.

As my eyes adjust, my gut twists—Leo?

No. Not Leo. The priest of the University's chapel.

Father Veer.

That one's not nearly as godly as he'd have you believe.

I think about dying suddenly. Father Veer: what on earth do you know?

You were getting fucked right next to him. Of course, he heard. You never could control your voice.

I resist the urge to crane forward or crawl towards them. As much as I want to hear this conversation in detail, I must pretend to be asleep.

Luckily, St Paul's is on my side, and those vaulted arches preserve the sound.

"Oh?" Drearton asks. Then, "No, actually, don't tell me. I already know. . . Of his preferences."

Father Veer says something soft, something I don't catch. But Drearton doesn't catch it either.

"What was that, Father?'

"Oh, no. Nothing," Veer says in the most unconvincing drawl. "It's for God to know."

"Hm." A beat passes. Drearton grows quickly frustrated. "Well? What is it?"

"Two things. Sutton D'Avore, and then a Blood Hunter. Name of Jenny."

Drearton sighs. "Jenny Pill?"

An uncertain noise erupted from Father Veer's throat. "Perhaps. She didn't share her surname."

"Blood Hunters are few. It was her." Drearton fidgeted with something, and then his voice turned dark and frustrated. "Well? Spit it out."

Veer spoke quickly. "D'Avore went to confession. Confessed she'd been having violent thoughts."

A snort from Drearton. "That's hardly a problem for a Hunter."

"Towards herself."

Drearton sighed. He sniffed and said nothing.

Cautiously, Veer continued. "Says she is ashamed of having them, but that it's hopeless. The *teras* will kill us, she says, and she's. . . living in the shadows of Angelica D'Avore."

"Well, if she stepped out of the shadow and lived up to her family name, as we expected, then perhaps we'd have a fighting fucking chance."

Drearton's voice is flat and angry. Veer is silent.

As if he'd said nothing, Drearton's tone lifts again to that light and airy nonchalance. "And this was after the executions?" he clarifies.

"Yes."

"I thought—morale should have improved."

Veer doesn't answer.

Sutton is struggling. I don't know why that surprises me. I suppose I thought, in a way, only the first-years were. On patrol, Sutton was incredible. It's in her blood the way it isn't in mine. So far, I've survived through sheer fucking luck. But Sutton? Agrawal? The fresh graduates, the third-years, even the second—I think it frightens me to realise we're all in the same boat.

"Fine," Drearton murmurs. "Fine. What about the Blood Hunter?"

"She came after. . . An incident. Not for confession. For comfort, in the pews. I found her. . . Sobbing, sir."

"She's always been emotional," Drearton says dismissively.

"No, it was. . ."

Something about Veer's tone gets the dean's attention. I watch as Drearton's silhouette reaches out to touch Veer's shoulder in a hollow comfort. "What is it, man?"

"A Hunter fled. Meant to be on watch at Chelsea but took the opportunity to desert—or at least, that's what they thought. The blood orrery showed him running, so Jenny Pill and a few others rode out to meet him."

"And what," Drearton murmurs, "she's the one who killed him?"

"No, sir. He was already dead. He'd been pulled into the Thames."

My panicked mind thinks of the *nuckelavee*. The Thames is tidal, its water brackish. If the *nuckelavee* fears fresh water, could it traipse through the Thames?

"*Kelpies? Morgens?*" Drearton asks.

"Something like that. I think Ms Hill was more concerned with the proximity than the *teras* class."

"As she should be. God. Alright. We should think about moving behind the threshold."

"Sir?"

The Janus threshold—that nebulous force inside the

University itself, only crossable by those enrolled in the University or its staff. In Veer's unanswered question, I hear the rest of his concern: what about what remains of London?

The Workers. The remaining families. We fought for their place—I fought for their place. I did things I shouldn't have done because I had promised my mother. I promised, and even if I never want to see her again, even if they've wronged me, it's complicated. It's not—I can't abandon them.

Drearton's suggestions mean that only the University is safe. And what happens when those wards fall? What about food? Resources? Are we locking ourselves up to die?

"But London's wards. . .are fine," Father Veer says. It's almost a question. Drearton's silence is an answer.

Then I was right.

Vengeance in my mind's eye; seeing the wards fall. The unknowable magic of them is being drained. How? And how does Drearton know this?

Drearton needs not to answer, because God interrupts him. I hear the clang of warning bells outside, and now I can't help it. I sit upright. Drearton turns to look at me, the shadows darkening under his eyes. It's as if he sees right through me, sees to the very core of me. I am an exposed piece of flesh, more human, more fragile than ever.

The colossal doors to the cathedral scrape open in a screaming groan of wood and metal hinges. Several sets of footsteps pound over the marble. I watch as the silhouettes of tricorn hats and cloaks pour in. They're all carrying lanterns; the cool blue light is chased away by the pulsing fire-light. They are led by Fraser, a friend of Agrawal, who led my patrol.

"A patrol?" Drearton asks in reference to the warning bells.

"We returned," Fraser says, "And Agrawal's. No sign of Claypoole. Except... two of their horses."

"Damn it, woman," Drearton hisses to himself.

My heart is racing. This is so much like Thaddeus' death —so much like watching that party of Hunters return after leaving my brother gutted and dying.

Father Veer says, "Who is among them?"

"Petunia Claypoole. Graduated last year—first patrol she's fucking led," Drearton answers. "Six of them. Seven, maybe. The others. . .?"

He gestures for Fraser to fill in the other names. But Fraser shakes his head. He doesn't know.

I throw the sheets off me and stand. My head spins, and every part of me screams in protest. My arm—my new arm— throbs at the joint. But I stagger forward. The patrol party all flinch at the sight of me; someone curses under his breath. They hadn't realised I was here.

"Leo?" I ask, but he would have come to me by now. The only other hope I have— "Is Leo Shaw with Agrawal? Victoria Bennet?"

I know they're not. I know. I know.

Fraser ignores me. I see his brow quirk, like what little respect I earned on patrol with him has just been snuffed out. He turns back to Drearton. "They're dead, sir. Or they must be. Agrawal wants to head out; I disagree. I don't think we should risk anyone more. What should I tell him?"

"Ah," Drearton says, without any kind of emotion. "A shame."

After a beat, he says, "Mr Jones won't be happy at all."

I realise what he means. The patrol that's gone out tonight has Leo Shaw in it. Has Victoria Bennet and her unborn child. But more importantly, I realise Drearton will do nothing about it.

Please. Please, do something. Send them out. Send the whole of London out. Send the fucking priest out—everyone who is able should go and find him.

I am standing there half naked and shivering, and I realise my heart is breaking and there's nothing I can do. After everything, everything I've done and felt and had done to me, I think this is the worst of it all because I know for certain that I don't mean a thing to Leo Shaw, but the thought of him dying is tearing me apart. It is breaking my heart.

If God wants me to worship him—if God wants me to tear myself apart before He ensures that Leo Shaw is safe, then I should do it. I think about kissing Father Veer's feet in case he might spare a prayer for Leo. I think about all the things I would do. I think there is nothing I wouldn't do if it meant I could see Leo Shaw's perfect face one last time.

And Victoria—

"Get a hold of yourself, Jones," Drearton snaps. I'm—sobbing. I'm hyperventilating. My hands are tied up in my hair, and I'm *pulling* hard. Drearton shakes me, but it does nothing. Faces crowd my vision, a haunting of disappointed Hunters, noses upturned in revulsion.

Slap!

My cheek stings where Drearton's palm has slapped me. My gasping stops. The prickled skin divides my attention, and I'm grateful for it. I get a hold of myself.

"Fever must have scrambled your brain," he says. "Yes, it's a shock; it's all a great shock. But these things happen, Mr Jones, in this world. And especially in war."

I look up at him. The tears in my eyes soften the outline of him, reducing the dean to a shadow licked at by the lantern light. It makes him seem far gentler than I know him to be. I wish I had the weight of the dagger in my hand. I wish I could raise it and push it through his neck.

I'm meant to accept this, and so I nod and keep nodding until he pats my back. "That's it. Good lad," he says. His grip on my shoulder is rough, and he shakes me good-naturedly. "Fraser, tell Agrawal we will not be following after Claypoole.

No rescue efforts are to be attempted. Then send letters to the outposts. We are pulling back. London is the final defence."

Fraser blinks at him and then throws himself into a half-bow. I wonder if he understands, if any of them understand what Drearton is doing. Abandoning the watch towers. Giving up, letting the *teras* advance right up to London's walls.

It's a step before a full retreat beyond the University's veil, a thought Drearton has openly shared with Veer. He's planning to leave the rest of London behind.

But the weight of that barely registers. I am thinking of Leo, sweat-sheen skin glinting under lantern light. I am thinking of his laughter; I am thinking how little I really know. How much I want to know.

I'm not leaving him to die. I'm not abandoning him or Victoria.

I'm going to ride out of London's wards and make sure Leo Shaw is alive.

But to do that, I know who I need to talk to.

LESSON TEN

Behind the University's threshold, in the bowels of that institution, away from the rest of London, which is rotting like some bloated drowned body, I can pretend there is no threat but the University itself. No *teras* army prowling towards us. No last stand on the horizon. I can imagine I am here to learn, as I'd once wished to. Think of the books I could have read. Think of the knowledge I might have spent my years poring over.

Instead, I have to do this.

It's still night. I throw on my uniform and run as best as a sick man can run, lungs burning a minute into my scrambling return to the world behind the veil. My personal wardstone lets me pass as normal, but the nausea—on top of the already dizzying effects of Vengeance in my head, a fever freshly broken, and panic and grief—means I go to my knees and dry heave into the grass for minutes until I can pull myself together.

Get up. Get up! He needs you!

Which might be true or a pipe dream. Leo could be dead. I

imagine Leo's body, perfect and mine, torn asunder; the stringy tendon, the limbs cracked and pulled from the strong torso. He briefly becomes Thaddeus in my mind, and I see his stomach ripped open and warm red intestines gathered in his arms. What will I do if I go and find him like that? Should I crawl between his guts? Drape them over me? The closest I'll ever come to having him again is crawling inside the cavity of his wound; I could put my head between his ribcage and kiss the dead heart.

What is wrong with you?

I'm crying. I don't even know the truth yet, and I'm crying. I miss him.

I miss him.

Nolite timere. Do not be afraid. I have to imagine God is in my ear before I can bear to lift myself from the ground.

Don't judge me for this weakness. After everything, after turning away from God's guidance, this is like a treat. The grace of a God that might love me even now—it's a tantalising fantasy, and it allows me to forget everything I've sworn and everything I tried to reject. It's easier to imagine the Holy Spirit entering me and urging me to stand than to think I have the strength to do it myself.

But I only let it go that far. Once I'm up on my own two feet, I shake God from my shoulders. If I'm going to invoke Him again, I better make it count.

The grounds are quiet. Very few students linger here; many are on patrol, and the rest, I gather, are either studying, training, or fucking. After the events of this morning and what we've all borne witness to, I'd imagine a lot of people would be drinking, too, using the last of the alcohol and the cigarettes to bear another night.

My hand itches, eager to pull the cigarettes free from my pocket, eager for the ease tobacco will bring me, but I'll have to confront Leo's gift if I do that, and I'm simply too fragile to hold such a sentiment in my hands. Instead, I start up in a pathetic run again.

The dormitories are set close to the Janus threshold, parallel to the quadrangle on the opposite side of the veil that hosts Meléti's library. Then there's the academic wing, the Hunter quarters and training courtyard, and the apothecary tended to by Healers, who have their own quarters in the building nearby. Beyond a set of strangely disjointed sandstone buildings, there is the realm of the Artificers.

It is a mismatched jumble of structures. One is their quarters, and another is a deep storage building meant to house all their materials. Then there are a series of interconnected rooms where they work from.

I've never been here before. I've been avoiding it like the plague. And she might not be here; she might be drinking; she might be elsewhere; I almost want her to be.

There's only one way to know.

I put my hand on the door. It's open, and I press against it until the hinges whine. The door opens onto a long corridor. I can see at least four wooden doors flush to the sides. A few lanterns burn in sconces, but otherwise, it's dark, the kind that creeps: the shadows are dense as they cling to the corners.

"Hello?" I call out. No answer.

I step over the threshold of the Artificer's building. My whole body is braced the same way it tenses when a *teras* is nearby. I close the door behind me and try to make sense of the way my heart races. Stupid. Ridiculous. Unnecessary.

Leo, Victoria, and the rest of Claypoole's patrol need me.

My footfalls are loud and unsettling, and I flinch every time the noise rebounds back to me because it seems so disproportionate a noise. There are distant clanging sounds. Someone humming from upstairs. I don't know where to go.

Then, a head emerges from one of the rooms. I freeze. It

appears to be a head on its own, a shadowy decapitation; my reactive scream is maudlin and unnecessary; I put a hand over my mouth after the noise escapes me.

I can't believe I'm still so concerned with embarrassment.

"Oh," the head says—the voice is not Fred's, thank God, not hers. It's a man's voice. It's familiar, too, somehow. I can't quite place it. The silhouette shifts as the man moves out of the door frame and steps into the hall. He is fiddling with something, wiping his hands on a towel with near-obsessive precision. "Oh, I'm sorry, I've forgotten your name. Is everything alright with your arm?"

I walk forward, and the silhouette resolves into Abraham, the Artificer who attached my prosthetic. The low light makes his brown skin appear ashy and sapped of life; there is indeed a hollowness to his cheeks, noticeable only because he was already so wiry. He throws the towel over one shoulder and adjusts his spectacles, and then he's not sure what to do with his hands. He half reaches for me, then stops himself, glancing back over his shoulder.

"Did you, uh. . ." he begins. "Did you need me to look at it?"

I could just get his opinion. I could ask him to clean the infection, and I could leave and pretend I came here only for that. But I owe it—I owe it to Fred Lin. She needs to know.

So I shake my head and ask for her by name.

Abraham leads me onward. I glance at the room he emerged from as we pass by and see dozens of prosthetic beauties suspended on metal contraptions. Fingers, arms, legs. Most of them are made of wood and ceramic—articulated but sturdy.

Is he making some in advance? Or are more injuries happening than I'm aware of?

"Winifred is with Anastasia," Abraham says like I might know who that is.

"It's Fred," I say, more defensively than I have a right to be. "Winifred is a stupid name. Her words."

Abraham makes a low noise at the back of his throat, and I get the sense he's been told this before and, for whatever reason, has decided to ignore it. He leads me the rest of the way in silence up the stairs of the building. Each step groans and creaks, with the near-silent patter of dust falling every step we take.

"Your name?" Abraham asks with a glance back. "Ah, Jones, right? Thaddeus' brother?"

"Don't introduce me," I say and push past him. All these manners, all this routine, will just give Fred a chance to say no. I can't give her that choice.

I've apparently never been able to give her that choice.

I hear the room they're in before Abraham has a chance to tell me their location. He slows behind me, an affronted noise dying in his throat when he realises that I'm simply not affected by the same sensibilities he is. The corridor upstairs is carpeted and smells damp and old. There are yellowing cornices coloured further by the lantern glow, and the wallpaper peels and curls like decaying petals, an inescapable age that has seeped into this place.

Light spills from one of the open doors, and I perch outside.

"I can't."

It's Fred's voice. She sounds... frustrated. Furious, even.

A woman, soft and familiar in her own way, says, "You can. It's simple. You just have to—"

"I *can't*."

Something clatters; someone throwing something or dropping something with disdain.

"I wasn't meant to—I wasn't supposed to fucking be this, alright? I was born to shape soil and plant wheat and goddamn potatoes. I was meant to be angry—I don't have the focus for this. I should have... I should have chosen Hunter."

A scoff, a tired sigh from the other woman. "Then why didn't you?"

"Oh, you know why," Fred spits sharply.

"Well, I think that Si—"

"*Don't!*" Fred's scream is shrill. A panicked bark, a wounded dog howling and thrashing in fear. "Don't say his fucking name. I will kill you."

My heart lurches. *Silas,* I think. *I'm sorry.*

Now's as good a time as any to step forward.

Fred has a blunt tool to the throat of another Artificer, who I recognise immediately, because she saved my life. My new arm throbs, the infection at the join burning hot, and the phantom pain of my missing arm flares brightly in a kind of remembering: in the jagged teeth of the *Nemean Lion* crunching down upon the ulna and radius and severing them in half.

She is as I remembered her, if not somehow smaller; shorter than Fred, her pale hair run through with thick silver strands. She looks like she's dying, and I realise there's a great chance she is. She can't be more than twenty-seven, but her body is brittle, her skin lacklustre, her arms only a little more than skin and bone.

"Anastasia," Abraham says. He breaks the spell. Fred's pained eyes jut over to the door and find me immediately. A new, enraged pain burns within them as she pulls back from Anastasia.

Abraham continues like he hasn't noticed Fred's reaction. "We have a guest."

The room smells of sweat, dead air, and the stench of soldering. Anastasia clears her throat and walks slowly to the opposite side of the room. I'd initially thought her graceful, but now that I'm really looking at her, I wonder if her movements are this slow because she simply can't move in any other way. When she reaches the other side, she pushes her whole body weight against the window to open it. It squeaks as it moves up, letting in a gust of chilling air.

"Probably not here to see me," Anastasia says with a short cough. "Unless you want me to apologise for not getting that salve to you quicker. I heard a friend of yours died. And I can see. . ." she gestures to my arm, then looks past me to Abraham. "Though Abraham always does a good job."

"You worked on it, too," Abraham murmurs, and I can't tell if his tone is full of pride or concern.

Do they think I'm here about the arm?

It's your cover, isn't it?

I glance up at Anastasia, but I'm inevitably drawn to Fred. Now that I can see her—and really see her, not in amongst the cowled sea at the execution—my body spasms. Unbidden memories lurch forward in my head; I see her prone, leg gone.

I wish we'd never met you.

I hear her screaming for her brother, screaming with fear, with rejection, with the strange amalgam of a body comprehending loss the way humanity has for centuries, and simultaneously revolting against the truth of her brother's death. I see the decapitation. I hear the moment Silas dies, the severing of the spinal column. The way his body went limp. The red pulp of his head extruded through *manticore* teeth, dripping in rivulets down the wilted body.

I want to live happily, Fred had said once.

And Silas, always the pragmatist, gentle yet firm, said, *Well, that's nice. But it's a pipe dream. The closest you'll get to that is here.*

I remember Fred's rejection—*have you ever seen an old Hunter?*

Silas, frustrated, shouting back, *Then declare something else!*

She had. She did.

She took up the mantle Silas had told us he would pursue. She is keeping him alive now the only way she knows how.

My fault. But what isn't these days.

I want to reach out and put her head against the side of my neck. I want her to relax against me. I want her to allow it. But she can't even look my way.

Fred Lin wears the grey trousers of the men's uniform and a white shirt a size too big. She's rolled the sleeves up and has most of the buttons to her chest undone, exposing a clavicle that gleams with fear-sweat. Up close, her shorn head no longer looks clean. Someone—most likely Fred herself—has taken a razor to it. Haphazard chunks have been shaven off in uneven strokes. Days-old cuts have scabbed over and now line the scalp in raised brown-red bumps.

"Fred," I say.

She makes a noise, this wounded, panicked sound. Both her hands go to her face, and she shakes her head, sniffling when she stands again to roll her shoulders back. "Why are you here?"

"I wanted to—I need—"

I need your help.

I realise I can't say it. Or that, if I say it, she'll laugh at me. She'll have every right to. So I panic and take off my shirt.

"The arm," I say. "It's infected."

Fred stares at me. Her brows come together slowly. Is that disappointment? Anger? I can't parse her expression. She clenches her jaw, shakes her head slowly, and starts to walk out of the room. "Anastasia can put a salve on it," Fred says. "She's good with salves."

This isn't what I wanted to happen. Fred is going to walk out, and—then what? I go after Leo and Victoria alone?

"Victoria is pregnant," I say.

It gets Fred to slow down.

"Okay," she says.

She doesn't need me to spell it out, but I do anyway, just to make her linger a little longer.

I tell her, "It's Bellamy's."

"Okay," Fred says again.

This isn't what I expected. I don't know. I'm still naive, aren't I? Hoping everyone will do what I need them to because it's convenient for me. I come to Fred after not speaking to her for months, and the last time we talked she was recovering from the loss of her leg and the loss of her brother, two wounds that won't ever heal quite right. Now I'm back, but only to drag her away again. I'm back because I want her to forgive me. Maybe if she helps me now, she'll forget what I had to become to have us survive the trials.

But if I go, then what?

Anastasia and Abraham are caught in this mess, both awkward and silent, looking between us.

"I need to talk to you," I say to Fred. At this point, I'm practically begging. "Alone."

She puts both her hands up in a kind of exhausted surrender. She looks to Anastasia, then squeezes her eyes shut. Her hand goes down to her right leg—where the join between the flesh and the prosthetic is. A phantom pain I relate to. She curls her knee in and out, moving the prosthetic in its socket. "I don't think I want to be alone with you."

"I can stay," Anastasia says. She puts her hands out and gestures to my arm, but I jolt as the Artificer approaches me, wrenching the prosthetic away from her. I don't care about the infection. I need to keep Fred here—I need to give her my bleeding fucking heart. I need to kill myself before her right now, an offering to a new god; I need her to forgive me.

I must look mad as I stagger into the centre of that workroom. Shirt open, hair a mess, on the verge of wracking sobs.

"Fred Lin, I have asked too much of you already. I have hurt you in a way that I can never expect your forgiveness, even if I... want it. And I am here to ask something more of you. You can say no. But I can't—I couldn't not tell you." It all comes out in a rush—I make myself speak fast in case she finds the will to leave. "Victoria is pregnant and keeps volunteering for patrols. I think she wants to hurt herself. I think Leo is with her—*was* with her—tonight. And they haven't. . ."

My voice goes high. Fred's shoulders slacken. She's guessed the rest; I don't have to say it aloud.

But I do because I need to, in a way. My chest is seizing. "They haven't returned. Drearton's giving the order to abandon their patrol. It's not just Leo and Victoria. The whole party is missing."

Fred says flatly, "Then they're dead."

I stare at her.

She folds her arms and shrugs them high. "What do you want me to do, Jones?"

"Come with me," I say. "I'm going after them."

She doesn't even do me the service of scoffing. Her stare is pinched and flat. "For Leo Shaw, what wouldn't you do?"

She looks like she wants to say more. I see her mouth working, nostrils flaring. It irks her.

I can almost hear it. *You'll risk yourself for Leo. You risked the rest of us for yourself.*

Instead, Fred says, "Well, I'm missing a leg. I can't outrun anything anymore. You want me to, what? Ride out of safety to fuck knows where and let the *teras* kill me? I've had enough of that. Enough of leaving the wards. I left everything to come here, and I've come here. Here's where I'm going to stay."

She gives Anastasia and Abraham a nod of farewell.

I start panicking. I reach for who she used to be a few months ago—but I remember later that Fred distracted the

Nemean Lion by offering up a table of trial takers to it. She chose Silas over everyone else in that hall; she's always been more ruthless than me. Silas was her buffer. I just never realised it.

She was always like me, and she hates herself for it.

But before I realise all this, I say, "I saw you earlier. At the execution. You watched it so carefully—you hate Drearton just as much as I do. He killed those innocents today, and he's killing our friends now."

"The *teras* have killed them," Fred says. "And you're wrong. About today, I mean. You're wrong. Those cultists deserved to die for the sheer fact they would worship those fucking beasts."

Her voice goes high and cracks as if she's lying. It can't be true. She was just as horrified as me, wasn't she?

She starts to go and means it this time. I charge after her and pull her back by the arm.

"Fred—"

She punches me in the face.

It's a brutally quick hit. The jab gets me beneath my left eye. Something crunches. I feel my eyeball bulge unnaturally in the socket and have a wild fear of it spilling out in a milky paste from the force. Pain explodes across my face, throbbing incessantly across my cheekbone, the side of my nose, and the entire eye socket.

"Fuck," I gurgle.

I reel back and bend over.

"Oh, Jesus," Abraham whispers.

This time, when Anastasia comes and touches me, I don't throw her off. The waifish woman delicately helps me stand. When I peel my hands away, Fred's finger stabs forward towards me.

"Don't try to spill your guilt onto me, you asshole. I am done with you."

I do the inevitable. I say—the worst thing I possibly can. Because in this moment, I don't want to convince her. I just want it to hurt the way I'm hurting.

I say, "The Fred I knew would have done something about this."

Fred looks at me. Looks through me. "Well, she died in the snow with her brother. I am someone different. Someone who keeps their fucking head down and does their job."

"Like on the farm?" I say. "You should never have left."

"No," she laughs. "You're right. We should have never left."

She doesn't look at me again, but she does slam the door behind her.

In the ensuing silence, I laugh.

Anastasia looks at me. "The Healers had a go at you, huh? Okay. I can work with this. Let's treat this infection, then," she says.

And this time, I let her.

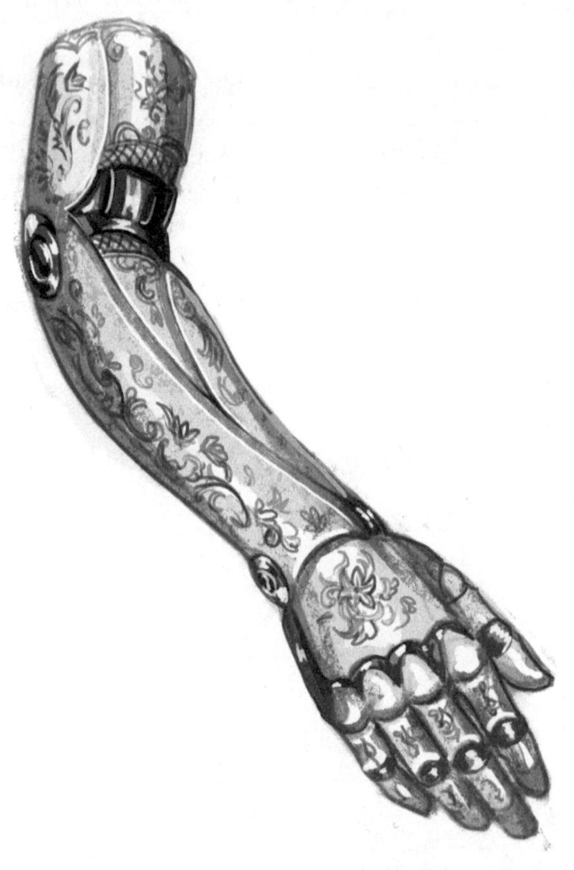

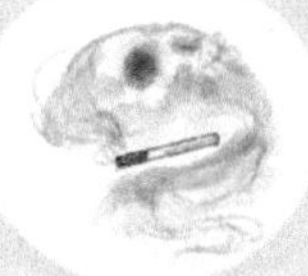

LESSON ELEVEN

I pull Don Wamsley out of bed.

The hand of my infected arm on his mouth, the other on his shirt, I tug him up and awake.

He thrashes immediately. Against my mouth, his breath is hot and rapid. Saliva and teeth graze my palm as he tries to bite. I don't let him.

"Stop it," I murmur, trying to keep my voice down. There are six other beds in this dorm, and whilst I'm sure two are empty, I don't want to wake the others. Not out of the goodness of my heart or a wish for their undisturbed rest—but because I don't want anyone to know what I'm doing. Who knows who belongs to Drearton. I don't want to risk it.

Don Wamsley recognises me and goes slack, but his eyes are aflame; those pupils hold a challenge. I stare back at him, waiting for the anger and shock to dissipate. It doesn't.

I try a new tactic.

"It's Leo. I need your help. Follow me," I whisper, and he shakes his head emphatically, trying in vain to get my grip on his shirt loosened. Even in the dark, I can see his cheeks have begun to flush.

"Not for *sex*," I hiss, furious that that's what he's thinking. But his fingers stop their onslaught, and he looks up at me now with curiosity.

I let go of him and gesture with my head to the door. Before he responds, I walk out and down into the chilly night air.

Ten minutes. Fifteen at most. That's all I'll give him—or give myself to convince him. I wasted too much time with Fred, and there's the matter of the horses. Supplies. God, there's no time. The longer they're out there, the lower the chance that they'll survive.

"What do you fucking want?"

I spin. Wamsley's thrown his Hunter cloak on over the loose get-up he was sleeping in. I run a hand over my face and get right to it.

"Leo's patrol is missing. Drearton won't launch a rescue. Will you help me?"

It's the most economical way I can say it because Don's a fucking idiot, and I worry I'll lose him if I take too long to explain. He blinks at me slowly, face lit only by the pale moonlight and muted lantern light haloing him. Each blink chases sleep further out of his eyes, but it still lurks heavy over him.

"I don't have much time," I say. "Don. Please."

That seems to get him. His brow furrows. "You're serious, aren't you?"

"Agrawal wants to search. Fraser and Drearton said no. I can't leave him out there." I make sure Don sees me. I say it again. "I can't leave him out there."

I could play on Don's obvious but suppressed attraction to Leo. I could—and would—try anything. *Use me*, I also say. *Use my mouth, any part of my body. I will whore myself to you if it means you'll help.*

But I don't need to do any of it. Don bites his lip and looks up at the moon. "I hear you, Jones, I do. Leo's a—good man. It's just, it's a war out there, and—"

"And they're coming for us anyway. Drearton wants to abandon London. Have us all retreat behind the Janus Gates. Siege warfare: tell me you realise we will all starve to death."

"So it's death or death, is that what you're saying?"

I don't know what I'm saying. I just want his help. I'm not thinking of the logistics, or the long-term, or how terrified I will be the instant we ride outside the wards.

"I'm saying I want to see Leo Shaw one last time before I die, and you're the only one I can think of who might help me."

The admission is sad. It's blunt. I don't want to think about how high and strained my voice has gone.

Please be brave, I think. I pray. *And if you can't be brave, please be stupid.*

I don't want to think of Don Wamsley as my friend, but when he nods at me, when he looks at me and says *yes*, I think he is the best one of all.

⁂

THE STABLES ARE on London's side of the Janus Gate. Most of this side of the University is a secluded circle from the point of the entrance hall—everything left of that appears to be a sprawling mess of buildings, but really is self-contained. If you push further and further into the University, you eventually hit the quadrangle with the massive willow and Meléti's library, the same quadrangle that houses the Janus Gates. This was where I spent the entirety of the trials. To the right of the entrance hall, beside the campus gates themselves, sit the stables in a long, freestanding warehouse.

I've only been here a handful of times, and none of the horses belong to *me* or to any one of us. The lot kept by the University have a mild temperament, and they are bred specifically to accept the touch of strangers. In theory, they should withstand the presence of *teras* to a degree, but not spooking when a winged beast thrusts its claws at you is a skill most humans have yet to master, either.

The stable exterior is all wood panelling. The building rises at least ten men high, and inside, exposed beams run the entire length as supports. In the dark, the building is a blue-black shadow emerging from the grass, the chill of London's night fogging around it like we're on the moors.

Or it should be like that.

Tonight, of all nights, I can see torchlight ahead of us. A soft orange haze emits from the high windows of the stable, and a line of flickering torches rushes across the grass, bobbing up and down and disappearing only when close to the stables.

"Three," Don Wamsley mutters next to me. He sighs and puts his forehead against the grass. I turn to look at him, and he flinches. "Don't touch me."

"Don't flatter yourself," I say, knowing full well I'd touch him if he asked me to. I'd touch most men if they asked me to.

But I'll be saving this flirtation for whoever's inside the stables.

"Three at a minimum," I tell him. "There's already light inside. Could be a whole lot of them."

"Great," Don says. His voice muffles against the grass, and he sighs rather dramatically as he lifts his head. His fists are balled in the grass. "Fucking great. You know we'll have Blood Hunters after us, right?"

"Let them come." I push up from the ground and kick the

side of his leg. He swears at me, and I have to resist the urge to kick him again but harder. In truth, I don't think Drearton will let the Blood Hunters come after us. He's just made a show of protecting his resources. The only reason I think that he might send them out is because it's me; Cassius Jones is the one defying him. But even then—we're all going to die, aren't we? Why does it matter if I die first?

Because he's holding on. Because without Drearton, there's no London.

"They might feel inclined to help us," I say, returning my thoughts to the Blood Hunters.

"Uh-huh." Don's not convinced and makes no attempt to hide that from me. He sniffs and pushes himself up, dusting grass blades from his Hunter cloak. "Who do we think's in there?"

I don't answer him. I stare at the stables for a long moment, as if the longer I look, the more obvious the answer will become.

"Come on," I tell Don finally, and he mutters beneath his breath and storms after me.

We crunch through the crisp grass. Every step screams our approach, but I'm too strung out to worry. I'll find a way to talk my way out of it. Or I'll—hurt them.

I have the *manticore* poison dagger strapped to my left hip, weakened by its use on the *barghest* but with another vial of the stuff on my person. Thaddeus' flintlock sits at my right. I have a can of black powder and four lead balls in my pocket, which is the extent of the ammo for the flintlock I've been able to scrounge up. Using one or more here to get out of London would be a waste—but I feel as I did when I rode after Thaddeus. Like I'll do anything to save a man.

It almost doesn't matter. I don't know how I'm getting back. Don and I will be on two horses, and there could be six

or seven injured students and graduates waiting for rescue—
we can't take them all.

Stop it. You're getting ahead of yourself. You're losing focus—
which is the core of it. Leo is my focus. Then Victoria.
Everyone else—

I'm simply not thinking of them.

Still, we try to stop being so obvious as we get close. I
urge the dagger from my side and raise it high, close to my
chest beneath my chin, the way Thaddeus taught me. Don
presses himself to the wall of the stables beside me. Ambient
chatter hums from inside, voices lost to the snorts and quiet
agitation of several horses. The torchlight flickers and the
shadows in the grassland flee. With a flick of my finger, I urge
Don closer to me, and the pair of us carefully skirt our bodies
right next to the stable's door frame.

Voices—the middle of a conversation—comes to me in
fragments.

"Don't understand. . .Shouldn't Fraser be. . ."

"No, you're not. . ."

". . .no time to. . ."

"Because Fraser is the one who told Drearton."

The last voice is clear and strong. Whoever it belongs to
might as well be standing in front of me, telling me himself.

Whoever it belongs to. . . I know the voice. Of course, I
know the voice. I throw a look back to Don, who shakes his
head emphatically.

"*Jones*," he hisses.

Don's fingers slide impotently off my shoulder before he
can get a grip. I step forward into the light of the stable's
opening and the three people inside are haloed in a murky
orange aura. Three hammers are pulled back, and three guns
are pointed at my pretty face.

My hands are already up. I see Sutton, her dark waves
pulled into a ponytail at the back of her head and tucked

beneath her tricorn hat. Len Hayes, who delivered my first patrol notice when Don was my overseer, stands with his thin lips pressed firmly together. Leading them is Agrawal himself. Half of his face is obscured by the shadow cast from the tricorn hat. His Hunter cloak is raised high, the neckline suffocating in appearance. It takes everything in me to not look down to where the embroidered *manticore* dances, but my mind goes there anyway.

You will ride out now, Agrawal? You left Thaddeus to die alone, and you'll ride out now?

Sutton makes a noise and lowers her gun first. She walks forward and pushes past me.

"Don fucking Wamsley," she says—how the fuck did she know?—and grabs him by his cloak, hauling him into the stable. The other two lower their guns, too. Both Len and Sutton look back to Agrawal, dogs to his command.

He cocks his head at me and raises the naked flame of the torch closer. That assessing gaze surveys me, all pinched and open in its scrutiny. "Jones," he murmurs after a moment. "Isn't it? Hm."

"Yes."

And then, "You killed the *manticore*."

Vengeance killed the *manticore*. I distracted the beast as the four of us threw ourselves at it, desperate to strike past its armour. I lay in the snow as Silas' head was pulverised in its mouth. I watched in abject horror as a *teras* twice its size calmly lit the *manticore* on fire and watched it burn to death.

I say none of this to Agrawal. Whatever the rumour is, whatever he knows, I did more to kill the *manticore* than he did, and he wears its mark proudly on his cloak.

"Yes," I say.

He nods. "Then it makes sense that you're here." He turns away from me and gives an invisible command to Len, who peels off from the rest of us and gets to work on saddling the horses. Agrawal clarifies, "You *are* here for Claypoole, aren't you?"

"For Leo Shaw and Victoria Bennet," I tell him. I need to be clear. There shall be no confusion about my motivations.

If Agrawal is offended by this, he makes no show of it. "And you? Mr. . . Wamsley, was it?"

"What Jones said," Don murmurs. He sounds like a school child after a chiding, terrified that he's been caught. I can imagine him standing with his hands stuffed in his pockets, chest bowing forward under the weight of his embarrassment, but I don't turn around to check.

Agrawal takes this at face value, which is either reflective of his stupidity or his desperation. I'm not looking this gift horse in the mouth; I can't tell you the sheer amount of *relief* that's filled me now that I know someone else is in charge. Call me any name you want for that—I just like being told what to do.

"Objective is the same," Agrawal says. "Does Drearton know you're here?"

He looks directly at me as he says it. I freeze. Why? Why is Agrawal asking me that?

"He was the one who told me," I say slowly. "Knowing him, he wants to see what I do."

"That's what you get for being Drearton's favourite," Len Hayes calls out from somewhere in the stable. Sutton shifts uncomfortably, and Agrawal is still staring at me, unmoving.

"You aren't going to elaborate?" I murmur.

"You already know," Agrawal says, but then, after I refuse to look away, he sighs. He takes off his tricorn hat, revealing dark mid-length waves squished flat by the tricorn's pressure. "Thaddeus wasn't the favourite," Agrawal says. "I'm surprised Drearton took an interest in you. But it must have been after. . .you retrieved your brother's body."

Were you there? Were you at the gates when I was screaming his name, begging for an answer? Was that you, Agrawal? Did you run straight to the embroiderer to embellish your fucking cloak whilst my brother held his own guts and died in the snow alone?

"Stupidity must interest him," I murmur.

"People interest him," Sutton says. "Especially when they do something unexpected."

"Well, this won't be unexpected," I say. "I don't care if Drearton knows or not. I don't care if he sends Blood Hunters, and I'm not sure I care if we don't make it back. I can't sit here rotting behind the wards—which are failing anyway—not knowing what happened to him. I can't do it!"

Don says *Jesus* under his breath, and I spin around with violent intention. His eyes go wide, the whites of them bulging, glinting orange in the torchlight. It takes everything not to punch him. I want to take my rage out on his body. Don't belittle me. Don't question me. You are here for the same reason, only you can't be honest with yourself about what you want.

"What do you mean they're failing anyway?" Sutton asks. I feel the room freeze, like the others hadn't quite heard what I'd meant.

There's no point in lying. "I've seen them flickering," I say, which isn't as nearly convincing as what I say next. "Drearton's ordered a retreat of all outposts. And he's told Father Veer he plans to retreat beyond the Janus Gates."

I'm surprised by their reactions: their lack of reactions. Sutton has perhaps the most dramatic, which is to look up at the stable ceiling and close her eyes. Everyone else sort of accepts this as something Drearton would do, and thus, barely anything worth reacting to.

"A problem for later," Len calls. "Fucking bastard."

"Agreed," Sutton says.

"Alright," Agrawal nods. The horses whinny and kick as Len leads them out into the night. "Good enough for me.

Here's what I know. Claypoole was in Southwark, but if that location was clear, her orders were to scout further south. Sussex or Canterbury way—too much ground for a single party to cover, but we're few and far between. Personally, I think she would have gone Sussex way, gone back west towards the Thames, and then up, ridden along the river until she was back in Southwark."

"How can you know?" Don murmured.

"It was her first patrol," Len announced. "It would be the smart thing to do."

The rest went unsaid; what would happen if Claypoole *hadn't* done the smart thing? If she headed out Canterbury way and was lost somewhere in that great stretch of land? She might have gotten close to an outpost, but so far, no messages had arrived.

There wasn't enough time to wonder.

"We head to Southwark first," I say, and Agrawal nods.

"Here." He throws me a pack—his own pack. "Split it between the pair of you."

Don appears over my shoulder, and I open the burlap sack to see there's a sparker, a salve, torn shreds of fabric that are either extremely yellow or made worse by the lantern light, and a loaf of bread that's already stale. I realise I haven't fucking eaten all day as soon as I look at it, but before I have to convince myself not to eat it, Sutton's pushed a flask in my face.

"For good luck," she says. The smell of it is intense; not a clean distillery. Something perhaps homemade. I take it without question and suck down two rough, burning mouthfuls and shove it into Don's waiting hand.

"Good," I croak, and Sutton laughs. She reaches forward and touches my nose with the tip of my finger.

"I think you're nothing like your brother," she whispers,

like it's a compliment, and I shudder, watching her walk out of the barn.

There's nothing left for us to do. We mount up on a horse each.

Agrawal gives the order.

"Ride out!"

12

LESSON TWELVE

The Romans built a pontoon bridge in early AD, a floating crossing to get to Camulodunum in Essex, one of their major ports. By the time the Romans were done in the 5th century, the bridge had fallen into disrepair. It was rebuilt, fell to fires and age, and rebuilt again.

It was remade just before the *teras* invaded in the early 1800s; a rather boring and conventional-looking bridge raised over five stone arches. But with the invasion, construction shifted rapidly towards defence.

There used to be a cathedral on the bridge itself. Houses, too. Now, there was a series of gates in a fortress style, with a gatehouse and portcullis at every turn. Four portcullises spanned across the bridge at even intervals, if just to be inconvenient to invading forces. None of these structures were protected by the wards, and certainly, a winged *teras* would have no need of the bridge itself. But nevertheless, the bridge was built like this.

We ride over it in silence. The night is cold, a wet chill that has me shivering even with the Hunter cloak on. Rain slides off its greasy exterior, but the shiver feels deeper than that, like nothing will make me warm again until I know Leo Shaw is alive.

Don't say anything to that. I know it's embarrassing.

Agrawal has us ride at full speed out of the wards to the first gate, which is manned by three bored-looking Workers.

"Business?" one calls down.

"Agrawal, Hunter. Business is a retrieval of lost party."

"Haven't heard nothing from Drearton," another voice calls. I notice they've set up metal sheeting over their turret. It must be their only defence against the *teras*.

I wonder if they fought for this job. If it meant they could sleep in London half the time instead of being kicked out entirely, would they have been desperate for it?

"If he asks," I say, "Tell him Cassius Jones insisted. I'll take the fall for any of you."

I mean it. Agrawal's head shifts towards me, but not so far that he fully looks around. What is he thinking of me, I wonder? That I'm a lovesick fool? An idiot? Perhaps he thinks I expect Drearton will take it easy on me since the dean has an interest.

But I said it because I want Drearton to know. I will invoke his name the way he expects to be invoked: as London's God. And I will blaspheme against him the way I will against the Lord Himself. I will take His name in vain. I will do whatever it takes to get what I want.

Which is Leo Shaw alive.

"Fine," someone calls from the gate after a whispered conversation. "Too bloody cold for this. It's your head, boy!"

The gate groans as it lifts, heavy iron shuddering upwards as it opens. Agrawal puts his horse into a canter as soon as he can clear it, and we ride forward again to the next, and the next, until we reach the last gate—which is completely unmanned. We have to dismount and lead the horses through the side door. This whole bridge is more of an inconvenience than a defence, but what do I know.

I almost miss it when we reach the end. We emerge into Southwark, and the night creaks—I can't describe it any other way. The way ice snaps at a sudden change in temperature, so too does the entire night react to our intrusion. Southwark had been built right up against the bridge and it spills out like a stain into the Thames.

The borough had been a slum; mills, warehouses, entire families stacked into tiny houses—this was how it was before the *teras*, and it only got worse once they punctured into our world. Something about the proximity to London, I theorise, kept the place growing. There are so many buildings it's impossible to see the streets between them in this low light, so the township rises out of the marshland like some hulking Behemoth, whose "strength is in his loins/His might in the muscles of his belly. . ./His bones are like tubes of bronze/His limbs like iron rods," if we are to believe Job. I don't know why I think of that.

Agrawal pulls a gas lantern out of the horse's pack, and everyone follows suit, except for Don and I since the pack Agrawal gave us lacks one. I snatch the sparker for myself and run my hand along the dagger's hilt, just for the comfort of the touch.

In silence, we push forward. The buildings closest to the Thames sit upon floodplains, and the ground is soggy, taking our weight with quiet acquiescence. The horses huff quietly; they sense nothing. No reason for concern yet. In the quiet, I find myself wondering if Leo walked through here—if he's holed up in one of these terrible, crumbling buildings. And really, they are quite terrible. The constant flooding, the marshland, and the lack of care and repairs mean Southwark is little more than wooden ruins. Most of the structures are slanted, and the smell of brackish decay permeates the ground around us.

The whole township has fallen into disrepair. No one technically lives here—and I imagine the *teras* have driven people off.

But that doesn't explain the blood.

The moonlight picks it up, the dark sheen of it mixing with mud in the marshy ground. I click my tongue, and Agrawal acknowledges it with an answering whistle. Sutton and Lee bring their lanterns close, illuminating the ground. Light roils over the muddy indents—footprints. Blood that's still fresh and red coats the pitted earth like a glaze. The footsteps dash further into the winding borough of collapsed buildings, and the horses stamp as soon as the wind sprays the scent of the blood towards their flaring nostrils.

"We should dismount," Agrawal says. "Keep the horses back until we canvass the town and know what happened. Know what the danger is. Hayes, you'll stay."

"Will I, now?" Len Hayes grumbles.

"We don't have time for this," Sutton hisses as she dismounts. She thrusts the reins into Len's moodily outstretched hand. "If we all start dying, you'll at least get a head start."

"Unless they come for me first," Len says, but he takes all the proffered reins nonetheless and begins tying the horses off to a wooden post near something that might have once been a warehouse. The wood is rotten, and the post groans at the sudden weight. I stare at it, watching it give and bend as the horses settle, and this feeling settles in me: not fear, not worry, exactly, but a kind of inhuman sense. I feel like I'm looking back on a memory, with the distance of a decade; none of it matters to that version of myself. I think, "*You're going to die, you know.*" And I do know. I do. But I don't—feel anything about it.

"Jones?"

My attention snaps towards my name. Agrawal and the others have dismounted and are waiting, and suddenly, I care about everything far too much again. I flush as I fumble and dismount, giving Hayes the reins.

Don stares at me. "What the fuck was that?"

Do you feel it? I want to ask. *Can't you feel it?*

But Don is twitchy already. Paranoid. I keep my mouth shut as we walk forward.

We try to be quiet, but the ground is icy in parts and slush in others. Every footfall makes a sound. I hunker forward naturally, trying to find cover in the slant of awnings, and I pull the dagger free, careful to hold it away from my body.

"More," Agrawal whispers back to us. The lanterns cast our elongated shadows onto the wooden walls, and I use the fleeting light to spy down at the footprints we're following.

"Shit," Don hisses. I glance his way and then past him. A spray of arterial blood has splattered onto the outside wall of a hovel. Sutton raises her flame to it, and it glistens, still wet. She gives us a worried look from underneath her tricorn hat, then dips her head and turns, following Agrawal onward.

"Ah."

The tight alley opens onto an intersection of four diverging paths. In the dark, we must have reached the equivalent of the town centre. I expect to see a fountain, a landmark. But there's a building the size of a warehouse that's caved in on itself, splintered from a great force. It's not decay that's done this. I think of the *manticore* crashing through brush and how the land would break before it. I think of Vengeance taller than the trees.

There's no mass of flesh lying in the ruins, which means whatever crashed it into has gotten up and moved on.

"No," Sutton murmurs. The hand holding the lantern shakes, but she quickly rights it. She holds it long enough for all of us to see the shattered leg torn asunder from the rest of a body that's nowhere to be seen. The leg is swathed in Hunter blacks. The shoe is missing. The exposed foot is muddy but somehow clean of blood.

"Claypoole's party," Agrawal says because it must be said even if we all know. "Draw your weapons. Nothing has changed. We search for survivors."

Nothing has changed, but everything has. This confirmation that they faced something—that Leo is out here, Victoria is out here—drives me nearly insane. I wish I could hold more weapons; I wish my hands could do more. To feel useless when holding a knife reminds me how pathetic I am. But if I could just arm myself to the teeth so every limb was overflowing, maybe I could—

"Alright?" Don's thick voice whispers in my ear. His hand is flat on my chest, holding me back as if I was about to go sprawling. He must feel the swift flight of my heart, and I can barely bring myself to look him in the eye. He's slipped his own flintlock free and loaded up the iron ball. One shot. One chance. I count my own bullets. Four. One loaded. I squeeze my eyes shut.

"Cassius," Don cautions. He sounds like Thaddeus. "You're getting all worked up over nothing."

It's not nothing, asshole, I want to say. *That was a limb. You know what comes next.*

I remove his hand from my chest somewhat roughly and shove past him without answer, catching up to Agrawal and Sutton, who are pushing close to the collapsed building.

In the dark, the shadows are worse. The marshland buckles, the houses shudder, and the wind shrieks through the alleyways and serpentine paths. All our Hunter cloaks flap wild behind us, and my nose wrinkles involuntarily at the scent: putrefied, hot rotting fish.

Agrawal freezes: my body reacts the way it always does.

Immediate tensing. A memory is scraped out from the bottom of my mind—that is *teras* breath. That is the smell of something half-eaten and mouldering in the gaps between animalistic teeth.

I try to become someone else. The Hunter in me. The man I've been on occasion. It hurts to leave Cassius behind because, briefly, I must stop thinking about Leo. Faith rears up; a Psalm struggling out from the crannies of my mind to shout, "My heart is in anguish within me/And the terrors of death have fallen upon me,"—I ignore it. I become nothing. I let it all slip away. And as Agrawal signals silently for us to flank the destroyed building, I roll the sparker between my fingers and settle into the cold, sure embrace of apathy.

The four of us spread out and surround the building, with Don and I spaced between the two lantern bearers. It's barely enough light, but it's enough to parse the hefty lump of shadow from the rest of the rubble.

I raise the flintlock.

But I do not have to shoot.

The horse is still alive somehow. It's in the centre of the building; it might be the cause of the destruction, like it was thrown. Its breathing is erratic, and great plumes of breath bloom from its nose, turning to white smoke in the cold. The thick flank has been peeled back with meticulous precision, so careful and clean I'd almost suspect a human is behind this. The innards have been lovingly pulled out. Great care has gone into the arrangement of the intestines, which wrap bow-like around the liver. The lungs are still attached but edged slightly out of the way; the whole ribcage has been cracked open. Each rib bone reaches up to the sky, reaching for God. Not thrown, then. Placed. Or injured from the force of the throw and picked through after the fact.

"Why?" Sutton asks aloud. Her eyes are shadowed by the tricorn hat, brows twisted; she's shaking her head, and even that tiny movement makes the lantern light bob over the dying animal in undulating motions, waves of light. I am transfixed by it. The warm hue softens the scene, both literally and metaphysically. I am reminded of warmth and fireplaces, reminded of things that never happened, like true safety, family, joy in front of a fire. My fingers are so cold and my prosthetic creaks in the chill. I think about crawling inside the horse's flank. The ribcage has been opened up. I could sleep in there now. I think about fishing its heart out and eating a warm meal before laying down to sleep in its stink.

"Cassius!"

I flinch.

When I blink back the spots in my eyes, I realise I've— moved. Crunched over the rubble. I'm standing over the horse. The animal is looking up at me, its eyes panicked and wide. The breathing is shallow, quick, in-and-out-in-and-out. I watch the exposed lungs expand and contract.

I've stepped in its viscera. The smell is sweet, like cakes, like bread and jam. I want it in my mouth. I drop down to my knees and put my fingers in the blood.

"What are you doing?" Don hisses.

There's enough horse for everyone. I frown over my shoulder and stare at Don. "I—"

"Sutton," Agrawal hisses. I turn.

Her face is slack and her body near rigid, but she climbs forward into the rubble all the same. I watch her approach and feel absolutely nothing about it. I don't understand why Agrawal is concerned. I'm not sure why Don is hissing at me. It's. . .fine. The horse is large. The air is sweet. There is enough for all of us.

The horse whinnies. It thrashes on the ground impotently, its back legs kicking weakly against rotten wooden beams. It tries to get up, front legs pushing against the earth. Half its torso lifts before it crashes back onto the ground. Something compels me to turn around.

"Jesus Christ," Don says. He sees it, too.

Looming high above Southwark is a colossus. Part of me panics—*Vengeance?*—but the acrid fear is quickly softened. The air grows sweet and heavy, and it smells to me like dozens of bakeries. The smell—and the creature emitting it— is coming towards us.

"*Phrygian!*" Agrawal shouts. He yanks his shirt high and desperately tugs a bandana from his pocket which is tied around his nose and mouth. "Sutton, look at me. Jones! *God damn it!*"

The great colossus resolves into a thick-bodied snake with the same towering height as Vengeance. Taller than trees, it slithers forward, and the rotten disrepair of Southwark splits open for it like a bastardised, wooden Red Sea. When it's close, it rears up briefly and sits on the coiled end of its tail.

A memory is dislodged at the sight. Agrawal said *phrygian —draco phrygius.* The Phrygian Serpent.

I know it from a Greek history—Aeolian, I think. He mentions it in passing: a giant serpent whose breath was so sweet it hypnotised birds into flying willingly into its mouth. It ambushed shepherds, too—it's rare. It's barely in any myths and, thus, barely in our world.

Part of me starts to scream. It's not a particularly strong part of me, but perhaps it is the most logical. It knows instantly that I should get up. It tells me to hold my breath and dash away—that I am delirious and famished for horse viscera, which is *not normal.* But I can't describe what the scent does to me. I haven't had the luxury of sweet food very often in my life. Perhaps I shouldn't crave it—or perhaps I've had so little that the mere scent is enough for me to lose my mind.

I lick my fingers clean of the viscera and relish the warm,

wet taste of it, which blossoms in my mouth, a layered spark of flavour. Tongue coated and sticky like honey—I want more.

Don ruins it. He crunches over the rubble and pulls me backward so hard we fall together. Fury rushes through my system, and my heart is straining at the bit. How dare he?

"Get off!" I shout. "I want—it!"

"Well, you can't have it, you gross fuck!"

Don crawls on top of me and holds me down. But I've fought him before, and I know better than to go slack. Don is heavier than me, larger—but he gets fatigued fast. I start thrashing beneath his grip.

"There's plenty for all of us!"

He wrinkles his nose. "Shut up!"

The *phrygian* gives a mournful bellow, and all of Southwark shakes. Its body is so large that buildings seem to fall away from it like damp paper crumpling. Does it want the horse? That thought upsets me. The *phrygian* is too large to share it, and Don is pinning me down.

"Get off," I hiss at him. "Get off me, *get off, get off!*"

"Cassius, please!" Don shouts, and something in his tone tells me he means it—that he's genuinely worried, truly upset. He shifts so his forearm is crushing my clavicle. I try to sit up and end up choking myself on his firm, immovable forearm. Don is rummaging for something in his boot. Sutton is lowering herself beside the horse, both hands outstretched. She lovingly scoops a handful of its intestines into her mouth and takes a bite.

Jealousy floods me. I howl. Agrawal rushes forward and gently tugs her back—a mistake. Sutton is strong. Rage flickers across her face and she spins violently, decking him hard in the face. Agrawal stumbles back.

All this distracts me, and I don't notice what Don is doing until it's too late. Something bright flashes in my periphery—

my head spins back in time to see the knife hurtling towards me.

No.

I have just enough time to close my eyes. I don't want to see the means of my own death.

Sharp white pain flashes behind my eyes. Searing, stinging —several things happen in my head, and I lie there confused, even as Don is saying my name and tugging at my arm. My shoulder burns, first with the sting of an open cut and then with the warmth of the blood that flows from it, clogging around my Hunter blacks. A severing happens. Tangy metal in my mouth. The full, round taste of the inner body, which smells vaguely like bowels and vomit and blood, all rolled up together. It's in my mouth. The back of my throat. Thick like paste on the roof of my mouth.

I roll over and throw up nothing but a spray of bile.

"Pain works!" Don is calling out above me. "Pain works!"

I don't see what's happening, but suddenly the weight from my chest is lifted as Don stands up. A shot blasts through the air: the hammer of Don's flintlock rolls forward and, thunderous, the iron ball hurtles out and is swallowed by shadow.

*Phrygian—draco phrygius—*I only know of that one tale. It dawns on me in a quiet, creeping horror that I don't know how to kill it. That perhaps there's no recorded way of killing it.

And does that mean—if all our sources are from myth, if these creatures are from myth, and there's no record of how to defeat them—that it cannot die?

Sutton screams and crumples over her forearm. I tear my eyes to her. Everything from her forearms down is blood-soaked, but I see Agrawal pulling away with a knife. Sutton blinks, discombobulated, and ends up staring down at her hands. They shake minutely.

Then, she vomits, too.

The *phrygian* shrieks. I wrench my own shirt high and will myself to breathe shallowly. I shout, "We have to run."

Don listens to me with something akin to joy and dashes over the rubble. Wood creaks and splinters beneath his feet. Even Sutton starts to move—until Agrawal speaks.

He's turned to face the great snake. Half of its body is submerged in shadow, and I think if he could see the extent of it, he would be running.

Agrawal says, "We stay. We need to know what happened."

"We know what happened!" Don shouts.

I agree. I say, "And there aren't enough bodies—so either they've been eaten, or they've fled!"

"We stay!" Agrawal spits. He aims his gun and cocks it. "We're Hunters!"

Fury. Heat rushes to my cheeks. I can't stop myself. "Like you stayed for my brother?"

It just slips out. Agrawal turns and looks at me. Only his eyes are visible over the makeshift mask he's fashioned from the bandana, illuminated by the glow of the lantern at his feet, but they are blown wide. Shock, anger—I can't parse the expression. But I know that, even as I sit in that awkward stretch of time, I feel no shame for speaking.

He left Thaddeus to die. *Now* he wants to stay? For what? A sinking, decrepit borough? A horse that's already dead? If there are survivors, they aren't here.

And I won't waste time pulling body parts from the stomach of the *phrygian*, should we even manage to kill it. I will spend my time tracking down the rest of Claypoole's party, and if Leo Shaw is not amongst them, *then* I will kill whatever fucking *teras* hurt him.

But for now, Leo is alive. He must be.

"I'm going," I tell Agrawal and immediately dash backwards. Don follows me, and Sutton is torn, still blinking away confusion.

As soon as I turn around, Agrawal shouts.

A dense shadow passes over him. My breath stops. I blink —that's all it takes. Quick as that, I blink, the shadow passes over him, and he is gone.

Only he's not. The space where he was is empty, but I see his body as it's lifted high, a speck of the unnatural black of his clothes spanning out against the night. A sparker goes off above us in a blinding flash, Agrawal's struggling fingers desperate to save himself, attempting to stun the serpent colossus. In the space of that second, the mystery of the *phrygian* resolves. Its skin is mottled, oscillating between white and black, but not in the way a natural animal might be patterned. It looks like the skin of a reptile that's been drowned, and all the colour leeches out into the water like life fading from the vessel—the scales have that flimsy quality as if a single touch would slough them off. The black fades in and out around its mouth, which is open, yawning wide. The chin drops low, frighteningly low, stretching until it sits close to the belly. Its eyes are pitch black, an iris that's exploded out and bled into the corners of the eye. The tail lifts Agrawal, whose shouts become strangled pops of sound as the pressure crushes him. Gently, almost reverently, it plops Agrawal into its mouth.

There is no struggle. That's perhaps the worst part. No blood, either. No biting, tearing, crunching. Agrawal is just swallowed whole, a morsel for this *teras*, and without much fuss at all, his life and his legacy are snuffed out.

But Sutton screams. It's not fear—it's anger. She loads her gun and shoots. A thumb-sized amount of scale and flesh blows off the *phrygian*, which is now illuminated by Agrawal's dropped lantern. Sutton pauses, hesitating as the giant maw gapes open towards her. She hasn't covered her nose and mouth. She's still exposed to the sweet-smelling trance.

"Get to the horses," I tell Don. "Get Hayes and get them ready. And cover your damn face."

I don't wait to see if he's listened. I just dash forward and grab the lantern. I raise it high and take Sutton by the arm. She hisses like I've burned her, eyes wide and flaring in panic as I wrench her back. We both stumble in the rubble, feet rolling—she hisses again, but there's no time to check for injury.

"He's dead," I say plainly. I reach forward and put the end of her Hunter cloak to her nose and mouth, urging her to cover up. "We're not. *Run.*"

There's half a moment where I think she'll say no, but her loyalty is overridden by the desire to survive. I see her ancestor in her, the first Hunter Angelica D'Avore, and what-ever instinct has maintained her legacy spurs Sutton away from the *phrygian.*

We run.

The *phrygian* moves.

Don't scream. Don't think. Just go! Go!

Sutton and I hold hands for as long as we can before it becomes impossible. Panic has me rip my sweaty hand away —I want the added momentum of it swinging at my side. Everything I can take, every extra second. But the ground is jolting beneath me. The *teras* approaches, and Southwark quakes; the vibrations jostle up my legs and move pebbles. I hear its thick body gliding over the ground, crunching across rubble. A building topples behind us, sending a plume of dust and wet wooden splinters flying into the air. The beast shrieks, this upset cackling. I smell sweetness again. Breath burns in my lungs; we turn, my foot sinks into marshland— and I realise we've gone the wrong way.

Sutton says, "No."

Wet, marshy earth hugs my ankle. I pull it out; the ground sucks me down, holding fast. Out of the corner of my eye, something rushes me.

I pull. I pull my leg again. But I don't move.

The *phrygian*'s tail slams into my torso.

I am torn out of the marshland. My right knee locks out as I'm thrown. I hear something snap before I've even landed, and I brace myself, eyes shut, but nothing prepares me. All the air is knocked out of my lungs. Spots in my vision—I can't breathe. Something's been punctured? Broken?

Calm down. Calm down. You're okay; you're alive. Cassius— stand up.

I look where I've been thrown. A collapsed building lies broken behind me. The soggy marsh stretches out, bits of rotten houses already half sunken into it. An old, decrepit dock—the *phrygian* has thrown me back towards the Thames, perhaps thirty meters. It hurts to breathe. My jaw aches from the force of the landing, but I don't think I've broken anything, somehow. I know I will be heavily bruised.

The lantern I carried has cracked open. Oil and flame have spilled out and lit the reeds alight. The entire side of my left face is exposed to light and heat and the smoking of the reeds as they burn.

You'll be fine. When you're back at the University, you'll heal. So get up.

I can't. I can't.

You stupid, pathetic boy—get up!

It hurts.

Get the fuck up!

I stand up. The voice is motivating. Is it mine, my father's, Thaddeus'—does it matter? So long as I don't think about the pain scalding around my knee and up my thigh, I can move. The animal part of my brain takes over, and the floundering human closes his eyes and is gone. The animal gets up. For the first time, perhaps *ever*, the animal's instinct is not to flee.

The *manticore* dagger is in my hand; the handle is weighted, and the texture is *good*. I feel strong. Sure of myself. Sutton is firing her gun again, having pulled herself free of the marshland.

"Look at me, you right bastard!" she screeches. The chamber clicks empty over and over, and I see her drop to her knees. The *phrygian* whips around to her and its head is snapped back by the force of a thrown rock. "Come on! *Come on!*"

She's a fool, or she's brave. She reminds me of Leo attacking Meléti in the library—this anserine action that blisters my heart.

Whatever compels it to turn and abandon me as its main prey, I am grateful for. God, or the beast's own ego, or its instinct for moving prey. Sutton's distraction worked, and in the end, it doesn't matter. I don't wait for it to turn back around to me. There's such a great amount of effort needed for that thick form to rotate that by the time it's facing Sutton, I can dash close.

The *phrygian* rears up on its own tail. The chest expands with drawn breath, and when it hisses, a visible plume of sweet-smelling scent plummets toward Sutton.

Her cloak hangs free at her side. She isn't covered. She drops her gun, and her limbs go slack. That dazed expression glazes over her eyes again.

Looming above me, the *phrygian*'s jaw unlocks once more, dropping low to its belly. The undulating flesh of its long body writhes as the neck descends towards Sutton. It doesn't hear me approach; it doesn't care even as my feet slap over the marshland, even as rotting wood creaks and snaps between the weight of each step.

I run at it. I pull out the flintlock and fire the single

loaded bullet. It barely reacts, and I have no time to reload. Instead, I raise the hooked dagger high, glinting with *manticore* poison, and I plunge it into the body.

The neck whips towards me. Its head is a weighted ball at the end of a string—all the muscles in its jaw freeze up and creak as it hisses. Spittle sprays over me. I scrunch my eyes shut and hold my breath, worried that its power will be concentrated in its saliva. Then I brace myself for another attack, teeth or its tail.

Neither come.

I risk a look.

The burning reeds have been reduced, now burning low as the marshland snuffs it out. The fire still throws enough light that I can see every part of this monster.

The *phrygian* is alive and breathing in shallow, stilted gasps. The tendons in its neck are visible, bulging and strained. The jaw is locked open, and its snake tongue lolls in a saliva-drenched pool growing in the divot of its lower jaw. The breathing is laboured. It sounds like a death rattle, the terrifying wheezing as air trembles in dying lungs, trying and failing to find purchase. Beneath its thin, sickly skin, organs seem to shift. Muscles convulse in obvious spasms. Up close now, I can see what I mistook as a dark, soulless eye has a gleam to it, a pupil darker than the rest that is tracking me as my fingers curl around the hilt of the dagger and yank it free.

I back up. Sutton is still approaching the *phrygian*. I watch her walk around beside me, turn to it, and haul herself up its body. She puts her hands on its teeth and begins to put her body into its mouth.

I dash up after her, running along the slimy body. Hands around her waist, I pull her out of the mouth, and we fall together, bouncing off the *phrygian's* back and onto the marshy ground. The pain from the fall shocks her back into control.

"Shit," she says and quickly pulls up her Hunter blacks to protect her nose and mouth.

"Are you with me?" I clarify.

She jolts back violently from the gaping maw. "What did you do?" she asks. Sutton turns to me with new eyes, cocking her head. "What's on your dagger, Jones?"

"*Manticore* poison," I say plainly. "You have a vial, don't you? Leo traded it for cigarettes. For me."

I don't know why I tell her that. I don't know why it matters. Except maybe, if he hadn't traded that vial, he would have had his own weapon coated in the poison. He could have protected himself. He could have made it back to London safely. Back to me.

And instead—

I shudder. Tears well up—stop it. *Stop it.*

Sutton's expression shifts, and she looks away. She doesn't press. "How long do we have?"

I don't know, so I shrug at her.

Sutton pulls back the cloak of her Hunter blacks and tugs her own dagger free. Then she walks up to the *phrygian* and tries to meet its eye. The sizing is off and makes the whole exchange at once terrifying and ridiculous. The *teras'* head is the size of most of Sutton. But fearlessly, she walks up to it. I understand what she means to do and nod at her, walking to the opposite end of the *phrygian*.

I don't wait for her. I just plunge the dagger into the underbelly of the colossus. Its breathing changes as the whole body shudders violently, its voice guttural and sour and squeaking out a cry. I have to carve it open; I cut and saw along the flesh, which is thick and ropy, all whilst walking towards Sutton. She walks towards me and does the same. The flesh of the *phrygian* begins to bulge as layered organs press against the slit. The air steams, and that sweet-smelling lie of its breath is tainted by the scent of the vivisection.

Bowel, digestive fluid, slick, warm intestines. The horse was bad, but this—this smells like hot, old fish and forgotten food left to cook in the sun. It smells like almost-death, like disease prickling the body, sickness locked in a room and opened after months: not the vacant smell of decay, but of life clinging on to an infected, ulcerated body. A living corpse.

I gag. The scent is everywhere. It crowds up my nostrils, claws into my sinuses. My eyes water with it. My throat is clogged with its filth. I squeeze my eyes shut and focus on the scent of the sweat-soaked Hunter blacks I am breathing into, walking until I can hear Sutton's footsteps.

When we meet, we step away quickly. All the beast's innards tumble out into a steaming, stinking mess. The bowel has been punctured—my fault—and shit coats the marshland. The stomach has been opened, too.

And we see four bodies. Two horses.

"Claypoole," Sutton says. She nudges a body with her foot and then seems to think better of it, kneeling to roll the bloody corpse over. She has been bisected. Ropes of intestine cling to her upper torso, which is the part Sutton has rolled over. Her eyes are open. Claypoole is maybe twenty. She's Sutton's colleague. Sutton sighs and closes the woman's eyes, wiping her fluid-soaked hand on the ground before she stands.

I—I look for his hair. For the blond. For his body, which I know as well as my own by now. I scan the digested pile and wait for the shock to hit me. Recognition does not bludgeon me, though. One of the bodies belongs to Agrawal. Another to Claypoole. Two to people I don't recognise.

It takes me a moment to comprehend that Leo Shaw is not in the creature's stomach.

Neither is Victoria Bennet.

"How many in the party?" I ask. "Six? Seven?" I vaguely recall Drearton saying that number.

Sutton nods. "So three or four left."

I swallow. "Two horses returned to London."

She looks at me. "If most of them are on foot, then they can't be too far."

"We need to—"

"You're alive."

I stop talking and turn. Don looks hollow. By the light thrown by the low embers, I can see the fear, relief, and exhaustion stitched into his face. His eyes glance down towards the dead *phrygian,* and his body visibly slackens. I half expect him to say a prayer—but Don is not that kind of man.

"We're alive," Sutton says. She walks back to retrieve the gun she dropped under hypnosis.

"Hayes?" I ask. Don is still staring at the exposed contents of the *phrygian*'s belly.

I glance at the bodies and then back to Don. "It's not him."

"What?"

"It's not Leo."

He blinks and turns to look at me. "Hayes knows where they are."

My heart. I can't describe what that organ does; I can't tell you what those words mean to me. Angelic, with the same power as God Himself telling me.

Hallelujah. Hallelujah. Hallelujah.

13

LESSON THIRTEEN

Hayes isn't where we left him.

From what I can tell—and from what I suspect—he had been planning to flee. He must have seen the *phrygian*, gargantuan form shadowing the night, and untied all the horses. It's a miracle none of them fled, though I know the *phrygian*'s hypnotic breath enticed the horses. The dying vivisected mount that lured me in is proof of that.

I can't blame him for considering fleeing. I wanted to run, too.

The other reason I can't blame him is because of what he's found.

Don leads Sutton and I back through the dark corridors of Southwark. We walk in silence. Sweat plasters the hair to the back of my neck in thready pieces. My Hunter blacks are uncomfortably tight and clinging to my body that the motion of walking tugs at my skin. I can feel the bruise blooming beneath my kneecap. Every step makes it scream, and so I end up telling myself to focus on the wet tightness of the clothing. Better to feel the uncomfortable pull of hair against cotton and leather than to taste the latent viscera in my mouth, the pain in my body, or to fall into a spiral of panic the instant I think about Leo.

Our single remaining lantern glows in the distance where Hayes stands with four horses. He clarifies as we get closer, and he's just standing there, the epitome of a lost man. His stare is vacant, but I know a facade when I see one. Those are the eyes of a man who will fall to ruin the first moment he's alone.

"Good," Hayes says, mustering a false happiness at seeing Sutton. He puts out his arm, and she clasps it, thumbs firm over forearms. I catch the look they give each other and attribute meaning to it for my own benefit.

I couldn't save him, Sutton seems to say.

I know, Hayes tells her, *but it still hurts*.

Maybe I'm wrong. Maybe they didn't care for Agrawal much at all, and maybe this is just a generalised shock at seeing a man eaten whole. But it comforts me to think human connection is worth something still—that in acknowledging one another's pain, they prolong a good part of humanity, a part that is dying more and more every day.

I glance at Don, unsure if I should offer paltry words or a limp handshake (both insubstantial and both all I can manage). But Don is staring ahead, past Hayes, and when I open my mouth, he flinches as if his periphery has caught me, as if he's frightened of what I might say.

"They killed it," Don says. His voice is high and shaky, and he clears his throat aggressively to bump it down an octave. "Opened it right up."

Hayes looks to Sutton. I suppose he's leading this thing now.

"Right," she says with a stiff nod, pulling her hand away from Hayes. "Three dead. Not including. . ." She clears her throat. "Claypoole herself is amongst the bodies. I think there was a Scholar, too. . ."

Hayes' eyes flutter closed. He swears under his breath.

"They're all dead," Sutton says solemnly. "That's it, isn't it?"

"No," Hayes says, rather confidently. He steps aside to show us his find.

It's another body. The man lies in Hunter blacks, face down. His tricorn hat has been thrown five metres from his head, exposing a ring of dark curls. Not Leo. Thank God. The dead Hunter's cloak has been embroidered with a spattering of smaller D-class *teras*, and that's it.

Hayes tells us he wasn't with Claypoole's party.

"How do you know?" I say, a little too sharply. Sutton glances at me, and I can tell my tone is unwelcome, so I shift and try again, saying, "It's just...Fraser wasn't sure who was in the party."

I ask because, obviously, I want Leo alive. I want Leo alive. I am struggling to care about anything else. The shock of the *phrygian* is already wearing off—it's not enough to dull the *want*, the *desire*, the fear knitted into my very gut.

I want him! The closest I've ever been to calling a boy 'mine'. I want him! And if he dies now, after that fight, after the fight, after the last time we touched being shared with another—it won't be fair. Out of everything unfair thing in this fucking world, losing Leo will be the thing that ends me.

"Well, Fraser didn't care enough to come, so can you really trust his judgement?" Hayes mutters. It's so abrupt and damning that I snort despite myself, and I see a ghost of a smile flit across Hayes' lips before happiness gives up trying to take root in him. Hayes turns back to the corpse with a sigh and nudges the arm with his booted foot.

"A messenger. You can tell by the band."

The band is a red bit of cloth—a strip, really, that's been tied haphazardly around the man's left arm. I notice immediately that said arm is like mine—he's an amputee. Only his prosthetic is made of wood. The hand has splintered like it was caught in the jaw of a wild dog, but otherwise, I see no wounds.

I frown up at Hayes. "Theories? What happened to him?"

Hayes bends down and turns him over onto his back. The answer is obvious: the man's right eye socket has been destroyed by the force of a bullet ripping through it. Gore splatters around the gouged eye.

Before anyone says it, I think.

Leo Shaw—was this your work?

"Killed. Most likely by Claypoole's party. He's too fresh to have been here long." Hayes says all this with a sure and calm assessment. He clicks his tongue and pushes the man's head up with a carefully placed finger. "Think his name was James. Poor James."

"Killed. . ." Sutton says with a sigh. I understand what that sigh is meant to mean. What a way to go.

"You said he was a messenger," I say. The urge to know increases. I get to my knees beside Hayes and start rummaging through his clothes. "What was he trying to deliver? What outpost is he from? Is the armband code, or. . .?"

"Jones," Hayes says. "Stop."

I don't stop. *Fuck you for telling me to stop.*

"He must have a letter," I say. "Or an object."

"If it was an object," Sutton says, "he was killed for it."

Don gets down beside me. His eyes are fixed on the man's fist, clenched tightly from its death spasms. Don and I share a look, and together, we move our fingers to the fist.

There's something intimate about desperately prying open a corpse's death grip. Our fingers keep touching, gliding alongside one another. I think—and I hate this—but I think Don might be the only one who would understand if I broke down now. He can't really understand because he's never experienced Leo the way I have. But I've been Don before. I've been that pining boy in denial of his own desires. The first man who ever looked at me and smiled when he saw what I wanted from him—I thought I was in love. To be seen, to be acknowledged, to be wanted in return; it's all enough to briefly triumph over the shame.

I'm momentarily grateful to have Don with me. But the instant I get Leo back, I think jealousy will overcome everything else. I will carve my name into Leo Shaw's back.

Don't you dare go anywhere ever again. Don't you dare ever scare me like that again.

The fist opens with a crack of the fingers.

It is not an easy release. The messenger held onto this crumpled paper in his death throes, and every bit of his final intention locked that grip into a claw. The paper we rescue from his palm has been scrunched up and soaked by the rain, rendering the ink scrawled on it nigh intelligible.

Don squints at it, and I pry it from his fingers, raising it closer to Hayes' final lantern.

The scrawl is hurried.

It reads:

. . . again.. . om. . . waves, skinless m. . . . ne talked. Southend. . . Ma. . . deaths.

I don't have to know what the rest of it reads. It's not important, not necessary to understand. Skinless. That's the word that jumps at me, claws outstretched.

Skinless.

I remember the report that came to us when Liverpool fell. I read that damn near thirty times with Don breathing over my shoulder, looking for accounts, looking for anything that could explain what happened to the outpost.

Came after first strike of midnight. Black dogs, monstrous teeth, howling. Men on horseback, no skin, screams like ocean waves. We flee —Liverpool has fallen.

Godspeed.

"Why is he on this side of the river?" Sutton murmurs. "Southend's on the opposite side of the Thames, isn't it? Northeast."

My stomach drops. I look down at the body. "He crossed it," I say. "Because it's the only way to deflect the attention of this particular *teras.*"

They turn to look at me. Sutton frowns, but her eyebrows soften after a moment.

I let her say it.

"*Nuckelavee.*"

The encounter I read said the man was hemmed in by seashore on one side and a freshwater loch on the other. I recall, "*Nuckelavee gave a wild, unearthly yell of disappointed rage as Tammie fell senseless on the safe side of the water.*"

The Thames is brackish, but maybe it is fresh enough.

"Shit," Don says. "You're shitting me."

Hayes looks out to the north, in the general direction of Southend. "Why are they back?" he murmurs. "Greco-Roman overpowered them. It's been, what? Fifty years since other subsets of *teras* have been roaming around, and they've always been few and far between. So why now?"

"It's a fucking army," Don is saying, panicked. "This skinless fuck—Jones researched it, and it had no skin. Just flesh. White tendon. It's breath—something about disease. God." He looks at me and opens his mouth. I see the words before he says them. *Let's go back. How much do you really want this?*

I fix him a look, strong and dark enough that I hope he can read how angry I will be if I lose my ally. I want Don's closeted desire to spur him on; I want to manipulate it to search for Leo. I want him to hurt the way I do, just so it means he'll join me in this search.

Don closes his mouth, and Sutton says, "How are we supposed to kill it?"

I stop listening. My heart is racing, my body reacting either latently to the fight with the *phrygian,* or I am panicking about Leo. About him being torn into by this skinless beast—and a part of me, the stupid, insane part, is jealous. A man-shaped thing will be the last to touch Leo Shaw. I'd rather it was me. I would rather be the one to take his life. How complicated is desire? How strange? It never makes any sense except the fact that I want him to be mine.

Rain starts above us. I gasp, air shuddering through my constricted lungs, and I look up at the night and close my eyes against the patter of the droplets. They roll off my cheeks, and I try to breathe in that earthy petrichor, as if taking it into my lungs will help me to be as grounded as the land itself. But my heart can't stop conjuring visions of the Orcadian *teras.*

It's takes me a minute, I'll admit.

Everyone is loud and skittish, and their anxiety affects me. They talk about it and what it could mean, and it's only when Don says, "But why would they? Southend's fucking miles away," that my heart constricts.

Why would the rest of Claypoole's party head to Southend?

Because Leo is from Southend.

My mind is flooded with the image of him smiling next to me on the bed before I let him crawl inside my body, smiling pleasantly like what he's saying is nothing. He opens his mouth and tells me the reason he's come to this place.

Oh, it's very simple, actually. There's no one left that I love.

But he never told me more. He still hasn't. And I haven't pressed because it's his business, his life, and he wanted me to know then I would.

But if Southend-on-Sea is being attacked, Leo would go, wouldn't he? He threw a spear to protect me from Meléti within days of knowing me.

But he's also ruthless. Leo Shaw is above everyone. Above all else.

Unless he isn't as ruthless as he says he is. Unless he's like me; lying to himself, holding onto the protection that lie offers him.

I say, "Leo Shaw is from Southend," and then, when everyone looks at me with an inquisitive stare, "He can be quite persuasive."

I glance at Don, whose face wrinkles up like he's sucked on something sour. He offers a noise of agreement, and I wonder what he's thinking about.

That's a lie. I know what he's thinking about.

"So he would have ridden out even further after a *phrygian* killed his party leader? Fool." Hayes spits. He runs a hand along the flank of his horse, which snorts appreciatively.

I bite my tongue and glance at Sutton. "Our party leader is dead, too."

Hayes freezes. I see the muscles constrict beneath his cloak. He half turns to look at me but doesn't fully commit; agitation blares hot through my stomach.

If Hayes says we are to turn around and head back to London, I will steal a horse and ride alone to my almost certain death. I did it for Thaddeus—Thaddeus!—whose love was brittle and unsure of itself. I do not think Leo loves me, but I—

I—

I can't leave him. That's all.

"Victoria Bennet is pregnant," I say next because no one's secrets are safe when Leo is at risk. "And who knows how many people are in Southend. It's a holdout. A decent settlement. Fisherman, farms. If it falls, we'll lose more food. Then we've probably lost the whole north."

Am I exaggerating? Probably. But Liverpool's gone, and we heard nothing from anywhere north of there.

No one is making a decision. Len Hayes is a wet rag of a man. Is it up to me? Really?

Fine. I'll damn us all. I'll kill us and do it gladly.

I walk to one of the horses, a gelding, and slip his reins from Hayes' grip. I lead the horse away and snatch our one remaining lantern before Hayes has time to protest.

"I'm going," I say as I'm slinging the lantern through the harness placed around the horse's chest. "Are you?"

I decide not to invoke anything or anyone. Not God, not Drearton, not obligation. But if any of them is unsure, I'll tell them to mount. Ride with me to save a man who might, at best, find me dull or overbearing. Risk your life so I might crawl into his bed once more. Sacrifice it all for my desperation. Do it, cowards.

Don hesitates. His feet slip in the marshy ground before he sighs heavily and joins me, mounting his own horse. At this point, I don't bother to wait. I put the horse into a trot and, reaching into its pack, pull out a compass. Northeast. It's probably a day's ride or more. Logic tells me we should rest and not risk breaking the horses' legs—or our necks—in the dark, but when has logic triumphed over obsession?

"You're going to get us all killed," Hayes calls out after me.

And God, I don't know who I am, but I look back at him and say, "Like we have much time left as it is."

I hear someone else mount—Sutton. And when the three of us put the horses into a gallop, led by the single lamp, I hear a fourth set of hooves join us in the distance.

We ride to Southend.

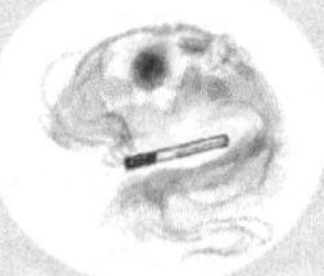

14

LESSON FOURTEEN

It takes nearly eight hours to ride out to Southend.

We don't know the state of bridges further east, and I grew up much farther north in Hull.

So we cross back over the bridge towards Cripplegate, wait for the wardstones to drop, ride through London—which feels at once cramped and empty, all the houses hosting ghosts more so than the living—and go out Aldgate to the east.

No Blood Hunters yet.

After, we ride through the night as best we can, but even if most of the ground is long stretches of flat expanse, the rain makes the ground soft, and I am soaked to the bone and shivering.

"Gonna get a chill from this," Don mumbles maybe three hours in. "Can you imagine dying to rain? Rip my throat out instead."

"Don't tempt me," I mutter.

Don scoffs. "What did you say?"

I don't reply, but a few minutes later, we pass a haven of a village. A lot of it is like Southwark in that it has been long abandoned and left rotting, but we find a structure that's mostly dry to sleep in. Hayes gets to work on starting a fire, and I agree to stay up for the first watch, which we each take in intermittent shifts.

But I stay awake for as long as I can. Because I'm worried about my dreams. About what they'll show me. I can almost feel Vengeance, like a weight or an anchor. I feel the tug.

I stay up long enough to sit with Sutton through her shift. I think about overhearing Father Veer say she has thoughts of violence against herself, but I don't speak to her about that. We've been through too much the last few hours to warrant bringing up another difficult thing.

So I sit in silence, sucking on a cigarette. It's been kept dry by Leo's gift of a case, which I worked up the courage to open, and my stomach clenches with every inhale. I imagine I'm breathing him in or exhaling into his mouth; less than a week ago, I was watching smoke curl out from the wound on his face, tendrils clawing from between his teeth. Sutton sits in silence, which I'm grateful for, and eventually says, "You should sleep."

I shake my head and wait until she wakes Don, and I choose to sit through most of his watch, too, before he calls me a faggot idiot and orders me to go.

"I'll call you the same if you like," I tell him.

He flinches, fixing me with a look of disgust. The others are asleep; I glance down at his crotch.

Don't—judge me. It's not a true desire. It's not the way I want Leo. This want boils down to comfort, and it's teasing, a bit of control I can wrench from someone hurting in a different way than me. Heat curls behind my eyes, and I know from the sickly nausea in my stomach that I don't really want this. But I lean forward anyway and pull Don into a kiss.

He freezes against me. My eyes are closed, so I can't see whether he's staring or shocked or loving it. I wait for him to push me off, but he doesn't. I imagine he's Leo. I try—I try so hard to imagine he's Leo. But when I breathe in, the scent of Don Wamsley triggers a reaction in my gut. Wrongness fills me with its swampy thickness. My stomach is coated in it. If he reciprocated and leaned in, I think I'd still let him do whatever he wanted, in case I could find a sliver of the heaven Leo pulls me into.

After a moment, Don gently pushes me away. The pity in his eyes is much worse than his earlier disgust.

"You don't want me," he says. "You're crying."

I reach up. Warm tears coat my cheek. How pathetic.

In response, I exhale shakily.

Don says, "I don't know why I'm here. You have a reason, and I have—I have something else. I might be better off if both you and fucking Shaw died out here. 'Cause whatever it is you do together—"

"—you saw what we do together."

"—is not something I should—it's not something I want."

His voice cracks high at the end of the lie, but his eyes take on a mean edge. Don searches my face. His hand hovers between us, outstretched to stop me the way one might a wild animal.

Pathetic! Even Don Wamsley rejects me.

I laugh and look up at the roof of the hovel. For a moment, I let myself listen to the rain and the howl of the wind outside. I almost wish it was a *teras* howling, but it's just the cold swirling up a storm.

"You're right. I don't want you." My head lolls down, and I stare at him as he shifts uncomfortably under my gaze. Firelight pulsates over his skin like floral blooms. His hair has grown out a bit, and fine stubble shadows his jaw. "You could be handsome if you tried," I tell him, and he punches me lightly without looking my way.

I snort and sigh. "You're like me maybe ten years ago. Before I realised the feeling would never go away."

"I'm. . ." he snorts and puts the base of his palms against his eyes. "I don't want to be. . .like you."

"I know."

"I want—I mean, there's no time, anyway."

"You should make the time," I say. I wait until he turns to look at me, brows pinched and eyes searching. I tell him: "I think you're a bit of a shit, Wamsley, but you deserve to feel good at least once before you die. You deserve to know what it feels like."

He reddens. His voice is pitched low into a hiss. "I know what it bloody feels like. I've done it before."

"With girls?" I clarify, and he nods. I shake my head. "It's not the same."

"How is it not?" he hisses, but his voice is cracking. I'm pushing him too far, and I've lost the thrill of it. I don't want to hurt him. I'm too tired, too sad. Maybe there's a bit of that Christian love in me—the real kind, not the insidious kind. I want to tell him it's alright to feel this way. I felt it, too. Disgusting. A burden. Unnatural. The fear of being wrong. It's a lot to handle when monsters are crawling through the world. I imagine it would be suffocating to work through when those same monsters are waging a war.

"Why did you come?" I ask, and he aborts an attempt to stand up. Don sighs and opens up his palms.

"Do I really have to say it?"

"Yes."

"Fuck you."

"You might, if you weren't such a coward. . ."

That makes him snort and roll his eyes, but maybe I do mean it.

Don inhales slowly and deeply. "You both saw me. . .like that. And you. . .you didn't. . ."

He can't finish the sentence; he just starts pulling dried skin from a callous on his hands. He sniffs, looks away, and buries his cheek against his shoulder.

"Will you just go the fuck to sleep, faggot?" he murmurs. All the bite is sapped from his words. He almost says it lovingly.

I don't say anything more to him. I do what he asks because I'm good at taking orders and because I'm exhausted. I curl up by the fire and fall asleep almost instantly.

When I come to, I realise I've dreamt of nothing. Pure blissful black—that's it.

But the other thing is this: nothing tried to attack us. Not one thing. F-class *teras* are an infestation, and yet they are nowhere. If I didn't know any better, I would guess something—someone—is telling them to stay away.

I worry that Southend is a lure.

I worry it's a trap.

⁂

THE SUN RISES and refracts a peachy pink glow through fluffy white clouds. A lone pair of sea birds chitter as they fly overhead. Their white breasts are stained with blood—not their own.

They've been dancing in the viscera, tearing strips of carrion from the bodies. And there is a great deal of bodies.

I think there's something incredibly raw about seeing destruction in the daylight. Night adds a horror to it, a layer of something unavoidable. Claustrophobic. Seeing them laid out like this, bodies scattered as if mown down whilst fleeing, seems so fucking unceremonious. There is no ritual to their deaths. No meaning. Forty odd people are lying in various states of decay, and they haven't even been wholly eaten.

In fact, very few of them look like they've been eaten at

all. Most of the wounds I can see from this vantage have flesh flapping in the wind as madly as the scraps of clothes still covering their bodies.

They weren't killed for food.

I see someone's exposed chest and dismount. The ribcage has been cracked open and her heart lays there, pink and unbeating. I think: "*He heals the broken-hearted, and binds up their wounds,*" Psalms 147, because my subconscious apparently has a sick sense of humour.

We are standing on the beach in Southend-on-Sea. The whole place is dreary probably at the best of times. Overnight, the rain stopped, and we rode out here so fast that the dampness of our clothes has been wicked away by the wind. Wildflowers clogged the old road, but otherwise, the land was free of dense trees. We rode past abandoned farmlands with razed, burnt crops. The dead husk of an unidentifiable *teras* lay in the centre of one of them, and the earth around it was scorched black. Every moment made me panic further—where was Leo? Where was *anyone*? The whole approach smelt of brine and fish, the scent blown in by an angry sea air that howled in my ears. And to the shore, we went.

Now, it is overcast, and the sun has a gaslamp quality to it, making the world muggy and hazy. Heat strains through the thick cloud layer. The pink sunrise looks beautiful.

"What the fuck happened here?" Hayes murmurs.

My gut churns. I leave the baying horses further up the beach and walk forward onto the sand. The first body I come to has had his back flayed open. Long talons would have done that—I count the cuts. Four talons on a single hand, the wounds evenly spaced. I glance back over my shoulder and see Sutton and Don dismounting to join me or offer their own interpretations of the carnage. But what's the point? We had a warning before we even arrived.

"It's the *nuckelavee*," I say as they get in earshot. "Has to be."

Don slows and grows cautious. His hips shift minutely, and he lowers himself, bracing for the unseen threat. His eyes dart around. "Then where the fuck is it?"

I nod back to the ocean. "Comes at night in the old tales. Stalks about on land. And its only. . .motivation is destruction. That's the whole point of it. That's all it wants."

Which is worse than the others, I think. Or perhaps reminds me too much of Vengeance. A creature whose entire purpose is destruction, with malignance knitted into its very core—that is so much worse than the *teras* that just exist. The *harpies* that want food. The others that just lurk here, the way they did in myth, who attack only when provoked.

Sutton is on her knees inspecting the body. She slips her gloves off and touches the sickly dead flesh without hesitation. The skin looks thick and unreal, discoloured with a greyish tinge.

"Could be a week old," Sutton says after a moment before glancing back at me. "These might be the first victims."

I look back over my shoulder at Hayes standing vigil with the horses. "There must be survivors," I say. All I'm thinking is that anyone here should be able to point me towards Leo Shaw.

We trudge up the slight incline away from the beach and walk into the town centre. In contrast to the way bodies look in the day—stripped of their power—the empty town and its eerie quiet is much worse. What could be explained away by the night is an unfortunate reality now. The town is abandoned. Or everyone is dead. Or. . .

"Is there a town hall?" I ask. "Or a church?"

"Must be," Hayes says with a nod. He looks around. "But you're right. Survivors would have turned to God."

There turns out to be very little in Southend, which grew

out of the end of a village called Prittlewell. A quarter-hour ride brings us into Prittlewell village, which is also eerily quiet. But there, beautiful and tall, a tower looms above the scattered structures.

The tower is tiered, indented three times, and flares out slightly at its base, where an old arch frames the door. The tower has a parapet and knapped flintwork. Stone, red, and other bricks make up the facade, and the tower joins to the long base of a church.

As we approach, we hear voices.

My heart lunges out of me. I offer both God and the Devil my soul then, just for a chance to see Leo Shaw again.

Hayes takes the lead. As we approach, someone appears on top of the tower, a little speck inspecting us.

"Hunters?" they call down. Their voice is pitched, and their tone—Excitement? Dismay? Horror? I can't tell—makes their words come out clipped and rushed. "More of you?"

More of you, more of you, more of you: he's here? He's alright?

"We are here to retrieve some of our own," Hayes says, "from a scouting party."

"Some of your bloody own, eh?" the figure calls. I can't see much of them. A male's voice, gruff and old. The sun reflects off a bald scalp. He says, "Why should I let you in? You'll be good fodder. Keep the *teras* busy when they come back tonight."

"How long have they been coming?" Hayes asks.

"What does it fucking matter to you, boy? London abandoned us! We wrote for help weeks and weeks ago. Now look at us! Dead. Or fled. Or holed up in this here church. But no —God's gone. Gone, gone. . ."

He shifts, and a second later, something is hurtling down towards us. Hayes sidesteps his horse, and a stone narrowly misses her flank.

"Jesus, man!" Hayes howls.

I push forward before Hayes can speak again. "Leo Shaw!" I call out. "Just tell me if he's in there!"

"Don't know," the man says. "And wouldn't tell ya if I did!"

I look at Don, who stares back at me with wide eyes. Then I calmly dismount, open up my cloak, pull my flintlock free, check the gunpowder is dry, load one of the three remaining bullets, and aim it at the top of the parapet.

The man squawks, "What're you—"

I fire.

Sparks fly from the flintlock as the ball is shot free. It misses the man's skull, exploding into the stone of the parapet by his hand. I'm fairly proud of that shot.

He screams something unintelligible and screams again. Then he's ringing some bell hidden on the parapet from this angle.

"What the fuck are you doing!" Hayes screams at me. The horses are baying and whinnying behind me. But my mind is blank. The fury and the sadness and the worry have whittled me into singular focus: I will not stop until I find him. I am sick of everything else. We are so close, and this bastard won't tell me? Who the fuck does he think he is?

I strip the Hunter cloak from my body and let it fall gracelessly onto the grass before I walk up to the stone tower. The stone isn't worked enough, and the mortar is uneven— once, it might have been maintained, but we are long past that now. Rot has worked its way through the smooth surface, and my anger is grateful for it. Dozens of stones sit at mismatched lengths and breadths up the wall, creating open pockets where I can easily put my hands and feet. Fuck it.

I start to climb.

"Jones," Hayes says, sounding unimpressed. "Get down."

I don't listen to him. I don't listen to my body, either. I am bruised, and my knee begins to throb instantly. Tears prick at my eyes—I can't focus on anything else. *Think of Leo. Get to Leo.*

"What are you doing?" Sutton adds.

I grunt out, "I'm going to fucking kill him."

I mean it, I think.

Don barks out a laugh and starts to climb up beside me. I'm in half a mind to kick him down. I want this for myself; I want to get up there and beat a man to death if he doesn't tell me what I want to know.

Who are you? Where is the child of God you used to be?

Leo told me to be ruthless. Ruthless! The only way to survive is to become this—but if I want to *live*, if I want to grab any kind of true life for myself, then I need to push beyond necessary action.

I need to kill to get what I want.

The stonework is mossy in places but otherwise dry. I've never climbed anything in my life, except for trees when it was necessary to hide in Hull. A fear interred deep in my subconscious begins to burrow out—if I look down, I might vomit. Hayes keeps calling out to me, and then the man above joins in.

"Get down, fool! You'll kill yaself!"

"I'll kill you first!" I scream back. My voice cracks. "Tell me where he is!"

I realise this behaviour is not sane. I can identify at least that much. But I keep climbing.

It's only a few minutes in that everything starts to burn. I am not conditioned for this. It's only been a handful of months since I started training in earnest, and what little muscle I've gained from that is competing with my nineteen years of—

My twenty years, now. I realise with a short start that my birthday has come and gone.

Ignore that. You're here for him.

But it feels good to take something into my own hands and *push* beyond. Even when the skin of my fingers is scraped or sloughs off as the rough surface of the stone tower pulls on my dry hands. Even when the red, raw flesh starts to sting, and every time I haul myself up, I'm on the verge of tears. My arms start to shake. The muscles in my forearms feel brittle and spark with stinging pulses. My hands spasm and curl inward like claws, made useless as whatever tendon connected to it starts to give up. Half the time, I'm hanging on with my prosthetic, and I am grateful for that indifferent, manmade arm. Now more than ever. I tell it to hold on, and it does, but the ache in the join—still slightly inflamed by infection—is more bearable than the searing overuse in my flesh forearm.

I won't give up. Of course, in a way, it's easy not to. If I give up, I really will fall to my death.

Wind picks up around me, and I lock eyes with the man standing on the tower's parapet. He's old—one of the oldest people I've ever seen, though that could be the work of wind and sand more so than time. Harsh conditions have carved deep lines into his face. His under eyes sag, and he looks mildly shocked to see me.

I put my hand on the top of the parapet and use my last strength to haul myself over.

The man shudders away from me. He has a metal rod—a fire poker?—which he brandishes, backing up against the opposite wall.

"Please, son," he says. My hand convulses. I am no one's fucking son.

My flintlock is empty. I quickly reload with one of the two remaining bullets, cock the hammer, and point it at his face.

"What do you want?" he babbles. "What do you want?"

I say it without thinking. I say it because something compels me to. "Vengeance."

There's nothing up here but the watcher, a trapdoor, and a makeshift bell. A string runs from it down to beneath the trapdoor.

Suddenly, shouts spring up around us. I turn in time to see Don pulling himself over into the safety of the parapet, but he himself turns and throws his head over the edge to look.

"Church door's open," he says. "Fire and pitchforks—this town's so fucking angry."

I glance at the watcher. "Call them off."

"I can't—"

I walk forward and press the barrel between his eyes. "Call them off *now*."

He shivers and drops the poker. With both hands raised in surrender, he skirts around me and goes to the bell—which he pulls twice, waits a beat, and pulls twice again.

I flash a look to Don, who is still folded over the edge. "That did it," he says, looking back at me over his shoulder. "But did you really think you could take on four Hunters?"

The man gulps. He's shorter than me but still bristles, somehow. "Your other lot wasn't much to deal with."

That doesn't sound right. Leo is far stronger than me. Victoria is smart. Whoever else they were with, too, were strong enough or smart enough or lucky enough to survive the encounter with the *phrygian*. So unless they're injured—

I freeze. I glance at the trapdoor.

"How bad?" I whisper.

I don't have to say anything else. *How bad are their injuries?* The man's eyes soften just a fraction. Then he sighs and looks up at the sky.

"Go down the ladder. They're in the sanctuary chapel."

I don't wait for anything else. I throw open the trapdoor and climb down.

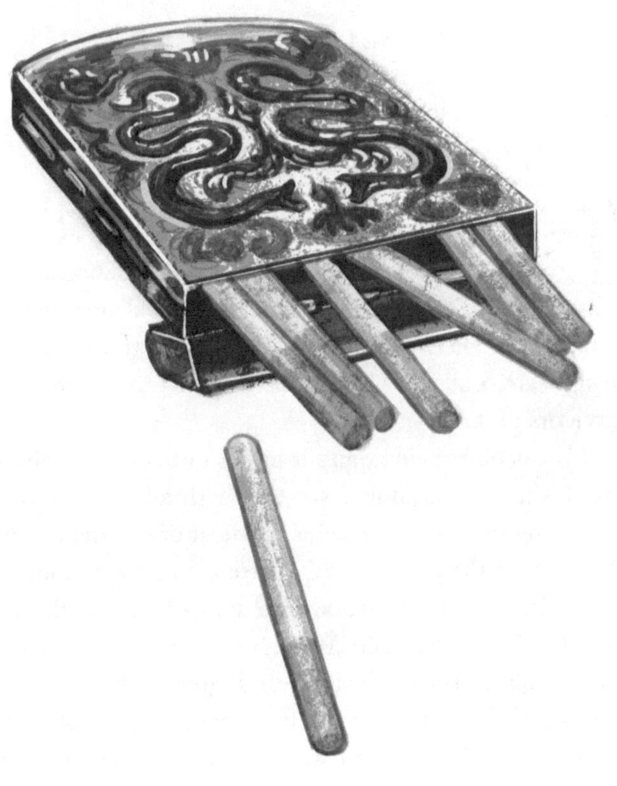

LESSON FIFTEEN

The ladder deposits me in the tower clock room, in which a series of pulleys, valves, and a mechanism sits unused and dusty. The door from here opens into the ringing room, where smaller bells have been set up to ring when their strings are pulled. This must have alerted the gathered survivors of our approach.

I press on the door, and it opens onto the church proper. The inside is beautiful. I say this with all the awe of a boy who clung to God in the wilds for most of his life: this is what God's home should look like. There are no *teras* submerged in the fucking walls. There are no symbols of anything other than God and Jesus and Mary. It's all tile, wood, stone, and stained glass. Brown, yellow, and green tiles tesselate the ground, and the pews are a deep mahogany, a colour that is mirrored in the wooden arches that separate the smaller internal chapels from the central nave and altar. The ceiling is vaulted. Exposed wooden beams run the entire length and remind me, as most churches do, of the inside of a boat. Noah's Ark comes to mind, and with it, the flood waters of my faith.

I don't know. Relief is perhaps the wrong word. I'm walking up the aisle of a church, and the sun is refracting through red and purple and green glass, and incense in the air masks the scent of injury and sickness, but—it feels—safe. Like I really am being held by the Lord.

Don't be ridiculous. This is all learned; this is all memory.

Maybe it is. Or maybe I will find Leo Shaw—a man I don't love but can't stop chasing after—safe in the house of God. What greater show of forgiveness is that? I ran from God; I denied Him like Peter denied Jesus, and now He houses the one I've been searching for. Now, I am walking up the aisle to find him. My chest hurts.

Survivors of Prittlewell, and presumably Southend, have gathered in the pews. Some of the other chapels pressed against the walls of the church are brimming with people. Most of them refuse to meet my eye, but those that do are angry. A few stand defensively and grab whatever they have near them. I can tell there are factions of a kind: families, some community groups. Women, children, and the sick are watched over by the fit and strong, which are mostly men. And it's these men, too, that don't seem to like the look of me. First, I think it's how I look. The long hair, the pale skin, the litheness without brawn or bulk. I am a kept pet in appearance; no tan, neither starving nor necessarily strong. But then I remember how I'm dressed. Tricorn hat, Hunter blacks, waltzing into their church—their last haven —to rescue our own. Even without my cloak, I am recognisable.

I can't help but wonder what kind of legends have been generated about us. The students and graduates of London's University—it is a different world. I remember this type of life. I remember cowering; I remember the consistence fear. I look at these people, and with all my empathy dried up, I do not envy them.

Even when the University is cursed in its own way, I would never willingly go back to this.

But if I were them, these survivors so thoroughly abandoned by the world, I would be furious.

You can't think about them. You can only think about yourself.

And that voice in me is right. Every person in this church would die if I decided to take matters into my own hands and ferry them back towards London. There's nothing there for them. Pretty soon, there will be nothing anywhere for anyone.

Light haloes the chancel. The window doesn't look like it was the original. Wooden supports surround it as if Prittlewell had been in the middle of replacing it. The glass has four panels depicting Mary and baby Jesus, and I wonder which soul here is specialising in something like stained glass even now. Humanity, sometimes, can be beautiful like that.

The roof above the chancel must have been beautiful once. Hammer-beamed, with gilding and colouring long ago faded. I see all this in seconds, but my focus is on the bodies beneath the altar.

The sanctuary is where the Holy Sacrament is kept, though the candle denoting its presence is not lit. I imagine they ate the bread and wine long ago. I do find it curious that this is where the Hunters are, and I think about the symbolism of that, and yes, I am stalling. I am thinking about anything other than the fact that the Hunters are lying around on the floor, their cloaks draped over them as blankets. I'm trying to ignore the fact that they are sick. Or injured. That they might be dead. So I approach slowly. If I take longer to get there, if the knowledge is still uncertain, then maybe I can prolong their lives.

I hear footsteps behind me and spin defensively. Don skids to a stop in the middle of the aisle.

I mouth, "Don't," at him. His brow furrows in confusion

as he looks past me. The expression on his face doesn't change when he registers the four covered lumps. Behind him, Sutton and Hayes have negotiated their way in, but now are locked in conversation with the man from the parapet and a stern-looking woman who stands with her hand on the hilt of a knife at her belt.

I just want a few moments alone. I just want to go to my knees and put my hand on his shoulder to wake him. I want Leo to roll onto his side and blink away sleep. I want to watch the dawning realisation in his eyes, for him to see that it's me. That I came for him.

I could tell him: *Forget about that fight we had the last time I saw you. I never want to fight with you again. You said there was nothing I could offer for you to tell me about yourself. Well, I don't need to know you, and you could have me anyway. I will offer everything I have just to see you smile again. Keep your secrets, Leo Shaw, and hold me. Don't go anywhere again. Don't get hurt. Don't die.*

I say nothing to Don. I just look at him. But he sees through me, and his eyes soften. I hate seeing him looking at me like that. Pitying me.

"Go," he says and has the decency to turn around.

My stomach flips. I turn back to the sanctuary. I bow to the altar, and I ascend.

I hate how much they look like corpses. Four of them, four left out of the whole scouting party. I stare at their thick cloaks and search for Leo. When I see the wheat-coloured hair splayed on the ground, my heart jolts.

God.

I don't look for Victoria, or check on the others, because I truly can't care about anything else. Leo—*Leo.*

Shakily, I lower myself to the ground. My face is hot, my eyes stinging already with pre-emptive tears, and my chest is clenching around nothing. I don't know why I'm so scared. I can see the rise and fall of his chest beneath his Hunter cloak. He's alive.

He's alive. Why are you scared?

On my knees, I gently pull away the cloak from his face.

His torn cheek glints back at me, teeth ground together firmly. The leather patch is nowhere in sight. I reach out and press the back of my fingers against his jaw.

He startles.

In a flash, the cloak is thrown back and out of the way. Leo holds a dagger, hilt jutting under his chin. His knuckles turn bone white with the strain of his grip. He sees me. He sees that it is *me*. Leo doesn't lower the dagger, which is nowhere near me, but his hand begins to quiver.

I see tears well up in his eyes.

I feel like vomiting.

He's shirtless beneath his cloak. White bandages envelop him. Skin pulls at the edges, wrinkling at his armpits and chest like the bandages are wound tight enough to keep him together. Which, perhaps, they are. Brown-red blood has soaked the bandages around his stomach. More bandages loop over his left shoulder also caked in dried blood. He's injured. He's injured badly. Now I see the sweat sheen on his forehead and the paleness to his skin. An infection, maybe. Or a fever—he's fighting something.

The *phrygian* must have hurt him. Must have—

God, how close was he to death? How close had he come to that nothingness?

Leo looks at me for a very long time. Neither of us speak. I want to, though—I want to move. I want to place my hands on him, make sure he's real. I want to say *I'm here. I'm here, Leo.* I want to cry, I want to laugh, I want to kiss him. But I just sit there looking at him, looking at his eyes and the darkness of his expression.

At some point in that stretch of seconds, something

changes for him. His nostrils start to flare, and his eyebrows edge up fractionally, buckling under the weight of this new emotion.

He drops the dagger. It clatters onto the tiled floor. Now free, his hand shoots to his mouth, and he presses his palm firmly against his cracked lips to suppress a whimper. A wail. He closes his eyes, and tears squeeze out and over his cheek.

I can't stop myself now. He's here and he's hurting and even now, he can't bring himself to let me in when it counts. He doesn't lean into me. He doesn't cling to me or ask me to hold him. If it's too much for Leo to tell me what he needs, then I will hold that feeling for him. I take the risk that he'll push me away. I reach out and hold his face with both my hands. A kind of calm washes over me: a stillness, a certainty. Even if it hurts, and even if he rejects me, and even if we die, and even if we live and he no longer wants me, I decide in this moment that the risk is worth it.

He is worth it.

"Look at me," I whisper. But he shakes his head viciously and curls in on himself, trying to make himself smaller. I know the pain that causes this reaction. Stomach aching, grief tearing through your chest—you fold over just to try and make it hurt less.

When he starts to cry in earnest, Leo curls his hands into fists and starts beating the sides of his head. He's grunting and sobbing—I try to pull his hands away.

"Leo, Leo, stop it. Leo—"

"I c-can't," he murmurs. "I can't, I—"

He starts to hyperventilate. I know the feeling of this panic, and know better than to try and keep touching him. I slide my hands away, and I lay down on the tile next to him whilst he cries and shudders.

"You're okay," I tell him. The pads of my fingers press into the tile as I try to resist holding him. "I promise you. You're going to be okay."

I keep speaking to him like that. Small promises, small reminders that whatever has happened, it's not happening right now. These fractional moments of safety are all we have. I've been like Leo is now. Every human left alive has briefly succumbed to the panic. It's inevitable. But I want him to know I think of him no differently. I do not love him, but I am here.

It's not love—I just can't stand to see him like this.

It's not love—it's something else.

When his crying becomes disjointed, and his breaths are shaky and gasping, he glances at me. Slowly, I reach out to touch him again.

My hand glides across his, which has gone bone white from the force with which he's pressing it into his face. I gently peel it away, and he lets me, though his hand stays slack even when I squeeze it and slip into my own. He keeps his eyes closed.

"Leo Shaw," I murmur. "Look at me right now."

He doesn't open his eyes. I see his tear-stained cheeks redden. Is he ashamed? Embarrassed? This is the most vulnerable I have ever seen him, and all I want to do is hold him.

"Please," I whisper. "Look at me."

His eyes crack open just a fraction, and immediately, his face contorts again. His eyebrows crash together, and his lip quivers.

We say nothing for a second. Then, croaking, Leo says, "You came."

You came.

"You idiot," I said. My voice cracks. "Of course I came."

He shakes his head. "You shouldn't have. You shouldn't

have—it's—it's dangerous. It's worse than ever. And—I —*Cass*. . ."

He's trembling. I reach out and very slowly push his head into the crook of my neck. I hear him take a shuddering breath. He wraps his arms around me. It is the most intimate we have ever been. It is the closest I have ever felt to him.

"I didn't think you would come," Leo tells me. His voice muffles against my neck, which is growing wet with his tears.

"I couldn't have stayed," I say truthfully.

He shifts minutely, pulling away to look at me. "What do you mean? Has London fallen?"

Is that what he thinks? Does he understand nothing about what I feel? About what I want from him?

I hold his face. He stares back at me. I say, "No," but I want to say more. His frown only deepens.

"I don't understand," he says. "We fought. I said. . . Things to you."

"Would you have come?" I ask, and then immediately, "Don't answer that. I don't want to know."

Of course, I very desperately want to know. But fuck hearing the wrong word pass through his lips.

If you don't want him to talk, then you better.

I clear my throat. "I couldn't have stayed if you weren't there. Don't you get that? I came for you, Leo Shaw, because I couldn't live knowing you were out here all alone. Okay? Drearton refused to look for you. It wasn't fair."

Leo is still frowning at me. I realise he doesn't understand, or perhaps can't comprehend that I came here for him and for him alone. That I disobeyed Drearton and the University and London. That I chose *him*. And that I regret none of it.

He says, in wonderment, with a boyish voice, "You like me."

And I start to laugh.

He grabs at my face and pulls me close. Leo kisses me hungrily, breathing in deeply as he presses our lips together.

There's noise around us as the others shift. Sutton, Hayes, and Don have climbed up into the sanctuary, I guess. I pointedly don't check. Or rather, I can't look anywhere else. Light shines over Leo Shaw's face.

"You look like an angel," I whisper to him.

This makes his face twist again. Tears fill his eyes, and he blinks away. He says, "I," and then stops. He clears his throat. "I've spent the last few nights thinking about what I would say to you, if I ever saw you again."

"What did you come up with?" I ask. "Dirty Latin poetry?"

He flicks his gaze to me, unamused. My smile falters.

Leo murmurs, "I thought, *all he's done is want to know me.* But I'm. . .I don't talk about it. Why I'm like this. I don't—I don't like remembering. And sometimes, I don't know what the point is. You look at me sometimes, the way you're looking at me now—" Leo is glowing, angelic, perfect; I want him, "—and I think, *Shaw, if you tell him, that look will turn to pity.* Which isn't what I want. Alright?"

I nod at him. He glances away. When Leo starts to talk, its matter-of-fact, blunt, and slow. He has practised this; that's what he was telling me. "My father's name was Ellis. My mother's name was Adelaide. She was pregnant. Six months. My younger sister was Maria. I think you would have liked her. My younger brother was Paul. He was four. I had two sisters and a brother who were stillbirths. My aunt was Agnes. My cousins were Florence, Jeremiah, and Peter."

I swallow. I say, "What happened to them?"

Leo's brows buckle.

"Right," Hayes calls, clapping his hands together. The sound echoes out in the chapel. Leo squeezes his eyes shut and I reach over, kissing him gently on the lips.

"Later?" I murmur, and he nods against me.

I have never seen him so frail.

I pull away from him, and in the quiet echo of the church, I feel empty. Empty of sacrament, holiness, goodness. Instead, I am filled with a hunger. I have him back.

What he has offered me is more than he has ever offered. That tiny detail of who he was before London befell him is enticing, and I am pulled towards him. When I see Hayes standing over us like a priest before his congregation, I almost forget that none of us are really saviours. Agrawal is dead. Most of the hunting party we have come to rescue is dead. But I have what I want. I am so blinded by the relief of him that I forget about *her*.

One of the bodies pushing themselves up is Victoria Bennet. As she sits up, the cloak shifts and pools around her pregnant belly, gathered there as if it were ruching on a fine gown made to emphasise the waist. All it does is shock me. Her hand goes over the bump, and I can't believe the child has survived where graduated Hunters have not. But perhaps that is the lingering force of Bellamy's blood. We lock eyes and I think about crawling over to her, ignoring Hayes and Sutton and the others. I think about apologising again, but we've done this dance before and there's no point. Perhaps as Bellamy's baby grows, so too will the chasm between Victoria and me. It's inevitable. The child is the last remaining link she has to him, and so I cannot fault her if she will always hate me. Which is why, when her eyes well up with tears at the sight of me, I accept that she's upset to see I'm still alive.

She even says it. Her voice cracks. "Cassius. You're alive."

"Are you. . ." I don't finish the sentence. My voice sounds weak and tinny, and Hayes is staring at me. Sutton, too—the remains of the hunting party. Leo, Victoria, a man, and a young woman about my age. All eyes are on me.

Hayes speaks into my momentary silence with a quickness. "Here's the lay of the land. Drearton didn't send us out here. We came alone. Which means no one else is coming. Agrawal is dead. I don't know who killed that messenger, James, the one in Southwark? But in any case, you're the last of Claypoole's party, and the *teras* are set to attack again. I will overlook James' murder, because we need Hunters."

"They attack every night."

I cut my eyes to the man who has spoken. He lies next to Leo and looks a haggard thirty years. His age strikes me as profound in its own way. I look for any sign of his mantle and see the Hunter cloak strewn over him. Much too small for his body. I wonder whose corpse he took it from, and if it matters; if it matters what skills the University purported to bestow upon him.

The man grimaces up at Hayes. "I killed the messenger. On accident. He stumbled out of the shadows screaming 'Southend' over and over, but I wasn't—I didn't hear that. I thought he. . .I thought he wanted to eat me. I was so certain of it." He glances around at the others, brow crumpling together. He shakes his head, "Something about the *phrygian.* . ."

I glance at Leo for confirmation. He closes his eyes with a nod.

The man continues. "Mr Shaw knew Southend. I don't know—we just had to move. We came here."

"The *phrygian* injured you?" Hayes clarifies.

The man's jaw pops as he grinds his teeth. "I should have died on the road."

I glance over at Victoria and know without being told she saved his life. She probably saved Leo's. I owe her everything.

"You went to Southend?" the man clarifies, and Hayes nods. "Yeah. We saw it too. Stumbled up here. And the remains of Prittlewell are here. Remains of Southend. Probably most human settlements in the area." He nods to the pews, to the small congregation. "This is it."

Don balks. The gleam in his eye is one of horror as he scans the pews in a quick count. "There's maybe fifty."

"There are a few more people in the basement," the graduate whispers sheepishly. He puts his face against his arm and sniffles. "God is the only thing stopping them from getting in. They scratch at the windows. Howling and groaning. Every bloody night."

No one bothers to ask why no one's tried to fight. All four of these people are injured, and they're the only ones trained. One of them is pregnant.

Sutton asks, "Why did you flee here?"

A few heads turn to Leo. It's as I expected, then—his connection to Southend-on-Sea swayed him here. He's cornered the lot of us, and I still can find no fault with him.

But then the other woman next to Victoria says, "He said it was important we went. That we'd be safe here."

Hayes laughs. "Safe? No one's left alive out there!"

"Leave the Shaw boy alone."

We all turn to the new voice.

A woman stands with her hands clasped before the sanctuary steps. She's, God, fifty? Nearly sixty? Her hair is straw thick and silver-white, peppered faintly with dark hairs. She has it all bunched at the back of her head in a low, tight bun that does nothing to stop unruly stray hairs flying about her head. She wears a dark blue velvet dress that buttons up to just beneath her chin. Her nose is small, and her lips are thin. They peel off her teeth in a dissatisfied grimace as she hikes up her dress and starts to climb up, bowing before the altar. A gold crucifix sits proudly against her chest, and she makes the sign of the cross even though I'm fairly certain this church isn't Catholic.

"Ma'am?" Hayes' voice is clipped and stern. He cocks his

head at her, asks her nothing. "These are my charges, and I—"

"Four of your so-called charges came to us injured, weakened, afraid, and on the verge of death. Young mister Shaw vouched for the other three—one of whom is pregnant!—and as such, they were granted sanctuary in the church. But make no mistake, boy. Just because you wear the mantle does not give you authority here. We are well beyond London's reach."

She says it all sullenly and folds her arms, coming to a stop in front of Leo, who has shifted. His arms are wrapped around both his knees, and he buries his wounded cheek against them.

"Well?" she says.

Leo shrugs.

"What does Leo have to do with this?" Don says.

'Leo' he said. 'Leo'—not Shaw. I drag my eyes over to Don and then flit them back to Leo. I grab his hand and squeeze, but he ignores me. Gently, he shakes his head. Is that shake for me? Or for the woman?

"Who are you?" I ask her.

Her eyes drop to me and then graze across my hand as it rests on Leo's. Her nose wrinkles. "Deaconess Margaret," she says glumly. Sniffing, she raises her chin. "Leo. I need to know."

Leo exhales shakily. His cheeks are wet. He shrugs helplessly, angrily. "It's not happening. I know you don't like the answer, but from what I remember, it's a no. You can't move it. It doesn't work that way."

The deaconess does not like this. Her face contorts, and her hands, which are swollen and bony, turn white from the pressure with which she grips herself. "I see. I shall inform the congregation."

"We don't have time for this!" Hayes says. "We need to leave. We need to *go*."

Hayes is scared. And an idiot. I stand up and brush myself off. "Look at them and be smart."

He doesn't tear his eyes from me, which is petty but expected of him. So I turn to the older man next to Leo. "What happened to you?"

He grimaces and throws the cloak off his body. It had been covering the bloody stump of his right leg, which he reveals to us with a humourless flourish of his hands. "Ta-da."

I glance back at Hayes, who looks a bit pale, before I turn to the young woman next to Victoria.

"Oh," she murmurs. "I'm alright, I—"

"She's broken her wrist," Victoria says with a sigh. "Head trauma, too. And her spine is bruised."

Without looking down at him, I say, "Leo. How bad is it?"

He takes a deep breath and laughs, and I hear the ghost of him there in that dry chuckle. "Oh, well. I think I saw part of my insides at one point."

My stomach flips. What? It takes everything in me not to turn and stare at him and his blasé fucking attitude.

"Oh, is that all?" I ask, pretending like I'm not seconds away from shaking him, checking on him, holding him. The unwritten rule here, to keep any sense of credibility before Hayes, would be not to look Leo's way.

Leo continues with, "A deep laceration over my heart, and another wound on my arm. But otherwise, dandy."

The hole in his cheek shows me how his teeth gnash together, a forbidden insight into the truth. He grinds his jaw in a tense display of faux brevity. I know anxiety. He's being truthful about what's happened to him—but he's more scared than he's showing now.

"Hayes, we aren't going anywhere," I say with a shrug. "Not for a while."

"If we get them to the University, behind the wards," Hayes says, then falls silent. He won't reveal to the deaconess what the rest of us know: there is magic in the University, a magic that could help them heal faster.

"We'll be dead long before we get to London," I say firmly. Hayes' nostrils flare.

Sutton, always the pragmatist, turns to Deaconess Margaret. "If we were to stay—"

"You can't," the deaconess snaps. "There's no food. No water. No supplies. We can't save you."

She speaks without looking away from Leo, which prompts me to glance back at him, too. He refuses to meet the older woman's eye.

Something has happened. Do they. . . know each other?

"This was your church?" I murmur to Leo.

Leo scoffs. "You know I never went to church."

"Leo Shaw," I say. "Tell me what's going on."

The deaconess' throat bobs. She steps towards us. "Don't."

But Leo is mine, and he knows it too. He looks up at me, eyes defiant and bloodshot.

"I'll tell you," Leo Shaw says. "Prittlewell Church has a wardstone."

❧ 16 ❧

LESSON SIXTEEN

"My father was a mystic. Or a conman, I don't know. Depends on who you talk to, I suppose. But around these parts, that's sort of what they thought of him. Eccentric at best, malicious at worst. Preying on people's fears and the like.

To me, he was just my father. I was fourteen when he died, so, you know. It's fairly fresh in the grand scheme of things. I don't really want to be talking about this, actually. I don't want to tell any of you anything about me, but I guess I led you all here, and now we're stuck, so. Fine. I deserve to feel uncomfortable for a moment.

Prittlewell Church—it's always sort of been here, in one form or another. I never really went. To Mass, I mean. None of my family did; my father was adamantly against it. In these parts, you can imagine. . . Well, look at Margaret. She's got a lot she wants to say to me now, and—yes, yes. *Deaconess*, I apologise. What I'm trying to say is that if the Shaws are known for anything around here, it's for blaspheming. And maybe for. . .

Some people say we got what we deserved.

Anyway. I didn't know why my father disliked the church until his death. Which I won't—I won't get into the hows, but at the end of it all, at fourteen, it was just me. He was dead. My mother and my brothers and sisters, and my aunts and cousins—they were, all of them, gone. I got left with the empty house. And before I decided what to do with it, before I figured out how I was going to survive, I tried to. . .go through everything.

The house, as it were, was a shack, really, back in Southend. Three rooms and my aunt and cousins lived with us. A tight fit, but a home, nonetheless. I wasn't concerned with the rooms and the clothes. It was everything beneath the house. There was a trapdoor since the house was raised, and we kept a lot of bullshit down there. Just extra storage, I thought. Never really thought about it until everyone was dead. But that's where I started. I went down there and pulled boxes out and went through things.

A lot of it was damp. From the. . .from what happened. It could have been much better taken care of before that, but. . . Well, I found some very old belongings in a chest. Generation of Shaws kept alive in that dank space. Old books. Tomes. Diaries. Some of the records went back to the beginning of the century, and it turns out my great-grandfather was a rather diligent writer. He kept journals from the time the *teras* materialised in our world. So, the Shaws had recordings of what things were like before. And the horror of the early days. Which, to be honest, isn't much different to now. Back then, money still had some meaning. They clung onto it as best they could. The rich stayed rich, and so on, until settlements rose, and London became what it is today.

Anyway, some men were contracted to research ways to defeat the *teras* or defend against them. I like to think of them as the first Scholars, though the University was still forming at that point. My great-grandfather was among those men.

Took a while before they turned to the myths. Tried every other avenue, tried to think about it logically, as men of science. Then, when that failed, most of them turned to God. It took a while to understand that they were seeing *brownies* and *chimeras* as they were recorded in legend. Some began to work on how to stop them—straight from the source, like we do now. But then others tried to find a way to survive.

My great-grandfather discovered the first Wardstone.

I suppose that's the short of it. He found this one, the one in Prittlewell. It grew naturally out of the earth, apparently overnight. The story goes that he camped out here. He tried cutting into it and moving it. Talked to townsfolk. No one knew a thing. Then, one night, the *teras* attacked. *Harpies* came, a whole swarm of them, looking for food, and he and two others took shelter by the stone. One *harpy* chased a woman and child out this way and, in their desperation, they ran towards the soft glow. One of the men sheltering with my great-grandfather rushed out to help them. The *harpy* swooped down and tore at his face and neck, but when he stumbled back and collapsed against the stone, the attacks stopped.

They saw the *harpy* land and squawk, but it couldn't get to them. No shelter, no weapons—nothing but this strange stone.

So that was how he learned about it. Reported it immediately, and his next job was to find out why. And how.

In the meantime, the church just expanded to accommodate it. Made it part of God's protection. I don't know if they knew what it was; my great-grandfather doesn't say except for a few instances. Something about God coming to Prittlewell; something about the faithful being saved. These weren't his words. Just what he recorded.

His focus in the journals turned to the 'why'. Why did a strange crystal emerge from the earth? And probably more importantly, why did *teras* not like it?

My great-grandmother was the one who turned him onto fairy paths. They're the paths fairies apparently take straight lines a lot of the time, from one point to the next. They're all over England. And whether they were there before the *teras* occurred, I don't know, but anyway, she seemed to think so. Of course, that would mean there was a natural magic, one that occurred before the *teras*. If *teras* and all their magic belonged to Satan, well, you can imagine. The church didn't like that.

Didn't matter that her husband had found the fucking thing. Prittlewell was up in arms about dear great-grandmother Shaw. Who was something like seventeen at the time, mind you—but I digress.

All this to say, the wardstones, from what I could tell, are natural. Don't ask about London's—I don't know how that happened. I don't know if they've moved them, but I don't think moving the stone here is a good idea. Or if it's even possible. My great-grandfather couldn't find a way.

Besides, I'm fairly certain the only thing stopping the *teras* from ripping into this church is that stone.

But what the deaconess wants to know is: can we move it? Can we pop it on a cart and become a wandering troupe? I'm thinking *no*. We can't.

The bigger question should be about London and the University. I don't know what they took from my great-grandfather's research. I don't know what else they figured out. But clearly, it's working. The wardstones are still up."

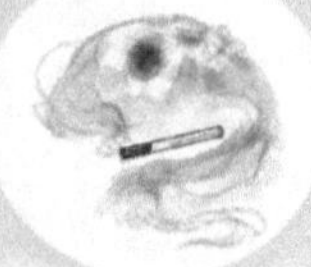

❧ 17 ❧

LESSON SEVENTEEN

"Except they are failing," I whisper. I make the decision to tell the others what I saw the morning the cultists were killed. Not Vengeance, not that vision, but the flickering of the barrier between London and the rest of the world.

Leo turns to me. "Yes," he says. "Well, that would make sense."

The others do not react with nearly as much grace. Both Hayes and Sutton already know, of course, but Leo, Victoria, and the other Hunters have no clue what's been happening. The man with one leg and the injured woman both make noises of panicked protest. They mutter about returning to nothing, and I feel their sudden dismay. If even London is weakened, then what hope does humanity really have?

In any case, I tell them the truth of what I saw. I say that I've seen them flickering. That Drearton has ordered the graduates manning the outposts to retreat behind the wards. That they plan to move even further back behind the Janus Gates. Hayes had said this was a problem for later, but now that I've brought it up again, and now that Leo has mentioned the origins of the wardstones, his face crumples with the sudden weight of the implication.

"You think this is an orchestrated attack," he says, gesturing around Prittlewell's church. The sentence falls flat: it's not a question.

"So, the *teras* are trying to destroy a wardstone in Prittlewell of all places, and the wardstones protecting humanity's last bastion are weakening, and hybrid *teras* are emerging as if the barriers and the rules they've abided by for decades no longer mean anything, and some of them are sentient enough to—to have a fucking army. Is that right?" Victoria says. She looks furious, brown cheeks flushed dark. She shakes her head. "There's no way this is a coincidence."

"Wait," I murmur. "You said they're trying to destroy the stone?"

Leo looks at me and nods. "Yes. After lying here for several nights and hearing them attack, it's clear. They want it gone."

"Is that why you came back here? You heard Southend was being attacked?"

He flushes. "Honestly, I don't know why I came back here. I thought it would be safe. But maybe I just wanted home."

No one who was with him interjects, but Margaret makes a noise. He turns to stare at the deaconess, whose face is squashed in an open scowl.

Leo snorts. "She doesn't believe me about the wardstones."

"Why would the *teras* want to destroy them?" Don asks.

"Why, hello, Wamsley," Leo says. He raises his chin, exposing the sharp jawline. *Whore.* "Fancy seeing you here. Did you come all this way for me?"

I stare at him. "Leo, answer the question."

His expression deflates, and he glares at me. "Yes. Obviously. It's the only explanation. They come every night. They try to get in. And some of them even–"

He cuts himself off and glances at the deaconess for approval, but Margaret has turned away from him and is staring up at the sunset hues leaking through the stained glass. "It will be night soon."

The man with the severed leg speaks next. "Some of them even talk. Call me crazy, I don't care."

Of course, no one calls him that. Victoria and I look at one another. We know he's not crazy.

"Well. . .what do they say?" Hayes asks.

Victoria hasn't looked away from me. She tilts her head, and her eyes glint with tears. She looks—somehow, for some reason—apologetic. "They want to come in. It's as simple as that. They knock sometimes and ask. The first night I thought it was a townsperson, someone trapped outside in the cold. But when Margaret said not to open the doors, the voices became a lot less. . . sweet. They got agitated, then angry, demanding, and the aggression began all over the church. Every possible angle, they tried to get in. But so far, they haven't smashed anything. The windows are intact, and even the trap door from the tower hasn't been opened. So the stone here must work the way the ones in London do."

She means their shape. Together, the wardstones form a kind of dome-like barrier that stretches across the whole of London. The wardstone here must do the same.

"Where is the wardstone?" Sutton asks.

"In the crypt," Leo says, which makes Margaret turn around and mutter snappishly under her breath.

Leo snorts at her and sits back on his haunches. Suddenly, I catch a glimpse of Leo—*my* Leo—who is proud and unbothered and shining.

"Don't think for a second you have any of my loyalty. You've never once been kind to me! In fact, you only know me because I. . . because I didn't die that day. Or maybe because you knew what my great-grandfather did and, like most churches, you uphold a tradition without giving a shit about its continued relevance. You hate my whole family for suggesting your God isn't real. Well, deaconess, as much as you might want me to be, I am not Satan. The *teras* are not my fault. If you want someone to blame for this mess, blame your God."

The deaconess regards him with the most scathing look I have ever seen. For a while, it looks like she might attempt to grapple him. Baptise him in holy water, make him succumb to the word of God. Even part of me quivered before Leo's declaration, but I know this man by now. No threat of God, or Hell, or Heaven, will sway him.

He is his own. He is without a master.

Deaconess Margaret eventually says, "May God be with you, Leo Shaw," and turns on her heel, stomping ungracefully down the sanctuary steps.

"So, what are we meant to do?" Hayes asks. It's funny that in any moment that requires a decision, Hayes refuses to lead us, but will happily declare his importance every other time.

"Well, wait a minute," Victoria says, flapping a hand for our attention. "Don't just move on so fast. What about the personal wardstones? Why are they portable and the bigger ones aren't?"

"The University must have found some way to replicate the magic," I tell her. "Besides, they only work for the Janus Gate. So they're hardly useful now."

"You're not understanding," she says. "If they are replicable, then surely that means the wardstones surrounding London do not have to be natural."

Leo says, "I'm not sure it matters now that they're growing weaker. Perhaps it matters for prosperity's sake, but in our reality, I don't need to know the why. I don't think I even need to know the how. All I want to know is what we're going to do to stop the *teras* here and now."

"Short-sighted," Victoria says stiffly. She rests a hand on her belly and glances away. "If we could move the stones. Or make more stones. If we could. . .figure out how they protect us. . ."

"Drearton has a plan for when our wardstones fail," I say and risk a glance towards the deaconess. She seems already skittish. An additional reason to panic—that the University intends to retreat so secularly—would do nothing to help us now.

Victoria narrows her gaze at me but seems to accept my words with a curt nod. I wish I had better news for her—I wish her child might grow up safe.

But as short-sighted as this may be, I think Leo is right. I say, "If we leave, we doom this town. And before you say anything, Hayes, yes, I am well aware that much of England is succumbing like this anyway. Pretty soon, there will be nothing left to save except London itself. But we are here now, and we came for these Hunters, and we know we can't leave until they're better. Or at the very least, until the threat to their well-being is reduced."

"So we kill as many fucking *teras* as we possibly can," Wamsley says.

We all turn to look at him, and he shrugs like it's the simplest thing in the world. He makes an aggressive gesture over his shoulder, jabbing his thumb towards the church pews where agitated towns folk sit and pray.

"Won't be long before they're too fed up to sit there doing nothing. We should take advantage of it."

"What?" Sutton laughs. "Put a pitchfork in one hand, a

brick in the other, and hope for the best? They're not trained. They're just cannon fodder."

"Which is exactly what we are," I say, "when it comes down to it. Drearton likes to uphold the idea that the University and the mantles mean anything anymore. Partly that's because he needs the relevance. Perhaps it would have been better for him to give everyone in London a pitchfork and a brick and send them out to hunt *teras* knowing that the majority of them would die. From a resource perspective, it makes more sense. But no one would ever buy into it. That's the kicker—that's the reason the University still thrives. He has made himself God, and whether London really needs him or not no longer matters. Whoever is left, us included, are part of his design. What Drearton isn't counting on is people being too angry to think about things like preserving London. Preserving society. He wants there to be divisions not only between the University, the Londoners, the Workers, the *xenos*, but whole schisms *within* those groups as well. Half of us are only in the University because we felt like we had no choice. So that's what we give these people. A choice."

"And then what?" Hayes mutters. "Four Hunters, two barely out of the womb, facing an entire horde of *teras?*"

This man...

"We know they can't get in the church," I say. "So all we have to do is dissuade them from camping out at this point. If we can clear enough away from here, encourage them to focus their attacks somewhere else, then maybe the people will have a chance to flee."

Hayes tilts his head. "And if not?"

At this point, I think Hayes is being a contrarian for the simple joy of it. I blink at him. *Are you serious?* I want to say, but instead, I tell him, blankly and as straightforwardly as I can manage, "Hayes, if we don't do this, sooner or later, us and them will starve to death."

That, at least, shuts him up.

"All right," Sutton nods. "Wamsley, Hayes, and I will talk to the townspeople. See what weapons they have here, see who's willing to fight and yes, Jones, I'll make sure they know the risks."

I nod at her. "Thank you."

They leave me alone with Victoria and Leo, but both have lapsed into an exhausted silence.

"We will talk later," Victoria says. Part of me smiles at that, if just for the simple pleasure of her wanting to talk to me at all.

I pull Leo close, and I'm surprised when I feel him relax against my chest. He sighs almost contentedly, and I briefly feel him nuzzle closer, jaw pushing into my pec. My bruised body lights up but I do not care. It's Leo. It's Leo and he's alive. I'll let him give me a hundred more bruises and be glad for them.

We say nothing. I don't want to ruin it.

But I do press my lips against his forehead.

In the growing silence, my thoughts scream loudly because I'm almost certain that tonight when I meet this army head-on, Vengeance will be there. That hulking colossus will lead them, or, like a general, will lurk in the back. Either way, I feel like it will speak to me again. I feel like it will recognise me as I ride out.

I don't want to tell the others about that, and maybe I'm doing them a disservice by keeping that to myself, or perhaps I'm preserving what little hope they still have for my sanity.

In any case, if I do meet Vengeance on the field, I will listen when it speaks to me. I will try to talk back to it. Maybe I can figure out what it wants.

What I don't want to think about is the reality of the wardstones being destroyed. From the way Leo described it, many are dotted around England. But if this army has already swept down from the north, then there's a good chance all those northern stones have been demolished. Is that why the wards around London are weakening? Are all the stones connected?

And if they all fall down, will London fall next?

❧ 18 ☙

LESSON EIGHTEEN

I wake only two hours later in the early twilight when a woman I don't recognise comes to take Leo away.

"Need to get a bit of walking in," she says, accent thick and sweet. She nods down at him, and he blinks up blearily at her, groaning something incoherent beneath his breath. *Don't want to*, I think, or something just as adorable. I smile at him. He shuts his eyes again and burrows close to me.

"Come on, Mr Shaw," she says again, all smiles, before a broad-shouldered man appears beside her to help haul my broken boy to standing.

"I'm tired," he says, but he's ignored, and they both lean down to help him up. We lock eyes before he stands, and some waking awareness comes back to him. Leo gives me a wink, like everything is okay and everything will be okay. I just smile back, watching him limp down the aisles with the woman's arms out to steady him.

I lie in that uneasy state between wakefulness and sleep for a handful of minutes before I decide I can't sleep any longer. I press myself up and look over to see that Victoria is gone from her spot, too.

The other two Hunters are still curled up around their cloaks. I stand and look out at the church where Don, Sutton, and Hayes are in the middle of training broken-looking townsfolk with a series of makeshift weapons. They're going through set drills, things I've learned only a couple of months ago. How to block. What to do when a greater force is bearing down on you. How to extricate yourself, how to dodge, what to do if you're down, what to do if you're disarmed. It's a deluge of information. Something that takes years to perfect.

The University's methods are growing weaker and weaker by the day. It is inevitable that any training at all will be a luxury.

There won't be much longer to worry.

I blink away the despondence and pull away from the scene before me. As preoccupied as I wish I was, I probably can't ignore her much longer.

I decide to seek out Victoria Bennet.

The deaconess informs me that she's made her way down into the crypt to see the wardstone 'for some reason'. For some reason—those are the deaconess' words.

"I just don't understand why a woman of her condition would walk all the way down there, especially if she's without God. If she believes the stone to be magic, well, subjecting a child to that. . ."

With the way she speaks, I believe Deaconess Margaret expects me to agree with her or, at the very least, engage in some type of conversation. I find it very hard to read her. She has all the markings of a religious woman and, in that regard, is recognisable and familiar to a boy like me. But in most other respects, she reminds me too much of a predator. I see in her a reflection of the University's strange *scylla* chapel: not the warm embrace of God, not the Lord that I once chose to love, but something else. Something fundamentally darker.

She seems symptomatic of the institution's corruption: the gangrenous limb on the Body of Christ, the stigmata rotting, an unhealable wound—all of which I believe are inevitable facets of the church now.

"Thank you," I say without engaging further, and I move away.

But then she says, "You're Christian, aren't you?"

The question throws me. I look back at her over my shoulder and see her standing there with an outstretched arm. A peace offering of sorts.

I turn around; I take the bait. I carry with me no rosary, no cross. I wonder what she sees in me that makes her say this. Whether she can smell it. Sense it. See it. Some holy aura, something that tells her I was like her once. It makes my skin crawl to think of a shared body, a shared identity.

I don't reply immediately. In fact, I take a moment to formulate a response, and as I'm struggling to explain the complexity of my faith, the deaconess takes my silence as admittance.

She says, "Yes, I thought you had the air about you, you know. Hope."

Comradery. She's reaching for it with me. Why?

To get to Leo. She didn't like his answer.

I could laugh. Although I thought I wouldn't engage with her, although I didn't want to, something in me snaps.

I feel an unnecessary amount of rage when I say, "I haven't been hopeful in quite a while, actually." I say it with learned politeness, an almost convulsive response to someone whose status I've been trained to respect. Even if I find her uncomfortable, my body reacts to her religious authority nearly as if she were divine herself. It feels like confession—is that what this is?

I think so. I think so even more when her lip quivers.

"If you are Christian, why do you concern yourself with a boy like Leo Shaw?"

My head spins. I'm not sure what she's implying, and I don't particularly care to know. If her greatest concern right now—with the *teras* bearing down on us, with battle a certainty come nightfall—is that Leo Shaw and I might do things to each other's bodies, then her priorities are exceptionally screwed. It's so very Christian of her. Still, that age-old fear sparks through me like I've been caught: the wrongness of it, the sinfulness, the blasphemy. Shame, shame, shame.

Stop it.

I make sure that thought can't take root.

"Love thy neighbour and all that," I say—a saying which is slowly becoming an aphorism. First Drike, now the deaconess. "Though from what Leo says, you've done a mighty poor job at following that commandment."

She blinks at me, and her eyes lose that friendly gleam. "Quite a corruptive force, the Shaw family is," she says. Her voice sounds like she's doing me a kindness. Like she believes she's helping me. "Sometimes, I don't know if I believe his story. What do you think?"

His story. His *story*—like it's something easily made up. The loss of his bloodline, everyone in his family slaughtered by the time he was sixteen. I swallow the other thought— that this vile woman knows the details where I don't—and I take a breath.

Who knows if she really doesn't believe Leo's story; who knows if knowing the truth would even change her mind about him. She dislikes the Shaws because that's apparently what people in Prittlewell do. But she hates Leo even more because of what he is. Who he is.

The deaconess is baiting me, and still, I want to ask, *what on earth could Leo Shaw have done to make you think that? How would loneliness benefit him in a world like this?*

But I don't trust her to answer me truthfully. She's just like Drearton. Just like all these authorities who have survived too long in this dying world.

I say, "On whose authority do you have the right to speak on corruption, when your own tongue betrays the morals that you claim to uphold?"

"Big words for such a young man," she says.

I snort. *What does youth have to do with it?* She wants my age to undermine the truth. She wants to discredit everything I say by pointing out that I'm only twenty.

"I'll be lucky if I last the year," I tell her. "At this point, I'm practically an old man."

Neither one of us says anything about her age and the anomaly of it, but I want her to realise the exceptionality. She is surrounded by fresh adults who have only just scrabbled out of the dangerous pit of childhood, a childhood fraught with war and blood and violence. Can't she see that has made us older? Disillusioned? Angry?

She wants her relevance, but she is a relic now. Perhaps I'll be one soon, too.

There's not enough time, and this isn't a hill I want to die on. Doesn't she understand that?

"Perhaps we would all benefit from your prayers," I whisper before I turn on my heel and make my way down the steps to the church's crypt.

Deaconess Margaret doesn't say another word.

There are three rooms down here: two offshoots to the left and right that house smaller chapels, and then the centre atrium. The air is dank and damp with that stagnant, dense feel to it. Air left too long to rot in stillness. Distantly, I can hear the dripping sounds of groundwater, which is unbecoming given the floor is tiled in a tessellated array of orange and cream. Is there a leak? Is there a way in? Suddenly, age and rot and decay frighten me. Can the wardstone be affected by erosion? By time itself?

The central nave displays a mosaic of Genesis. The word CREATION is detailed in black tiles, though the word has been made stilted and wonky by the hand who placed the tiles.

Several sconces line the halls, and all the candles are lit. The only other source of light, of course, is the wardstone.

It glows faintly and only at certain angles, as if the shell of it is iridescent, but really the light seems to be emanating from within. Veins glow intermittently and pulse through the stone. It is only about as tall as Leo, and is much, much smaller than the ones around London.

Victoria stands in front of it, her neck craning and her brows pressing together. If I could have captured that moment. . . She looks like a bastardised version of Mother Mary, a portrait of the Holy Virgin, haloed in unnatural blue light. The saint with child, frightened for her future.

Victoria stands with one arm bracing her back and the other draped gently over the rise of her belly. She hears me approach but doesn't look over. Eyes transfixed on the stone, she tells me dryly, "It's kicking."

Her tone surprises me. There's no excitement, but neither is there sadness. When Victoria speaks, her words sound flatly resigned to the point I can't tell what she feels about the child.

It's because it's you. This is a moment she should be sharing with the child's father.

Which isn't possible and therefore not helpful. Bellamy is dead.

The instant I get close to her, she turns to me and grabs my hand to place it wordlessly on her stomach. When I feel it

—when I feel the baby inside her jolting—a strange amalgam of feeling erupts in me.

"Oh, God," I say, and she smiles a little private smile. Maybe she's secretly happy that I find this horrible. Not the baby. Not Victoria. But this situation.

Here I am, responsible for the death of this baby's father, trapped with its mother in a church mile from London's safety, and I have the privilege of feeling it kick. Or the responsibility. This feeble life, this unexpected fighter. Nausea swarms me, and I think I might be sick. I try to pull my hand away, but Victoria holds it fast.

I can see her in my periphery, watching my expression and my reaction, and I am too cowardly to meet her eyes.

"Uncomfortable, are you?"

"Obviously," I whisper. I have the urge to say something cutting or mean. I want to ask her if she really thinks the baby will survive. If not the stress of its mother's injured, exhausted body, the reality of this world. I want to ask: *do you really think* you *will survive?*

Because that's another thing we haven't thought about yet. What will labour do to her? Does she want that?

I say none of it because Victoria doesn't want this moment to be about that. She wants me mildly uncomfortable, shifting my feet. But if she seeks an apology, she still won't get one. Really, if I had left her, then both her and this child would be dead instead of Bellamy.

I saved two lives that day.

I am not sorry for my choice.

We stand in silence for a moment, and I eventually give up trying to pull away, relaxing instead into the feel of Victoria's firm stomach and the occasional twitch of the thing inside her.

Then she says, "I'm uncomfortable too, sometimes. And I don't mean just physically. That much is obvious. I mean that it doesn't feel real, that I'm still here, that I'm forced to carry this thing. His child. Four or five months of it, now, I'm guessing. I don't know what I'm meant to feel about it, Cassius. I don't know what I meant to feel about *you*. Because I know when I sat up a few hours ago and I saw you sitting across from me—I saw you *here*, and I realised you'd come for us—the first thing I felt was relief. It was like I'd forgotten what you'd done. I woke up, and Bellamy was still alive, and I wasn't pregnant, and I was safe again because of you, because you'd come. And then I remembered, and I couldn't quite figure out if I should hate you. We both know you didn't come for me this time."

"That's not true—" I try to say. She just shushes me.

"I think you should cling on," she says, "as hard as you can, because we really don't have much time."

She takes my hand off her belly and looks down at the swollen rise, running her own fingers over the bump. "I can't believe it's still holding on," she says. "The stress, the lack of food, the horse riding, the fighting, the *teras*. I thought it would be gone by now."

I swallow. "Did you want to be gone by now?"

She pulls a face and looks up at the ceiling. "I think he would have hated it. Having a child, I mean. He wasn't, I mean, he wasn't going to be father-material, was he? He's too young. He *was* too young, and I'm...well, I guess it doesn't matter because I'm stuck with it now. But I do get scared. Not even about the birth, though that, honestly—I don't know if I'll survive it. No, I get scared that it will be a boy. I'm scared it will look like him more than it looks like me. I'm worried I will love it. Is that silly? Of course, I'll love it. I grew it, and loving it will be inevitable. But then I'm not sure because a part of me doesn't know if I'm keeping it out of love or hope or obligation or despair. And the pragmatic part of me, the realist thinks 'well, it's just a game now, isn't it? It's all a game'. We're all playing with borrowed time, and I probably won't even make it to labour. I probably don't have to worry about this at all. Yet as it gets closer and closer, the more it feels more inevitable, Cassius."

What does she want me to say?

Or is she hoping I stand here and say nothing, that I hear the confession like the statues in the church, the gargoyles perched high above? Does she want me without opinion, without agency, unable to even comment?

I say, "Victoria, what do you want from me?"

She scowls at me. "I could try to get rid of it now. I could ask you to hurt me. Hit me in the stomach, Cassius. Do it."

I stand there. We don't look away from one another.

She says, "Or I could cut it out, or I could find some herb that would do the job. But I think it's too big now. Isn't it? It's too big." Her eyes well with tears and her brow furrows; she's furious. "I worry it's like a parasite, and I'll lose myself to it. It will just eat me up from the inside out, just like its father." She cuts herself off in a high-pitched hiccup and squeezes her eyes shut. Both hands go to her swollen belly, and she presses down on it firmly. "God, that's mean of me."

She puts her head in both her hands, and this is so reminiscent of her breakdown beneath the willow tree that I curse myself for not seeing it sooner. She gets like this because she's even worse than me. She won't tell a soul what's wrong until it's too late.

Not that you ever ask. Too busy swallowing cock to give a shit.
Stop it.

I tell her, "If you don't want to keep it, we will find a way."

"We," she says, shaking her head. Her sigh is heavy and loaded. "It's just not that simple, Cassius, if you've been listening at all.

We lapse into silence.

I put my hand on her shoulder. She doesn't flinch away.

And because it's uncomfortable for me to sit in it, because I don't really want to feel what she's asking me to feel, I turn my attention to the wardstone. The size of it confounds me. It looks like a stunted growth, something that should have been much taller but failed somewhere, a plant that didn't get enough sunlight and is now withered and small. I realise I've never looked too closely at the wardstones surrounding London. They are colossi forms looming over us, so tall that they blend easily into the architecture and the wall protecting the city. I think my human mind puts more emphasis on the physical wall as the thing that keeps the *teras* at bay, but standing before this malformed crystal-like structure, I see, perhaps for the first time, the true magic in it. It is a grey stone, although the outside of it appears slightly transparent like a shell, beneath which I can see the rock veins shooting over one another in jagged intersections. Mystical geometries, all sense of which falls apart when I stare too long. The air around it thrums as if the stone is vibrating with infinitesimally small motions.

I think about touching it. Instead, I lower myself to the ground and squat, tilting my head to get a better look at where the growth emerges from the ground. Although the human-placed tiles around it are neat and cut at deliberate angles, the stone still looks as if it has ruptured out of the earth. Great cracks run through the floor around it, which tells me something about how the wardstone has changed since its emergence. Either it has grown, or whatever frequency it emits that protects us influences its surroundings. Has it emanated such power to break the tiles? The foundations? Could this thing bring the church down on top of us?

Anxiety is getting the best of me. I shake my head. Leo is right. The stone is properly rooted in the ground. I wouldn't be surprised if there were roots anchoring it or perhaps even feeding it. Whatever magic it draws upon, I suspect it must be in the earth. Pools of natural magic, deep beneath the ground, brewing away from human hands.

"There's no taking it," I whisper.

Victoria makes a noise. "No," she says and then sighs. "But that's not why I'm down here. The deaconess only wants to know because she's frightened, and besides—moving it would probably damage it anyway."

I glance back at her, rolling out of my squat position and standing. "Which might be what they want." I'm talking about the *teras*, of course, and the sentient rage that seems to be guiding them to destroy this wardstone. "Soon enough, this siege warfare will make someone snap, and suddenly, they'll be trying to haul this stone out of the earth thinking it will still protect them when it's on a cart."

I know this because I have been this desperate before. If I had learned about the existence of loose wardstones scattered about England when we lived in Hull, I know I would have tried to find one. I know my whole life would have been spent living around them. I know this because the stones are the reason we moved to London in the first place.

"They must be few and far between," Victoria says. "Not that I have much knowledge of life outside London, but surely we would have heard about it."

"Drearton would have killed that myth," I say.

She shrugs. "Probably. Who needs London if you find a wardstone to protect your family home."

"Maybe they are that small," I say, and nod down at the one before us. "Just big enough they can only protect one building, if that."

She rummages in the pocket of her Hunter cloak and flashes me her personal wardstone. "Or big enough for one person."

As if hearing us, something keens so loud outside that we

can hear it reverberate beneath the church itself, the sound scratching the walls of this dank, stuffy crypt. The haunting cry of a creature pulled from myth announces its arrival, and then, like the leagues of hell, I hear answering cries resound. Rumbling, howling, chittering, screaming.

The world seems to shake with the noise, and I realised we've misjudged this army.

Victoria and I turn to stare at one another. She seems almost unfazed, like this has been every night since her arrival here.

She glances down at her belly, then away. "Good luck," she tells me.

And I wonder if she hopes I'll die out there, just so we never have to have another of these awkward conversations again.

LESSON NINETEEN

I've just climbed the stairs out of the crypt when the slam of the tower trapdoor echoes throughout the church. Sutton rushes back into the church's body, storming through the central nave.

"Can't see much," she announces, out of breath. She gestures her head towards Hayes, who is stalking up from the opposite end. "Vision's shit. But they're everywhere, surrounding the place. I can just feel it."

She puts her arm out and shows us the goose-bumped flesh, hairs electric and standing on end.

"Anything tried to swipe at you?" Hayes asks.

Sutton rolls her sleeves back down. "Wasn't up there for that long. I'm not sure how close they can get."

Hayes sniffs and nods. "How many will you station up there?" he asks, eyes rolling over the huddled mass of towns-folk, all clutching their makeshift weapons close to their chest.

"Only three," Sutton says. "Two have archers' blood, or so they claim. They have sturdy bows, well taken care of, and they've hunted—just rabbits. Food. Another man claims to have used a bow once as a child, and so be it. They're willing, and they're the best we have. The deaconess offered the church's hunting bow, and he took it up. If they die, at least the weapons won't be difficult to reclaim."

My stomach drops. I glance over to the pews and see two men testing their bows, pulling the string taut, bending and stretching to accommodate the force. Beside them, a man watches. But he's my age. He's a boy in the right lighting, a boy when the wispy moustache is shaved. I know he'll be a boy when the *teras* attack; I can already hear his scream.

I look away. "That one seems young," I whisper and hope there's enough weight in what isn't said so I can be a coward and not tell Sutton what I really think.

She glares at me. "He's University age."

"He looks like a weasel," I say. "How's he survived out here this long?"

"Had three brothers." Wamsley appears out of nowhere. He's chewing on a piece of stale bread, which he offers to me. I take it, too hungry to be picky, and attempt to gnaw at the corner. Part of it is damp already with Don Wamsley's saliva, a new level of intimacy for us. Wonderful.

Wamsley continues oblivious. He picks at his teeth. "Died in Southend to the *nuckelavee*."

Hayes folds his arms. "Told you that, did he?"

"No, but no one's shut up about it. Everyone's a gossip. You're just not paying attention, Hayes."

Hayes grimaces, and we all turn back to Sutton, who shrugs.

"It's the best we can do."

"Come on," Wamsley says. He takes the bread off me—I managed a single, uncomfortable bite—and stuffs the hard slab in his cloak. Then he fishes for his gun and picks up a simple hammer he'd placed on a pew. I'm surprised to see him raring at the bit, but he looks genuinely excited. Perhaps the knowledge of a safe haven so close fills him with a needed confidence—he could retreat at any point. Slip back over the threshold of the church and be made safe. How true that will be in practice remains to be seen.

I am surprisingly calm. After finding Leo, I think nothing else really matters. All the panic and upset of the last days is muted behind the haze of sheer relief, and now, even if my logical mind is thinking, "Cassius Jones, you might die," another part thinks, "So what?"

But I at least don't want to walk straight to my death. I take stock.

"I'm out of bullets," I lie, flashing Thaddeus'—my—flint-lock. I have two iron balls left. Wordlessly, Hayes gives me three that he pulls from his pocket, all of them prewrapped and ready for the chamber.

"Part of the communal stash," he tells me, pointing vaguely to the right. "But I would recommend finding a different weapon."

I nod. I have my dagger at my side, and I take the time to recoat it in my second and final vial of the paralysing poison. Still, I choose to take Hayes' advice, not willing to waste the stuff on the first *teras* to get the best of me.

Hayes points me towards the back of the church where I see gruff, exhausted-looking men rummaging through a pile of makeshift weapons not yet claimed by others. A few women stand with kitchen knives, fireplace stokers and cast-iron pans clutched to their chests. They talk in low tones.

"Well, you'll take care of Mary if something happens. I'll take care of Stephen."

"Okay," another woman says with a nod. "Okay, that's fair."

They clutch each other. Someone starts to cry.

If there is a commonality between all these people, it is the exhaustion. Their eyes sunken and lifeless, skin pallid as if sick, and I recognise the bone tiredness that has whittled these people down to nothing but rage. The quiet kind, the one that simmers, a low burning fire. It is the only fuel they have that keeps them going.

I can see how broken they are. They would have to be, to risk their lives, to choose weapons and stand fast, even after hearing the choral cries of the *teras* waiting for us in the dark.

The plan, as I understand it, is this. Us Hunters will go first. We will call for reinforcements if or when we need them.

We hope not to need them, but I know we will.

I say nothing to any of the gathered townsfolk, but I do nod at them, hoping to share a brief bit of camaraderie without lying. I refuse to tell them it will be alright. I refuse to promise that I can protect even just one of them, and I am grateful when no one asks me to make those promises.

I take out another fireplace poker and test the weight of it in my hand. Good. Sturdy. Dense enough to bludgeon and maybe to stab with from afar. The dagger will have to be for close quarters. The gun. . . I'm not even sure if I'll use it. The *teras* are close, packed around us, and a gun might do nothing to help in such chaos.

I draw the hunter cloak tighter around my body, and I turn and join the others by the front door.

But I don't know where the horses are. I was too preoccupied with Leo to think about it. But if they're injured or gone, we're stuck here.

"If they killed the horses," I say, but Hayes shakes his head.

"The deaconess says the stables are protected."

I imagine the poor things out there, getting hounded all night. Smelling blood, traumatised by the noise.

"Let's just make this quick," I say.

I do one last check before Hayes and Sutton open the

door. Inevitable adrenaline blisters in my gut, and my heart rate quickens.

I have with me my flintlock gun pre-loaded with a single bullet. The other four roll about in my pocket. I have the sparker, the *manticore* dagger strapped to my hip, and a fire stoker in my right hand.

"Tactics?" I prompt. "Any plan whatsoever?"

Sutton says, "Hayes and I will go left. You two go right. The side doors to the church are unlocked. We retreat there if anything happens—not to the front. If we're overwhelmed, call for the deaconess. The townsfolk will attempt to help. But start small and keep the search area manageable."

I can't help but imagine how it will happen. The *teras* will lure us out, deeper and deeper. We call for aid, and it comes to us. We are cut off from the church immediately when the *teras* swarm around the reinforcements.

"They will try to lure us out," I make sure to say. "Don't take the bait."

Sutton nods.

"I'll protect you," Wamsley says with a wink.

"Then you can go first," I say with a wink of my own.

His shit-eating grin crumples, and his throat visibly bobs as he turns towards the door.

Hayes and Sutton nod at one another and shoulder the door open. The cold night air wells into the church with a whistling howl.

All the candles at the entrance are blown out.

The night air is bitter and suddenly deathly quiet. No insects, no animals, no rustling. Not even the chittering of *teras*. There is only an uncomfortable silence, one that feels heavy and false. My body reacts like it can tell the difference between the calm of a quiet night and whatever lie this is. Instantly, my hands are clammy, and sweat pricks at the back of my neck, lower back, and chest. My heart tightens, and I brace myself instinctively, my mind searching the shadows and finding silhouettes every second. Jolts of fear run through me at each imagined shape.

Get yourself together, Jones.

I know they want to lure us out. What better way than to stay quiet, hoping we will edge out of the safety of the church. We don't know how far the wardstones' protection extends, but since the injured Hunter said he'd heard scratching at the doors, I imagine it ends the instant we cross the threshold.

Sutton leans down beside the entrance where several horse lanterns are stacked, having been stripped from the mounts. She passes me one and gestures for me to string it about my neck for the light. It's a beacon but a necessary one. This isn't like the *barghest*—there are too many *teras* for us to give up the advantage of sight.

"Wear it," she says, "and stay close to Wamsley."

I nod, and then there's nothing left to do but step into the night.

I take the sparker out of my left pocket and raise it high, poised to blind whatever comes at us. Wamsley steps out of the doorway, and I flank him, pressing close.

Instantly, the air changes. There's a heavy sense of expectation, the night thick with bodies and creatures and eyes.

"I can feel them," Wamsley says. His voice shakes.

I press my hand to his upper back in a quiet display of agreement.

We both instinctively begin to lower ourselves, finding a centre of gravity where we can move defensively. The ground shifts beneath my feet, grass giving way to the squish of mud beneath. The soles of my shoes aren't so well textured anymore, worn away by overuse. One slip and it's death.

A resonant cry booms somewhere, deep amongst the stretch of grass and hills. Prey instinct flares to life in my body. Agitation sets me alight, and I am breathing heavily, flinching against the sound that vibrates in my chest; this haunting, abyssal howl threaded with sonority as it echoes around us. Disoriented, I fling myself about searching for the source. Just one? One *teras*?

"Don't," Wamsley murmurs. *Don't fall for it.*

Immediately, that first cry is matched. *Yip-yip-yip.*

A high-pitched chittering is drowned out by a triumphant squawk somewhere to our left, and then it is a chaotic chorus.

A gun goes off, cracking through the air. The sky lights up in a bright flash of light. Hayes yells.

Wamsley spins back to me, shaking. "Cassius, I think—"

Something sends him hurtling to the ground. I see it in a flash, a dark shape smothering his form, and then he is prone. He screams. Another shot booms as Wamsley fires; a flash of white illuminates the dark, and his bullet spins uselessly to the right over the *teras'* shoulder. In that tiny bit of visibility, I note Wamsley's other hand is pinned to the ground, and a *harpy* crushes his chest. It trills and screams, raising its taloned foot to Wamsley's chest.

In my mind, a flash of my own wound—the blood, the spray, the vivisection—urges me forward. I kick the *harpy* square in the back. Its scream gurgles in its throat, and it whips its head around towards me. The horse lamp offers only a soft glow, an orange haze, and in that light, I see the *teras'* fury. It goes to dive at me when Wamsley rolls, arms locking around the creature's torso. He crushes it into the ground, and the noise of outrage and panic from the *harpy* shrieks through the air.

I don't see what happens next because several things break from the tree line. *Chimera.* Several *cerastes* wriggle over the earth.

A whole horde. My mind blanks. I don't know what to do

first. I make several aborted motions, raising the fire stoker and then the sparker. In amongst the chaos, I press the sparker in my left hand, and white light blinds me. A chorus of shocked and angry screams squawk around me, clarions shrilling for revenge, for food, for death.

But my vision swims with white dancing lights, and it's only the noise of bodies moving along the grass that alerts me to the attack. I swing low with the stoker and meet flesh. The dull thud of iron against a body becomes a squeal, and my eyes clear in time to see a *cerastes* thrown across the field from the force of my strike.

The sudden stench of rot clogs my nostrils, and I look to my right to see the oozing entrails of the *harpy*, Wamsley stabbing over and over into its exposed belly. The creature dies unceremoniously, open mouth exhaling the stench of days-old flesh. Wamsley groans; he's covered in blood. But the other creature has pressed forward.

I turn back to face the *chimera*.

My scholarly mind summons what I know. I recall Homer's *Iliad,* which describes it as *a thing of immortal make, not human, lion-fronted and snake behind, a goat in the middle, and snorting out the breath of the terrible flame of bright fire.*

I step back. All three heads bulge from the flesh of the torso. The lion head is bulbous and familiar, sporting that same uncanny weight and power as the *Nemean.* The goat head is poorly supported. It bleats and shouts, neck floppy; the head rolls side to side, trying to assess its prey. The snake tail culminates in the last vicious head, which spits at me as the *chimera* sizes me up.

Coughing and retching, the thing begins to stumble forward. I know what's about to happen, and I back up fast until I feel the cold stone of the church pressing against me.

The *chimera* vomits flame and the ground roasts. Sudden, blinding light. The intensity makes me squeeze my eyes shut, and I spin to shield my face. It's so hot that even the damp grass sizzles and catches. When I risk a glance, the sudden visibility shocks me. I can see twenty meters ahead, thirty, further. I can see the horde, the army. At least fifty *teras* on the ground. Probably more lurking. The fire makes a temporary wall, holding them at bay.

And flush with the shadows, body creaking distantly, I think I see it.

Vengeance.

The *chimera* screams at me, demanding my attention. Terrified, I pull my eyes from Vengeance's gravity. The *chimera's* body convulses and storms forward, lion head snapping. The goat head bleats in panic, and its snake head, which emerges like a tail off the distended creature, hisses viciously at me. Wamsley scrabbles up and rushes to my side so he and I can face it together. The snake head snaps out in Wamsley's direction, and I have no time to see his reaction, for the rest of the body launches at me.

Giant lion paws swipe down. Distantly, I remember this beast is related in some way to the *Nemean Lion*—in myth, not just in its appearance. For some reason, that truth makes my brain betray me. I don't know what happens, but it happens quickly. My mind is overwhelmed by a vision.

Bellamy on the ground, trying to stand up. His leg torn away from his torso. He looks up at me, eyes bulging in their sockets, shot through with veins. "Cassius," he says. "Cassius, don't, please don't—"

Pain shakes me back into reality. I scream. Claws have swiped down my chest, and blood oozes free of the wounds, pooling black on my Hunter's cloak. I stumble back and swing wildly with the fire stoker. The iron cracks over the lion's face, and the force shudders up my arm, blow landing with a dull crunch that has all three heads screaming. The *chimera's* whole body recovers in time for the goat head to register as something hurtles down towards it. Wamsley's hammer comes down through the air in a whizzing rush. The goat bleats, terrified, eyes wide and tongue quivering through its shout.

The hammer crushes its skull.

Blood and brain matter explode out of the eye sockets and the tongue lolls dead out of the mouth. The neck goes limp and the remaining two heads scream in terror and referred pain. The creature dashes backwards, but not before the snake head can spit venom in Wamsley's direction. The spray of it touches the knuckles on his right hand, and he drops the hammer in open surprise, shouting as the skin bubbles and lifts. His scream becomes brutal. I catch a glimpse of white bone in my periphery, yellow fat bubbling and dripping away down the flesh of his hand. Wamsley begins to crumple to his knees, and I have to turn away. The *chimera* is close enough that I think I can aim. I drop the sparker, fish around for the flintlock, and push every other thought out of my head. Once raised and aimed, I send the bullet flying towards the lion's head. Before I've even registered whether or not I've hit it, I rush forward and whack it across the face with the fire poker. I don't let up even as I hear the sounds of other *teras* around me. I bring the steel down again and again on the lion's cheek until I feel the bones break from the force, until the jaw dislodges and bone puckers through the flesh, gleaming white amongst the bloody, fatty viscera.

The lion's scream becomes a gurgling, upset roar that chokes in its throat. The paws flex on the ground, twitching, turfing up the soil as it struggles. Its rapid breathing causes the torso to pulse violently and then it's only the snake tail that's still alive. The rest of the body shuts down slowly, half crumbling. The limbs go heavy, and that small brain of the final head tries to move. Legs trip over themselves. The heavy bulk of the lion crashes into the ground, lower end upright as the snake hisses and whips about, spitting venom every way it turns.

Wamsley screams and rushes close, smashing his hammer across its face.

The thing dies and slumps, but we barely have time to recover.

"My fingers!" Wamsley is screaming. "My fingers! It took my fucking fingers!"

"At least they're cauterised!" I shout back, and he bares his teeth at me, sweat coating his cheeks with shiny streaks.

The next wave of *teras* comes forward.

From somewhere I can't see, Sutton cries out, "*Barghest!*"

My heart thuds in my chest. If we are caught by that thing, none of our wounds will heal. Several *teras* are spitting and screeching behind the wall of fire summoned by the now dead *chimera*, but the fire is slowing. Soon enough, they'll be able to cross it, and another battle will ensue.

I see a dark shape fly over the flame and head to Wamsley. It tackles him to the ground. I go to turn to him—and shudder.

"Oh. Don't look at me like that."

I go completely still. What am I looking at? What am I seeing? This isn't—this can't be—

"For fuck's sake, Cassius. Pull yourself together."

But I can't. I can't move. I can't think. Because it's Thaddeus. It's my brother. And not my brother how I left him, not with strings of his intestines looping in the snow, not with death and the smell of his guts exposed to the world, but as I knew him.

He is dressed in his Hunter garb, large tricorn hat drawn low over his eyes, shadowing his face but not obscuring the gleam of his expression, the searching bitterness, that look of inquiry he always had for me. He looks disappointed, upset, and frustrated, all of which were looks he had in his repertoire. It seems some tricks last through death.

The battle continues around us, but I am oblivious to everything happening. Logic tells me to put another bullet in the flintlock.

You know it can't be him. You know that he's dead.

But why couldn't there be ghosts? Out of everything that came through the rift, every myth, legend, folktale, why could there not be ghosts among them?

I wet my lips. "Is it you?"

Thaddeus scoffs. He pushes away the side of his cloak to reveal the very same flintlock I have in my right hand.

"Stop looking at me. Pay attention. God, I haven't been gone a year, and you've already forgotten everything." He says it all as he fiddles with the flintlock, adjusting the hammer, inspecting the barrel.

I take the opportunity to move, slipping my hand into the pocket of my cloak. My remaining bullets are prepared, wrapped in papers. They crinkle under my touch as I pluck one out and, without pulling my eyes away from my brother's ghost, I pop it into the gun.

Thaddeus scoffs at me. Finally, he looks up.

"What is it, Cassius?" he says, drawling. "Been too busy getting your asshole fucked to learn anything useful? Did I die for your cheeks to be spread? For you to be used on University couches?"

I breathe deep, pull back the hammer, and shoot my brother between the eyes.

Thaddeus' eyes go wide with shock, pupils expanding. He hadn't expected it. Before the body crumples, it transforms, flickering away to reveal nothing more than a tiny humanoid creature. I don't know its name, but there are plenty of shapeshifters in folklore. The *gytrash*. The *hedley kow*. I stare at it. I think I will vomit.

"*Cassius!*"

I half turn towards the sound of my name when something knocks me to the ground. My lungs contract, and all the air is blown out.

Weight bears down on my chest, and I begin to writhe instinctively. Panic sets in when the smell of rot and fetor fills my own screaming throat. A black dog, a possible hybrid: big teeth gnashing, its eyes aflame with the reflection of the dying *chimera* fire. I struggle beneath it, pushing helplessly back as it chomps towards my neck. I push. I try to fight it; my arms press weakly against the force of it. I wrap my hands around its thick neck and squeeze, hoping to choke it, and then all I'm doing is keeping its teeth from my throat. Thick claws tear at my thighs and belly. The old scars left by the *harpy* begin to sting. I think this will be the time my gut is truly and irrevocably opened.

And then my shoulder gives way. There's just suddenly no fight left in it. The muscles are exhausted. There's nothing I can do. I am still kicking, I'm still screaming, but nothing is able to prevent the sheer strength of the hound as it shoves past my defences and buries its teeth into my right shoulder.

My vision goes white with pain. It's blinding, immediate, and not even shock is enough to blunt it.

I start hitting the *teras* with the only thing left: my prosthetic. I curl my left arm and use the fist to bash the side of the dog's head. It begins to whine and growl, and then it shakes. Its teeth sink further into the flesh of my shoulder. Hot blood pours out over my skin, which goes sticky with it. I change tactics, riding what little adrenaline I have left before I allow myself to die. I move from punching the side of the head to smashing my fingers against the bared teeth.

The open snout means I have access. I throw my weight

behind every punch. Tears are in my eyes, but the shock has set in now, burning away the raw ache of the flesh wound.

I feel the first tooth dislodge as a sudden stoppage to the force of my punch, so I drive my fist forward again and again. A crack sounds and then a shattering. At once, both its teeth and my fingers crumble. The ivory cracks along my arm, porcelain splintering instantly. From the force of my punches against the hound's teeth, the forefinger and the middle finger come apart and fall into the hound's bloody maw.

I am left with jagged edges just below the knuckle, and I stab them again and again into the hound's neck. The dog breaks off my shoulder. At least two teeth are left behind as it rips its face away and screams.

The howl splits the air, and I am momentarily shaken. I don't even try to push it off me. I let the moment pass, and I'm going to die when it recovers. All at once, the hound's cry becomes a pitched whine, a shocked squeak interposed with bone splintering and the squish of the brain and then —silence.

Brain matter leaks from the ears and the nose, mashed and thick, the consistency like undigested vomit. The smell is borderline rot, undercut by a musty metallic tone.

I don't realise I'm panicking until the dog is dead. It collapses onto me, and the sheer weight of it begins to strangle me. My cheeks are wet and my shoulder throbs, the adrenaline and the shock wearing off and no longer numbing it. I need to get out from underneath it. I begin to struggle and push. The brain matter slops onto my neck and face. I'm sure I eat some of it; I taste it, creamy, buttery, but still gamey—the metallic, salty inevitability of any organ. Perhaps it's the heat from the fire, but I think it's dissolving in my mouth.

I hear someone grunting from the other side. Two voices, maybe. I kick and squirm and keep my mouth shut, desperate to prevent any other fleshy material from falling inside. The dead eyes stare at me, clouding slowly, the reflected fire fogging up as death takes hold.

"One. Two—"

The weight is lifted, and all the air rushes back into my lungs. Breathing hurts like the air is searing the inside of my lungs. I cough and roll onto my side, scrabbling backwards even as my shoulder aches.

My eyes adjust. Wamsley stands panting. He kicks the carcass. Some other dead *teras* lies to his right.

But the other voice, of course, belongs to Leo Shaw.

"Darling," he says. "What would you do without me?"

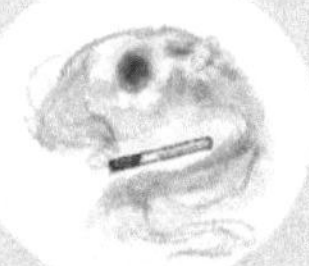

❧ 20 ❧

LESSON TWENTY

In the end, there's no time for romance. Leo rushes forward and drags me back towards the church even as he grunts. His abdomen presses to the back of my skull as he drags, arms loped underneath mine. My prosthetic hangs shattered, and the flesh near the join aches, but most of my attention is on my bloody shoulder. I can feel my jaw spasm with the force with which I hold it. Every moment of the drag aches—until I feel the wet warmth of blood pooling at the back of my head.

I didn't land on my head. It's not my blood.

Leo's stitches are splitting apart.

I exhale, upset. "What are you doing?" I cry. "Leo, stop. You're hurting yourself."

He doesn't answer at first, only grunts low with the effort of pulling me backwards. My shoulder is on fire, the pain searing where teeth have ripped my flesh asunder. I pull out of his grip and struggle back, trying to get my bearings. He's yanked me back to the centre. The church doors sit behind us. The *chimera's* fire is to the right, and Sutton and Hayes must be to my left.

The fire is beginning to fade, and a new wave of *teras* begins to push forward through the embers.

"Go back inside," I tell him.

"How dare you tell me what to do," he says playfully. He's not looking at me. He keeps re-adjusting the weapon in his hand, flexing and unflexing around the metal rod.

"Please," I say. My voice cracks. "'m ashamed of how desperate I sound, but I don't want him out here. Not now. Especially not now.

I watch his expression when the howling starts up again, the chittering chorus of happy monsters, gleeful as they march towards us. He does not falter. Not an ounce of fear flashes over his face. I wonder, as I often do, what he's seen to make him so jaded. I even start to believe him. *Maybe he knows what he's doing. He got this far. He's seen enough. He can fight.*

But then the deep call sounds. Both our bodies react and react poorly. The sound is old, low, and resonant, closer to drowning wind than noise. A chord vibrates through the ground, feeling like tremors beneath the Earth. My body shakes. I have the urge to run. I can't hold a weapon in my right hand—it's useless. I'm useless. My prosthetic is destroyed. I have the spiked remains of my forearm, and that's it. The helplessness douses my mind.

Leo is no different. He looks pale and unwell. He places a tentative hand against his belly, where blood has already seeped through his blacks. He shuts his eyes, and his brows crash together. Hesitantly, he takes a step back to the church.

I know he sees it too when he sleeps. I know he dreams of that thing in the woods, Silas' headless body, the flattened leg still attached in tendon ropes to Fred's body.

"Cassius," he says. I hate hearing him like this. I hate it.

"I know."

"Talk to it," he says. "Say something. Maybe you—maybe you can stop this."

Who's speaking now is that new version of him, the one that's scared and small, the little boy I've never met until now. Leo seems to realise that his fear has broken through. His cheeks go red with shame, and he shakes his head and steps forward to meet the crowd of *teras* coming up beside Wamsley.

"Leo," I murmur, and then someone cries to my left.

Sutton's voice is high and strained. "Oh, God, oh, God, oh, God," she says over and over again. She drags Hayes out of the shadows, and as she does, church dwellers surge out of the church to take their place. No need to call upon them—they've chosen.

"You're okay, you're okay," Sutton is saying.

I scream, "Victoria!"

She appears in the doorway and casts over the scene, eyes wide. But when she focuses on Hayes, her expression shifts, and she nods. "Bring him in," she says, gesturing to Sutton to haul him over the threshold.

As the rest of the makeshift soldiers pour out in a throng, the sounds of fighting escalate. Steel on flesh, the occasional crack of a bullet splitting the air, cries both human and monstrous, screeching through the night.

"Stop this," I say quietly under my breath. I envision Vengeance in my mind's eye. I tried to speak to it. *Stop this. Stop it.* But why would it? It wants destruction. It wants vengeance—on humanity. On everyone complicit. And none of us is innocent.

"*Claude!*"

Stop, in Latin.

The voice is unfamiliar. It booms with such force behind it, such authority, that even I stop breathing. The fight continues for half a second before a kind of cry goes out—a neutral sound, like a pitched hiss—and then the scrabbling stops. There's an uneasy moment where the townsfolk stand there shivering, weapons pointed, and the army of *teras* bare their bloody mouths in frightening grins.

Then, they turn. It's an immediate shift. All the *teras* spin, bodies whipping around and dashing back into the shadows. I do not see Vengeance, but I feel its presence fading. The air becomes lighter. The ambient creaking stops.

The world feels like itself again.

We don't move for a long while. All of us are locked in anticipation, bodies hunkered low to the ground as we expect the next onslaught. It doesn't come. Not for minutes. Not at all.

"Inside!" the deaconess shouts and this booming cry is what breaks the spell.

The townsfolk chatter. There's a quiet, non-committal cheering that peters out and dies before it's really begun. Most head back to the church, but some lean down and strip what they can from the dead *teras*.

I overhear a few debating whether or not to eat the flesh of the dead monsters. The morality of it, of consuming Satan's creatures. The desperation of the hunger overriding old opinion. I don't pay much attention, though, because my body is still locked up with fear.

Leo looks back at me. "Was that you?"

When I shake my head, his eyes go wide. He flinches, half turning around. "Did you hear that?"

Footsteps. The sound of twigs snapping underfoot. Something heavy trotting through the brush. Wamsley, Leo, and I get close, all braced as we face the direction of the sound.

"Get inside, you idiots," Wamsley hisses to the people still scrounging for scraps. They get up and rush inside. One carries the carcass of a dead *cerastes*.

Out of the shadows trots a mounted rider.

I freeze immediately. *Nuckelavee*—it's here. It made no appearance in the battle, but I realise now it must have been biding its time. I make a strained noise and cast about. Fresh water. I need fresh water. It's the only thing that deters it.

Leo's hand shoots out to my arm and prevents me from moving. "Wait."

My nostrils flare. The skin around my eyes feels too fine, suddenly, like it's weak to the elements. Everything in me aches, and Leo still clutches his stomach, and I am thinking about the skin around my eyes.

The rider resolves, and I realise they really are human, mounted on a horse. This alone confounds me, but then I look further. Their horse looks well-cared for, brushed, fed, and watered, which strikes me as significant because very few outposts have horses so healthy. The bridle, the saddle—it's more than well cared for. It's a London horse.

It must be.

But as my eyes raise up to the rider's face, I know it can't be. This person—this strange amalgam—cannot be from London. I know this because of how they are dressed, and it's not the cloak that grabs my attention, for it is as bland as any other travelling Macintosh, but it's what this person wears on their face.

They wear a mask that's malformed and patchwork. The dried skin of *teras* plucked free of feather and scale has been pulled taut across both eyes. Tufts of *harpy* feathers fan above both brows in symmetry, and fur lines the whole thing, a maroon red, like *manticore* fur. The lower half of the mask is leather, still its natural tan colouring. Scales have been sewn delicately over the leather in certain places, like baubles for decoration. At once, I'm struck by the mastery of the design and confronted by the fear that I feel upon seeing it. *Unholy*, a voice inside me squeaks. *Unholy and blasphemous.*

This is a cultist. A rider from the Cult of the Rift.

I watched most members driven out in the dean's first purge before my final trial confronting the *manticore* in Sherwood Forest. What feels like a moment ago, I watched several members executed in bloody ritualism, stragglers left in hiding.

I do not understand these people. That's the first thought that strikes me now. At first, I don't even question how or why the *teras* have left at the command of this cultist. I can't comprehend it, and so my mind focuses on the most tangible problem: who the fuck is behind that mask, and what do they want with us now?

Leo stands up straight. He storms forward without any pause or worry and gestures at the rider, finger punctuating every word as he drives it through the air. "You vulture. These people are townsfolk. They're hungry. I know you cultists take the remains of *teras*. I know you'll want some of these carcasses, but both Southend and Prittlewell haven't eaten in fucking weeks!"

The rider says, "I'm not here for the *teras*."

Leo pauses and lowers his arm. He glances back at me. His open cheek exposes his teeth, which glint under the moonlight. I look between him and Wamsley.

I say, "Don, check on Victoria, see what you can do to help."

The man bristles and flashes a look towards me. "But—"

"Please."

He kicks the dirt and sighs, but he at least sulks off in the direction of the church entrance.

I take a moment to watch him as if I'm worried for his well-being when in reality, I'm trying to breathe through the nausea and the fear that's sprung up in me. As the adrenaline from the battle wears off, I feel a rush of suppressed emotion flood my system—and pain, too. My prosthetic is completely destroyed. When I try to flex what remains of my fingers, I'm hit twofold: first by the ache near the join, and then by the memory. The ghost outline of my old arm burns suddenly. I can feel it hurting, like it's been the thing torn asunder by *teras* teeth rather than the flesh of my shoulder.

It's not real. Breathe. You need to focus on the cultist.

The truth is, I don't want to focus on the cultist. I don't want another complication; I want something in this world to be easy.

But Leo is waiting for me. He clears his throat politely. "Mr Jones?" he mumbles.

I turn back to him with a smile and get as close as I can without obstructing either of our hands. I refuse to let go of my weapon—but I want to feel him.

"What *are* you here for, then?" I ask the rider as soon as I'm settled by Leo's side.

The rider's horse senses something and whinnies uneasily. The light from the horse's lamp and my own dance along the ground. The rider mutters something—nothing to soothe the horse—and begins to slip the mask from their face.

Wait. Wait. I don't know why that word comes to mind, but I am suddenly chanting it. The moment stretches achingly long as the patchwork monstrosity is peeled from the face. I don't want to know because I already do.

Leo gasps beside me, then scoffs. His grip on his weapon goes slack.

But I tighten mine. Lying, selfish twat. How—and why— and *what is going on?*

"I'm here to get you back home alive," the cultist says.

And the person beneath the mask is Fred Lin.

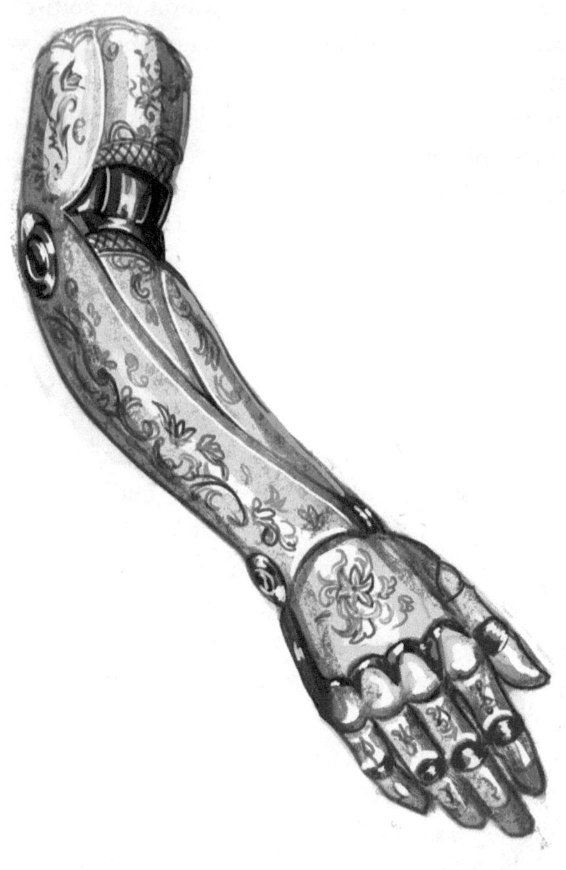

LESSON TWENTY-ONE

"Don't have much in the way of luxuries here. But it's the best we can do."

The deaconess sounds different as she stands before Fred Lin, her knees soft and her body half bent in a non-committal genuflection.

Word of Fred's interference in the battle has spread throughout the church already; she has been made a legend in a moment. Now, the people of Southend and Prittlewell have scrounged through their stores and found something—a true gesture of good faith.

A thimble-sized serving of rum.

My mouth waters, tastebuds jealous for some kind of numbing hit. Laudanum. Alcohol. Fuck it—I've been so very good. I rummage in my pocket and pull out the cigarette case Leo gifted me. I've only had a handful—six, maybe?—since he gave it to me. I count them out roughly; fourteen left. Okay. Plenty. That's plenty.

Leo leans over to me. "You kept it," he whispers.

"It's cigarettes, Leo; of course I kept it," I murmur back, but I'm flushing like he can somehow see how I've cherished this. How difficult it became to look at this when I didn't know if he was alive.

He says nothing, so I meet his eye. I think about being truthful, but it's hard to speak. I reach out for his hand and squeeze it once, hoping I can convey in that brief touch that I missed him. *God, I am so grateful...*

I pull away and strike a match along the stone floor to light the cigarette, inhaling tobacco laced with stale incense and God's judgement. I can feel Him watching.

When I look, though, it's only the deaconess. Her glower is impressive.

"How dare you," she seethes.

I want to tell her my relationship with God is my own, that I can't begin to unpick the complexities of it myself, let alone explain it to someone who clearly hates me.

Her eyes crinkle as she assesses me, and I choose to stare defiantly back at her whilst smoking my cigarette, which certainly dulls the calming sensation I was hoping it would muster.

But it is at least funny.

"What do you think you're doing?" she says. Her voice has a quaver in it that tells me she believes in reverence for the church and that it's not just for God. She's become part of this place, I guess. Perhaps she's furious at my defiance of her authority.

You have no idea...

I say nothing, but a short laugh still escapes my mouth. The deaconess baulks, horrified, and Leo leans forward, tilting his head with a grin.

"I promise you," he says, "Cassius has done much worse things in a church than this."

Cheeky bastard.

I resist the urge to slap him and continue smoking my cigarette. Everyone else is watching us, watching this display with the interest of a quietly desperate crowd. Like a waiting horde at a gladiatorial stadium hoping for a blood bath. Here is the scene: Leo's stitches have ripped open. I saw briefly the smooth, glossy flesh of an intestine before Victoria stitched him up again. She herself is very pale, the lone Healer in a sea of wounded people. A few of the townsfolk have tried their hand at wrapping wounds, and Don Wamsley is doing his idiot best, offering water to people recovering. The flesh of the fingers on his right hand are gone. The knucklebones peek out of the skin, and the remaining flesh is blackened. He has the hand bandaged up, but still decides to work. I know he's the type to enjoy distraction.

At the sight of Fred Lin walking over the church threshold, Victoria stopped everything.

It is the four of us and the deaconess bundled up in the sanctuary whilst other wounded townsfolk are scattered in amongst the pews or laid out on the floor.

The battle was neither a victory nor a great loss. A handful of the people from Prittlewell and Southend died. Sutton is alive, and Hayes is, too—for now. A great gash of a wound has cut down his sternum. We aren't sure what's done it. But if it was a *barghest*, he won't be long for this world.

All this to say: Fred Lin is here, and I wish she wasn't.

Call me petty; I don't care. I asked her to come—I fucking begged her. I needed help to save Leo, and she turned me down.

But now—now she's here, speaking Latin, communicating with the *teras*, and wearing a mask that signifies she is not quite on our side.

"Thank you," Fred says, interrupting the silence to take the cup of rum from the deaconess' hand. She won't look at any of us, but she stares down into that stormy liquid with melancholic intensity.

"Well?" Victoria asks. When Fred doesn't say anything, Victoria glances up at the deaconess.

"Deaconess Margaret," Victoria murmurs sweetly. "Would you mind giving us all a moment to catch up?"

The air shifts around us. Barely concealed rages flicker momentarily across the deaconess' face, hard lines forming over her forehead. Abruptly, they're smoothed back out again. She pats her apron down and nods stiffly. "Why, of course," she says, tone cracking as she slips past us. The sound of her shoes clacking over the marble bounds until they become just another noise, blending with the moans of the injured and chatter of the survivors.

We wait for a minute in silence. Fred swirls the liquor around in her cup and sips gently at it. She makes no reaction when the liquor touches her tongue. God, she seems different.

Fred already told me that, though.

Well, she died in the snow with her brother. I am someone different.

I wonder how true that is.

She still isn't speaking, like this is some game. *Perhaps she's anxious*, the good part of me thinks. Well, fuck that.

She had plenty of time to do the right thing.

Into the silence, I speak. "You refused to come."

I say it because I'm petty, and because I'm angry, and because I want the others to know Fred wilfully abandoned them. Not me. I came—I came as soon as I could. But Fred comes not as our friend, but as something else. An envoy.

And an envoy for whom? The cult? The *teras*?

This, at least, gets her attention. "Yes. I refused to come —for you."

I meet that angry glare and tilt my head. "Do you mean me, Cassius Jones, the man you blame for your brother's death? Or do you mean all of us? The three of us here?"

Fred's jaw moves silently. She doesn't blink. Then she sighs and stares down at her glass again. "It's not that simple."

"I think it would be simpler if you spoke," Leo said with a broad grin. The look in his eyes betrays that smile.

Victoria leans over stiffly, groaning with her hand on her belly, sliding Fred's mask back along the floor. She picks it up with both hands and turns it over gently, with reverence. Victoria looks like her old self for just a moment. Her eyes are soft and sweet, and she looks at Fred not with anger but with a kind of sorrow. I suppose the two of them have something in common.

Victoria offers her hand to Fred, who takes it instantly. They squeeze each other like that, and Fred nods.

"Okay. Okay, I'll tell you everything."

She downs the rest of her liquor, snorting as some of it rushes up her nose. After she's done shaking her head, she slips the mask free of Victoria's fingers.

"I joined the order."

"The cult," I correct snappishly.

Fred stares at me unhappily, and Leo loops an arm around my neck, pulling me close.

"Heel, boy," he murmurs against my ear. I'm his dog; I'm still his dog. I close my ears and press my cheek closer to his lips.

Fred takes this as acquiescence.

"The Order of the Rift is not what you think it is. It's not. . . A *cult* any more than your Christianity, Cassius."

I raise a brow; I have a lot to say to that.

"What it is—what we do—is. . . .it's not worship. Not quite."

"It's propitiation," I say. Like the worship of Apollo Smithers, god of mice, god of plague, divine disfavour is averted through appeasement. It's what the cultists have always done, isn't it? Worship the danger in the hope of protecting themselves. Wearing the flesh and the skin and the fur of dead *teras* to mark themselves as special. A giving up of their humanity, a renouncement of mortal flesh.

How should I see it as anything except that?

Fred shrugs at me. "In a way. Perhaps it's also respect."

"Respect?" Leo's voice has gone bitter. His teeth are bared as his lips curl off them in disgust. He says nothing more and doesn't have to. Why should any of us respect the creatures that are killing us?

"I know you want me to justify myself," Fred says as she sets her jaw. "You can't think me a turncoat or a traitor in truth, can you? You all watched my brother die with me. I have no love in my heart for the *teras*. But I want you all to think for one moment. And it might be hard for you two," she gestures to myself and Leo, "but perhaps Victoria will better understand.

London, England, too much of this world, will see the likes of us and assume us savages. Don't say anything—I need you to listen. It might not be overt now that the *teras* are the main focus, but it's insidious. I will be a savage in the minds of many because of what I look like, no matter my accent. Victoria will always be brown first. Even now, even with the world on the brink of collapse, that mindset finds a way. We already know Drearton has no issue culling undesirables from London. Useless people. When it really comes time to trim the fat, do you expect he'll choose me? Even if I ingratiated myself to him, in the end, I would not survive Drearton's London."

She takes a breath and tilts her head back, holding the empty glass to her lips with desperation. I've been there. One last drop. One last bit of oblivion.

Frustrated, Fred sighs and says, "But the reason I speak about this. . ."

She trails off. Fred sucks at her bottom lip and then moves

her attention to the cross-body messenger bag at her side. She drags the battered leather to the centre and opens it before she pulls out a battered volume, small and thin. The pages are yellowed and browned and crumbling in parts. It must be fifty years old at a minimum.

She places it on the ground for all of us to see.

The Teras and the Savages.

It's a treatise I haven't seen before. I curl my lip at it and glance up at Fred. "Who wrote this?"

"Gerald H. P. Brynes. In the first decade of the *teras'* appearance. Compares the Chinese in London to all sorts of *teras*, which he says are worse than animals."

She reads:

"The savage is not as proud as civilised men, for whom comparison with the animal form would be a slight. Many of the savage folk find comparison with the beasts, save for the accident of bodily form that diverts them.

In this same way, I purport the teras *to be another link, between beast and the savage man. A comparison of these peoples and their base beliefs should reveal mythologies in line with those whose mythologies have been made real in the world of the civilised.*

We are now heirs to this suffering, and we know who to thank."

What is there to say to that? No defence, no rejection. The University arose in these conditions. I take Fred's meaning—they would have blamed whomever they could have for the *teras* invasion. But it would never have been a white man.

"Maybe you can't understand why I would see intelligence where you are so certain there is none," she says as she turns to a particular page. "But in truth, it was you, Cassius, who made me shift my thinking."

Fred pushes the book towards me.

I take a moment before I look at it. I meet her eyes. *I*

want to be happy. She said that once. Silas told her it was a pipe dream. Maybe he was right.

Feeling somehow guilty, I glance down at the treatise, expecting another deluge of bullshit. But it's a sketch. A sketch of wardstones set up around something that looks like a wound, a cut in the skin pulled wide.

"A rift," I murmur.

"*The* rift," Fred says, and then quickly amends that with, "Well. Artist's interpretation, of course."

I do not understand the correlation. I go to open my mouth, but Fred says, "Several things happened very quickly after Silas died. I realised I couldn't. . .think about things like dreams. That I'd end up even more miserable if I kept thinking I could live a good life in a world like this. I. . .focused on the practicalities. The truths of this world. Only, what I'd thought to be true clearly wasn't real. Because you, Cassius Jones, could talk to a *teras*."

"And now so can you," Leo says.

"So can anyone," Fred says. She takes the book back from me. "It's only Latin."

I suck the rest of my cigarette down to nothing and lean my head back against the wood of the divider that keeps the sanctuary somewhat private from the rest of the church.

"Do all *teras* understand Latin?" I ask.

"Only the Greco-Roman genus."

Victoria frowns. "So the British folklore. . .can understand us as is?"

"I'll be honest—I haven't tried. And the rifters are focused on Greco-Roman genus, because they were the focus for decades. Maybe the others can speak an older English, I don't know. The point is: the *teras* are intelligent. And no one has been smart enough to ask what they want."

I see where this is going. I get up a little and tilt my head at her. "Except for the rifters."

She splays her hands like it's obvious.

"Fuck," I say, and pinch the bridge of my nose. Could I have begged for Thaddeus' life? Would the *manticore* have even listened?

Is it worse to know I can be understood, and to have those beasts tear me apart anyway?

"What does the rift have to do with this?' Victoria asks.

Fred sighs and wrings her hands. She has this air about her suddenly, like she's elderly, like she's seen too much and is weary from life. "When I learnt it. . .I was angry," Fred whispers. Fred is always angry, so I can only imagine the rage. But she is telling us this because she worries about how we'll react. I sit up properly and put a hand on Leo's thigh. He thinks I'm being sweet (I hear him make a low noise of approval) but actually, I need the added security. The gravity of another person.

"Alright," Fred says, but she won't meet our eye. "The rifters believe that it was no natural occurrence. That someone found the natural magic in our world and manipulated it. That they. . . tore it open deliberately."

My stomach drops, but not so dramatically. Instead, it's like lanterns turn on inside me, and I can see the truth for a moment.

I think there is a significant difference between feeling like you've been betrayed and knowing it—a certainty that is made so much worse when the people who have betrayed you are the ones meant to protect you. In the end, nothing will stop humanity from trying to live as normal. The *teras* came into the world, and it didn't stop all those strange human idiosyncrasies from mattering. Fred proved it just now: race matters. London's very existence proves that class matters. The shame I fight every moment to show my desire—my care —for Leo is proof societal normalcy matters.

What are we fighting for except normalcy? A chance to

live the life we've been promised, spoon-fed as children? What are we fighting for except to perpetuate this very system?

If London were to fall, what then?

We sit in silence for minutes. It's neither comfortable nor awkward. There's a pained neutrality to it; the air somehow feels nauseous.

"Why are you telling us this?" I ask Fred eventually.

Now she meets my eye, and makes sure to look at all of us, makes sure we're all seeing her.

"Because we know where the rift is. And I need your help to close it."

LESSON TWENTY-TWO

He finds me on the roof not ten minutes later, smoking another of those precious cigarettes.

I haven't run away exactly, but neither have I stuck around. Fred Lin wants something from me, and the Christian part of my soul says: *do it. Jump. As high as she asks.*

The rift is in London. The rift is behind the wards.

And the way my stomach twisted and sank at that, my intuition tells me—

It's in the University.

The trapdoor to the tower smacks onto the stone as it's roughly opened from below. I spin around, hackles raised, but I breathe easy once I see that mop of blond hair bobbing up the ladder. Under the moonlight, all of Leo is awash in a blueish haze.

"Leo. Stop it, you're injured. Go back to bed. I'll only be a minute." I try to keep my tone harsh and scolding, but I want him here. God, do I want him here. My voice betrays me, and as soon as he clears the opening, he looks up at me and grins. Boyish and youthful and perfect. I worry that his smile is false; I worry about everything these days.

Stop worrying. Stop ruining things.

"You're injured too," he says, gesturing to the new and strange stump I have at my side and the wounded right shoulder. The remains of my prosthetic has been roughly bandaged, if just to dull the knife-like edge of them before we're on the road again. Victoria was convinced I'd cut myself up in my sleep. She was likely right. The shoulder is throbbing, but Victoria put a salve on it, made from local plants. It should stave off infection, she says.

When Leo gestures to my prosthetic, I feel that phantom ache again. Briefly, I feel the limb as it was when it was flesh, and then as it was when the *Nemean Lion* bit it off. Burning pain, sharp and stinging through my nerves. The tears of tendon, brittle as it stretched and cracked. I squeeze my eyes shut, calm myself, and open them to Leo Shaw.

Leo winces at the angle he has to take to push out of the hole and up onto the parapet.

"Fucking hell," he mutters, hand on his belly.

I turn back around just as he clears it completely. I smoke quickly, clinging to the rasp of tobacco, hoping it will calm me. Being around Leo tonight makes me want to cry. I don't know—I was worried. I am still worried.

A blood stain smears over the stone edge to our left and runs down the tower before abruptly stopping. I don't want to think about that, so I've moved to the right, facing back towards London.

Leo comes up and wraps his arms around me. I jolt, like my body is fighting the calm that often comes with Leo Shaw. After a moment, I relax into him and squeeze my eyes shut.

He snakes his fingers through mine and steals the cigarette from me, leaning his sharp chin on the soft indent on my shoulder. He takes a few breaths and smacks his lips.

"Still not a fan?" I whisper.

"Only of you," he says, and he nuzzles close, pressing his nose against my neck.

My heart begins to race. This affection. . .is new. With all the anxiety of a prey animal caught in a trap, I press the tips of my fingers against his skin.

"I can feel your heart through your back," Leo murmurs. He doesn't prompt further but the question is lingering. *What's wrong? What is it?*

How am I meant to tell him I just—feel—scared?

"Long night," I say.

"Cass."

I sigh and collapse down on the parapet. Leo does not untangle himself and instead laughs, kissing my back as he rests his head there, his body stretched at a strange angle. But after a moment, he hisses and he presses up slowly, hobbling to my right to lean his weight on the wall.

"How bad is it?"

"Barely a scrape," he says without humour.

I tut. "I saw your insides."

"I've felt *your* insides," he says with a small smile. His eyes are still closed, and his hand is pressed firmly on his stomach. "Cassius—I will let you know if it gets too much."

I hesitate to believe him because I'm not sure if he *will* tell me. But I see this conversation going nowhere. "Alright," I say, when what I really want to tell him is: *Please take care of yourself. Please. I almost lost you.*

"Are you upset about Fred?" he asks. "Or about the battle?"

"Can it be both?" I take another drag and hold my breath until it burns. The edges of my throat feel raw and scratchy, as if I've been screaming.

"Tell me what she did exactly," he says. "Apart from the joining-the-cult thing."

"I can't tell if you're being blasé because you think it's cute or if you actually don't care."

He senses my anger—and it's real anger, too. I can't help it. I have no sympathy for Fred Lin's new plight. Even if what she says is true, and we are more aligned than I expected, I refuse to—to align myself with—

"Cassius," Leo says softly. He touches my hand. "They're just people. I saw you at the execution. I saw how it affected you. You don't hate the rifters. You hate everything else about this world, but you don't hate *them*."

I grind my jaw. This isn't quite right. "It's not that they exist. It's that she—"

I don't know how to explain my distress. I'm not even sure if the distress is real, or allowed, or if I'm just an idiot for thinking it. But Fred refused to talk to us, refused to listen, refused to help me. Is that selfish? Are her sights set bigger? Is that all it is?

Leo assumes what I was going to say. "She didn't come? Cassius, that's just this world. I don't fault her—I wouldn't have faulted you, either."

You cried when you saw me, I do not say. *You were so relieved I had come. Why are you being stoic now?*

Everything is so muddled. I put my head in my hands. "Leo, I could not have left you."

He pauses. I know that he understands, that underneath the understatement is a maze of complex emotion. I could not have left him. I couldn't have. I would have broken. I would have been different if I'd chosen to stay and wait and never know.

He doesn't say or do anything, and we stare out at London for a bit.

"I'll be honest," I say. "I didn't even. . .I have never really put much thought into the rift."

Leo snorts and shifts. "No, me neither. I just—I didn't

think they were still coming through." He pauses. "*Are* they still coming through? Or are they breeding here, and breeding wrong?"

He means the hybrids. I haven't even thought about *them*. "If the hybrids *aren't* coming through the rift, then that's worse, isn't it? Because then they're just. . .made here."

The implication—that even if we closed the rift, some remnant of the *teras* might still exist—is beyond unsettling.

"I thought I saw. . ." Leo starts. He clears his throat and gestures his head out to the plain where we fought an hour earlier. "In the battle, I thought I saw, or I heard. . .the one from Sherwood Forest."

Chills dance up my spine. I swallow hard and nod. "Vengeance. Yeah, I. . .I felt it, too."

"It listened to Fred."

I know he doesn't mean that it understood the language. It understood me perfectly as well. But it left when she told it to.

I don't like where this is going, but I need to hear it.

Leo shrugs. "All I mean to say is, those *teras* wanted to tear down the wardstone here. And they'll want to weaken them until the wardstones around London buckle, too. But then what? Because Vengeance told us what it wanted in the snow, and it wasn't wanting to go home."

Fuck.

"It has no home to go to," I murmur.

"Exactly," he nods. "Its body is incomplete. It's neither here nor there. It can't return through the rift because it has no home to return to."

"No myth it's been pulled from," I continue. "Which means perhaps the hybrids want something different to the other *teras*."

My stomach churns as I finish the sentence. *Teras* politics; no part of me thought I'd ever be thinking about that.

I wonder what Fred told them. Why *claude* was enough to dissuade them. Had she made promises before this? Had the rifters? Did they promise the *teras: We will close the rift for you,* and that is enough for them to listen?

"We should ask Meléti," I say, "when we get back."

"And what could we offer it, do you think, to earn that kind of information?"

I stare at him. *Things you won't tell even me*—I don't say that. *Things you're scared to admit to yourself*—I also don't say that.

His father's name was Ellis. His mother's name was Adelaide. He mentioned brothers and sisters and aunts and cousins, and I know that all of them are dead. I know it must have been *teras*.

Later, I told him, and now it was later. But. . .I don't want to ask him again. I want him to tell me.

I clear my throat and shrug, turning back towards the faint speck of light on the Thames, the distant London. "We'll figure something out. First step is getting home."

"I suppose we ride out immediately. Tomorrow, I mean."

"We don't know if there's a real amnesty, or if Fred can hold them off again. So, yes. I imagine so. And besides. If we can't close this rift, then I don't think there's much time left."

I shouldn't have said that. The air shifts. It's thick with sudden, hefty expectation. I should *not* have said that.

Not much time left. Do I say anything more? How I wish to spend it with him? Or does he know?

Does he know?

"So we should sleep," Leo says.

I nod without turning, shutting off those other rampant thoughts. "We should."

Neither one of us move.

My body knows before my mind does, or rather, my body *hopes* with an openness my mind denies, that something is about to happen. The movement of the air has shifted. My skin can feel it. There's weight to it, and not just the weight of my own interest or expectation. A heaviness fills the air. The pit of my stomach—which only a moment earlier was overrun by dread—now curls with delicious interest.

He's like an anchor. I turn to face him.

And Leo Shaw is already looking at me.

We don't say anything. I don't want to cloud this with my anxiety; I don't want to tell him what it means to be able to touch him again. I let my body lead.

I move towards Leo. He lets me come. Warmth emanates off his body, and I am compelled to touch him. As gently as I can, I glide my hand over his stomach.

"Does this hurt?" I say, watching his face in case he winces. He shakes his head, fingers gliding over the underside of my arm to gently angle it towards the back of his head. I wrap my arms around him and let him hold my waist. His fingertips press into my pelvis. He digs them in, and I squirm forward. Eagerness floods me. My cock jumps: a rush of warmth fills my groin, and at the same time, sorrow builds in my chest. It's the most unusual feeling. Desire calls for my attention, and my body wants it, I want it, but my heart—

"What is it?" Leo asks, pulling back to look at me. The moonlight glints off his canines, making him a predator. I lean forward hoping he will crush my neck in his jaws.

He avoids my kiss. "Tell me."

I knock my forehead against the sharp edge of his collarbone. "I don't know," I say truthfully. "You frightened me. You upset me. Perhaps I'm latently feeling that."

He offers nothing but a gentle touch, nails dragging up and down my back in a slow rhythm. He kisses the side of my forehead and I push closer until he grunts from pain; I've pressed too firmly on his stomach.

"Sorry," I murmur, pulling away.

He only shakes his head and smiles, but then his eyes glide down lower, and both our trousers are tented. He presses forward, makes our cocks touch through the fabric, which is at once arousing and very stupid.

"You and churches," he whispers, pulling me forward gently until he is smiling against my lips.

"*You* and churches," I say. "You're the fucking instigator."

"Can't help it. You're so handsome," he tells me. My stomach twists: I'm not used to him saying this. Sweetness turns sour on his tongue. I pull a face and he laughs at me, grabbing the bottom of my chin. "I want to fuck you."

That's more like it.

"You're too injured," I say. "And if you open your stitches up here, Victoria will kill me."

"We'll blame the ladder," Leo says, still holding fast. He shakes my head for me, grip firm. I feel like a doll. The pressure on my cheeks becomes an ache. "Scapegoat it. Let it take the fall."

I snort despite myself. It's not like I don't want him. It's not like I can't imagine him shoving me into the groove of the parapet and fucking into my hole, holding me by my hair as we rut together on top of this church.

It's not like that thought alone did nothing but get me harder.

I sigh, and I shake my head. He lets go of my chin and assesses me. I turn my hand and press the palm over his cock. "Use my mouth," I say.

His eyes soften. "Shouldn't I be the one thanking *you*? You came all this way."

"And you saved my life not an hour ago. We're even." I lower myself to my knees.

"Then this is. . .?"

"Because I want to," I murmur—and I do. More than anything. I want to slide his pants off and feel the head of his cock against my tongue. I want to make my throat wet and take him slowly; I want to please him; I want Leo Shaw to be happy.

Leo settles himself against the parapet, and I let him shift and squirm for a moment as his aching body settles into some comfortable position. He looks down at me and he's cast in shadow. The right side of his mouth is lit up by the moon; his eyes and the pearly teeth peeking through his cheek wound glint, and the rest of him is in shadow. I wonder what I look like, which parts of me catch the light, whether or not he can see my eyes and the emotion in them.

God. I feel like crying. Why do I feel like crying?

I ignore the feeling because I know I want him, and I begin to undo his trousers. He lets me take control and watches me silently. My fingers slide beneath the waistband and gently tug the trousers down. They catch on the bulge of his cock, and I push it down until they're free. I watch his cock bounce up, spot the wet stain growing on his pants. He steps out of his trousers, kicking them ungracefully to the side, and widens his stance. His eagerness is palpable, then; like the way incense smokes up the church, I breathe his desire into me, and let it mingle with my own. My body reacts. My heart is eager, my cock wanting, and my mouth is watering for him. But I still move at that slow, teasing pace. It takes several slower movements to drag his pants down and over his thighs, finally exposing his cock. Leo's head is arched back. His chest rises and falls rapidly, eagerly, and his hands grip the parapet stone so hard they begin to shake.

"Please," he mutters without looking down at me.

I exhale over the head of his cock and watch it twitch in response. Even in the dark, I can tell it's blushing a bright pink. So swollen. How many days has it been since he's touched himself?

He's surprisingly wet. The precum that stained his pants

was only the beginning. A deluge of it has leaked out in stringy beads and now slides slowly over the head, coating it. I lean forward and drag my tongue over it.

Leo shudders. He curls forward, hand tangling in my hair. The precum is sweet with a tinge of salt. I tongue up into the oversensitive slit of the head just to have Leo moan again.

I know he won't last long, and so I'm slow with him. I edge him for minutes, sucking his balls, licking up the shaft and around the head. Once or twice, I take him to his full length in controlled, smooth motions, but each time he bucks into my throat, I pull back and return to teasing.

"Cassius," he grunts, and his voice is a shadow of its usual self, stripped of bravado and attitude; a sapling fading in harsh weather. He sounds helpless. Beyond eager. Leo's desperation makes me shiver; my cock strains.

"Tell me that you want it," I whisper.

"I want it."

"*What* do you want?"

"You," he says breathlessly. "You, you. Please."

"Leo," I say, voice scolding.

"Suck it," he growls, folding over himself, trying to force me onto his cock.

And it feels like coming home again to the embrace of my new church; holy prayer on my knees, communion on my tongue. I go to him willingly as a servant.

Mouth-soaked; I take Leo to the hilt. He thrusts, and I gag, choking on him; he doesn't care. His grip tightens in my hair, and he keeps my head still as he fucks down into my throat. He moans and ruts, and I desperately move a hand into my own pants just to squeeze myself.

Saliva drools from my mouth, and I'm moaning with him, my eyes rolling back into my skull each time he thrusts. Exhaustion hits him, and I take over, rolling up onto my knees and bearing the discomfort of the rough stone as I bob my head back and forth, mouth sloppy.

"Cassius, Cassius, ah—*ah*—" He jolts forward with a soft moan.

I strain to look at him, eyeballs craning against some orbital bone. He looks heavenly. I rub my hand against the lower part of the shaft, grazing at his balls. And Leo *whines*.

"Don't stop," he begs, and then, not a second later, "Oh, fuck, I'm coming."

He cries out as he rides the wave, and his hips roll. I keep my mouth on him, moaning too, and wait until he's slowed to swallow the tangy cum and slide my mouth off of him. His cock pops out, the skin glinting with my coated saliva.

I give him a moment, remaining on the ground as I bask in his ecstasy. He looks so good like that, stretched out and gasping, cock exposed.

I run my hands up his strong thighs and squeeze them, feeling them quiver despite the muscle.

"Fuck," he says after a moment, though it comes out with a gasping moan. His hand reaches for my head and lands heavily, tangling again in the hair. All the force behind his touch has been sapped away. His limbs are laden. I love him like this.

"Cm'here," he slurs, mind made fuzzy by orgasm. His sudden sweetness makes me laugh. I stand and push close to him.

Lazily, we kiss like that, both our weights supported by the stone. His hand droops from my hair and gently tugs me forward by my shirt. I moan against him.

There's something different about kissing after orgasm; the little death strikes away the sensible, put-together mind, and leaves this silly, enervated version of the self. I like seeing Leo like that whilst I'm still composed; even if my cock is rock hard and leaking, I have some sense of mind to take this in.

He pushes his tongue into my mouth, and his other hand snakes up towards my hair. Leo pushes me close.

"My darling," he murmurs.

I go cold.

I know—it's something I should want to hear. Perhaps part of longs for it. A lot of me longs for it. But the reality of hearing it—that word 'my', with all its weight and all its meaning—makes me shudder. It's like I stand before a *gorgon*, frightened that I'm turning to stone. Why can't I say anything?

Leo laughs, not recognising my expression. "What is it?"

It's unfair, I want to say. *I want to be yours. But am I really?*

"Leo," I whisper.

"I missed you," he says. I pull away from him.

This isn't right. This isn't the narrative he has been feeding me. Where is the ruthlessness? The refusal to commit? Where is the unknowable man who keeps me at arms' length?

I step back and push against his chest. My cock begins to soften, all desire rushed away by dread.

Leo's smile falters. He looks me up and down. "What is it?"

I exhale shakily. Tears start to well up, which feels stupid —*do not cry. Do not.*

I sniff and say, "I don't understand," which doesn't explain anything to Leo. He shakes his head, and I rub my hands over my face.

"You're confusing me. You keep confusing me. You tell me to be ruthless. You won't tell me about your life. You are mean to me if I ask. But then you trade something that might save my life for cigarettes, and you start calling me your darling sincerely, and the way you're looking at me—the way you've looked at me since I found you—it's been so. . .so *sweet*. So genuine. And it frightens me. I'm *scared*, Leo, which sounds completely idiotic to say aloud, but I don't understand you, and I'm afraid to feel anything for you, and—"

"Cassius, I like you."

I slam my jaw together so quickly all my teeth clack. My breath stutters to a stop in my throat, every muscle tensing. "What?"

He reaches out and snakes a single finger around one of mine. It is here that he focuses, not on my face or my eyes, but on this single point of contact.

"I don't know if it means anything more than that. I don't know if it *can*. And I. . . I can't promise I won't be confusing. Sometimes I do things without knowing why myself. But I. . ." He rubs the back of his neck and glances away. "I don't think I want to be reckless with you."

I don't know why that's so hard to hear. I don't know—I don't know why, but my body begins to convulse. It feels strangely horrible to hear that. It is exactly what I've wanted him to say, and I just want to tear my skin off. It's like it's being said to someone else, someone more deserving. But I realise quickly it could be anyone saying it, and I would feel the same.

I have never in my life expected to love openly or freely or honestly. I've never expected to be loved in return. It turns out that doing things in the dark is not conducive to stability. Someone like Leo Shaw—someone not quite perfect, and in many ways broken—deciding he will see me: it feels like confession, when you're pouring out your sins, when you worry the priest on the other side of the booth is putting marks against your name, counting your wrongdoings, knowing you, seeing you—

I am frightened to be seen.

"Cassius, what's wrong? What is it?"

I'm crying. I let myself be pulled forward and bury myself into his neck. This is more intimate than what I've just done for him. I feel so vulnerable, a shaking lamb in the cold, that when Leo wraps his arms around me and murmurs sweet nothings into my ear, I feel *worse*.

"I don't know—I don't know why I'm—" I keep hiccupping. Leo soothes me and slowly lowers himself to the floor of the rooftop. I go with him and, once he's comfortably positioned, rest my head on his shoulder. He lets me stay silent for minutes as I try to regain my composure and my heart swells around that truth. Such little displays of kindness, but they are pure. They are genuine. Because of that, they feel mighty.

Perhaps we are just finding solace in one another as the world ends. But as I shake and cling to him, I try to let myself feel briefly safe. If I can feel at peace in the oblivion of sex with this man, then this quiet moment should surely be no different.

"Talk to me," I say. "Tell me anything. I'm sorry about this."

He kisses my forehead, tells me it's okay. Then he gestures down to his stomach. "Should I tell you about this?"

I'm almost scared to know, but he is offering it to me freely. I nod eagerly and try for humour, as I always do when I need to lighten the mood. "At least we'll both have matching scars."

It ekes a smile out of him. His eyes dip down to my belly, and he reaches out, ghosting his finger over my clothes, above where the scars from the *harpy's* attack are crisscrossed and raised. "We'll be equally beautiful," he says. "Or equally unfortunate in appearance."

"Which is the real reason you've decided to like me," I say assuredly. "You're completely hideous now."

"Oh, as are you, Hunter Jones," he laughs, and then I

laugh because I can't stop looking at him. The moon kisses his skin, and I am jealous of her; I want him to be mine.

He sighs and knocks his head back against the stone, stretching out his leg. He undoes his shirt, which has grown damp with sweat.

The bandages will have to be changed soon. They've grown brown with old blood. So long as there is no pus, I decide not to worry.

"It was the *phrygian?*" I prompt.

He nods, but his brow furrows instantly. "I wish. . .that I'd read about them. Or that we'd had a better Scholar. He died. . .very fast. Before he identified it. Before we even knew. . ."

Leo's speech is stilted. His breathing is laboured, like it's a battle just speaking about it.

"Hey," I say, putting my hand on his arm. He squeezes his eyes shut and nods.

"I'm alright," he says. "It's just a blur. That thing rose out of the shadows, and it barrelled through us. We had no formation. Claypoole was shouting orders, someone else was screaming to retreat. The horses smelled blood and bucked a few of us off.

"I don't care how it's possible. I care that it happened."

Leo rolls his eyes. "Thank God for me, would you?"

"You know we aren't on good terms," I murmur back.

He meets my eye, smile fading softly. Then his lip curls up, and he glances away. "Anyway, it must have clawed at me at one point. I remember being in the air and then on the ground. I was lying there in the mud, and I could. . .feel the blood leaking out, and I knew." He swallows hard. "I mean, I thought I was gone for good. And sure, I thought about my family first. My little brother. I thought, '*I hope I've done a good enough job*'. Part of me really wanted to go. But then I—"

He chokes up and grunts, shifting uncomfortably. He's frowning so intensely now it almost looks comical. Leo shakes his head. "Cassius, I thought about you, and I felt. . .so terrible about leaving things how I did. I thought it was the end, and I'd never get to tell you, or apologise, none of it. I just thought, *'This is the one person, the one lover, who's ever tried to. . .know you. And you can't help but push him away'.*"

Leo drags one of his legs up and uses it to lean on. I think he's secretly trying to hide his face.

There are so many things I could say to that. But I end up saying, "I was worried about you," and it comes out with an accusatory tone. "I was really worried about you. I—"

I could think of nothing else. For days, there was nothing else. It was just you, Leo Shaw.

I clear my throat. "Leo?"

He turns to me, cocks his head. "Yeah?"

"I like you too."

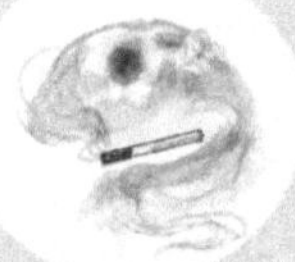

LESSON TWENTY-THREE

I want to cry hysterically after I say it. It feels like some awful admission of guilt, like I am a morally abhorrent person, like I have done awful things, and I will happily do them again.

The stone in my stomach corrupts all the good parts that come with the admission. I feel weighed down, ugly, anxious. I want another cigarette; I want another fuck—I need a mind made blank. But instead, Leo and I stand and stare out at the distant London in a silence we pretend is anything but awkward. We don't touch each other, but I can feel the warmth of him. Queasily, I shift away.

"Bed?" Leo asks innocently.

"Yes," I say and muster a smile. My mind rolls from detail to detail as I look at Leo. His mouth quirks up at the corner as he looks at me. He has a graze on the back of his knuckles I hadn't noticed before. When he turns his body towards me, the movement is slow and focused, as if he's trying not to frighten me. All these details are irrelevant, but they are burrs for my senses to catch on. I feel untethered, and Leo is suddenly a stranger.

Why did I say that?

As we head towards the ladder, Leo does the silly thing of rushing forward to wrench the trapdoor open for me. I know it causes him pain because his knuckles clench against the bloody wound on his stomach.

"After you, Hunter Jones," he whispers to me, and he presents his other hand to me as a gift.

I take it, using it to balance as I climb down, but as I'm letting go, I make sure to tell him, "You're a fool for coming up here."

He slips his hand free with a simple smile. "Why? I had a rather nice time. Was something not up to your standard?"

He climbs down. I crane my neck and catch the silhouette of him lowering. As the womb-like tower room welcomes us again, candlelight illuminates him, and suddenly, I'm watching the way his legs work as they pop down each rung, the way his hips move, the bulge of his right arm as it takes the bulk of his weight.

"You seem to have stopped," he murmurs, and I jolt down the last few rungs, flushed to the bone.

"Momentarily distracted," I say unconvincingly, padding out of the way for him to climb ungracefully off the ladder.

"You're insatiable," he laughs and then winces. In the light, I can see how pale he is.

I step forward and slip my hand over his. Pain may be instructional, but in this instance, it is an enemy. I don't like that Leo's hurt.

I don't mention his wound, though. Glancing up, I find he's looking at me, eyes searching.

"And you're easy on the eyes," I murmur. "What do you want from me?"

He visibly swallows, the apple of his throat bobbing. Then he tips forward, big hand gripping my left shoulder for support, and though his fingers dig deep in an attempt to find purchase in the flesh, the way he kisses me is gentle.

"That," he says as he pulls away.

"You did it wrong," I tell him. "Very wrong."

"You're right," he says, and he adopts this adorable expression, tightly knitted eyebrows and pursed, serious mouth. "I should try again."

He leans forward again. I close my eyes.

"There you are!"

We break apart.

Victoria stands with her hands splayed on either side of the tower room doorframe, looking about as pissed as I've ever seen her.

"You two are the worst patients I've ever had. I mean it. I've worked hard to keep Leo alive, and I don't need you tearing your stitches through—through rigorous activity."

Leo laughs.

"Oh," she steps over the threshold. "You're laughing, but I'm *very serious*."

She wrenches Leo's shirt up, and his laughter dies in his throat. The stitches are coming loose again. Blood pools at the seam of his flesh.

Victoria wrinkles her nose and looks over at me, unimpressed.

"Don't look at me like that," I mumble. "It's not like I fucked the open wound."

Victoria turns back to Leo. "You know, I fucked him once, too," she says, gesturing her head towards me. Leo's eyes go very high, and I flush. I think the way I have sex with a woman—had sex with Victoria, the only woman I've touched —is remarkably different to how I approach having sex with a man—for a variety of reasons, but most importantly, *I am not attracted to women*. Victoria does not hear my inner monologue and tells Leo, "I wouldn't be ripping out my stitches for it."

Leo cocks his head. "Well, no offense, Miss Bennet, but I can assure you Mr Jones is perfectly enthusiastic under the right circumstances."

Victoria flashes him a look, but her mouth betrays her, quirking up in a small smile. They share a silent moment, but I know they're both thinking—in different ways—about what those 'right circumstances' look like.

"Come on," she says. "I have to fix you up."

We move out of the tower room, and Victoria turns on her heel. "Not you," she tells me.

Maliciousness or something else? I freeze, but she answers my question a beat later. "You'll only distract him again."

The church is mostly quiet at this hour. Lumpen bodies lie draped across pews or huddled in corners of the church. Big woollen blankets are shared between many bodies; it somehow feels colder in here than up on the roof.

Victoria walks away with Leo slowly, accommodating both their necessary paces, and I watch for a while. She's leading him to another chapel where she's set up with some supplies. A makeshift triage lingers nearby, and the deaconess helps with some of the other townsfolk.

Leo looks back once and winks at me, and I smile despite myself. It's like my insides flare to life, like they lie dormant and uncaring until he looks at me, and then joy spores in my flesh.

I like you. I like you.

He is not perfect, but neither am I. Perhaps if things were different, if we had the luxury of choice, we would never be together.

Or maybe it is fate that we *are*. Maybe this kind of affection is inevitable. Maybe this kind of love—

Not love.

I go back to the sanctuary and curl up on the floor, balling my body beneath my Hunter cloak in the space next to Leo's.

The other two Hunters are already asleep. The floor is cold, hard, and unforgiving, but a woollen blanket has been laid out for Leo and me to share. I take it and try to snuggle down under it, pretending I can't feel the tiles pressing on my body or the way my broken prosthetic aches in the chill.

I close my eyes with the intention of sleep. Barely a minute later, I start crying.

The tears well easily and quickly, and I know there's no point in trying to stop them, so I quickly give in. Reflexively, I curl in on myself. All the pain is pulsing in my chest; my heart resonates with it, and I can feel each pounding beat against my ribcage. It *hurts*. But I make sure to cry softly.

It's a skill I've learnt by necessity. A hovel-sized home, living on top of one another, with a father who would gladly beat me for any indiscretion and a mother who didn't care what he did so long as we all woke to a new day.

Don't antagonise your father.

She would tell me that when I was young. You learn rather quickly that wailing and crying and giving in to your emotions do you few favours in a household like that.

In a strange way, I'm thankful for that treatment now. I can sob and do it quietly.

I let the emotion blossom. I dislike it—I dislike feeling it —but it has its roots in me. My body rocks back and forth beneath the blanket, and I press my hand over my mouth, where snot and tears gather at the seam between my palm and my lips.

My mind is fuzzy. Rough impressions of the feeling—*pain, sadness, worry, fear*—flit through my mind, but they all seem untethered and without cause. Vaguely, I know the reason: I have exposed my underbelly. It's frightening to care for someone. It's frightening in a world like this and for a boy like me. I don't think I've ever let myself get this close, and certainly never with a chance for it to be reciprocated.

It is all I've ever wanted. Why is it so hard to hear?

I cry intermittently for about an hour. Every time I think I've stopped or put away the dreaded emotion, it just starts up again. The feeling comes unbidden; I keep my mind blank and focused on sleep, determined not to spur another upset, and yet, as my body relaxes, something deep in my chest refuses to let go. That thick knot of feeling, terrible in its convoluted twisting mess, refuses to detangle.

Ruthlessness, apathy, stony-hearted.

Some part of me has always thought the only way to survive is to be like that, and Leo only seemed to confirm it. But it's all Thaddeus, in the end, isn't it? And behind my brother, it's our father. And behind him, it's God knows who. I never met my grandparents, but if my father's personality speaks of their character, I am glad for it.

All this to say, one after another, I have found myself told again and again what I should be feeling. How I should be feeling it. Who I should be showing it to.

For someone who feels so much, I somehow don't feel enough. I don't allow it to sit long enough to know it, or to care for it. I just close my eyes and pray and hope it goes away. I just raise a cigarette to my lips, or a cock to any hole, and I let oblivion dull emotion; fuck it all back behind a wall I've long forgotten should not even be there.

It's a terrible revelation to have—and even worse to have in this church. The site of the Shaws' struggles. The symbol of my own tortured religion. What a place to find myself.

You know what lulls me in the end? The smell of him.

He must have been using this blanket as a pillow. It smells of his hair, and when I inhale, it's like I'm burying my face against his neck, breathing in at his nape.

My body reacts to it. I stop crying.

Leo Shaw is both my danger and my bastion.

LESSON TWENTY-FOUR

When I wake, I wake in his arms.

It's a unique bliss. He has pulled me against his chest, encased me in a warm cage of arms. He's managed to push his leg between both of mine, just for another bit of closeness.

The both of us are hard, but I don't want to do anything about it. Thinking of moving away upsets me; this moment is ours. Huddled beneath the blanket, I breathe in our mingling scents, and I focus on the way my body feels. No tension. None of that strange, messy knotting around my heart. I feel perhaps the most at peace I've ever felt in my life—and that just makes me want to cry more.

God.

Too much crying.

"Get up."

It's Hayes who says it.

In all honesty, I had practically forgotten about the man. Call me cruel, but earning scuff marks on my knees and a cigarette under the stars occupied my mind more last night than checking on Len Hayes.

I dislodge myself slowly from Leo. He hasn't woken and frowns with genuine annoyance. His lip curls up.

"Stop," he mumbles and flips onto his stomach. Instinctively, his hand moves to the flat of his belly, and his face contorts again from the pain of his stitches.

Around me, the others are slowly waking up. Victoria sits up carefully, her hand on her belly. Her hair is dishevelled, and she looks pallid. She scrunches up her face.

"I'm going to be sick," she announces. Sutton—who looks comparatively very well put together—launches forward to help her stand. Hayes has the gall to look mildly miffed that no one is listening to him, but he isn't a pregnant woman who's saved all of our lives at one point or another, so he can keep sulking.

The other two Hunters are just as slow, but they look somewhat better from yesterday. The haggard man pulls their shared woollen blanket away from his leg and hisses. Blood has soaked through the bloody bandages around the stump of his leg.

I have a rather cruel thought, then, that there is no point in this man trying to survive. That he will slow us down—and the woman, too. What was it Victoria had said she'd broken?

It doesn't matter that they're graduates. It doesn't matter if we could use them once they're healed. The best thing they could do for us is to die as bait.

I sit in silence after I have that thought. I don't like knowing I can be so cruel, that even after saying such dark things to myself, I can feel no remorse for them. I know it's the truth. How are we meant to bundle up injured people on the few remaining horses we have available to us, trek back towards London through *teras*-infested lands, and not expect some of us to die? Would it be better to leave them here as part of this final stronghold? Or is that an abandonment more sinister than how the University intends to abandon the rest of humanity?

What if you get back and the dean has already slithered behind the Janus Gates? Does everyone here have a personal wardstone? Does Leo?

"Stop staring at me, kid."

I blink out of my reverie. The older Hunter is staring at me. His lips have gone pale from the pressure with which he presses them together, and I have this inane fear that he's figured me out. One of my thoughts has leaked through into reality, or something just as impossible.

"It's Cassius," I tell him, glancing away. "I never got yours."

"Dog meat," he mutters.

"Interesting nomenclature." *Dog meat.* Does he know how easy I already find it to think of him like that? If it came down to it, if a *harpy* swooped us and wanted blood, if I had Leo Shaw to protect—there'd be no fucking thought.

"I know what you're thinking. I know you think I can't make it."

So, he had heard me, then, in a way. I open my mouth reflexively, an old, learned behaviour. My body is ready to defend itself, my mind eager to sway the man's opinion of me back to the positive. But I pause because why does it matter? Especially if he won't be making it back.

"Your name," I press again.

"Philip," he says with a heavy sigh. "But dog meat might as well be it."

His other leg is tangled in his cloak, and he angrily tries to rip it free. Philip lies back, panting, and squeezes his eyes shut. I hear his teeth clack together.

You know this type of anger, Cassius. You can recognise helplessness anywhere.

God, what is wrong with me? What kind of person have I become?

"Get up," Hayes says again.

"I can't fucking stand!" Philip shouts. The two of them stare at one another.

Hayes is pale. Sickly looking. I hadn't realised, but Sutton is supporting a lot of hit weight.

Don't say it. Don't say it.

"How bad is it?" I say anyway.

Hayes' gaze flashes to me. I'm undermining his authority at best and enticing fear in the rest of us at worst.

"I'm fine," he says stiffly but I see the way Sutton's mouth quirks down, and the way his hip quivers from the sheer difficulty of remaining upright, and I think, *Cassius, you might have to be prepared to leave them all.*

I look over at Leo. Behind Hayes and Sutton, I can see the shambling return of Victoria Bennet.

Would she be an exception? Or would I leave her, too?

Leo's warm fingers come to rest on my chin. Very gently, he drags my gaze back to his. "What is it?"

I shake my head, lacking the words to tell him and too filled with fear to speak regardless. He furrows his brow and cocks his head at me in an explicit assessment.

"Why are you lying to me?"

Because I'm thinking about leaving people to die. Because I'm scared of how easy the thought of it is, how willingly I would prioritise you.

"Later," I murmur, and I move my gaze away.

After the last night and after minutes of complete and utter disrespect, Hayes finally loses it.

"If you won't all get up, you will at least give me your fucking attention!"

His voice came out in a strangled cry.

Sutton said, "Hayes, *please*— "

But I can see the cracks in him. Agrawal is dead. He has come out here to be a hero, and now he is thinking, "*What was the point?*"

I have what I came for. Hayes, though, is shaken.

"What's with the ruckus?" Don Wamsley murmurs. He climbs up into the sanctuary, eyes falling on Leo and myself and how close we sit. He nods at us, face firm and unyielding, and when Leo nods back he comes over, slipping behind us and hovering. It is not at all subtle. I can hear how heavy he is breathing.

"We leave today," Hayes says. He has regained some control over his voice, which shakes marginally less now that he isn't screaming. Half the church's eyes are on us. The air starts to shift; it won't be long before we are no longer welcome here.

"And if the *teras* aren't really gone from here?" Victoria murmurs. She stalks up the stairs, pale and sweaty, with a hand splayed on her belly. A smear of vomit has been missed across her cheek. She says before Hayes can interject, "The army wants to destroy the wardstone. Whether Fred really managed to deter them—"

"—is that what happened?" Hayes asks. His question remains unanswered.

"—is irrelevant to the question: will they stay away?"

It seems to me that there are several questions. How well protected is the wardstone? Are the people here willing to stay to defend it? Can they actually go anywhere else?

Most importantly, if we leave and return to London—if we pool our focus on closing the rift, on siding with the cultists—will that be enough to save these people?

"Hayes has a plan," Sutton declares. She sounds desperate, like she's beyond hopeful we'll fall for her false assuredness.

Hayes shifts in place, which in turn makes her scramble to keep them both upright. "Tell them."

Hayes grunts. "If we leave now, we could be in London's vicinity before it gets too dark. We'll cross the Thames at Greenwich, maybe. Or go through Whitechapel. Whichever ends up being quicker."

"How many horses do you have?"

The voice belongs to Fred Lin, whose face has peeked into the sanctuary. She hovers as if avoiding stepping up into the space, which I find curious. She was never devout, but this feels. . .pointed. A little rebellion in God's house, or a kind of honouring for the altar she will not bow to?

"Well, we each rode in on one," Sutton declares. "But four people will have to ride abreast."

My heart sinks. "The horses won't survive that. Not at any pace we need to get back in time."

"Then. . .then I'll negotiate with the deaconess," Hayes declares. He turns around but even that motion looks sloppy. I look at Philip again, and he's staring back at me.

I cringe away from him, but he tuts. "Go on, Cassius. Say it."

All eyes turn to me. Of course, they turn to me.

"You have some plan?" Hayes asks, tone slightly mocking.

"No plan," I say, shaking my head. I gesture to Philip's state, and then nod my head to the woman whose name I still haven't asked for. "What did you break again?"

"My wrist," she says. "But I can ride. Or walk."

Her voice tinges towards panic, and I know she's clocked what's happening. Her eyes dart to Victoria, who says, "And a bruised spine. Probably a concussion. And—"

"I can walk!"

Very firmly, Victoria says, "Kathleen, stop it."

The silence stretches. No one moves.

Philip is still looking at me. I do him the service of returning his gaze. After a moment, he falters. Sighing deeply, Philip lies himself back down, stretching his arms out like a lazy cat.

"We all know I'm going nowhere," he says. "I'm not risking it. I'll die fast, or I will fall and die slow, and maybe staying here will be another 'die slow' situation, but at least there's other people. At least it won't be *teras* doing the killing."

It's not his belief that the *teras* won't attack here again that surprises me. It's his quite plain acceptance of his own death. Starvation. Sepsis. Disgruntled deaconess. Anything, really, could be his end.

And all I can think is *good*. One less body to worry about.

"We can ride abreast," Don says. "Take turns. Give the horses breaks. Just means we have to stay alert."

He sounds the way he used to, back in the University, behind the wards. That smarmy confidence tinges his voice—is he doing this for Leo? Pretending for a man whose cock I worshipped last night?

I lean back to look at him. "Kind of you to offer your horse to—sorry," I glance back at the woman with the broken wrist, searching for a name, "That's right. Kathleen."

Don's lips press together faintly. Was he imagining Leo at his back, pressing close, I wonder? Is that what he still hopes for? Is it?

Calm down. You sound insane. We are discussing life and death, and you are worried about this?

"Then we go," Hayes says. "And fast."

In the end, that's all it took to make the decision. Philip did not say another word, not even when I whispered to him that it was for the best, that I was grateful, that as soon as we closed the rift, we would return.

I said those things to an empty body. Philip's eyes were far away.

I said those things to appease myself, to sedate my own anxiety and guilt, the way I would in confession.

Just another way my faith stays relevant.

25

LESSON TWENTY-FIVE

We left and rode for hours, and during those hours, the weather stayed consistent, and the sun lit the way forward, and I had the naive thought that everything would be fine.

But the horses tired easily, and even with Leo, Kathleen, and Victoria switching themselves between horses, we had to reduce our speed to a snail-paced trot.

Victoria appreciated it. When she rode with me, I could practically smell her nausea. Her breathing came out haggard, and one hand stayed spread on her belly the whole hour she was with me.

"Touch it," she told me, and I reached forward around her. She smelled of sweat, and a sickly sweet something I couldn't name. She'd pushed her dirty hair into a bun above her head, and it exposed the side of her face which, meant I could watch her expression as my hand pressed over hers. She slipped her fingers out from under mine, and then I was pressed up against the hard swell of her stomach.

My own nausea swelled in me. The uncanny nature of this —the knowledge that it should have been Bellamy sitting here, that I was an interloper in this life—ate at me. Then the baby kicked, and I flinched away from it like I'd been struck.

Victoria chuckled a little, but her face fell when she looked back at me. She swallowed hard. "I know," she said quietly.

But whatever she knew, she never told me.

By the time the sun was setting, we were nearing Barking, which put us about an hour or so out of London proper. The relief I felt. . .was difficult to identify. It flooded my synapses so perfectly that I was dizzy with it.

You know, like a fool.

My brother had a saying for a reason, after all.

Noli dormire dum in speculis.

Light fades quickly at the horizon, an orange blare sinking below the Thames. We begin to head further south so we can press into Whitechapel and enter through Aldgate.

Leo is with me. I have him ride behind me because I'm worried about delirium setting in and him losing control of the reins. At some point in the last hour, he pressed his forehead against my back to rest and has since fallen into a kind of slumber, waking every so often to grumble about the uneven trot of the gelding or hiss at the hot pain searing across his midsection.

"Not long now," I tell him, and he grunts his acknowledgement. Hours under the sun with limited water and no food would make even the best of us upset, and so I can't fault his low mood.

As for me, my shoulder hasn't given me too much trouble, but I ended up releasing my left arm from the bandage. I could somehow feel the pressure of the bandage trapping what remained of the prosthetic, and it felt better to have it free. The infection at the join seems to have gone, which I count as a holy miracle given all the stress I've been under.

For a couple of seconds, everything seems fine. The

Thames stinks, and in a way, it's a homecoming. I know that smell. I know this safety.

Hayes starts coughing behind me. I glance over just as he spits blood over his horse's flank. It whinnies immediately, frightened by the smell.

Hayes frowns and wipes his mouth with the back of his hand. "Wait."

"Not waiting," Wamsley mutters ahead of me. He glances back.

"Wait," Hayes says.

Fred stops abruptly and turns towards the water. "He's right," she says.

Wamsley scoffs. He gestures rather violently towards London and shouts, "Oh, for God's sake, Hayes, let's just—"

Something red sprints out of the river.

It's so fast that none of us have time to register. The horses start screaming. My gelding bolts. Both Leo and I topple off. Leo lands badly and groans—but I'm still moving away from him. Pain pulses across my back, and my ribs scream. Then something shallower—the stinging pain of skin splitting open. I twist around and see my foot caught in the reins.

"Woah, woah!" I scream, which does nothing to calm the poor beast. I kick and flail and then heft myself up and hold onto the reins, desperately hacking through them with my severed prosthetic. I eventually manage to dislodge my foot, but the gelding is gone, ignoring my softer coos for his attention. No time for him, though. I am shaking on the ground. Adrenaline floods my system, and all pain is momentarily bludgeoned. Screams and shouting fill the air, and a snarl like water lodged deep in the throat, the sound of a man choking on it. I rush back the hundred-odd paces I've been dragged. In amongst the grass, I see it.

Red skin slick, glistening with the juices of something pus

infected, raw as if flayed, whole, elongated body an open wound. Its uncannily long arms drag over the ground. It looks as described: a humanoid body sitting atop a horse, the same fresh red flesh as the horse-like body beneath it. But they aren't separate creatures. They are conjoined. I can't tell which head is alive, for both the humanoid head and the horse's grin brightly at us. The equine mouth curls into a sharpened point, nearly impossible in its width. It opens its mouth and cackles. Both mouths are filled with multiple rows of human teeth. The thick pink tongue lolls out, coated in saliva, and the humanoid chest heaves with its laughter.

Both voices choke and gurgle on water as if a flood is in its lungs.

One of the beast's hands snatches at the leg of Haye's horse; the mare screams bright and loud as some bone snaps from the force of the grip. Hayes tumbles out of the saddle. Without looking back, the *teras* launches its long arm away, still clutching the mare.

The entire body of the horse flies into the water.

I baulk. Victoria is on the ground, crying. She's on her stomach, crawling away. Is that blood? Is that—

Wamsley is tugging Leo back from the scene. Sutton is shouting. I watch her fire one useless bullet into the creature's flesh. Fred has her guns out, and she's shooting, too.

Nuckelavee.

I bolt forward.

"Get away!" I start shouting. To it, or to the others, I'm not sure.

The Thames is brackish. The Thames is not fresh water, and we need to cross fresh water to get away from it. It's the only thing I know about it and the only myth I can recall. I thought the Thames was fresh enough.

The only fresh water I have is the little bit let in a water sack, which is in my fucking gelding's pouch.

My hand is shaking as I pull out my dagger. The *manticore* poison might be used up by now. I have nothing. I have nothing but the blade itself and, I suppose, the sharpened edge of my prosthetic.

Sutton screams as the *nuckelavee* rounds on her and darts forward. Kathleen, who was riding with Sutton, backs up and trips over. She falls on her broken wrist and howls, rolling over in pain. Hooves clop against the ground, and the *nuckelavee* shouts excitedly, its top half bouncing oddly as the torso rocks side to side. It throws its whole-body weight into its strike, claws slicing down over Sutton's cheek, which splits open far too easily like the skin of an old fruit. Blood gushes out immediately and she falls to the ground in shock. In the next motion, the hand grips Kathleen and wrenches her from the ground.

The woman shrieks. She lets out one unbroken scream that echoes around us. The *nuckelavee* takes its other long arm, grips her head, and pulls it off.

Her body falls limp. The head and part of the spinal cord are ripped free. Blood gushes in an arterial spray around her.

All of us scream at the sight.

Fred looks sick. I know this is like Silas all over again, but I can't focus on that. She takes out her daggers and rushes forward to attack—and I can't spare a thought for her.

One of the other horses has broken its leg in the chaos. It whinnies and cries, convulsing as it tries to stand and escape the fighting and the blood. It can't overcome the pain pulsing throughout its whole body. I run to it, but for no good reason. I know it can't be saved.

"It's okay, it's okay," I tell it. Its eye bulges as it snorts. We both know I'm lying.

I stop with the niceties, which are more to comfort me than the dying horse and put the knife between my teeth. I move my free hand to the satchel at the horse's side. There's a small skin with a few drops of water. It won't be enough, but it's something.

I pick it up and also grab the horse lantern from the dying beast's neck.

By the time I'm standing again, the *nuckelavee* has turned its attention from Sutton to Hayes. I don't know why. It could have killed us all very easily, but something about it—something about the myth of it—tells me it likes the torturous lengthening of the kill. The part where the prey is played with, where hope has not wholly been dashed.

The creature exhales. Fred backs up with a shout as part of the *teras'* breath touches her hand. Hayes, who has fallen beneath it, cannot move. I think one of his legs is crushed.

If this is part of its mythos, I never read of it. But I see the *nuckelavee's* breath curling from its nostrils. The air moves unnaturally in curling wafts that are tinged yellow. The colour is putrid, like pus, bright like the fat in the human body. The exhalation dances slowly over Hayes' face. He quivers just before it meets his skin.

Hayes screams.

The soft squish of his eyes begins to melt and bubble. The sensitive skin around his eyes turns pink and blisters. Pus and lesions form in seconds across his face and elsewhere; he jolts instinctively, nerves pulsing from the pain, and the hand he uses to shield his face turns the same. Diseased. His flesh becomes pockmarked, and he writhes from the pain, legs jerking and kicking the air to get out from beneath the creature's grip.

I know then we are being played with for sure. This being is as close to a demon as any other *teras*; if Vengeance can be reasoned with, this thing, resolutely, can not. It has no purpose beyond malevolence. It wants nothing except to cause pain. And if we don't get out of here—if we don't dissuade it—it will kill us all.

Slowly.

Victoria looks back at the scene and tries to scramble up. One of the *nuckelvaee's* long arms smashes into her back. She crashes forward onto the ground with a scream.

I rush forward, passing Wamsley and Leo, whose stitches have ruptured yet again. He looks up at me.

"Cass," he whispers.

He's losing blood. More than that, more than a little—he's fucking dying.

No.

I simply don't have enough hands. I drop, perhaps stupidly, the dagger. It falls from my mouth into the earth. Tucked into the crook of my shortened arm, I uncap the waterskin and push forward as close as I can. The *nuckelavee* glances up and makes no move to stop me. Either it thinks I'm an idiot—I am—or it's eager to see what I will do. It doesn't expect me to whip the remains of the waterskin over its flesh.

The water is barely more than a dribble. It arcs out and splashes over the *nuckelavee*'s face. Immediately, the beast rears up in horror. The equine part screeches out a deformed whinny, kicking up into the air. The humanoid part writhes, long arms grazing against the dirt as it splutters and screams.

What did that do to it? No skin is fizzing or bubbling or steaming. There are no signs of how its body has been damaged. Nothing except this reaction—a good reaction, a good *distraction*. It's long enough for Sutton to spring into action and try to drag Hayes away.

As soon as she touches him, his howls only become louder. I don't understand what's happening until I squint. Sutton's taken hold of both his hands, intent to drag him back towards safety. The boil-covered hand has split apart.

No—that's not right.

The skin is sloughing off from the touch. In a second, the

entire hand is degloved. Red flesh exposed to the world. Hayes' eyes bulge out of his head as he stares at it, screams quietening suddenly as shock overcomes pain. Sutton is shaking, horrified as she looks down at the sleeve of skin draped delicately over her palm.

I cast about. "Wamsley! Fred! I need help!"

Sutton, Fred, Wamsley and I are the only ones left standing. We must be the ones to do something. I have my jagged prosthetic, and this currently unlit lantern. I turn the valve until flame shoots to life behind the glass. Wamsley and I make eye contact, and he nods.

Whatever decision he's made, whatever silent conversation he thinks we've just shared, I have no idea what he plans to do.

But he does something rather brave, then. He runs for me and snatches the horse lantern from my grip. The *nuckelavee* recovers as he does this. They lock eyes. Still, Wamsley doesn't stop.

He bolts forward with a shout, slinging that lantern through the air like a flail. The *nuckelavee* snaps its arm out towards him—and Sutton, moving close, stabs through the flesh with her knife. Fred has flanked the creature and manages to shoot into its back.

The creature shouts. I run in, drop low, and skid over the muddy bank, half falling as my momentum slows. It gets me low enough that the wet flesh of the *nuckelavee*'s torso glistens above my face.

I drive my severed prosthetic arm into the equine heart and wrench it free in the next motion.

The horse torso rears up again with another scream. Hooves beat down on either of my face, and then the creature is bucking. I wanted to stab it again, over and over, to try and bring about its death—but the hooves are too close to my skull, and I end up rolling out of the way, just as Wamsley screams my name.

He strikes the lantern over the humanoid torso.

Glass shatters. The lantern explodes. Fuel douses the *nuckelavee*. An instant later, flame engulfs it.

A chorus of screams rages around us. Both the equine and human mouths are open, but the voices emerging from both sound layered, like three or four people are inside and burning alive.

The smell of scorched flesh hits my nostrils. I scrabble away from the scene, running towards Leo, who is curled in on himself. His hands are bloody and pressed to the wound on his stomach. If this keeps happening to him, infection will be inevitable. If infection hits him, even if we're behind the wards, will he be alright?

"Are you okay?" I keep asking, before the *nuckelavee* is even dead. "Are you okay? Leo, *Leo!*"

Flames reflect in the whites of his eyes. He's transfixed. I turn to watch the bucking, howling creature. It waves those long arms in the air, flame licking at the sky. Both mouths hang open, skin bubbling and melting from the jaws, dribbling like saliva onto the ground. Then, it makes the decision and rushes back into the Thames. There's a wild jerk as it orients itself and, still screaming, throws itself into the river. Steam rises from the water. The whole body disappears beneath the brackish Thames, and that last anguished scream bubbles away as the humanoid mouth dips beneath the waters.

"We have to go!" I say. "No telling how long it'll stay down."

"We've lost all the horses," Wamsley says. He puts his hand through his hair, turns to Hayes, and then vomits onto the ground.

"I'll chase them down," Fred says. She doesn't wait for us

and starts off in a run after my gelding and two of the others that fled towards London. I watch her go for a moment and wonder if she'll come back.

But she has to. She came for us for a reason.

Part of me is scared to get closer to Hayes. His cries are quiet, but they come with every exhale.

Don't think about him, not yet. Not yet.

I look towards Leo. He's shaking, not from fear or even from pain. It looks like his body is just doing it, adrenaline flooding his nervous system.

"Leo."

"I'm fine," he says. He even offers me a smile.

I reach over and peel his hands away. Involuntarily, he makes a noise like a hiss and squeezes his eyes shut.

"Don't lie to me," I tell him.

His nostrils flare. I think tears are welling in his eyes, so I press his hands over the stomach wound again and lean forward to kiss his forehead.

"The horses are gone," he says. "I don't know if I can walk."

"It's okay," I say. I look around. My gelding—perhaps he hasn't run that far. "It's okay, I'll find a way to get you back behind the wards. I promise you."

When I glance behind me, Sutton is waiting. She inclines her head, and I nod, going to her. She takes my arm and skirts us away from the water and the group so we're out of earshot.

"Hayes is a goner," she tells me. It's a matter of fact. Straightforward. No emotion laces her words, but I can tell she's frightened. Agrawal. Now Hayes.

I bite my tongue until it stings, and I nod at her. "Okay. Are we leaving him? Or. . ."

I leave the question unsaid and look past her to where Hayes' body lies.

Only it's not his *body*—not a corpse. Not yet. Hayes is still alive.

"I know what you're thinking," Sutton says quickly. "But the resources. . . Just trying to get him back to London when we have two others injured. . ."

"Would the magic behind the Janus Gates help him?" I ask.

Sutton blinks at me and then shrugs. "His skin is sloughing off, Cassius. How are we going to move him without killing him? Without dirt and disease getting into his flesh?"

Two things happen in me, then. The first is a resurgence of old, ingrained guilt. I feel religious in that moment, the way I might if God Himself had come down to me and said, "Cassius: this man is in pain. Cassius: you are meant to relieve him."

The second is an incongruent, angry feeling. Practicality and ruthlessness and necessity—I understand that it will not be a kindness to pretend that Hayes is going to make it, or that I will put half the effort into saving him as I would for Victoria or Leo. I walk to him.

Hayes shakes on the ground. Part of his skin and flesh surrounds his body. His Hunter cloak is slashed. Looking at it makes me think of my own: the mantle of the Hunter, the uniform, the prestige. I could embroider a *nuckelavee*, now. A *chimera*. Whatever else I fought at Prittlewell.

What ever was the point of embroidering the kills? What ever was the point of training, of learning behind London's walls? I feel as if we have only half a chance better than the rest of humanity. Was it ego? Have we all been groomed into thinking we could be *better* or *smarter,* that somehow, through the right combination of books, through the right number of years, we could survive against a threat like the *teras*?

That we could *win?*

"You listen to me," Hayes is saying. I snap to attention and look down at him. He's shaking and shivering. He's crossed his arms over his torso. The skin flays from them and then disappears beneath the Hunter sleeve. The skin on his neck and face are red and raw, or covered in blistering welts. The whites of his eyes are bloodshot. The lids of his eyes have half melted—he can't blink. He looks like he wants to cry, but with such dry eyes, I know he can't.

"You listen to me. Listen to me," he says. "I know. Don't say it, Jones. I fucking know."

I glance around. Sutton hesitates but steps closer. I go to my knees before Hayes. He reaches out and grabs my arm with one of his diseased hands. I'm ashamed to say I flinch from him.

Hayes ignores my obvious disgust of him. "I want my flesh to feed something. If it's you—if it's humans—all the better."

I stare at him. "What?" And then, as I recognise exactly what he wants us to do, I shake my head. "No. Absolutely not."

"Drag me back!" he says, voice shrill. Phlegm, or perhaps the flesh of his oesophagus, has coated his vocal cords. His voice oscillates from high and strained to a deep gurgling. Hayes shakes my arm weakly. "Do it. You don't know how long it will be until all the food is gone. And then what? Do you think you'll still have morals when your body starts to eat itself?"

"Hayes, I will not eat your body."

He looks upset with me. His eyes dart from me to Sutton, who is walking closer. "Sutton, tell him."

She can't meet his eye. Sutton nods her head to the ground, reverential. "You're diseased, Len. The flesh is diseased. We can't eat it. And I couldn't. . .couldn't do that to you."

"You will," he says, "that's an order."

"I won't," she says. Her voice is a whisper. She kneels beside him and puts her hand flat on his chest. "I can't."

Hayes' face convulses. He tries to smooth out the expression and regain control, but his voice cracks as he says, "Please. Don't leave me out here."

That's the crux of it, in the end. He doesn't want to die alone.

I look at Sutton, who is already staring at me. I open my mouth and breathe in deeply. "Hayes, we can't stay."

He seems to consider this. His face cycles through a range of emotions. At each buckle of his brow, the skin cracks. Half a minute later and a flap of flesh has peeled away over his temple. It now sits, curled under his eye. I give him the grace of another minute, letting him rage and dent and plead internally before he comes to the same resolute conclusion.

"Alright," he says. Regaining some control over his voice, Hayes sounds settled. He tries to stop his shaking. "Then end it here."

I expected him to ask it, but I am still shocked by the bluntness of his request. I glance at Sutton. She, however, must not have expected it—her eyes are wide, and tears are welling. She looks at me and shakes her head. Mouths at me, *I can't.*

Shit.

My dagger is lost somewhere in the grass. I ask Wamsley to find it, but I think I'll return one of Hayes' bullets.

"Hold my hand?" he asks Sutton steadily. She slips both her hands over his and grips tight, even when the pressure causes his skin to part from the flesh of his fingers. Sutton whimpers.

I shift. My heart is racing. Nausea screams in my stomach. I ignore it all, retreat somewhere deeper in my mind; none of this matters, I tell myself. There's no guarantee I'll live even another day. So this one death doesn't matter.

Besides—I've done it before. I put a bullet in the skull of a suicide attempt. I helped to spare his suffering. That's all this is for Hayes. The same thing. The same thing.

I get onto my knees and load a bullet into the flintlock. I've done it before. I've done it before. I push the barrel against his forehead.

I try to stay out of Hayes' line of sight because I don't want to be the last thing he sees. But I needn't have bothered. He's looking at Sutton, and she's looking back. They nod at one another.

"Thank you," I tell him. I want to say more, to thank him for going after Claypoole, to thank him for his efforts. In truth, I want to thank him for being the one to die.

At least it's not Victoria. At least it's not Leo.

At least it's not me.

Without further delay, I fire the bullet into Hayes' skull.

He dies immediately. I sink onto my haunches, watching the way the skin disintegrates around the bullet wound, the way his blood seems to melt away the rest of his diseased face, and when Sutton lets out a sob, I stand to let her have a moment.

When I turn around, though, another scene is at hand.

Wamsley has his back against a tree, arms folded. His brows are scrunched together in something close to disgust.

Leo has moved, the idiot. He's gotten up or crawled to be close to Victoria. Who is crying. Who is crying so hard that my stomach falls out of me.

As I get closer, I can see why.

Blood, viscera, pink. A trail of it leading between her legs.

Leo gently lifts her shift away from her stomach. The bruise there is near blue from the impact of the *nuckelavee*. From whatever trauma she sustained fighting the *phrygian*.

From the stress and the starvation and the horse riding and the fighting and everything else—

It was bound to happen, wasn't it? Even if the baby had lasted to term, could it have survived in this world?

I go down to my knees and crawl towards her, touching her knee. "Victoria."

She slaps my hand away with a scream, but then she starts crying again. "I'm sorry," she says, "I'm sorry, I'm sorry."

I don't think she's talking to me. She reaches between her legs and starts fumbling through the viscera, searching for the small clump of flesh belonging to her baby. I'm not sure if she finds it, but whatever bit of flesh she picks up, she cradles. But it's not the baby she cries for.

"Bellamy," she whispers before sobbing again. "Bellamy, I'm sorry."

26

LESSON TWENTY-SIX

"Well, I don't know a damn thing about babies. Except they kill a lot of people."

Fred found one of the horses—my gelding—and managed to calm it. Victoria is slumped over in the horse's mane, sleeping fitfully, waking every so often to sob.

"I want to know if she'll survive it," I say. I'm talking about the viscera. Of whatever might be left inside her womb. I don't know how it happens—if it will pass naturally, if it will rot inside her. Fred is the wrong person to ask. I see her shift uncomfortably at the mention of pregnancy or of babies, and after a beat, she turns to me and blinks.

"My mother died in childbirth," she says. The mask she wears is a veil hiding her emotion. I can't parse anything from her tone beyond a general sadness, one that's always lacing her voice. "That's about all I know of it."

Fred speeds up so she can get away from me, tugging the reins of the gelding to encourage it onward. I slow until I fall in step with Leo.

The fool has decided to walk. Something about giving Victoria her space or her privacy. It means he is limping, his body twisted over as he clutches the wound in his stomach. He looks like a wounded Gaul, that marble statue I've read about once. Or perhaps an *automaton*. He walks without Meléti's terrifying grace and occupies, instead, an uncanny middle ground. It frightens me to see him like this.

Strangely enough, Leo doesn't react much when I come up beside him. His eyes are fixed on the ground. Every step must be paining him. My eyes keep darting to his abdomen, where his fingers press firmly over the layers of fabric. I squint, waiting until I can see blood.

"I'm fine," Leo croaks out eventually. He rolls he eyes at me, aiming for nonchalance, emulating vapid immortality. I grimace at him, and his face falls. "Really."

"Really," I repeat and slip my arm through his, urging one of his hands off his stomach so it sits up and over my shoulder. Immediately, he slumps into me. A small noise escapes his mouth, sweet like a moan, and I wish I was strong enough to carry him. I imagine him, beautiful neck lolling against my chest, face sweet as he relaxes and falls into slumber. The boy in my mind is not quite Leo; I'm not sure Mr Shaw would let down his guard like that. But I love to think I might be the one he lets in.

"It's the better part of an hour back to London," I guess, by the way we're going, and he nods, grunting his acknowledgement.

By this point, Sutton looks like a ghost of herself. Her skin has that grey, sickly tone to it, and she breathes shallowly, walking sluggishly behind even Leo. I glance back at her and watch the rise and fall of her chest. Her breathing is shallow. The furrow in her brow deepens when she catches me looking.

I haven't said that I'm sorry about Hayes, and I don't plan to lie to her. I did something she couldn't do—did she want me to leave him to the elements? Or to fulfil his last wish, dragging his corpse behind us as if we would eat his infected flesh?

"She's just in shock," Leo says to me when I turn back around.

"I didn't even say anything."

"You didn't have to," he murmurs. He glances at me, smiles softly. "I know you."

I shiver, wondering if he does and what it means if he does. His grip on my shoulder becomes a squeeze, and he moves his hand to the back of my neck, where he squeezes again. The grip is possessive and yet somehow kind, like he's guiding me forward.

I feel an internal tug and involuntarily urge to go limp against his touch.

"Stay focused," Leo tells me, and I roll forward to do as I'm told. His low chuckle is half lost in the wind, but as he pats my back, I hear him murmur. "That's it. Good boy."

I try to dislodge my focus from Leo, because I think I'm rather good at focusing on him, and quite shit at focusing on everything else. I think he's like mildew, in a way. Some creeping, infectious disease. I think he's taken root in me, and maybe a part of me will always belong to him now.

I think I don't really mind that.

But in any case, I look forward. Wamsley is leading us. He has my dagger in his right hand. I can see the force of the grip from here.

The sun is like a cracked egg, yolk splitting over the horizon. Its beauty is tainted by the knowledge that night will fall soon, and our human eyes will fail us. I bite my tongue for a minute or so before I say, "We need to speed up."

Leo looks up at me, pained betrayal spotting his eyes.

"I know," I say. And then: "Leo, get on the horse."

He opens his mouth to protest, and his voice ekes out of him, falling into a flat sigh. His eyes fall on Victoria.

"I don't want to," he says. "You know why. I'm just as much responsible for what happened to her and Bellamy. And really, Cass, I already told you: I would have left her behind, too."

"It's not like she knows that," I say. I see the *Nemean Lion*; I see its jaws opening wide and tearing my arm free from the rest of me. I see Bellamy's body limp by the door. I feel again, as keenly as I had when I first realised it, the knowledge that he was still alive. That he could have made it.

It's not like she knows that. A weak argument—made weaker still now that Leo is pouring his heart out to me. *He is telling you why he can't, and you are telling him why he should.* I stop walking and turn bodily to face him. In this light, and now that I'm looking at him fully, he is more than a little unwell. Sweat beads at his forehead. And there *is* blood pressing between his fingers. Panic flares bright in me as I imagine his stitches popping apart and the skin flaring open, all his insides falling out and steaming at my feet—*stop it.*

God. Should I pray to You now, I wonder? I can offer You nothing anymore. I will sin again with this man if you save him. I will sin against You if you do not. What else do you want from me? What else do you want from this world?

Does any one of us deserve this kind of life?

Is any one of us innocent?

I rub my hand over my face and ask with frostiness, "Why are you so eager to pretend you're not injured?"

Leo chews on his lip and shrugs, a flippant motion made less so by the firm pressure with which he holds his stomach.

"I can't have you worrying," he says, voice light.

I cock my head in question. He sighs.

"I'm scared of injury," he says. "Is that what you want to hear? I do not like being weak, Cassius. There's not much weaker I can be than this. Unless, you know, I was dead."

I stare at him. I stare at my stupid, stupid Leo Shaw.

Plenty of animals act like this: hide pain, obscure their injuries, pretend to everyone and themselves that they are in fighting form. Anything less than that invites predators, danger, death. I understand why he's doing it—but around this group? Around me?

"You're not pretending for the *teras*," I say.

He doesn't deny it. He doesn't say anything. On the tower of the church, I told myself I wouldn't ask. I wanted him to come forward and tell me. But now I find myself asking:

"What happened to your family?"

His face contorts. "You would ask me this now?"

I grind my teeth. Is it a stupid time? Probably. Do I feel justified anyway? Yes.

"Leo, the only thing I can think of is that showing you are injured. . ." I don't finish the thought. Instead, I turn and call out to Fred, "Slow down! Leo needs to get on the horse."

He reaches for my arm, and I slap him away. I'm angry, but in that hurt way; this is care. This is compassion. I want him to accept it; I want him to *let me*. I hear the soft hoof beats as Fred leads the gelding back to us, and before she gets too close, I decide to tell him something.

"If we ever. . .complained. Or limped. Or showed my father we were injured, even if *he* was the one responsible, then he would. . ."

Leo isn't looking at me. I step forward and lower my voice, gently gripping his wrist as I say the rest. "He would make it worse. Tell us we had to be stronger. That the *teras* would smell the weakness in us and rip it out. And the worst part is, I stayed weak. Thaddeus grew some hard shell, and I just got softer and softer. More frightened. More broken. More desperate, for God, or for men, or for some saviour from it all. Then, one day, he doesn't come home. Then it was a week, then it was another. For a moment, I thought God had answered my prayers because I was that sort of child, praying my father would die for good. Praying all the pain would stop and the rest of us would move on. When he finally shows up on the shoreline, he's different. Half the crew is dead, and everyone else is like him. Empty. My mother—she's the type of woman who couldn't comprehend that he was a bad person. She mourned him and still mourns him, and fought to get all of us into London, even when it meant Thaddeus would have to be amongst the best. She treats that husk of a man like he is worth any bit of care in the world. Even after everything he did to us. Even after Thaddeus' death, even after I found him like that, I haven't heard from her once. So I understand why you might be acting like this, Leo, but I am telling you, you will kill yourself. You will rip the stitches free, and our Healer has just lost her child; she does not have the capacity to care for you too. Don't be a fool. Don't die. I won't ever forgive you. Do you understand me? Get on the fucking horse."

By the time I've finished, I don't care who's heard me. I can feel other eyes on me, and I know everyone has stopped walking, for I hear no footsteps, no crush of grass or squish of mud.

Leo's eyes are wide and searching, and he has this particular gleam in his expression. I don't know what it means. He leans forward, steepling his fingers against my neck, and he kisses me very firmly on the lips. When he pulls away, he says, "I'll get on the fucking horse, Cassius Jones."

And he does.

❧

AN AWFUL, creeping fog slouches towards us the closer we get to London. Night eats the runny rays of the sun quickly, swallowing it whole, and then the only bit of light is from my gelding's horse lantern. I expect to see London lit up, but as we walk, there's nothing to tell me where we are. So when we do stumble close to Aldgate, I'm shocked.

None of us say it, but we feel it. London is dark. The wardstones flicker, and I won't lie; the relief I feel that they're still upright nearly makes me keel over.

Victoria mumbles from her place on the horse. I don't hear her words, and they quickly devolve into sobs. Cautiously, Leo reaches out and spreads a tentative hand against her back. The rest of his body is tense and unmoving.

"We're almost there," I coo to her.

She presses her face further into the horse's mane. "Shut up, Cassius."

I shut up.

"Hello?" Sutton calls out. Her voice echoes, and the sudden loudness of it unnerves me. The phantom of her greeting shudders around us, returning on the wind as it ricochets off the stone structure.

We all go quiet, straining our ears as we wait for a response. Nothing. No reply at all. My nerves start up immediately. A pain begins in my left chest, at the rib just below the heart. Or perhaps the heart itself—I don't know, only that the ache is there and grows more prominent as the silence stretches. If Aldgate is unmanned, then we'll have to walk around, find another gate, and beg to be let in there.

"I don't like this," Fred says.

"You can say that again," Wamsley grumbles.

"Wamsley," I say. He flinches towards me. A light rain starts up, and he stares unblinking at me even as the droplets pool in his eyelashes. As I skirt closer to him, a hand reaches down and squeezes my neck—Leo, like an angel from above, sitting atop the horse.

"Careful," Leo says with a wink.

I swallow and turn to Wamsley, inclining my head away from the group. He follows.

"What?"

"If Aldgate is abandoned, does it mean the rest of the gates are?"

He looks down to where I've touched him. Without thinking, I've gone and gripped his forearm. Rain pelts down on that flesh-to-flesh bond, and I watch the droplets slide off our Mackintoshs, which in this dark light appear like strange, greasy skin.

Wamsley gently pulls his arm away and stands straight. "Why are you asking me? No, actually—why are we having this conversation away from everyone else?"

My eyes flit from him to the side door next to the large gate. "Press on the door with me."

"With you?" he frowns.

"Yes, with me." I take him by the shoulder again and spin him towards the gate. "I don't want to do it alone."

He snorts. "Frightened, are you?"

His tone is mocking, but he lets me guide him. I don't answer immediately. The cool breeze snakes over my skin, and the chill makes me shiver. There's the other thing, of course; the creeping dread. It moves with the fog which drags itself through the tree line, sinking closer towards London. Perfect cover for an army, for a thousand creatures to stalk towards this final bastion.

My body tells me something is wrong. I have lived my whole life with instinctual warnings; the dread in the stomach that won't go away, the persistent strain of anxiety on my nervous system. I know how to listen when something is wrong. Thus, I know, too, when something is *worse* —when something has shifted, and the usual threat becomes magnified. Something ticks in my brain, and I know it's not just the night I should be worried about. Not just the *teras*.

The wall surrounding London looks intact. The ward is

still up and shimmering. In the week since we've been here, something possessed the dean to retreat.

Is that what's happened? Has Dean Drearton made good on his promise and pulled all of London's survivors behind the Janus Gates?

But only students and graduates have personal wardstones.

So where is everyone else?

I finally answer Wamsley, "Yes, I'm scared. You're not?"

My honesty must shock him because his face falls. "Quite a bit, actually."

"Good. We'd both be stupid not to be. Now come on."

He walks in step with me, in tandem, and when I press close, he doesn't move away. Water drips in the grooves of Aldgate's side door, leeching an old scent from the wood. Together, we press our bodies against it. No force is necessary. The thing swings open with a groan, and I step back involuntarily, spurred by the sound. Not good. Not good at all.

I look over my shoulder to find Sutton has come up behind us. Her hands are on her hips. Rain drips from the edge of her tricorn, which shadows her eyes and makes her concern palpable.

"I know," I tell her before she's said anything.

She sighs and shifts her arms, crossing them across her chest. "Are they dead?" she asks, looking past me.

I spy Victoria, slumped over and shoulders shaking, and Leo behind her, gently patting her back. We lock eyes, and he cocks his head in question, then looks behind me at the gaping blackness of London's interior. The hand on Victoria's back stops moving.

I meet Sutton's eyes, but I can't bring myself to answer. How could I know? And what benefit would there be for Drearton to abandon them, unless he has decided there is nothing worth protecting more than his own life. It seems to undermine every action he's taken thus far, though. Completely uproots the power of the institution, which in turn makes Drearton untouchable.

"He wouldn't kill them," I say, glancing back into the bowels of the empty street. An image of my parents dead cracks into my mind. My mother slumped against the wall the way Thaddeus died, guts in her hands, pretty dress smeared with entrails. My father with his eyes gouged out, with his body made as hollow as his soul.

Wamsley plucks my sleeve and pulls me closer. I stumble in his direction. He lets out a gruff sigh, chews at his lip. "I fucking hate this. Alright? I don't. . .I didn't realise. That Drearton wasn't. . ." He lacks the word, but I understand his sentiment.

"You don't want to be punished?" I ask.

He glares at me. "I don't want London to no longer be safe."

I stare at him, and I think it might be nice to live with that kind of ignorance. In the end, it's not me that says anything. It's Leo. He's brought the horse trotting towards the entrance.

"It was never safe," Leo tells Wamsley. "Not unless you were the right sort of person."

This only makes Wamsley frown, of course, but he's been a Londoner all his life. In that way, he's worse than me—sheltered beyond the torment of years of exposure. But he's had a taste now, I suppose.

"There's nothing wrong with wanting to be safe," Sutton says.

And she's right, of course. Of course, she's right! Only when you think about it, when you *really* let yourself think about it, and you imagine the suffering of every person outside the wards—the deaths and the injuries and the trauma and the endlessness of it all, the helplessness that lingers, that's passed through generations—then it makes your own safety taste bitter. It makes God's love feel unreal. It makes Satan more tangible. Then, when you look close enough at the bastion you've poured your hope into, you can see the cracks. And the cracks become fissures. And then you realise the whole thing is built on the backs of Workers, who never experience full protection or safety or luxury, who live forever under the caveat of being useful. Which, in turn, is what the rest of us have to be. It was always like this; the University was about making scared people worth something. Now, they just happen to be more open about it. All of us are too scared and too lost and too helpless to do much else but accept it.

Except, I suppose, for the cultists. God. I am starting to sound like Fred.

When my own mind betrays me like this, I get uncomfortable in my own flesh. It's like a foreign gospel has taken root in me, the seeds of a new god's scripture blooming on my tongue. An infection. An interloper. I bite down hard on the fleshy thing until the pain turns my mind blank.

"Cassius?" Sutton prods.

I blink my eyes open and nod at her. "I'm alright. We should go."

It's then I notice the silence. Or the absence. I didn't even notice when she slipped away.

"Wait," I murmur, and the others turn to me. "Where's Fred?"

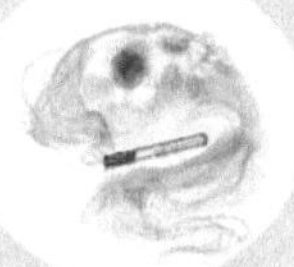

27

LESSON TWENTY-SEVEN

It seems odd to me that she abandoned us. Or rather, it just makes her story more inconceivable, and I am already doubting her heavily at this point. We stand like chickens, directionless and pathetic, squabbling amongst ourselves about what to do. I want to go into London itself, which Leo, of course, agrees with. Everyone else argues that we would have seen Fred Lin slip past us, and unless she'd been foolish enough to walk to some other gate, she should have been close. But no one dares to call out her name. It is dark and rainy. The fog keeps creeping closer. Visibility is poor, and after the attacks we've endured, we can't stand to call another *teras* to our location.

"Then we should step over the threshold," I say. "Head inside. Get to the University."

After that, it should have been up to Fred to lead us, in whatever direction her cult believes the rift to be. But since she's wandered off, I resolve to find Drearton.

"And if Drearton's unleashed some fucking *teras* into London?"

The voice is Victoria's. She looks unwell. The rain has

plastered her hair to her cheeks, and her eyes are puffy from crying. Her body is slouched over, hands gripping her stomach, face still pressed against the horse's mane.

"Another *Nemean Lion?*" she murmurs. She says it whilst staring directly at me.

I do not look away.

"Is that what you think he'd do?" Sutton asks. She takes out her dagger and flexes her hand around its grip as she peers into the dark streets beyond the ward.

"I wouldn't put it past him," Victoria mumbles, anger plain. "He'd do anything for power."

"Thanks for waiting."

We all swivel. Fred Lin rushes towards us with a sack in her hand.

"Fuck off like that often, do you?" Leo asks, voice pitched sweetly high. Fred flashes him a look and doesn't grace him with an answer.

"You can't do that, Fred," I say as she places the sack on the ground amongst us.

"I can do whatever I want," she says. "I spent the trials listening to you, Jones, and look how that turned out for me."

Leo laughs. "Ah, yes. The *manticore* was very much under Cassius' control. Look. I'm sorry Silas is dead, but—"

Fred moves swiftly. In the blink of an eye, she's shifted. Her dagger nips at Leo's belly. To his credit, he doesn't flinch, not even when Fred's eyes shimmer with fury, not even when her lips peel off her teeth in a snarl.

"You don't get to say his fucking name," she says. "I wish you had died instead of him."

"I'm sure you do," Leo says. "I don't blame you. When it happened to me, I wished something similar for a long time."

"What would you know of it?" she spits.

It's a chance for Leo to say something—to make strides to

repair this schism between them. To share something of his past with her. But why should he?

Leo says nothing. But he does smile.

Victoria is staring back at Fred, and the two make eye contact. Fred's nostrils flare, and she pulls the dagger back, turning instead to the sack at her feet.

I don't understand this exchange. Have the pair of them spoken that much since the trials? Maybe, and I wouldn't have been privy to it, for they both have the bond of being screwed over by my choices. Of losing loved ones. Of being changed forever.

"It's a Rifter drop," Fred says, replacing the blade in its sheath. "Stashed at various points along the wall, for anyone exiled, or anyone coming back from patrol."

"Any cultists, you mean," Sutton says. Fred doesn't even bother looking her way.

"What's it for?" Wamsley murmurs, voice so quiet that I think he's frightened of her.

Fred doesn't look at him either. No moment is spared for anyone not worth it. She drops into a squat and carefully opens the sack.

"Can be anything," she mumbles. "But this one. . ."

She pulls out weapons.

Fred makes a grunt of approval as she hefts out a crossbow and ten bolts.

"Jesus," Wamsley mutters, folding his arms, but he can't hide the interested tilt to his head. I'm the same. This is good. This gives us a chance to survive whatever is in London's walls—*teras*, Dean Drearton, the rift itself. Thank God for pagans. All hail the rift, or whatever.

"Load up," Fred says, snatching the crossbow and bolts for herself.

My eyes catch on something, and I freeze.

"Is that—?"

"A revolver," Fred says appreciatingly. She picks it up and palms it, rotating it as she inspects the casing. "Your flintlock has nothing on it."

And I love my brother's gun, but it's outdated and suffers in the rain, and Fred is right.

The barrel is a bright polished silver, and the grip shines pearlescent. *Is* it pearl? I can't fathom the expense of it, can't imagine from which rich bastard's corpse this thing has been pilfered.

Revolvers are rare. Most weapons manufacturing ceased when the *teras* threat simply became too difficult to manage. If anything, it falls to Artificers to tinker with and fix the weapons already in circulation. But nothing new has been made—at least not on a large scale—since before I was born. I've never actually held a revolver. It seems to me like a piece of technology far too advanced for a world like ours. What do you mean it uses cartridges? What do you mean it automatically ejects the casings? What do you mean it can hold six of them before needing to be reloaded?

Fred can see my hungry eye. I see my warped reflection in the whites of her eyes, and I wonder how I become this sort of man. Should I go down on my knees and pray for it? Should I let her put the barrel in my mouth, should I suck— would that Cassius be more familiar to her?

You'd do it, wouldn't you, whore? You're not above anything now.

"Can I?" I murmur.

She cocks her head at me and moves her fingers so the revolver swings in an arc, balanced on her index finger. I have this image of her throwing it, and then I chase after it like a dog.

"Ms Lin," Leo mutters from the horse.

It breaks Fred's revelry. Her face crumples, and she snatches the revolver close to her chest. "Don't call me that. No Miss, or Ms, or what have you. Just Fred. Okay?"

Leo blinks. "Okay."

Fred throws me the revolver.

I catch it and open it immediately, counting six bullets. Wamsley's already gone to his knees in the mud to rummage through the sack. He pulls out a gun of his own. A rifle.

"Better with distance," he murmurs, also snatching up another knife that he decides to strap to his ankle.

Sutton grabs a longer blade, a rapier. Leo asks for a gun. There's only a flintlock left, but he takes it. He also takes a dagger then gestures for another, which he then slips into Victoria's hand. She grips it so tightly her knuckles turn bone white.

"Alright," Fred says. She bundles up the sack and dashes off in the rain to return it from wherever she plucked it. I consider following her, but I can't justify the interest enough. My eyes fall on Leo, who's gripping his stomach with the same ferocity with which Victoria holds the dagger.

"Are you. . .?"

"I'll be fine," he says. Unsatisfactory.

"Everyone has their personal wardstones?"

To my great relief, everyone nods. Everyone except for Leo.

"Are you kidding?" I whisper. It comes out snappish and full of anger, which isn't quite my fault; I'm scared. He's injured. His guts are falling out. I may not understand much about the Janus Gate, but I know the magic inside it heals, and Leo needs healing.

I turn to the others just as Fred returns.

"I need to get Leo past the Janus Gate immediately. Victoria, too. They need to heal." Everyone stares at me. "Someone give up your stone."

Fred grimaces. She wants to go searching. She wants to find the rift immediately. "This can wait."

"It can't," I say firmly. I don't care as much about the world as I do about him.

"Then take mine," Wamsley says. My body reacts strangely, and I turn bodily to him. He fishes his out of an internal pocket and passes the small, pressed bit of crystal into my palm. My arm shakes as I accept it, and I look at him with more lust and love and gratitude than I've looked at almost anything. He could be God in that moment. I want to kiss him.

Wamsley recognises something in my eyes—of course he does, he's seen me getting fucked—and red springs across his cheeks as he flushes.

"Stop that," he mutters, scratching the back of his head. And then, "Come on."

With that, spurred on my embarrassment, Wamsley is the first one to cross the threshold into London.

28

LESSON TWENTY-EIGHT

The rain becomes a fine mist as we cross the threshold as if the world recognises the shift. The cold spritz clings to my cheeks and dampens my oily Hunter cloak until it clings to my skin. The lack of light is more noticeable inside the walls. Pubs, usually full of revelry, are silent as if abandoned. A door bangs somewhere, spurred on by the wind. The only sound is the intermittent clopping of the horse, and its hoofbeats rebound off the stone, echoing through the empty city.

The wind howls through thoroughfares. In the south part of the city, closer to the University, a few gas lamps remain lit. I freeze instinctively.

"You alright, Jones?" Wamsley teases, but my jaw is clenched so tightly I can't reply. Leo leads the horse over in my direction and touches the back of my shoulder.

"Cass?"

"It's nothing," I say. "Just a memory."

Which is true. I see Watford, that market town Thaddeus and I visited together. Where he risked Drearton's wrath by taking me out for patrol. Where I encountered my first *hybrid*.

Where the bodies of dozens of villagers lay mangled in a viscous soup preserved by the snow.

But Drearton wouldn't unleash a *teras* in here, would he? No *teras* except those used in the trials are kept within the wards. And those are protected, aren't they? Those are kept safe?

Fred is looking at me with something akin to disgust or perhaps pity. I wonder what she sees, whether she recognises my remembered fear.

But I think Fred managed to kill the scared part of herself and move on. I have never been able to do that, not really. As much as I try and as much as I tell myself I have, as much as I move away from God and the frailness I felt with my faith, I can't ever truly be this man.

"Remember it somewhere else," Fred mutters after a minute. I say nothing. I can't even muster the urge to feel annoyed. Leo squeezes the back of my neck, and I close my eyes.

Everything is fine. Everything will be fine.

We keep walking in this strained limbo, listening to the wind and the rain and the clopping of the horse.

London smells empty. There's no smoke or smog, no amalgamation of cooked meals stewing through the streets. The rank mess of human life has been washed away, and it feels wrong.

A screech shatters the silence. All of us freeze. It echoes out into a chitter and reverbs throughout the streets.

"It's not inside," Sutton says with a confidence I don't feel. "It's just so quiet we can't help but hear it."

No one says anything, not to argue and not to agree. By some silent signal, we all decide to keep walking. But my blood is hot, and my heart is racing. I feel that learned adrenaline, and every sense in my body lights up. I move, tense and ready, trying to remain as nimble as possible to spring into action. My eyes search every corner. There are shadows in vestibules and under awnings. Under the pale moonlight, they stretch and wane, becoming elongated like the arms of the *nuckelavee,* or stout and feathered like a *harpy.* I see every possible variation of *teras* hidden in amongst the umbral dark, coalescing with shadow, being born from it, bred from it. There are no people. There's no blood. But this is somehow worse.

Then, closer to the University gates, there's light.

It shocks me enough that it's not relief that I feel upon seeing it but fear. Several of the apartments and houses have firelight glowing behind transparent curtains. Sutton rushes up to one of them and knocks on the door.

No one answers.

Leo brings the horse to a stop, and we listen, all of us straining for sounds of life. For chatter. Music. Anything.

Sutton knocks again. "Hello?"

Her voice sounds foreign and frightening, if just for the loudness of it. It echoes slightly in the confined vestibule, but Sutton is not dissuaded. She knocks again. Fred takes her lead and chooses another door.

Not me. I look up at the sky. I see something—a *harpy,* maybe—fluttering angrily above. It screeches distantly, talons curling up violently each time its feet meet the barrier of the wardstone.

Like it's testing to see if it's still there.

"*Quiet!*"

The voice is muffled through the wood of a door. I drop my head—someone has answered Sutton.

Fred abandons her own attempts, and we gather close to the door.

"What is going on?" Sutton asks.

There's no reply for a moment, then a choked: *"Go away."*

Sutton straightens herself. Her face takes on this look of profound upset.

"I am Sutton D'Avore, direct descendent of Angelica D'Avore, the first Hunter. I've been on patrol, and I've just returned. To. . .to this." She waits a beat. "Tell me what happened."

Her voice doesn't waiver. I know what she's doing by invoking Angelica, and I still shiver when I hear how she steps so easily into legacy.

After a strained beat where the wind whistles through the thoroughfare, the voice finally says, *"Fine."*

It's pitched barely above a whisper and sounds male. The person refuses to open the door. "Dean Drearton says... that the *teras* are coming. That there's an army. That he's not sure how much longer the wards will hold! We are just some of the people left."

The voice pitches higher. The sound of someone sobbing in the same room cuts through, and the voice abruptly shifts to comfort them.

"People left?" Sutton clarifies, cutting the comforting short.

The person shuffles and sighs. *"People fought to get into the University. A lot of them are holed up in there."*

I can't imagine Drearton allowing that. I frown and look around at the others.

"The University is. . .not for outsiders," Sutton says carefully. But the person says nothing more except, *"Go on, now, leave us."*

So we go.

THE UNIVERSITY IS INDEED the locale where most of London has fled to, and their presence there feels, in an odd way, like a violation.

Don't judge me for that—I feel as if I've earned my place here through literal blood, sweat, tears. This institution does not belong to me, but my place here has been carved out; it required that I prove myself, that I follow its rules, that I become one of its students. I was confirmed by its rituals, and I participated. To see the people of London scattered about like interlopers throws into question everything I did.

If I could have just walked in and taken root, why didn't I? Why did all of us agree to participate?

Of course, it's not that simple. The Blood Hunters would have stopped us from leaving. Deep down, all of us craved confirmation and belonging because it promised us safety, too.

But if Drearton has let London in—and it appears he did, for the gates sit proudly open—then he has abandoned this facade.

"He let them in," Victoria murmurs from her place on the horse. She sounds as surprised as I feel and sits up straighter on the mount as if spurred to thinking by the sight of London's remains. "My family might be here."

She says it flatly, and I wait for her to say the rest—to ask to go and find them. She turns to look at me. Hair plasters across her cheeks, which are pale and sweaty. I know she feels the same as I do. There's no point in looking for people who did nothing to warn us or protect us, who welcomed the trials for us if it meant their continued safety. My eyes flick to Wamsley.

"You want to go searching?" I ask. He is breathing heavily. The rapid rise and fall of his chest catches my eye. For some reason, he looks to me and then to Leo, eyes lingering on the both of us before he finally shakes his head.

"Later." His voice comes out weak, cracking halfway through the word. Is it shame that stops him from seeking them out? I remember that feeling. Like my parents would see what I'd done, that I'd let men touch me, that I'd fucked them gleefully and then gone to church stinking of sin.

When Sutton leads the horse around to the left of the entrance hall, where the trial quarters sit, we see that most of the Londoners have set up here. A few tarps have been raised, but most of the people are sequestered in the colonnaded strip to the right, heading down toward the great hall. Where Bellamy died. Where I lost my arm. I notice almost none of them have slipped into any of the accommodation, and I wonder if that's to do with a reverence for the place or if Drearton's simply had them locked.

In any case, we give them all a wide berth. We all keep our heads down, but this only accentuates the silhouette of the tricorn hats. The Londoners speak out—I hear them call out *Hunter* the way one might *saint* or *angel*.

I ignore them and use this moment to sidle close to Wamsley. He shivers when I get close.

"What?" he hisses. His eyes go past me to the crowd, searching desperately. Is he worried to be seen with me? Worried someone will spot him close to another man and assume the rest?

"You don't have to do this to yourself, you know," I say.

He frowns and finally slides his eyes to me. Not for long, though. Very soon, he drags them to the ground, where I assume he finds it safer to stare. Wamsley stuffs his hands into his pockets.

"Don't know what you mean," he says.

Maybe there would be a better time for it, but when I think of my life over the past year, there's rarely been anything close to a good moment for complex conversation. I want him to realise what I have realised: that this world is callous and dying, and we'll all very likely die with it. Why give power to the forces who would not only see you dead, but praise a soon-to-be-defunct God for your demise? They will quote scripture at us when we're all dying of the same disease. They will find strength in their righteous fury without recognising they're suffering all the same.

"You should live," I say, and I put my hand on his shoulder. He flinches fractionally but then relaxes. "You should live whilst you still can. I will not fault you. Leo won't either. But you're not to touch him without me."

Wamsley's cheeks flush. Again, reflexively, he stutters out, "Don't know what you—"

"Of course you don't," I say, and I release him from my grip. "But if some sort of meaning does come to you and you think, perhaps, there's a bit of truth in my words, feel free to come and chat."

I leave him like that because it's all I can do. He might not take the offer. He might be content with the offer and not the action. In any case, it's not my burden; it feels instead like charity, offering him sex. Or another form of selfishness. Another man to touch me before the world ends.

Our party moves deeper into the bowels of the University's facade, through those colonnaded vestibules that lead to the quadrangle, with the ancient willow tree, Meléti's library, and the Janus Gate.

I give Leo Wamsley's stone and ready my own, turning the thing over in my hand. I pre-emptively try and brace myself for the inevitable vertigo I'll have to bear as we cross the threshold.

It turns out I needn't have bothered worrying about something as simple as the Janus Gate. Call me stupid, or cock-drunk, what have you. My focus has certainly been on other things.

I didn't really think, in the grand scheme of things, what

Wamsley, Sutton, Agrawal, Hayes, and I had done would register. But I was wrong.

London does not belong to God. It belongs to Dean Drearton. His Divine Will is law here.

We enter the quadrangle, and from the shadows emerge four Blood Hunters. The click of guns readying pops in my ears.

"Cassius Jones and crew," one of the Hunters shouts. "You are hereby under arrest for wilfully defying the orders of Dean Drearton."

I say nothing. I do nothing.

As my friends shout and the horses whinny, I look the Blood Hunter in the eye.

His face contorts. He takes the gun, whips it around, and then the thing is hurtling towards my head.

LESSON TWENTY-NINE

The next thing I know I am waking up.

Nausea flips my stomach. I roll and vomit onto the ground.

There's not much to expel. The bile that emerges is tinged tobacco brown.

There, shaking, I take stock. The side of my head pounds. I feel keenly the place where the pistol landed and knocked me cold. My stomach roils, either from being knocked out or because we've crossed through the Janus Gate.

Or because I haven't eaten in some time.

I breathe deep. I don't feel hungry. I feel displaced. Something in the air tells me I'm right; physically, I have moved from London's gravity to the more ephemeral pocket reality where the University sits. The air is a tad thicker, or stuffier, like a room without a window.

The next thing is that my hands—as it were—are bound. My one flesh hand has been strapped across my chest and tied to the remaining flesh of my shortened arm. It means the sharp remains of my prosthetic are nowhere near the rope, so I can't see through, and the whole thing is rendered useless.

I'm lying on stone.

With some ungraceful effort, I right myself.

This does nothing for my head or my body except make everything worse.

"Fuck," I mumble, dragging my knees up to rest my throbbing head against them.

"Finally."

The voice sounds—pissed off. Not even pretending to be concerned for me. I don't have to move at all to verify who it is. Instead, I say, "Hello, Fred."

Movement sounds nearby, the shuffling of shoes as she presumably gets up and comes closer to me. Only now that I have some awareness my surroundings, I realise she can't get very close at all.

We're in separate cells.

I look up and around the jail. Up until this point, I hadn't realised even existed in the University. It strikes me as odd. Or, rather, completely contrary to the image Drearton and the institution itself touts to the rest of the world.

London has a jail—for ne'er-do-wells, and thieves, and the occasional cultist execution. But in all honesty, crimes perpetuated by humanity are few and far between.

Or at least, that's what we're told.

To warrant a jail behind the Janus Gates suggests students and graduates could, or have, done things that jeopardise the University's very existence.

"You're thinking the same thing I am," Fred says

I don't feel like talking to her, though I should. She is perceptive. I'm sure she's noticed something I haven't in my bleary state. But all I want right now is Leo. I shift.

"Where—?"

"Not here," Fred says. "No one else is here. It's just you and me."

My stomach sinks slowly. It's not that I don't want to be

around Fred; it's that when I turn to face her, she is wearing her cultist mask, and I realise with some horror that means Drearton knows.

If I am kept in jail with the cultist, my crimes are on equal par.

I stare at her. After a moment, she decides to remove her mask. She slips it up and over her head—

—revealing a face so severely beaten I flinch at the sight.

"God. God, Fred."

"You slept through it all, lucky bastard," she says with a croak. Her left eye is swollen shut. The cheek beneath that has gone purple and puffy, and her lip has split. Blood is crusted down her chin. A laceration on her right cheek cuts dangerously close to her other eye, which is red but otherwise unharmed.

"Tell me," I whisper.

She smiles, but it's an odd smile. Her cell is to the left of me, and the bars are wide enough I could slip my hand through if I wanted to. Instead, the bars feel close to a necessity—it's a way for us to talk that means we can talk civilly. Closer to the way we used to. She shifts and pushes back along the dusty stone so she can rest against our shared back wall, the right side of her body leaning against the bars for support.

"They knocked you out and subdued everyone else. Leo and Victoria—they were led away almost immediately. I don't know what that means, but I told the Blood Hunters they were injured. Wamsley and Sutton were taken one way, and you and I were taken the other. They did a quick search and immediately found weapons and my mask. Cue beating."

She says it so matter-of-factly I almost miss the quiver in her voice. Fred roughly clears her throat and looks down at the frightening patchwork mask in her hand.

I check myself and find she's right. All my weapons have

been confiscated. The only I have left is Leo's gift, and I clutch the silver case in the palm of my hand until it grows warm.

"Drearton means to kill me," Fred says.

I swallow. I knew it as soon I saw her wearing it, but it still shocks me to hear. "When?"

She shrugs. "Something's happened. They're all nervous—Drearton and the teachers. It was Professor Dexter who. . ."

Professor Dexter? Fury bubbles up in me, though it is likely misplaced. Bedelia Dexter was never going to care for me. I suspected that she suggested the *manticore* for my final trial. And Fred isn't mine to worry about. Not anymore. Is she?

"Fred, I— "

"You don't have to say anything, Cassius; it is what it is." She swallows hard and sighs. "The only thing you can do now is get out of here."

I don't understand what she means. We came back here for a multitude of reasons, but mainly because Fred begged us to.

"Out of London?"

"Not yet," she whispers. "But out of this jail, certainly. Next time they come, whatever you have to say, say it. Just get out. Forget about me. You need to find the rift."

"How? How am I meant to find it?" My heart begins to race. I feel—tired. It's not an adequate description, but I can't explain the exhaustion that creeps up on me then. I want to get out of here, and I want to be Drearton's good little pet again, and I want to go back months earlier and kill him, and I want to go back to my teenage self in Hull and tell him, "There's no point."

I want God, suddenly. I want the comfort faith used to bring me. I want to feel the Holy Spirit, and I want to find comfort in every trial and tribulation Jesus endured, and I want to see myself in his care and believe it. God, in that moment, I want to be a believer again. I want my faith to be unshakeable and true and not defined by fear or guilt.

Please, I pray. *Please come back.*

It doesn't, of course. No great sense of peace fills me up. Nothing but a growing dread.

"I need to ask Meléti," I whisper.

Fred knocks her head against the bars. "I don't know what you could offer it."

"You sound just like Leo."

"Well, maybe Leo is right. What are you prepared to offer it, Cassius? A memory you offered freely hurt you last time."

"What do you want me to say?" I spit. My body aches suddenly, and the pain in my temple only intensifies as I turn bodily to face her. "You want me to find the rift. You say we have a chance of ending this. Do you want me to sit here now and say I am selfless and unafraid? We both know that's not true. But if it means stopping the end of humanity, am I even allowed to say no?"

She looks at me from under her swollen brow, eyes dark and close to fury. But she says nothing, only shrugging like I haven't said anything of worth.

"If you can stop it," she murmurs after a while, "please do."

I hear what she didn't say beneath those words; I hear her, or perhaps hear my own guilt. *If not for me, for Silas.*

I cleared my throat. "Yeah."

\#

I don't know how many hours pass. We talk and sleep sporadically. I wake up shivering on the stone and Fred wordlessly beckons me over. We sit close, sleeping fitfully with our backs pressed to each other through the bars.

She speaks to me about the execution of her friends, the Rifters hanged that day by St Peter's for a crime they didn't commit. She swears it wasn't them, that it was some *teras* taunting us, intelligent enough to stack multiple bodies into a passable human. She has no proof, but I decide to believe her.

But whatever creature made that man a patchworked figure terrifies me almost as much as Drearton.

At this point, I am not feeling anxious or upset or much of anything. A numbness has settled, a decent metre of snow in my stomach, a blanket of cold like what covered Sherwood Forest. The jail, or this part of it, has one lantern that slowly burns down to nothing, and then we are left in the dark and the cold.

When the door opens, I'm shocked by the bright light. It casts a ray of near-white clarity throughout the room. Fred shies away from it, and I sit up blinking sleep out of my eyes.

"Mr Jones?"

I don't recognise the voice. I don't reply at all.

"Mr Jones, get up."

Someone else comes in, and I hear the jangle of a set of keys as one is pushed into the lock. The grated door swings open with a groan, and two bodies come in to collect me. I decide not to aid them and let them haul me up to standing.

"Where are you taking me?" I ask calmly, with whatever flat severity is currently suppressing my other emotions.

"Dean Drearton wishes to speak with you," I'm told.

Before they close the door, I look back at Fred. She's slipped her mask back on and mock bows before the door closes, and then she is gone.

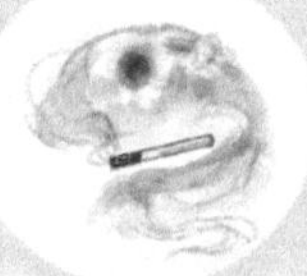

❧ 30 ❦

LESSON THIRTY

The place where Dean Drearton has made his office is well-lived.

I only ever visited his other office once and it was with my brother. We dirtied his desk with the head of the *hybrid* we killed in Watford. The one *I* killed.

Where the other office was cramped and seemed purely decorated for administrative purposes, this room has a hint of flavour. A very slight insight into Drearton's personality.

The first thing I notice is the orrery. It's almost identical to the one in the Janus Gate threshold room, the one presumably monitored often by Blood Hunters. This one is much smaller, though its scale is much larger. It spans the entirety of London, both this pocket realm and everything outside it. I squint at it as the Blood Hunter pushes me forward and manage to catch a glimpse of myself, Drearton, and the Hunter, whose name I learn is Frederick Powell.

"Thank you, Mr Powell," I say after I'm roughly pushed forward towards a chair opposite Drearton's desk.

Drearton is wearing spectacles, pretending to be very busy with papers and whatnot. I find that laughable. The *teras* have

345

an army and are hoping to tear down London's wards, and here he is, playing at his own significance. Papers and signatures and busying oneself with administrative bullshit—I've never seen such display of one's own self-importance.

"Whatever you're possibly signing," I mutter, "can't be more important than what's happening out there."

You see, at this point, I've given up on some things. I want to say: *I should have killed you when I had the chance*, but the last thread of logic keeping me together suggests this will get me nowhere.

Even the comment I made is risky, but it at least pulls Drearton's attention from the scribbles on his page.

"Mr Jones," he drawls. "How did you sleep?"

I take a moment to breathe. I think about what I wish to say and quickly put those thoughts to one side. I focus on what I need to do, what I need to know, and exactly what will get Drearton to relax.

"You can't seriously believe I'm part of those mad cultists," I say. I put a shake in my voice as if outrage or upset has broken through. "I'm a godly man, Dean Drearton."

"So Father Veer tells me."

I freeze. Fail to keep the flush from my face. I recall Father Veer telling Drearton, *"That one's not nearly as godly as he'd have you believe."*

I'd forgotten about that exchange entirely. Now I have to hope it hasn't buggered me here. But to save face, and to protect against any other things that have slipped my mind, I close my mouth and look as dejected as I can. I'm aiming for sympathy.

I don't know why. Drearton is not a sympathetic man.

"You defied my orders," Drearton begins. "You risked your own life and that of four other Hunters, both students and graduates. Two of our best have died."

"To be fair," I cut in, "Agrawal led the charge."

"Agrawal might have thought that he was being noble, but you defied me for very different reasons."

Does it hurt you to know you can't control me the way Leo Shaw can?

That thought at once warms me and terrifies me. If Drearton knows why I left, if he knows what I feel, then he has the power to control me better than anyone.

"I did not leave because I wanted to defy you," I whisper.

"Of course not, Mr Jones. We both know you're smarter than that. But at the end of the day, you *did* defy my orders. And at this point in time, what with a war looming, I cannot afford to have students or graduates who will not follow orders."

I stare at him. "I don't. . ."

"Sutton D'Avore and Don Wamsley have both admitted to being influenced by you."

He lets that sentence sit for a minute. I am stunned. Sutton said what? Wamsley said *what?*

"What did they say?" I murmur urgently after the silence gets too much to bear. "Sir, what did they say?"

"That you led the charge. That you put them in direct danger in regard to the *phrygian*, and—"

"—sir, that was Agrawal!"

"—that you encouraged them to then follow in Mr Shaws footsteps, all the way to a hub whose outpost we had already abandoned. The danger was *known*, Mr Jones, and you chose to go anyway."

I'm breathing heavily. In part, this is true, but he makes it sound like. . .like I forced them. Like I put a gun to their heads.

I murmur, "Len Hayes was in charge after Agrawal's death."

The dean sighs and leans back in his chair, which creaks as the weight shifts. He replaces his quill in the inkpot and folds his arms. "Unfortunately, neither Jahan Agrawal nor Len Hayes survived your little expedition to corroborate your story."

I feel gravity shift. Not literally, of course, but I know intrinsically that I am no longer on strong ground with this man.

Our relationship has always been conditional. But it seems he draws the line at a direct insult to his authority. Even now, with the *teras* threat encroaching so severely. . .

"The *teras* are coming. Surely you know that. Surely you know you need all the help you can get."

He looks at me and blinks, and I realise—that's simply not true. That's simply not the world Drearton cares to forge. If he wanted to focus on protecting all of humanity, he would have trained everyone who asked for it, even if he could not house them behind London's walls.

What Drearton wants is not so tangible. Power forged in helplessness and chaos. The god-like faith people offer him freely when their safety is threatened. The willful giving up of rights and individual freedoms for a chance at living. Drearton requires this particular brand of chaotic destruction. He has made of this pocket realm a Noah's Ark; he offers safety to the chosen few, regretfully opens the University gates for minuscule additional safety, bemoans the cruel fate of it all. He is God before the flood. This is his righteous destruction as much as it is the *teras'*.

"You don't have to do this," I say.

He cocks his head. "I haven't told you what I mean to do yet."

He doesn't know that I see him. That I know what he means to do.

"Mr Jones, as you may have guessed, this pocket realm can only hold so many people at any given time. Not only is this number limited by the number of wardstones we have available—which, might I add, often diminishes, given how many of us die in the field still carrying our stones—but by the simple matter of resources. We have limited food. It goes without saying this place must be culled when it becomes necessary." He pauses and looks at me.

I know what he's going to say.

"It *has* become necessary, Mr Jones," he says. I know what he's going to say; I know it, and still, my heart sinks. *No. No.*

The dean sighs, like this is an unfortunate truth, and leans forward with his hands clasped on the desk before us. "If humanity is to survive, then the people who stay behind the Janus Gates need to be people I can trust. Miss Lin is very obviously not such a person. Her wardstone has already been confiscated, and I hope to extract Satan's plans from her very lips."

"You believe that?" I ask.

Drearton raises a brow. "You don't? I thought you were a godly man."

"My faith has me see the good in people first," I say.

"Of course," the dean concedes. "Which is perhaps why you are sitting here now, with your fate in my hands."

I see no good in you, *though.* But what's the point in saying that? He's right. I have no power here.

What little I'd felt I'd gained by choosing the mantle of Hunter is now slipping from my grasp.

"I can't have people disrupting what will need to be a very tight society," Drearton continues. "Do you understand me?"

I think I do. He will punish me, or he will want me to swear fealty. I say, "You have Workers here?"

"The necessary ones, certainly," he tells me. "But everyone will contribute to the running of the Janus realm."

Another beat passes, but he still hasn't told me what he wants. "Dean Drearton. What exactly are you testing me on?"

He smiles and says, "Mr Jones, I think we are beyond

tests. Unfortunately, I no longer see you as someone who. . .*fits* here."

My blood runs cold. My body stops working. *No. No.* The suggestion in his words—is it—am I right—?

"Put your wardstone on the desk, please. And when you're ready, leave the Janus realm for good."

I stare at him.

"I don't. . ."

Drearton sighs and splays both hands on his desk. "I think you probably *do* understand; you're a bright young man and all. But it's quite a shock, I imagine, so you can take a moment. Or, perhaps I can say it more clearly for you. Mr Cassius Jones, considering you have defied me, have endangered several of your colleagues, have consequently affected the deaths of *three* colleagues in total—I almost forgot about poor Miss Kathleen Thorne—I simply do not think you are a viable member of the University. You will not graduate. Your mantle is hereby revoked. What secrets you have learned are not to be shared—and I'm breaking my own rule here, you understand, because, well, I thought you quite interesting at one point. In truth, I should eliminate you here and now, but I am not sure if you'll have much time left outside the Janus Gate, and I offer that time to you as a gift. At this point, whatever information you do or don't spread is easily deniable and, honestly, not as important as the entire *teras* army bearing down on London. So. As I said. Please reach into your pocket, pull out your wardstone, and pop it on the desk for me. Oh, and don't forget to leave your cloak."

I sit for a very long time. Probably a minute or more, I can't be sure, but Drearton only steeples his fingers together and lets me process.

Well, in truth, there is very little processing happening. I panic a great deal. My palms grow sticky, air feels thick in my throat, my skin itches in that way where I want to be rid of it, and I can't stand the way he is looking at me. Thaddeus comes unbidden in my head, and I can hear his voice telling me to pull it together.

The dean wants you to react. He's testing you, even now. Thaddeus' revenant voice scratches eagerly in my skull, pushing forward. What would he do, I wonder. Grovel? Blow up in a rage? In every way I experienced Thaddeus, I have no clue how he dealt with authority.

The only hint I have is that he defied Drearton himself. Taking me to Watford. Putting a *hybrid*'s severed head on the dean's desk.

Thaddeus wanted our family's safety secured. That was his motivation.

It isn't mine.

And yet, I think suddenly of my parents. Two emotions rise in me, and both are conflicting. The first is a gladness that this is happening. Would they be expelled from London? Would it even matter at this point? The way Drearton speaks about it, anyone not within the protection of the Janus Gate would almost certainly be killed.

"My parents?"

"Are free to live however they can," Drearton says. He has the decency to cock his head to the side. "I'm only sorry I can't do more."

"Are you?" I say, against my better judgement. Against the voice of Thaddeus, against the hard-on I have for authority of any kind. I think about what to do, face turning to the window. My legs feel leaden, and the concept of moving is so exhausting I genuinely am not sure I can do it. It's that threshold moment again, the one that delineates this world from the rest, us from them: I leave this room, and I am one step removed. I cross the Janus Gate, and I am a severed limb. Part of my brain is worried about liveability—I should be worried about what I can do while I'm still here. I should be worried about weapons, pulling from ammunition stores, sequestering food. But the rest of my mind thinking—

—I don't want to die.

"You are killing me," I whisper. Drearton stares me down.

I feel the empty space at my side where a gun should be. I yearn for it. What do I have? My severed prosthetic, maybe. Could I dive across and skewer him at an angle before Drearton or the Blood Hunter manage to stop me?

Drearton stares at me, and somehow, he knows what I'm thinking.

"Mr Powell," Drearton says. He gestures absentmindedly, one finger licking through the air. I hear the barrel roll and the click of the hammer being pulled back. Very slowly, I peer back over my shoulder at the Blood Hunter and see Frederick Powell has pulled a gun on me.

What else could I have done?

I abandon all hope of fighting my way out of this. I stand. Very slowly, I remove the wardstone from my pocket and place the bright humming thing in Mr Powell's hand. The cloak is harder to let go of. My fingers graze over the silver embroidery, and I think: *Most* teras *I've faced aren't even on here yet*. My pride, my ego, the identity I had begun to mould—

Leo won't be calling me *Hunter Jones* ever again.

Leo.

I glance back towards the orrery. Somewhere in amongst those dozens of dots is Leo Shaw.

I slip the cloak off and swallow what little dignity I have left as I fold it up and place it on the desk, moving the wardstone to weigh it down.

"At least let me say goodbye."

The dean considers me. I decide before he speaks that I would do anything. Shame be damned; I would worship at his feet, kiss them, do whatever he asked. I would laud him as I once did God— "Please, sir," I croak out. "Let me say goodbye."

Drearton sucks in a breath. But he nods.

Relief floods through my brain, and my vision swims with the deluge of joy. "Thank you. Thank you."

The words come out breathy and pleading, and it reminds me of sex. Not of the love or the passion or the pleasure, but of the power. This game Drearton and I play is a type of sex; I am being fucked ruthlessly over his desk, and my life will never be the same.

"Mr Powell," Drearton murmurs, gesturing for Mr Powell to take my wardstone. "Escort Mr Jones to his friends. Do not leave his side until he is through the Janus Gate."

LESSON THIRTY-ONE

"Cassius?"

The University's medical ward is a small, tiled strip of a room with very high barred windows and an abundance of natural light. Healers move back and forth between patients—there are ten patients in beds that I can count, and I think they must be quite important if Drearton has agreed to try and preserve their lives. People who are good at their prospective vocations.

Leo and Victoria are among them.

Leo tries to sit up when he sees me. I shush him and put a hand out. Seeing him turns my stomach into knots; how do I tell him what's just happened?

"Are you alright?" he asks when he's the one in the bed.

I ignore the question. "How are you healing?" My eyes flick to Victoria. She lies flat on her back, eyes rolling towards me without shifting her head at all. "The both of you."

Victoria's lip quirks. Tear stains have paled her cheeks in thin strips. "I'll live," she croaks out. And then, begrudgingly, "Thanks to you."

I don't ask about the baby. There are too many layers to

that question, and I am no longer close enough to her to ask without opening new wounds. But I want to know: *Are you relieved? Are you heartbroken? Are you both?*

She has to handle these emotions alone because she will not lean on anyone, and that makes my heart ache for her. I don't deserve her trust, not after Bellamy. But a part of me wishes she could see I would do anything for her.

I would kill her lovers if it meant preserving her life.

Leo's eyes have shifted to Mr Powell. "You have an escort," Leo murmurs. He glances back at me. "He doesn't seem like your type."

Mr Powell straightens behind me and I fail to suppress my smirk. Any bit of discomfort feels like a blessing. Fuck Mr Powell. Fuck this whole place. Fuck it, fuck it—maybe I should pray. Maybe I should have gone to the chapel instead of to Leo's bedside.

My expression must be obvious because Leo's brow twitches. "Cassius, what is it?"

Instinctively, my body lowers itself to the tiled floor. On my knees by Leo's bedside, I slip my hand through his and say, "Mr Powell, could you give us a few minutes alone?"

Mr Powell does not move. I glance back at him, and he looks down on me with equal measures of disgust and pity.

"I will be escorting you—"

"I know." I cut him off quickly. He won't be the one to announce my departure. "But at least allow me this."

He does, for whatever reason. Most likely to get away from the sight of two men holding hands.

Victoria is looking at me, but when I meet her eye, she turns her head away politely and pretends not to listen.

It is the closest to privacy I can have.

Leo cups my face. "What is it?"

I don't explain. I push up, and I kiss him. There's this moment sometimes, in a kiss, where your whole body swells with the joy of it. You can smell the other person, and something in your brain floods the rest of your body with pure, unaltered pleasure. Everything feels right. You fit together, and your chest seizes with the severity of the emotion; joy is briefly overwhelming.

It happens now. We may not be perfect, and it may not be love, but I *could* love him. And I admit it to myself: Leo Shaw, I *could* love you. The admission is like flaying myself, peeling the layers away until my heart sits exposed and vulnerable. I feel nauseous with it.

I don't want to go. Please don't make me go.

Leo gently pushes away. The light in his eyes diminishes, and his expression shifts, taking on a more brutal, scouring look.

"Stop this," he says. Commands. "Tell me what happened."

I tell him.

I say it quickly because I can't stand to hear it longer than I have to. I tell him Mr Powell has my wardstone and that after this goodbye, I will be escorted to the Janus Gate and abandoned on the other side.

When I finish, Leo just says, "No."

For a long while, he just looks at me. His brows crash together, and he reaches out, thumb gliding over my cheek. "No."

I don't know how to feel in that moment. My heart feels heavy, and a panic that was once distant is now creeping up on me. "Drearton makes it sound like there's not much time left at all. This might all be over soon. Everyone in here will be. . .the last of England."

"Stop talking," Leo says roughly. "You're not going anywhere. They can't—he can't just— "

His cheeks are red and flushed. I reach into my pocket for

his gift, that silver cigarette case the Blood Hunters allowed me to keep. "Cigarette?" I whisper.

He stares down at it. Anger makes him flush, and I almost expect him to rip it out of my hands. Eventually, though, he nods, and I strike the match along the bedside table and light one for him and I.

Victoria sits up. "Can I?"

I light one for her, too. Six left now. Not that it matters. Maybe I should smoke them all now.

We sit in silence for close to two minutes. Leo and Victoria cough intermittently, and at one point Victoria lets out a single sob, but otherwise, no one makes a noise.

Leo takes my hand and rolls his head towards me.

"I'm. . .furious," he says.

I nod because I'm furious, too.

Victoria drags her legs up and puts her head on her knees. Her hair falls in brown waves over the white sheets. "Congratulations. Who isn't?" she spits. She sounds, I think, like Fred. But she shivers and presses her palms against her eyes, wiping away tears. "My anger has nowhere to go. Not anymore."

I wait for her to keep going. She sniffles and turns her head. "I hated the thing in me, and now I regret hating it. I think. . .Cassius, I think maybe I will swap places with you. Maybe it's better that way."

My stomach drops. "You absolutely will not."

"What's the point," she whispers. I know that tone. I know those words. I know the soft thrill of speaking them aloud: the admission that maybe nothing matters, that maybe you'd like to die, that maybe it would be better if you could. If you did.

But I don't know what to tell her because there was nothing that helped me. There was never any point except the guilt to keep going. No point except for stolen moments and fleeting pleasure. I worry about saying, "Stay," and she won't answer. I worry that I have no sway with her and no right to say anything. There is no point. The *teras* will kill us all. Your lover is dead. Your baby is dead. If the *teras* don't kill you, starvation eventually will. But don't go. Please.

Is it selfish of me to want that for her?

"I saved your life," I end up saying. "Please don't. . .please don't throw it away."

Her face crumples immediately. "I hate you," she says weakly. She wipes the tears away and shakes her head. "I wish you hadn't."

There it is: the crux of it. I've made her live, and in living, she continues to hurt. She hurts more and more. But I'm not sorry, and I tell her that.

"You won't ever make me apologise for that."

She looks up at me, glaring, but the fire dies in her eyes. "I don't know what to do anymore. I don't want to live here, but I don't want to die. I don't know what to do."

I feel this helplessness in my bones, but it's not real. Not now. Not now that Fred has told us what we *can* do. I check over my shoulder for Mr Powell, and when satisfied he's not stalking over, I say: "Forget me for a second. They're going to kill Fred. You have to get her out of there; at least you can do that. Sutton and Wamsley—don't trust them." I grunt after I've said that. "Well—honestly, I don't blame them. They needed a scapegoat to stay here, and they chose me—said I was responsible for it all."

Victoria stares at me. "In a way, you were."

"Fine," I say, putting up both my hands. "I'm already condemned. Don't think about me. Free Fred. And then, you can find out where the rift is and close it. There's a purpose. There's something to live and die for. You could close the rift and make our lives easier. Either the *teras* disappear, or we stop new ones from coming through. That's what I'm going to do: I'll go to Meléti now. I'll find where the rift is. But I don't know how to get the information back across."

"I'll come with you," Leo says.

I frown. I look at his stomach. "You won't."

"To Meléti? I will." He rolls his eyes at me and shakes his head. I hate when he gets this look on his face, like I'm an idiot. "What will you offer it? Another memory?"

"Yes," I say, growing defensive. I don't understand why he sounds so upset. Is he being obtuse? His stomach was opened. He saw his own intestines. He's injured. I am not the insane one for suggesting he rest.

Leo follows my gaze and touches his belly. "I'm nearly fully healed. That's why you wanted me to get behind the ward." He inclines his head to Victoria and then to my shoulder, which has also healed as best it can. "The both of us. Please— "

"He's coming," Victoria murmurs languidly.

Leo shuts up and takes a long drag of his cigarette. I follow suit. Behind us, I hear the slow footfalls of Mr Powell coming to take me away.

I'm proud to say I experience no drop in my stomach. It's quite possible my stomach has fallen as far as it can, and I am now numb to the fear of my new reality.

"It's time," Mr Powell announces. "Let's go."

"I'm coming," Leo says. "If that's permitted, of course."

Mr Powell looks at him, then at me. "Mr Shaw, is it?"

"Yes," Leo says.

"Mr Shaw, if you mean to join Mr Jones in his exile, I will need to discuss it with the dean first."

"I have no intention of joining his exile," Leo says sternly. "I mean to go Meléti's library."

Mr Powell cocks his head, disbelief written plainly on his face. "Whatever you mean to do," he says slowly like Leo is a small child, "should you in any way aid or abet Mr Jones in interfering with his exile, you *will* be joining him. Do not forget Dean Drearton, and every Blood Hunter has access to an orrery. We can see where you are, how long you've been there—if Mr Jones is ever on the wrong side of the gate—"

"That won't be happening," Leo said flatly. He smokes and crushes the butt against the metal bedframe. "I'm not so suicidal that I would give up my place here."

I believe him. My stomach sinks, and I believe him. Of course, he's well within his right to preserve himself, and I know in my heart that I would hate if he chose exile for me. But it's the romance of it, isn't it? A part of me longs for him to say: "No, I will go with you. Of course, I'll go with you. Curse this place, curse this supposed safety: you are what I want."

But that's not Leo Shaw. That's some ideal I've envisioned in my head. And despite every flaw, Leo Shaw is the one that I...

I wring my hands together. He is risking something by seeing me out or accompanying me to Meléti. It's not my decision to make, and yet I... can't stop the urge to stop him.

"You shouldn't," I whisper feebly as he throws the covers back.

"I can walk."

"You shouldn't get out of bed. The Healers—"

He cuts me off. "I can walk," he enunciates slowly. There's a bit of bite behind his tone. Stubbornly, Leo Shaw swings his leg over the side of the bed. His hand clutches my shoulder, and without another look at me, he pushes down on it to hoist himself up.

A grunt escapes him, but he bites it off, I suppose in an attempt to sound in control of the pain.

"Lead on," he says, voice grating.

Mr Powell nods and looks down at me. I'm still on my knees, a bastardised supplication.

I say, for myself and in my head, a small prayer. The verse that comes to me is this:

Hebrews 4:16. *Let us then approach God's throne of grace with confidence, so that we may receive mercy and find grace to help us in our time of need.*

But I have no confidence in the Lord anymore.

I stand up and follow Leo and Mr Powell down the long corridor. I glance back at Victoria, still smoking slowly. She raises the cigarette to me like a toast, and I raise mine back, sucking on the end of it until it burns, until it's all ash, and before I leave the ward, I drop it on the tile and crush it out.

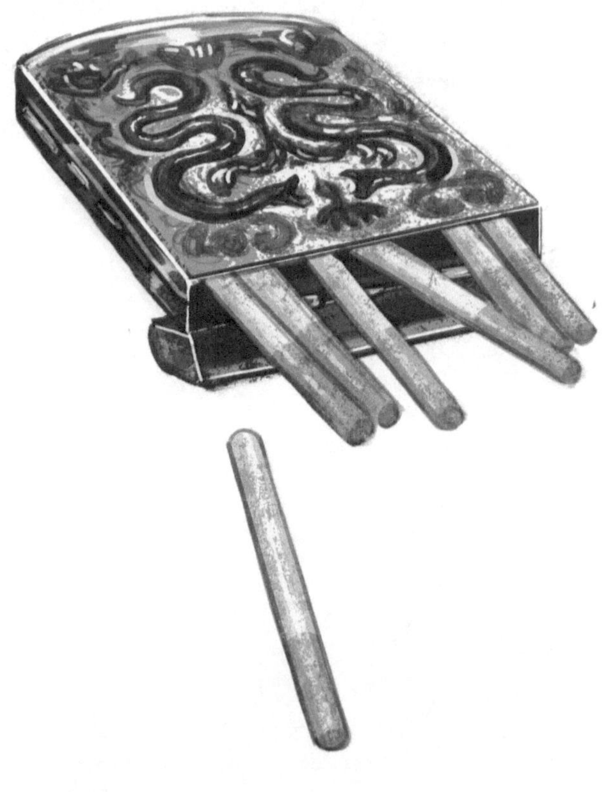

LESSON THIRTY-TWO

At the Janus Gate, Mr Powell goes first.

This strikes as me strange until I think about it. If he let me through, I could run, wardstone in hand. Indeed, the brief whimsical thought flares in me: *oh, I could find a place to stow away. I could hide.*

As if the orrery doesn't exist. As if I didn't give my blood to this place.

Mr Powell passes the wardstone to me with a severe finality, pressing it firmly into my palm. He looks me in the eye. "Do not dally," he says gruffly, and steps through.

I don't look at Leo because part of me is upset with him for coming, and the rest of me is thinking about how a few weeks ago we were doing this. Slipping through the ward, pressing up against each other, heading to Meléti's library. For entirely different reasons, of course, but you can't fault me for thinking about them. I'd naturally prefer Leo's pretty mouth around my cock than permanent exile.

"Well?" Leo murmurs.

I look at him. The hole in his mouth exposes those teeth and the pink of his tongue. I pull him close and bury my face in the side of his neck, breathe in the scent of him, kiss his jaw, the edge of the puckered flesh—I feel his teeth part as he exhales—and then bring my lips to his.

There's something in his eyes. A nervousness or a fear. I refrain from asking him and turn to the gate, squeezing Leo's hand once before I let go.

The gate pulsates. Waiting any longer is pointless. I don't even give myself a chance to turn around and take in the sight of the University—my stomach twists, but I won't say good-bye. They won't keep me out. They won't.

I am meant to be here.

I hold the wardstone out and cross.

My head spins. The pressure shifts behind my eyes, and I hear a faint popping from someplace internal, the shifting of organs or bones, a readjustment to a different plane of exis-tence. As always, it's a disgusting feeling. I nearly keel over when I pass through but manage to stop myself, blinking away nausea.

When I look up—

"What did you do?"

Mr Powell is crowded close. Instinctively, I step back-wards. My eyes flicker down, and I realise belatedly he's pulled a knife on me. It's trained to my neck, and he only steps closer with it now that I've backed up.

Metal presses against the skin. It's cold. I stop breathing.

I think any other man might have tried to defend himself. But my stomach drops out of me, and shame rushes up to fill its place. Like my body is saying: *well, you must have done some-thing*. An internal betrayal—I don't think he's wrong, I think, *Cassius, what did you do?* Call it old instinct, but I hear my father's wrath echoing in my mind, and I know the best defence is to say nothing at all.

Noise warbles behind me, but I don't look away from Mr Powell, who's pressing ever so firmly against my neck.

"What are you doing?"

A hand appears in my periphery; Leo's. His arm grazes over my shoulder, grips Mr Powell's wrist, and shoves him backwards.

The knife scrapes away from my neck, and Leo shouts, "Don't touch him."

Mr Powell's face is plain rage. He hasn't taken his eyes off me. Two Blood Hunters dash across the quadrangle and push through the gate. Their bodies disappear with a warbled groan, but I don't dare turn around to check.

"Give me your wardstone," Mr Powell says.

I still don't move. Not out of bravery, but out of fear.

Three more Blood Hunters emerge from the colonnaded path on the opposite side of the quadrangle. They dash across the damp grass, two men and one woman. One of the men I recognise from his gaze alone. He sat in the Janus Gate tower when we participated in the trials. He knew my brother; he brought the Artificer through the ward for us. He sees me, and his eyes widen with a recognition he quickly attempts to hide. I let him.

"Secure the perimeter," the woman shouts. She flicks her wrist, and the two men dash behind me. Once again, I don't turn.

"Cassius Jones," Mr Powell says slowly. "Give me your wardstone."

"Cass," Leo urges.

I put both hands up and away from my body. The wardstone is clutched in my right palm. "Alright. Alright, hang on."

Very carefully, I step forward into Mr Powell's range and drop the stone in his waiting hand. I feel the loss of it keenly as the pulsating pressure disappears. Gone with it is my safety. Gone with it is my future. My life. Then I walk backwards, not dropping my gaze from Mr Powell's until Leo grabs my arm.

"Is this necessary?" Leo asks. I can hear how heavily he's breathing, but his voice remains calm. His grip on my arm is tight to the point I can feel the pads of his fingers pressing in, rolling over the bones in my right arm.

I look down at my left, at the sharpened bit of bone protruding from the puckered flesh and wonder if I should have stabbed Mr Powell in the eye.

"It is very necessary," Mr Powell proclaims. "I. . .you have. . .tricked us."

I stare blankly at him. Fuck this. I push forward out of Leo's grip and say, "Mr Powell, you've been following me around for an hour, and before that, I was rotting in your jail. I'm flattered you think I've managed to do anything without your knowledge, but I really need you to be more specific about what you think I've done."

He doesn't reply right away. Voices of the Blood Hunters drift over, and I catch bits:

"And the orrery?"

"Is confusing. The location isn't precise. It shows she's still inside. She won't be getting out."

I turn towards them. She?

"Winifred Lin has escaped."

I turn back to Mr Powell. My stomach flips, dread and excitement competing inside me. "Has she now?"

Mr Powell doesn't like my tone and tells me so by jutting that knife forward, pointing at me. "What did you do?"

"Ms Lin has nothing to do with us," Leo says. "We discovered she was a cultist when the dean did."

Leo folds his arms, and his brow quirks with something close to disgust, as if the mere suggestion of knowing Fred is ludicrous.

"Mr Powell." One of the other Blood Hunters—the woman previously shouting orders—sidles close to him and whispers in his ear. Feverishly, disappointedly, he drops his knife and shoves it back into its sheath.

"Fine," he mutters. She slinks off, and Mr Powell turns back to us.

"Mr Shaw, if I learn you have anything to do with this, the dean will hear of it. You will not help Mr Jones. He is exiled. Unless you wish for the same fate, I would avoid him."

"Should be easy," Leo said with a shrug. "I barely like him."

I spin to him, but he's smiling softly, and I want to eat that grin off his mouth.

Mr Powell says nothing more to us. He spins on his heel and dashes after the other Blood Hunter. More orders are shouted, and one other Blood Hunter disappears through the gate. I've counted ten, the most Blood Hunters I have ever seen.

"Drearton's attack dogs," Leo mutters. "Sell-outs. That's what they are."

"It's fine," I murmur. "Powell doesn't matter. But if Fred got out. . ."

"There's no way she managed that alone."

We look at each other. Leo mistakes my expression and clarifies: "Not that she's incompetent. Only—"

"I know. There was no getting out of there."

Neither one of us question if it was Victoria. We left her lying in the hospital bed, knees tucked up under her chin and cigarette burning down to a stump. Who, then?

Wamsley? Sutton? But they betrayed me, had me jailed.

"Something more's at play here," I settle on. "And I don't have time to think on it."

"Then don't." Leo grabs my arm and spins me. Bodily, we both turn towards those grand double doors, and I recall standing here months ago in the rain, watching Blood Hunters track an escaped trialee.

The *automaton* waits.

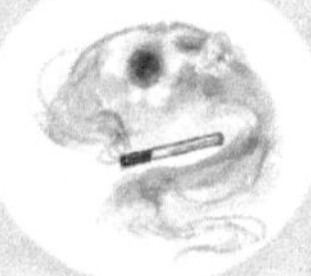

LESSON THIRTY-THREE

"Hello."

The unsettling body of the machine is waiting when we enter the library. The *automaton* stands motionless, holding a red cloth in its hand. After it speaks, it falls eerily quiet, waiting for us to reply, but my eyes skid past it. As always, all of the library is illuminated with a bright yellow light. It seems empty. Even now, with London's dregs camping on the grounds.

And then I look at the ground.

A body is crumpled at Meléti's feet. Blood from a wound I can't see has spread circularly out from the head. Matted hair is smeared across the dead woman's face, hair that is clumped with brain matter and blood. She is positioned so that her head and neck are facing me, but her body and limbs face the *automaton*. I know without seeing it that there must be a bulge in her neck where the bone pushes against flesh. Her eyes, though lifeless, are somehow captivating. I glance at the one glassy orb visible in between the strands of hair, intending to pull my gaze away quickly, and I end up staring at her for several silent seconds.

Her mouth is open. Her tear-stained cheeks have yet to dry.

My heartbeat is all I hear in that moment. She stares at me, she stares, and I see myself.

"You have caught me cleaning." Meléti's voice is upsettingly calm. Its head drops once, twice to the side in descending clicks. "How rude of me."

I jolt and take a step back towards the door. As if seeing me for the first time, the *automaton* drops the bloody cloth and whirrs towards me, moving indiscriminately over the corpse on the ground. Bones crunch, and the cadaver folds briefly inwards from the pressure of Meléti crushing it. It's one of the worst things I've ever seen.

"Mr Jones." I blink, and Meléti stands in front of me. That uncanny, permanent semi-smile presses close to my face. The *teras* is so close my breath fogs its face. "You have been exiled. You are not permitted in the library. You will leave."

My eyes flick to the corpse on the floor. I think: *Yes. Yes, of course, I will leave.* I open my mouth to acquiesce, and suddenly I am saying, "I won't."

I have no time to feel regret.

Meléti's hand whips forward. Cold metal curls around my neck, and then I am choking as it hoists me high, cutting off my air, letting me kick and strain. When my foot grazes its chest, it simply extends its arm, positioning me further away from its body. I can't breathe. I can't.

As my vision blurs, I hear, "Dean Drearton has opened the gates."

Meléti stops. Almost curiously, its body shifts and clicks, its top half whirring towards the sound of Leo's voice.

I open my eyes. The edges are blurred but I can see Leo standing defiantly. He speaks calmly. Even as I'm choking, or dying, he speaks calmly.

"Put Mr Jones down, Meléti, whilst we discuss this."

Perhaps it's because Leo is a student, or perhaps the *automaton* just happens to like him. In any case, I am dropped.

Not gently.

The floor hurtles up to meet me, and I splay my right hand to stop the fall. Something gives way in my wrist, and my face meets the tiles unceremoniously, pain reverberating through my severed arm where the pressure of the force strikes a nerve. I roll with a groan.

Leo calls out, "Alright, Mr Jones?"

And to please him, I say, "Wonderful, Hunter Shaw."

"Oh, don't start that," he says with a laugh. "I'm trying to save your life."

Meléti, for all intents and purposes, ignores me. I'm able to crawl back and stand without it stopping me, but I decide there's no point in aggravating it, not when it's so easily spurred to violence.

"What are you suggesting, Mr Leo Shaw?' Meléti asks.

"I'm suggesting you've made an error by killing this poor woman here. A mistake you were about to repeat with Mr Jones."

"I have made no mistake."

Some unidentifiable noise echoed in its throat. If I hadn't known better, I would call it a scoff.

Still unmoving, Meléti's head rolls downward to the cooling corpse on the tiles. "She attacked me. I eliminated her in self-defence, as is my prerogative."

"Fine," Leo said, folding his arms. "But now that Dean Drearton has opened the University up to London, anything on this side of the Janus Gate is public property."

"Public. . .property?" The *automaton's* head tilted violently to one side. A whirring starts up in its exposed chest, the cavity blurring with the sudden flurry of movement. "I am no such thing."

"Of course not." Leo splays his hand out, waving it to

encompass the multi-levelled library. "You're a keeper of knowledge. That stays the same whether you are from that other world or here."

"Other. . .world. . ." Meléti speaks slowly. It turns its head around on its axis without its body to follow, turning so it could aim its next question at me. "What is it you are looking for, Mr Jones?"

"I wish to close the rift between our worlds."

Meléti makes no immediate answer. I look to Leo, who gestures at me. *More*, he mouths. I drag my gaze back to the *automaton*.

"It would prevent new *teras* from slipping through. It would, I believe, also prevent the creation of *hybrids*."

I shut my mouth after that, not because I'm concerned that Meléti will kill me, but because I wonder suddenly—is Meléti a *hybrid* itself?

I recall Silas talking about Daedalus and quicksilver, but were there precise names for the *automaton* Daedalus produced? Is Meléti shaped by this world and its knowledge? Can it change and evolve and adapt; can all of them?

"The *hybrids*," I say. "What do you know of them?"

"You have not offered me anything. I will provide you with no answer until you do." It says this evenly, but I sense a firmness in its tone. It turns the rest of its body to face me, seemingly to have decided not to have my body join that of the rapidly cooling cadaver sprawled on the tiles at our feet.

Meléti asks, "What do you plan for the *teras* who have already come into this world? If you were to close it, many of them would be stranded."

Them. It uses '*them*', not '*us*'. This strikes me as odd. Surprising.

But I say, "Meléti, I will provide no answers to your questions until you provide answers to mine."

It does not like this. In a near-stroppy mechanical huff, it spins back to Leo and whizzes over to him.

"I do not know how to proceed with Mr Jones. His presence in the library concerns me, but you have spoken truth about Dean Drearton altering the conditions of trespassing in regard to the University. As such, I am at an impasse. I feel I cannot provide Mr Jones the information he seeks."

Leo stares at Meléti for so long that I see the cracks forming in his expression. Tiny ruptures split across his forehead and his brow buckles with the weight of his thought. He glances at me and looks almost apologetic.

"I will give you a memory," he tells Meléti. "But I have conditions."

Meléti stands up straight. "Name them."

He quirks his lips, sadness attempting a smile. My stomach drops. My body tells me something is wrong.

"I want Mr Jones to see the memory, too. Do you think that will be possible?"

You could hear a pin drop in that room. Even the mechanical whirring seems to fade to nothingness as Leo and I stare at each other.

I want to say a great deal of things. I have many thoughts all colliding with one another. Is this what it's taken for him to finally open up to me? And is that what's happening, truly? Will he give Meléti a memory about—

"Your family?" I whisper.

Leo averts his gaze but nods.

Meléti rolls its head between the two of us. I wonder if it can sense the tension, if it revels in it because it seems to grow more certain with every passing second of silence.

I ignore the *automaton* and say, "Leo, I want to know about you, but not like this."

Leo still won't look at me. "I know. I know you do. And perhaps you deserve that, Cass, but I can't. . ."

He doesn't finish that sentence for so long that I think he's abandoned it. But then he adds, "I can't tell you about it. I can't speak about it because. . .I'm afraid I will lie to you."

I frown at him.

"Lie to me?"

Leo finally meets my gaze. His eyes are wet.

"I accept the terms," Meléti says and beckons me close. I hesitate for a long while because I'm not sure I want to know anymore. Why is Leo. . .why would *lying* be a concern?

"Hold hands, and then hold me," Meléti instructs. Leo grabs my hand. Squeezes. I can't look away from him.

And then he reaches out and touches the *automaton*.

RECORDATIO

"Raining again."

"When isn't it raining?"

"Well, I'm saying it's too wet to go out. So, there's no point trying to go to market; Martha won't be there. Mr Lidcombe won't be there either."

Leo Shaw, young and rosy-cheeked, stood with his face pressed to the cracked glass of a small, cramped, and forever damp house creaking in the windy town of Southend-on-Sea. Beside him stood his cousin Jeremiah who, at ten, was closest in age to fourteen-year-old Leo. Both boys had that eagerness that often came early in teenage boys: they wanted to be men before their time.

"Shut up, shut up," the true man of the house said gruffly. He was Ellis Shaw, nearly forty, hair greyed out already from the mere stress of living. A rough and wiry beard spread from his face and clung to his neck, poorly cared for in recent months. Dark circles made his blue eyes haunting, and the man sniffed and croaked as he woke. Leo immediately worried that his father was getting sick.

Ellis Shaw waved the boys away from the window. "Too

early for this bloody racket." He deposited himself on a rickety chair by the small dining table. There were only three seats now, though there had once been four—still far too few for a home housing nine. The fourth chair had been dismantled for firewood in the winter when it had simply gotten too cold to withstand without a fire.

"Here." A bowl of watered-down vegetable stew wobbled onto the table as Adelaide Shaw dropped it. Ellis looked unhappy, muttered something gruffly under his breath, and dragged the bowl towards him.

Adelaide had already turned away. She was Leo's mother, heavily pregnant, with long, mousy hair down to the back of her legs. Leo could tell she was aching this morning; she had pain in her joints, and the heavy swell of her belly only made things worse.

Leo could smell the tension between his parents, and he hated it. Often tried to ignore it. There had been love, once. Very recently, in fact, if two years could be called recent. What Leo had was a strong and severe memory of laughter. Of comfort and affection, and catching the pair of them slow dancing in their small kitchen as if the sleeping bodies of their family weren't crowded at their feet. Stolen moments of true happiness, despite the reality of the world. But his mother's most recent stillborn had seemingly wicked that all away. Now the pair of them had—this. Bowls of stew laid without care. Gruff words. No thank yous or apologies—which Leo had been taught were important things to say to people you loved. The dissolution of manners was the first true sign that love was lost.

A sniffle sounded from the corner, and then a young voice said, "I think she's dying."

Leo turned. His cousin Florence, a tiny thing, hunkered over a sleeping form. If he listened closely, that wheezing death-rattle Leo knew well sounded from beneath the layers of blankets.

Adelaide spun, tea towel in hand, and whipped it across Florence's face. The girl squealed, hand pressing close to her now red cheek. Adelaide pointed at her. "You invite death into this house. Do not mention it. Do not speak of it."

Florence wailed out, "I'm sorry," and her brother Peter whisked her off to another room.

The sleeping mass was Leo's aunt Agnes, Adelaide's sister. She was nearly thirty but had always been sickly, and this last winter—what with little food they had—might have killed her. A slow killer, sure, but killed her, nonetheless.

Leo's mother had started worshipping death after the first of her three stillborns. Worshipped it in the way some of the farmers worshipped plague, or those strange cultists worshipped the *teras* themselves. They'd tried not to speak on it, but the church had found out anyway, and Prittlewell had sent plenty a missionary down the road to the Shaw house to talk Adelaide Shaw out of it.

"They'll think you a witch." Leo had heard his father hiss that at his mother many times. She would say something back to him—that he was a conman, that he had enough people fooled that he couldn't be surprised if people started calling her a witch, that his family was already hated by the church, so what did it matter. He would yell back. But Adelaide would not be dissuaded.

"Girl's right," Ellis grunted now in between mouthfuls of his stew. This was not the right thing to say. A chill came over the whole room. By the door, Leo's little brother, Paul, only four, poked his head around the corner. Leo shook his head, waved him away, a warning. *Stay out of this. Stay safe.*

Leo and Jeremiah, though, would be forced to bear witness. Both froze like prey animals do, pressing themselves against the wall until the cold window met the bare nape of their necks.

"Don't," Adelaide warned.

The rattle of a spoon put roughly down, echoed by the rasping of Agnes' dying breaths. Ellis said, "Delusional woman. That's what you are. She's already dead, and you are wasting the best cuts on her. You used the last of the meat on her last night—she can't taste it. She doesn't need it."

"She *does* need it!" Adelaide said shrilly. "She needs to get her strength back!"

"She's long past that! Medicine, if we'd had the coin—maybe that would have done something. Now the best thing we can do for her is call a bloody priest."

This was a great concession on the part of Ellis Shaw, whose family was long mistrusted by the Christian priests. Leo didn't quite understand why, but he knew that much. Agnes was a Christian woman, and Adelaide had been too, at some point. But Leo's mother shook her head and slapped her tea towel down onto the table.

"She's my sister," Adelaide said.

"I know," Ellis muttered. His hand shifted, and Leo half-thought his father would reach out and touch Adelaide's hand to show an ounce of support for his wife. He did not. "But that's how this world works."

Adelaide went rigid. She sniffed and straightened, dusting her hands off on her apron. "Right. I need to. . .I'll be heading to market."

Ellis snorted. "With what coin?"

"See what I can trade."

"Don't matter anyway," Jeremiah said foolishly. All eyes turned to him. "It's raining. Market won't run."

"Boy, I swear—" Ellis' tone turned sour, and Leo never learned what his father swore on, because the roof of the house was torn off.

The rest of the memory occurred in flashes.

Dust, debris, the sound of screaming both distant and near. Leo's vision swam, became clouded as he was knocked down. A crushing weight pushed down on his chest, and he could not breathe, could not for the life of him move.

Adelaide screamed by the body of her sister, crushed by a beam, before she herself was lifted up. Leo saw this and simultaneously did not see this; his mind warped around the image of her being plucked up, a giant hand squeezing the life out of her, the bloody pop of the flesh, the yellow fat, the resulting viscera, and the wail abruptly cut off.

At this point, Leo managed to roll out from the beam laid over him at an angle, lucky enough to squeeze out where the gap widened. He stood and ran. He thought of Paul. Paul, who was the youngest and the best of them. Who stayed sweet even after night terrors and attacks. Who reminded Leo to smile.

Leo ran to the side room, where Peter had taken Florence to comfort her, and found them both screaming, staring up.

Leo twisted and looked up himself and he saw a great, enlarged face staring down at them, brow smooth and the place where eyes should be bump-less, and a single great eye emerging from the centre of the forehead, and all of them were screaming and screaming. Something held onto Leo's leg, and it was Paul, Paul who was bleeding and howling and part of his arm was missing, and then Leo saw in the giant's hand the dress of his younger sister Maria, who was seven, and who Leo hadn't seen that morning—he hadn't said hello or good morning and for some reason in that moment felt terribly sure he hadn't said good night to her either—and Leo wanted to tear his own flesh open and he started hitting the side of his head because the pain was too great, and then the other hand of the giant came down and plucked up Peter and tore his head off, and Florence screamed and tugged at the lifeless limp body of her brother and was lifted up off the ground as well, and she screamed, "Leo! Leo! Please!" as both Peter's bleeding body and hers were put almost delicately into the *cyclops*'s waiting mouth, and Paul was screaming, "Leo! Leo!" and Leo decided if any of them should live it should be Paul, and so he grabbed Paul up and dashed through the back of the house, and planks were falling and the back door was blocked, and he turned and ran back through the house, and a giant finger dashed down beside him, he saw the yellowed nail crash through the joining wall, and as he ran back into the main room over glass and Agnes's body he saw his father crawling, saw him crawl away from the bloody stringy mess of his legs, and his father was reaching out and babbling but no noise was coming out, and the front door had collapsed into rubble, and Leo turned around and around and couldn't breathe, and Paul was bleeding all over him, and a great roar sounded above him and Leo ran now to a window and put Paul down to smash through it, and he knew he would have to crawl over the broken glass, and as he turned to pick Paul up the *cyclops* had lowered its face down to them, and its tongue very gently licked over Paul's little body, and Leo probably could have grabbed Paul's arm and thrown him through the window, he probably could have saved Paul and sacrificed himself, but he didn't.

He didn't.

He looked Paul in the eye and pushed himself over the glass and had enough time to register the slow blooming horror in Paul's eyes before he dragged himself over the windowpane and cut up his stomach and fell into a muddy pile below. Leo was wheezing and screaming and crying and then abruptly all of that stopped. All that pain and all that terror disappeared, replaced by an eerie but welcome calm. He stood up and saw Paul be licked up into the giant's mouth.

Paul was dead.

Leo screamed again, this agonising roar of a sound, this blood-curdling cry, and he raked his nails down his face. Turning, he saw two other houses had been demolished and left bloody, and then he saw a crowd of people launching projectiles from the ground. Stones and bullets. A few ran in to stab at the giant's feet. And then the rest followed the great myth of the *Odyssey*, which Leo had been told most years of his life, and they wrapped rope around the giant until its next step made it fall, and it half crashed onto the beach and then it could be killed. Slowly but surely, it was killed.

The memory flashed forward.

Leo sat in the rain and watched its dead body all night until someone told him he was killing himself and brought him inside, but just for one night, because she couldn't feed him. But Leo didn't eat until the rain stopped and Southend could burn the giant corpse.

Leo watched it burn away over the course of several days, and he did not cry, not once, even when his body felt like exploding, even when he wanted to cut into himself, and even when he thought about praying to a God that he'd never believed in.

Leo Shaw watched it all and did not cry and thought he never wanted to cry again. He never wanted to feel any of it again; nothing painful, nothing that could turn to pain, nothing strongly ever again. He did not want to be vulnerable. He wanted to be nothing but strong.

He would spend the next years scrounging for scraps and living off goodwill and trying to find shelter and killing what he could, and killing what *teras* he could, and waiting for something to change.

And then the Calling happened.

LESSON THIRTY-FOUR

I can feel his shame. It's palpable, it oozes from him, like an illness.

I stare. This can't be. . . all of it. This is the selfish part of me, recalling him speaking in the church at Prittlewell, calling his father a mystic, a conman. Saying he learned the reason his father disliked the church so greatly upon his death.

This memory shows none of this. But perhaps this isn't the time to pry any further.

When the memory ends, Meléti whirrs backwards, and I am left holding Leo Shaw's hand.

He is crying.

There's no sound. He cries so quietly I almost believe I'm mistaken. But when I turn, I see the tears staining his cheeks, and my heart lurches with great severity, and I want to promise things I can't follow through on. *Leo, I'm here, I will take this pain from you.* It's not how it works, but I wish it could. I wish with everything in my body that I could divorce him from the pain of what happened to him.

Leo won't meet my gaze, and his cheeks are flushed. I squeeze his hand and try to stop my stomach from flipping. I feel impotent. I can do nothing. God, help me; what do I *do?*

"Your memory is accepted," Meléti says. "A *cyclops* in Southend-on-Sea is new information and perhaps proves the sudden dominance of Greco-Roman *teras*. Thank you for your contribution to the library."

Leo nods stiffly. His hand goes slack in my grip. I don't let go.

"Please re-state your enquiry."

I glance at Leo, but his jaw is tense, and he has that thousand-yard stare, and I worry about pushing him any further. I wanted to ask about the *hybrids*, but I focus first on the other thing.

"The rift. Where is the location of the rift?"

Meléti stares, and for a while, there is nothing but the whirring of its insides, churning around and around. Abruptly, it turns on its heels and guides us—not up the stairs, but instead to one of the statues framing the ascent. The spear Leo dragged out to defend me months ago has been replaced, but Meléti pushes past this and turns so we are under the winding staircase.

A hidden door waits.

Meléti extends its hand and twists a finger into the lock. The mechanism clicks over, and the door swings inwards. We are greeted by damp musk and the groan of unused hinges. Meléti moves inside and strikes its metal limbs across the stone until fire erupts and, somehow, stays lit on the edge of its hand.

In silence, we move uniformly down into the bowels of this crypt. All senses scream, and I ignore the instinct to run. Part of me thinks: *is it taking us to the rift?* But I can't imagine the Janus Gates being free of it; I can't imagine it being here in this reality.

Still gripping Leo's hand, with my heart twisting and a ridiculous urge to hold him shouting in my chest, I pull all my focus onto Meléti. The rift is my priority. And Leo's always told me to be ruthless, hasn't he?

He says that to stop his shame. He says that to quiet the guilt of surviving.

At the bottom of the stairs, though, is no rift but instead another library of its own kind. The temperature has changed dramatically. There is no longer any dampness, but instead a humid dryness. I spot Latin books, Greek, Armenian. Myths of the British Isles. Manuscripts and treatises—originals. These books are special. These books are rare.

Meléti whirrs over to a particular shelf and extends itself to reach the very top of it, where another locked cabinet sits. It opens this and takes from it an old set of papers.

The *automaton* says nothing when it hands the papers to us, not for a while. But before we open them up, it says, "I think I would like to stay here. I do not wish to return," and though I can make no promises—for I have no idea how the rift works, where it is, or how it was formed—Meléti moves to the other side of the room and leaves us alone.

Which is unusual for it. It does not vacate the room entirely, but every other work I have interacted with here, it watches over religiously. It's almost—almost—close to trust.

Now that we are semi-alone, Leo's flush has only worsened. When I touch his other hand, his face crumples briefly. "Don't," he whispers.

I say nothing. I want to know many things. I have many questions. But the potential of making things worse hurts me more than my questions do, so I look down at the book and say instead, "Let me open this up."

He lets me.

The paper is dry and fragile. Very carefully, I open it. It's a small manuscript, more of a treatise, on the rift itself. Most of it is in Armenian, which I can't read. But some of it is in English and Latin and a smattering of Greek. It tells me the rift is within the Janus Gates. That it sits in the eastern quarter, deep underground. That there are crypts there, a series of tunnels that ferry its contents out of London's wards.

Ferries its contents. . .

Teras are pouring into the world, right into the heart of London.

And from London, out into England.

What about the rest of the world? There are other Universities, other *teras*. They can't all come from this rift.

It is something we have known in a roundabout way from the instant we saw the first *teras* in the trials. But this knowledge feels sinister for the simple manufactured nature of it. The existence of the crypt, the tunnels, the Janus Gate. I don't understand what I'm learning. I don't understand what it means.

And I have no time to understand because Meléti rushes back to us with its voice a high-pitched alarm. "Get out!" it starts to scream. "Get out! Get out! Get out!"

Neither Leo nor I move for a time until Meléti grabs us both by the neck. It hoists us high, and I don't remember what happens, because all I experience is pain. Pain and suffocation, the bright blistering heat in my chest as my lungs scream for air I cannot give them. When I breathe next, it is a sharp inhale, and I am dropped to the marble floor of the library's ground floor.

Meléti spins in panic, and one by one the lights of the library are snuffed out. Darkness intrudes and creeps up on us, all the while the *automaton* screams, "Go! Go! Go!"

Now that we are upstairs and out of the muffling stone crypt, I can hear the screams.

Leo and I look at each other, and we run to the door.

The instant we are outside, the library locks. I hear mechanisms whirring shut and when I test the handle, the great doors shake but do not open.

Leo and I are panting. The quadrangle is empty. A light misted rain has started up and made the grass dewy. The air feels. . .wrong, somehow. A dread creeps up inside me, and my body tenses. Something has happened. What is it? Is it Fred? Victoria? Something to do with the Janus Gate?

A scream ruptures the air. It's curling, guttural. Several more go up only to be cut off abruptly. They sound near, within the University's grounds, and I realise no—this is here and now. This isn't the Janus Gate at all.

And then there are the howls.

Leo glances at me and starts to run.

There's nothing to do but follow him. My mind goes blank; there's nothing but the burning in my lungs and the urge to move. Everything in me wants to hide, but I ignore this urge, and instead, Leo and I run together through the colonnade, feet pounding against the stone.

We pass the chapel and find it overflowing with bodies. People scream and shove to be let in, but the chapel is simply too small. I hear a few garbled prayers, a flurry of desperation. Sweat and bodily stench permeate the small vestibule as bodies push and shove, at least thirty outside and still pushing in. I spy the overarching *scylla* sitting high, all its tailheads screaming, and a great flurry of desperate believers trying to push their way inside, crushed close to the *teras* skeleton. The doors won't close.

Leo squeezes through beside the opposite wall. My body is crushed against the stone as I move through, and when I'm expelled on the other side, I almost fall onto the stone. I right myself, and my mind is still blank, still as unthinking as I can make it. On instinct alone, I push forward, and we burst out of the colonnade to the accommodation side of the University, where many Londoners had begun to camp and the west tower I killed for sits high. We can see the whole stretch of green to the gate. Littered belongings cover the ground. Clothes are strewn about. A man is crying, rocking in the grass.

Past him, by the gate, a large black dog is ripping someone to shreds.

My heart stops. I hear a trumpeting noise from deep within London, a warning that becomes garbled and peters out as the trumpeter no doubt dies. The screams of the injured and dying echo around us, and the trilling noises of *teras* crowd my ears. Excited, happy, gleeful noises, far more potent than our battle at Prittlewell. This is joy. This is triumph. This is gloating over glory.

I see it, then. In between the rainfall, the usual blueish flicker of the ward isn't there.

My heart sinks, and with it, any bit of hope I still had. An eerie acceptance settles in my stomach.

This is it, then.

I grab Leo's hand. He grabs mine back.

"The ward," I say.

He exhales. "It's fallen."

And from between the buildings I see, and hear, and feel its approach; that creaking body slouching forward, its haunches strained near to breaking, the slow approach of our death. Vengeance in my mind's eye, in my ear, in my soul.

It speaks to me. I go to my knees; I am bound to listen. My soul wishes to obey.

"*Vae, puto deus fio!*" it screams, and I cry out, and Leo cries out too.

This is the end. This is humanity's doom.

Ah, I think I am becoming a god.

END

ABOUT THE AUTHOR

Lucien Burr has a background in the Classics and is an author and creator writing dark fantasy stories.

ALSO BY LUCIEN:

THE PRINCE OF LUST SERIES:
Prince of Lust
Hell and its Pleasures

THE TERAS THREAT SERIES
The Teras Trials

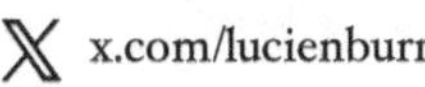

x.com/lucienburr
instagram.com/lucienburr

www.ingramcontent.com/pod-product-compliance
Lightning Source LLC
Chambersburg PA
CBHW050113120726
47904CB00004B/1329